The Unyielding Clamour of the Night

NEIL BISSOONDATH

The Unyielding Clamour of the Night

Cormorant Books

Canada Council **Conseil des Arts**
for the Arts **du Canada**

ONTARIO ARTS COUNCIL
CONSEIL DES ARTS DE L'ONTARIO

The publisher gratefully acknowledges the support of the Canada Council for the Arts
and the Ontario Arts Council for its publishing program. We acknowledge
the financial support of the Government of Canada through the Book Publishing
Industry Development Program (BPIDP) for our publishing activities.

Printed and bound in Canada

LIBRARY AND ARCHIVES CANADA CATALOGUING IN PUBLICATION

Bissoondath, Neil, 1955–
The unyielding clamour of the night / Neil Bissoondath.

ISBN 1-896951-87-2

I. Title.

PS8553.I8775U69 2005   C813'.54   C2004-906529-7

Cover design: Marijke Friesen
Cover image: © Paul W. Liebhardt/CORBIS
Author photo: Anne Marcoux
Text design: Tannice Goddard
Printer: Friesens

CORMORANT BOOKS INC.
215 SPADINA AVENUE, STUDIO 230, TORONTO, ONTARIO, CANADA M5T 2C7
www.cormorantbooks.com

.

*It is difficult to recognize that treason can be honourable
and loyalty wrong. There is so much one has to admit to in oneself
before one can accept that radical moral turnabout.*

— ALBERT SPEER

ALBERT SPEER: HIS BATTLE WITH TRUTH

BY GITTA SERENY (VINTAGE)

PART ONE

ONE

THE KEY TO the schoolhouse had been given to him without
ceremony the day before he boarded the train south.

The man at the ministry, plump, middle-aged, wavering between
exasperation and distraction, hadn't been able to find it. He had
dug through the disordered drawers of his desk, looked among
stacks of files fat with sheets of yellowing paper, searched through
several boxes stored in the toilet cubicle. He had ransacked the
desk of his assistant, a bony and listless young man — a southerner,
with the darker skin and oiled, curly hair of his people — all the
while muttering unhappily to himself over his wife's failure to pack
him a lunch that morning. Frequently, one of the five strands of
silver hair he had arranged over his bald head from the right ear
to the left would work free from its mooring and fall into his
eyes; he would lick his palm and slap it back into place with a loud

smack. His breathing grew laboured. Sweat slicked his forehead. The air conditioner, he complained, was broken.

Angry at his failure to find the key, he turned on his young assistant and sent him scurrying from the small and crowded office with a torrent of abuse. He turned to Arun. "These damned *rikshas*," he muttered.

"I'm going to be teaching those *rikshas*." The man who, in his frenzy, had awoken his sympathy, now struck him as vile and pitiful.

"Better you than me. You know what they're like. Like that one. A stone would make a better office assistant. At least it would be useful for something. Paperweight. Doorstop. Stones don't smoke the *ganja* to mess up their brains."

"So why'd you hire him?"

"Hire him? You think I'd hire that type? He's a two-percenter. I'm stuck with him." He stroked his chin, glanced around the office. Then he waddled over to a filing cabinet in the far corner of the room, opened the first drawer, glanced in, banged it shut, opened the second. "Your key," he said, fishing out a manila envelope. "I should have known it would be here, with the two-percenter files." He reached into the envelope, took out a small silver key and tossed it to Arun. "As far as we know," the man said, slapping a strand of hair back into place, "the school's still standing."

In the street outside, Arun decided he would walk back to his sister's house instead of hiring a jitney. It was midmorning. The streets were crowded, cars and vans and bicycles jostling for space on the narrow, uneven roadway, mangy dogs, tongues lolling from their mouths in the heat, trotting unsteadily among the vehicles through clouds of exhaust. The air seemed to boil in the howling traffic. On the sidewalk, he joined the flow of pedestrians surging one way — housewives out shopping, maids running errands, secretaries on their coffee break, businessmen with briefcases in one hand and cell phones in the other — while another flow surged in the opposite direction, parallel tides eddying with studied blindness around the occasional beggar holding up a palm or a holy man blinking up with bleary eyes or a peddler offering fistfuls of pens or combs or key chains.

At the roundabout at the end of the street the traffic thinned, the sidewalk bustle diminished. There were no more beggars or holy men. The circle, monumental in scale, had been the heart of the colonial administration. It was enclosed by large, solid, many-storeyed buildings — the Governor's residence, the Seat of the Local Assembly, police headquarters, the courts — which had been converted, at independence, into various government ministries: the Presidential Palace, the Ministry of Finance, the Ministry of Internal Security, the Ministry of Justice. From a pole mounted on the roof of each building the national flag hung limp in the heavy air, and at the main door of each soldiers in battle-dress stood watchful guard from behind stacked sandbags. It was said that the drapes at the windows hid plates of reinforced steel, and that each building housed troops drawn from the presidential regiment.

At the centre of the circle, where a granite Queen Victoria had once sat on a carved throne, a monument in white marble rose from a well tended lawn: Prince Aryadasha, the mythological conqueror of the south, brandishing a fiery lance from his blazing chariot. There were those who worshipped the memory of Aryadasha, who saw in his mist-shrouded figure the symbol around which a new nationhood could be built in the aftermath of colonial retreat. Teak and rice and minerals would provide the wealth, but Aryadasha — so mysterious anyone could make of him whatever they wished — would provide the spirit. Arun wondered whether the soldiers on guard duty drew inspiration from the statue of Aryadasha, whether they saw in his single-minded brutality — the epics told of rape, torture, and massacre — an example to be emulated. To him, the statue was a reminder that, while the south had long been captured, it still had not been conquered. An amateur student of history, all his reading had brought home to him that stories of the past, like the stories in the daily newspapers, were not to be wholly trusted. It was dangerous business, drawing lessons from tales too often told.

By the time he turned into his sister's leafy street, the sounds of traffic a distant cacophony, the two-storey houses secure behind high fences and chained gates, he was heavy with the thought that would remain with him throughout that last day and evening in the capital: that he had committed himself to teaching school to *rikshas*. Of the students he would face, no more than two percent of them would be given the opportunity to advance beyond rudimentary reading, writing, and arithmetic, no more than two percent of them would be offered places at the university or jobs in the civil service. His success with them would peak at two percent.

He rang the bell at the locked garden gate and, waiting for the maid to run down with the key, he knew he would have to somehow distance himself from that fat ministry man, his abused assistant, and dusty filing cabinet — and most urgently from the idea of two percent. His sister had invited several members of the family over for a farewell dinner. They wanted to fête him, she had said over his reluctance, they wanted to wish him well. He was aware that behind his back heads shook in dismay, lips twisted into smirks, whispers questioned his sanity. He's only twenty-one, some said, why is he throwing away his life? He's only twenty-one, others replied, he'll learn. They would celebrate him that evening in the way that the Christians at his high school had celebrated the crucifixion: as a salve to the collective conscience. The country was not large, but he was heading south, across the central plain and down into the mountainous territory near the coast. To the people he would see that evening for cocktails and dinner served at the table glittery with crystal and silverware, it was as if he were going into exile in some unstable foreign land.

IN THE PRE-DAWN darkness, the sky held no stars. Behind him the train sat heavy and silent on its track, curtains drawn across the windows. The platform was deserted save for the conductor farther down conferring over some papers with a couple of military men and, beyond them, motionless shadows beside his wagon, his sister and brother-in-law. In the ticket booth, a single lamp showed only the bony hands of the clerk. He wore a ring on each finger and, although he remained faceless, his voice was friendly when he told Arun that he would find the dining car at the rear of the train.

"This must be my lucky day," Arun said. First, his train ticket had been waiting for him as the man from the ministry had said it would be; he had not had to make a scene. And now this news about the dining car — the phrase suggested a kind of luxury that eased the thought of the long trip ahead. Trains to the south often had army wagons shackled to them, transporting troops and material to the garrisons. There had been some noise in the press about this — the army stuck stubbornly to its idea, many times disproved, that the presence of civilians would discourage attack — but the government had brought the debate to an end by invoking national security. On such trains, the dining car was sometimes left behind.

His sister had offered to pack him enough food to see him through to his journey's end. He had refused but she'd inherited their mother's concern with well-being, and well-being was associated with a full stomach. It was a quality that made her a good wife and would make her a good mother but it also meant that she and her husband had to make annual trips to the dressmaker and the tailor to have their clothes enlarged. She fretted constantly over Arun's slenderness. His father had liked to joke that Arun's ribs would make a superb xylophone. His mother, not generally known for her wit, once said that her mind was at ease knowing that, come what may, Arun could always earn a living as a live skeleton model at the medical school. He was good-humoured about the teasing, if slightly embarrassed that his parents seemed to have little of the dignified gravity that defined his friends' parents.

7

Earlier, as they had sleepily loaded his bags into his brother-in-law's car for the drive to the train station, his sister had pressed on him a new briefcase more befitting a university professor than a simple small town schoolteacher. He could tell just by its smell that it was expensive. It was made of supple leather the colour of dried ox blood, and had brass latches which he could lock, if he wished, by twirling two numbered dials. The gift amused him — it suggested that his sister had a grander idea of him than she let on — but he also felt it would mark him, would make him slightly ridiculous in the place where he was going. He had to suppress a ripple of irritation when she explained that the briefcase's inordinate weight was the result of food prepared by the maid: sandwiches and sweets and bottled preserves.

The man in the ticket booth switched off his light, and it was suddenly as if he was not there. Arun tucked the ticket into his shirt pocket, picked up the briefcase from the concrete floor and turned towards the train. Up above, the sky had turned a lighter shade of black overlaid with hints of royal blue. His bags were already in his compartment. His brother-in-law, adept at such things, had seen to their loading by one of the idle young men, mostly southerners, who hung around the station hoping to pick up some change by performing whatever task they could find. His sister had urged her husband to accompany the young man in case he tried to make off with the bags. "Don't worry," Arun had heard his brother-in-law say as he left them for the ticket booth. "They're lazy, but they're not thieves."

Now all that was left for him to do was to say goodbye. He was glad that the sun was not yet up. He knew his sister, and he did not want to see her tears.

His compartment smelled of dust and tobacco smoke and engine oil, the odour not unpleasant, even comforting in the way that the words *dining car* had been. The wood panelling had long lost its gloss, and in spots the stain had been thoroughly worn away. The curtains, drawn shut, were of a faded green fabric stiff with age and, he suspected, grime decades old. Little remained of whatever elegance it might once have had. Designed to accommodate six passengers, it had been reserved only for him. Not many people travelled south these days. The train, he had been told, was not even half full, and most of those passengers were in the cheaper cars closer to the locomotive; after just a few hours, they would begin to feel the wood beneath the thin padding of their seats and they would spend the better part of the journey either squirming or standing.

As they had shaken hands to the sound of Joy's sniffling, his brother-in-law, an engineer by training and a man who prided himself on his practicality, had pointed out that his wagon was well-located in case of attack. Bombs tended to go off beneath the locomotive, which often crashed over onto its side, pulling the next two or three cars with it. His wagon was far enough behind that it stood a good chance of remaining on the track. Arun wasn't sure what he was meant to do with this information, but he thanked his brother-in-law anyway. Perhaps, he thought, the observation was merely a gesture of kindliness towards Joy — an attempt to reassure her rather than Arun.

He stowed the briefcase in the metal rack above his head, beside his luggage — two old plastic suitcases that had belonged to his parents, each still identified by the swatch of red ribbon his father had knotted to the handle. Seeing the beauty of the brief-case beside the worn blue plastic of the suitcases, remembering how his sister had tried to persuade him to buy new ones, he wondered again at this idea she had of him — perhaps not a better one than he had of himself but the opposite, which caused her to want to improve him. The train shuddered, gave two raucous metallic coughs, and began moving off. On impulse, but knowing Joy would be disappointed if he didn't, he shoved the curtains back and looked out at the railway platform drawing past. In the grey, pre-dawn light, it was like looking at an old black-and-white film, the images hazy and uncertain, all shadow, not cleanly seized.

The light went on in the ticket booth. An old man was sweeping the platform, a stray dog slinking past him. Arun didn't see his sister until the train, picking up speed, sluiced past the small parking lot — and there he saw them, Joy and Surein walking slowly towards their car, his arm around her not in the way of a lover but as if lending comfort. Their backs were to him but he raised his hand in farewell anyway.

It was the train's speeding along the track, he thought, the regularity and sureness of its rhythm, its sense of forward momentum, which instilled in him a sense of well-being. The brown leatherette seats, like sofas for three facing each other, were as worn as the wall panelling, but their springs had remained firm and there was an appealing plushness to them. He sat on the seat facing the front of the train, eased off his right shoe and raised his stockinged foot onto the other.

The sun had risen into a fragile blue that quickly grew formidable. The mildewed apartment buildings, decrepit storehouses, and ramshackle shantytowns of the capital had been left far behind. The heat would be building out there in the tilled fields. Through the dusty window pane, he could see knots of people, the men shirtless, the women wrapped in swaths of colourful fabric, squatting or bending over digging and hoeing and weeding. But the air in his compartment remained comfortable and he enjoyed the sight of the rich earth and the rows of plants — peas, cucumbers, tomatoes, okras, and other vegetables for the market, their leaves moist and succulent, of a friendlier green than the forest darkening the distant horizon.

He pictured the train's progress the way classic films traced long voyages, the old locomotive and its line of rattling carriages smoking a path down a map of the scarab-shaped island, the craggy northern coast rising gently to acres of tea and vegetable plantations separated by the towns they fed, the southern coast rising past cliffs to a more daunting landscape of mountain and forest. To the east, across miles of placid sea, the fat tail of the Indian sub-continent, too distant to be seen yet, always, as looming a presence as a tank in the neighbourhood. To the west, farther away still, the shores of Somalia, Yemen, and Oman. Some claimed without proof that in the days of Aryadasha, trading dhows with sails swollen by the wind had regularly made the lengthy crossing to Africa.

After a while his eyelids grew heavy, and a creeping drowsiness threatened to encroach on his sense of well-being. Standing up, he slipped his foot back into his shoe, retrieved his book from the exterior pocket of one of the suitcases and gingerly drew back the sliding door of the compartment. The corridor outside was narrow and full of sunlight. Through the windows, cultivated fields and greenery moved swiftly by. At the door to the wagon ahead, a porter was sitting on a wooden crate rolling cigarettes. He was an old man, unshaven, squinting at fingers busy with paper and tobacco through the curl of smoke rising from the cigarette that dangled between his lips. Over a white shirt that appeared dirty even from a distance he had buttoned a threadbare navy blue jacket with the railway crest pinned haphazardly to the pocket. The unsewn hems of his khaki trousers climbed halfway up his shins. He was barefoot. Arun thought of his father, thought of how he would have enjoyed the sight of this old man who, with his ragged dignity, seemed a home-grown version of the Little Tramp who had always made his father laugh. His uniform was unprepossessing but it was enough to lend him authority in a land where uniforms had long inspired fear.

At the sound of Arun's door, the old man looked up, found him with his rheumy eyes and nodded once in acknowledgement. Those from the other wagons who wanted to purchase some food or drink from the dining car had to knock at the door, give their order and money to the old man who would fetch it for them in return for some small consideration. It was the custom that those enjoying the protection also reward the old man. Arun approached him and put a coin into his hand. The man clasped the coin between his open palms and, mumbling, raised them to his forehead in a gesture of thanks. His eyes did not meet Arun's. That too was the custom. In the tobacco smoke, intermingled with it, Arun smelled the sweeter odour of *ganja*.

As he turned and walked back down the corridor towards the dining car — the train rattling now through some small town: wooden houses collapsed in on themselves, broken fences, backyards riotous with rusted vehicles, a clutch of ragged children smiling and waving skinny arms — he wondered if what people said was true, that the farther south you went, the more interesting the landscape became. There were fewer towns, less urban desolation. The climate grew wetter, more humid, the vegetation denser, greener, more lush. The northern plains gave way to hills rising into mountain ranges, some inland, some defining the edge of the land in a rocky cascade into the sea.

The town of Omeara, to which he was headed, was set on a shallow bay, an unpromising location that had hindered its growth. There was a beach, but it was pebbly. The land around was fertile, but there was little of it to go around. A UN-sponsored plan to encourage terrace farming some years before had failed, jungle quickly reclaiming the terraces and their retaining walls of stacked rock. The people were reluctant to enter the hills; they were heavily forested, and the forests hid the bands of armed men they referred to as the Boys. On the outskirts of town was a large army base that housed the troops of the Aryadasha Regiment, unfailingly described in government communiqués, and so in press reports, as élite. He knew nothing of the military situation in the area. He knew only that the élite troops and the determined Boys had been at each other for years and that, again according to those communiqués, the troops scored only major victories against the Boys. He knew, too, that the children of Omeara had been without a schoolteacher for months.

The dining car — and he felt he should have expected this the moment he closed the door behind him, shutting out the swirling chaos of metallic shrieks and hot wind between the wagons — had seen better times. The seats were of unplaned planks of wood nailed together by a haphazard hand. Before each a narrow counter showed the dried stains of various liquids — hardly surprising given the sway and hiccups at the tail of the train. At the far end was the service counter, its faded red arborite suggesting that it was a leftover from the dining car's original, less modest circumstances. Displayed on it were bottles of water and soft drinks in a variety of colours. Behind the counter, a young man in the uniform of the railway service staff — maroon shirt with shoulder tabs, grey trousers — nodded gloomily at Arun.

"Good morning," Arun said. The decor neither inspired comfort nor encouraged well-being and the man's greeting made him feel like an intruder. He felt like fleeing. Still, he said, "Do you have any tea?"

The young man nodded but remained where he was, hands splayed on the counter, as if he had failed to understand that the question was a request.

"Can I have a cup of tea, please," Arun said. He thought for the second time that morning of his father, who would have lost his temper and denounced the man's indolence.

The young man turned away and busied himself behind a plywood partition. Arun dug into his pants pocket for change. A yellowed price list on the wall spoke of food and drink — pancakes, French pastries, soufflés, cappuccino, espresso — that were well beyond the capacities of this kitchen and that man. It was, to Arun, like reading a bit of public fiction.

He was counting out the change, legs unsteady as the train rumbled along what felt like uneven rails, when the man emerged with a steaming Styrofoam cup in one hand and a tea bag in the other. Arun shouldn't have been surprised but he was anyway — what his brother-in-law liked to call his little naive side. He paid, inserted the bag into the water and, eyeing the benches, decided he would return to his compartment rather than perch here under the deadened gaze of the attendant.

At that moment the door to the wagon slid open. At that moment, too, the train, beginning an ascent, gave a sudden lurch. The man at the door lost his balance and stumbled in, snatching at a table to break his fall. Arun, startled, felt hot water splash from his cup onto his fingers. He yelped — and he heard the man laugh. "So how bad is it?" the man said. "Second degree? Third degree?"

Arun looked up at a friendly, open face offering a glimpse of sympathy despite the mocking words. "Second," He said. "At least second."

The man eyed the Styrofoam cup and the tea bag cord dangling from it. "Is that the only tea they've got?"

Arun nodded.

"What's this country coming to, I ask you. We produce tons of tea leaves and what do we drink? Tea named for some English lord put into bags made in the USA. So what's this country coming to, can you tell me?"

Arun's instinct was to respond that this country had far greater problems than the tea that was available. It was the kind of comment his father would have made. But he saw that the man had spoken with humour.

The man put out his hand. "Seth," he said. His face was round, his eyes large and soft with a frankness, a directness, in their gaze. His cheeks showed evidence of childhood acne, but lightly. He was probably in his early thirties. He struck Arun for some reason as a man who should have been wearing glasses but who did not because — like the black hair cut neat and short, like the moustache trimmed with an exacting severity — of notions of vanity.

Arun shook his hand, mumbled his name.

"You dropped your book," Seth said, bending down to retrieve it. He glanced at the cover. "Conrad. Not the lightest reading. What do you make of him?"

"Have you read him?"

"A long time ago. I've come to think of this novel as a kind of instruction manual for the line of work I'm in. An instruction manual for what *not* to do."

"What line of work is that?"

"I'm aide-de-camp to Major-General Theodore."

"You don't look like a military man." But perhaps that explained the moustache.

"My wife says the same thing." Seth gave a theatrical sigh. "So much for making General. It's all in how you look, you know."

Arun joined him in a laugh. "So who's Major-General Theodore?"

"Commanding officer of the Southern Military Region. If you're going there you should know such things."

"I don't pay much attention to politics, to tell the truth. I'm a schoolteacher."

"The General's no fan of politics either. Still, that's no excuse. Especially not for a schoolteacher."

"I teach reading and writing, arithmetic. Politicians have a way of making two and two add up to five."

"They're the ones who give the General his orders. Ultimately. That's why he's not fond of politics."

"So we understand each other, then," Arun said lightly.

"Looks like it." Seth glanced towards the counter and the young man standing sullenly behind it. "How does the food look here?"

"I wouldn't chance it if I were you."

"I left home in a hurry this morning. Had a wonderful week-long visit with my wife. If we're lucky, the next time I see her I'll be well on my way to being a father. We spent the last minutes before leaving for the train station increasing the odds, if you see what I mean. Didn't have time for breakfast."

"Listen," Arun said. "If you'd like to join me, I've got a briefcase full of food back in my compartment."

"A briefcase full of food? You teach cooking, too?"

"My sister ... It's a long story."

"You're a funny fellow, aren't you."

"Perhaps. But I'm the one with the food."

Seth pursed his lips around a smile, gestured with the book towards the door.

Leading the way, Arun said, "By the way, what does an aide-de-camp do?"

Seth slid the door open and pondered the question for a moment. "I'm like his wife. His military wife." He grinned. "But I don't go all the way, of course."

Arun's sister had packed several jars of preserves, enough cheese sandwiches with the crusts trimmed away to last him beyond the trip, half-a-dozen hard boiled eggs and four family-sized bars of his favourite dark chocolate. He was touched to see that she had included a can of condensed milk, with a punch to open it. As children he and his sister, inspired by the English adventure books they both devoured, had occasionally put together a picnic of jam sandwiches and sweet biscuits, which they would transport to the shade of a tree in the yard behind their house. They had no hamper as the English children in the stories did — they weren't even quite sure what a hamper was — but an empty chocolate box served the purpose. They would sit together and eat, washing down the food with long draughts of condensed milk, a little unsure about the nature of the pleasure they were supposed to be experiencing. The English children never had to contend with suffocating heat or ants the size of erasers. And they never felt vaguely sick afterwards.

Seth, sitting across from him, bit into a sandwich, chewed, sighed. "You've saved my life. I seem to be always hungry. I even wolf down army rations. If it weren't for the morning calisthenics, I'd be as big as a transport truck." He dipped his fingers into a jar of mango preserves, extracted a piece and popped it into his mouth. With relish, he licked the juice from his fingers. Reaching for another sandwich, he said, "So what else do you read apart from our depressing Polish friend there?"

"Just about anything really," Arun said, wiping bits of egg from his lips with the back of his hand. "From the trashiest potboiler onwards. You?"

"I haven't got time for trashy potboilers. Not with my job. I picked up a complete set of Proust yesterday. Figure that'll keep me busy for the next few months. And with nothing else to read, I'll be forced to work my way through him."

"What's an army man doing reading Proust?" Outside, early afternoon clouds were gathering in the sky, white bellies with grey hardening the edges.

"The army's my profession," Seth said. "Reading's my passion. Apart from my wife, of course, but that's a whole other matter."

"You weren't drafted, then."

"No. I've always been attracted to the military. I seem to have a talent for it. I've made Captain and there's no reason I shouldn't rise higher, apart from my appearance of course." He gave Arun a wry look. "But the way things are, even that shouldn't be a problem. Plenty of room for advancement."

Arun wondered what he meant by that — that the needs of the war created opportunities, or that its battles created vacancies? He chose not to ask.

They fell into a mutual silence. Arun watched the forest outside darken as clouds began filtering the sun. Already he could sense a difference — as if this country seen through dusty glass were an alien place and not fully part of his nation as it had been defined so many decades before at independence. The air in the compartment grew close and he wondered whether he should open the window a bit. He decided not to. The noise would be deafening.

After a while, Seth, peeling an egg, said, "You going to Omeara?"

"Yes. Do you know it?"

"Very well. Too well. Not that there's that much to know. I'm based at the Southern Command headquarters just outside the town. The general prefers to be there, in the thick of things. He's a good man. He doesn't believe in leading from the safety and comfort of the capital like most of the upper echelon."

"Do you know the school? What's it like?"

"I helped build it. Part of the army's attempt to win over the people. When I first got there all they had was a kind of hut, four poles with a thatched roof. There were no walls, so when the heavy rains came it got drenched. There weren't even any desks. The children sat on the earth floor. So we ordered the materials and put a platoon to work. It was done in a week. It's a simple building, not much to look at, but it's sturdy. Just a single room, I'm afraid, but we had desks and a blackboard trucked in."

"So the army's part of the life in the town."

Seth sighed. "Not really. As I said, there isn't much to do. The troops make occasional forays to buy fresh vegetables or personal supplies. There's not much in the way of entertainment. You like films?"

Arun nodded.

"There's no cinema." He smiled. He seemed to be enjoying himself. "You like music, perhaps? A little dancing?"

"Music, yes, but as for dancing ..." Arun tugged up his left trouser leg and tapped at the plastic shin.

Seth's eyes flickered in surprise. "No dancing, I guess. Which is all for the best since there isn't any of that either."

Arun adjusted his trouser leg. "So what is there, then?"

"The occasional cricket match, some football. A wedding or two. A funeral once in a while, but its entertainment value is somewhat minimal. The townspeople are uneasy about getting too close to us. Not that you can blame them."

Arun searched Seth's face. He saw that the acne scars had darkened, and that lines had etched themselves onto his temples. He thought he saw, too, a kind of panic in the eyes. He said, "What kind of place am I going to, Seth?"

Seth thought for a moment and, as a sudden rain lashed at the window, he said, "It's a place that's full of shadows, Arun. A place where questions have no answers. It's a place where two plus two equals five."

The train station was a shuttered wooden shack. The dim light of a solitary bulb above the door revealed the town's name roughly inscribed in white paint. Seth, whose only luggage was a duffel bag, helped him with his suitcases. They were the only passengers to disembark. An old car — the town's taxi, Seth informed him — was idling beside the shack. Behind the taxi was an army jeep with its headlights on, the driver leaning on the hood smoking a cigarette. The rain had ended, but had turned the ground soft and muddy.

The train did not linger and in the wake of its departure the darkness closed in on them. The bulb on the shack seemed to diminish to the intensity of a match flame. Even the beams from the jeep simply gave out after a few feet, as if overwhelmed by the density of the night. From everywhere came the sounds of water dripping.

"Where are you staying?" Seth said.

"There's some kind of schoolmaster's house. I'm told it's basic but comfortable."

"Basic, yes. That's about it." Seth led the way to the vehicles. "If you like, you can spend the night at the base and, come morning, I'll have someone drive you over to your digs."

"I think I'd rather settle in right away," Arun said. "I'm eager to get a look at things."

Seth considered his words. "Are you sure? Arriving in the middle of the night ..."

"I'd like to make an early start in the morning."

"Suit yourself," he said.

The driver, tossing his cigarette aside, relieved them of the luggage and stowed it in the jeep. "Hop in," Seth said. "We'll give you a ride."

"Thank you, but I can take the taxi."

Seth climbed into the seat beside the driver. "You won't accept my hospitality. You won't accept a lift. But you're not in the capital now, Arun. You're not even in the north. Down here, you better decide who your friends are."

With some difficulty, Arun clambered into the jeep beside the luggage. Embarrassed, he said, "I'm not the most agile person, I'm afraid."

Seth ordered the driver to head for the town and the driver, face obscured by the brim of his fatigue cap, turned what felt like a long and searching gaze on Arun in the rearview mirror. Then he put the jeep into gear and stepped on the accelerator. As they surged off, Arun couldn't help imagining the taxi driver sitting there in the dark, resentful, watching his single fare whisked away by the army. But then it occurred to him that perhaps the driver had simply assumed they were both army men and that, this night, the train from the capital had left him empty-handed.

Arun stood in the middle of his digs — strange word that Seth had used but apt now that he had seen his accommodations; apt because the word suggested a burrow of some kind — and pronounced the word *basic*. Then he repeated it, and each time the two syllables filled the space.

The light switch beside the door didn't work and it was by the flame of the jeep driver's match that they had found the oil lamp, seen that the reservoir was full and the wick hardly used. The driver struck another match, lit the lamp. He placed it on the small wooden table that occupied the middle of the room. In the tenebrous light that was as much shadow as gleam, Arun looked around at walls of untreated cement blocks, the expanses of grey relieved only by a window that had been left in the middle of each wall and enclosed by heavy wooden shutters. He saw there was no ceiling, just the underbelly of overlapping sheets of corrugated iron supported by a skeleton of wooden beams. The air was musty with the smell of damp and mould.

The driver handed the box of matches to Arun and went to fetch his luggage. Seth, looking around, said nothing. Arun, embarrassed, avoided his eyes.

In one corner, beside a plain wooden chair that probably went with the table, was an armchair upholstered in a fabric so thinned and faded that its floral pattern appeared the product of some arid garden. In another, a cot so small it was almost a declaration that the inhabitant of the house was expected to arrive as a bachelor and remain so. A third corner held a kitchen counter on which a rusting two-burner stove offered little hope of food beyond the basic — there it was again, that word, fast becoming a theme of his new life — and perhaps not even that, for the rubber hose that would connect the stove to the gas cylinder hung uselessly to the floor. There was no sign of a gas cylinder.

Arun remained standing for some minutes, surveying his accommodations. The driver came in, put down his suitcases, left again. Seth told him to leave the door open, to let in some fresh air. Then he said, "The camp's no resort, but it sure beats this. And this time, I've got the food. Not to mention a well-stocked bar. Don't know about you, but I sure could use a drink right now."

Arun was tempted. As he had been tempted, in the weeks before his departure, by the offers of employment tossed to him like life preservers by family members. Manager of this, manager of that, with salaries far beyond what managers earned. But he hadn't wanted to be saved then — he knew this was how they saw it — and he didn't want to be saved now. He knew what he wanted to do. He forced himself to smile, forced himself to walk around the house in a show of animation. "Thank you, Seth. Doesn't look like much, I know, but I'm sure it'll look better in the morning. As for food — you haven't eaten all the sandwiches, have you?" He knew, also, that he was trying to reassure himself.

Seth looked at him and, for the second time that day, said, "You're a funny fellow, aren't you."

Arun smiled, shrugged.

"If you need anything, let me know. People in the town can direct you to the camp, it's not far. Madhu can drive you in his taxi." With a wave of his hand, Seth walked through the open door into the night.

When the sound of the jeep had faded, Arun shut the door, fetched the wobbly wooden chair from the corner and placed it at the table. He set his briefcase beside the lamp, took out the last of the sandwiches and had dinner.

TWO

HE AWOKE TO a darkness so unstirred that he thought with a rush of panic that his eyelids had failed to rise. He blinked twice, to no effect. *Blind.* His breath seized and he felt himself begin to suffocate. His mouth yawned in search of air. A rusty gasp rose from his throat, but his lungs filled in an instant, the air thick and close, leaving his tongue musty, and tasting vaguely like old mushrooms. The panic retreated. He breathed again, with effort, the way, as a child, he had had to suck hard at the clogged straw to draw up the last of the crushed-ice drinks he bought at the school's tuck shop. That had been part of the pleasure, the little slivers and balls of ice spitting cold onto the tongue. But this sucking at air was a different matter. It was effort without reward.

The cot rocked as he sat up. He had been dreaming that he was still on the train, the landscape flowing by at unaccountable speed.

From behind the counter of the dining car, the sullen young man — whom he also knew to be the jeep driver — suddenly smiled at him, as if they somehow shared a joke, and said, *Not too bad a burn, I hope?* He had slept deeply.

He lowered his foot to the floor, the concrete cool and damp, refreshing, and stretched his muscles stiffened by a night spent in an unfamiliar bed on a mattress so thin that his last thought before oblivion had been that it was hardly thicker than the pancakes his sister made for Sunday breakfast. The thought came back to him now, and his mouth watered at the memory of the sweet fruit-compote filling.

His fingers found the chair he had placed beside the cot the night before, found the matches, struck one, lit the oil lamp. The walls of the house leapt at him from the darkness and he had a brief moment of regret that he hadn't accepted Seth's invitation to spend the night at the base. Still, he was pleased to find a sense of well-being returning to him — something to do with the lasting voluptuousness of good food, with having slept well, with being here at last, in the south. As he strapped the prosthesis onto his left thigh — the sole of the shoe, he noted, was rimmed with dried mud — his feeling grew rich. He pulled on his trousers, got to his feet and avidly brushed his hand at the wooden latch that held fast the window above the cot. The shutters swung open of their own accord, to a stinging explosion of sunshine, a small kitchen garden choked with weeds, earth parched the colour of sand. And, when he looked up, to the startled eyes of a woman in the window of the neighbouring house not fifteen feet away.

Arun stiffened in surprise. She was not young, this woman. Her face was plump, with a scored forehead and pendulous cheeks. Her silver hair hung long and loose about her shoulders. She gazed at him as at some unearthly apparition — which, he supposed, he was for her. He gingerly raised a hand in greeting, although no smile came to him and he found himself incapable of constructing one. His open palm elicited no reaction and he felt the gesture to be that of an intruder, as if he had, by merely opening the shutters, unwittingly violated the woman's intimacy. Then she gave a single, sharp nod — more an acknowledgement of his presence than a sign of welcome — and let her eyes fall to the unseen activity of her hands, the washing of dishes, perhaps, or the kneading of dough. He would go over later, he decided, at a more appropriate time, and introduce himself by way of apology.

He stepped over to the kitchen area — the rusted stove, a small enamel sink with a lead spigot bowing into it. He grasped the tap, twisted at it, but it remained fast. He seized it with both hands and slowly, with a rusty squeal, it gave way. The spigot trembled, gasped, wheezed. To his surprise, water exploded from its mouth and thundered into the sink. There was a reddish tint to it, and the clotted smell of lead, but he cupped his hands under the flow and splashed his face again and again. The water was warm and thick, but refreshing nonetheless.

Then, with a certain caution, he turned the latch at the window and peered out through the parted shutters. Another garden, this one well-tended, with rows of healthy plants — peas, perhaps? — rising from mounds of soil dark with moisture. The house beyond it was painted pink; its window, gleaming white in the sunshine, was shut.

The third window at the back of his house, the most exposed, was the least sturdy of the three. Each shutter hung on a single hinge. Falling away, they revealed, beyond a backyard of arid, beaten earth, a lengthy stretch of cultivated fields that ended in the distance at jungle rising into mountains, folds of greenery growing darker and more dense as they retreated into the painful, azure sky. Somewhere in those mountains, he knew, was God's Nipple, the country's highest peak, sheathed in jungle so dense it was said that even on the brightest days midnight reigned on the ground. There, in perpetual darkness, lay the heart of the insurgency, the mythology that sustained it, the young men and women who served it.

He turned away from the mountains and the fields and, off to the side, the weather-beaten hut that he suspected housed his latrine and shower, and let his gaze wander around the little house. With the windows open and sunlight flooding in, a quick survey showed him that he'd been wrong the previous evening: it didn't look better in the morning. The walls of raw grey brick suggested a warehouse, and the furniture was of a quality his mother would have been ashamed to give away. He comforted himself with the thought that there was great scope here for improvement. He would begin by painting the walls white, which would make them friendlier, and he could have his sister send him some prints, something colourful, and framed photos of the family, and perhaps even curtains for the windows. He knew that would please her, would make her feel less abandoned. Although he wasn't much of a handyman, he could acquire a few basic tools — a hammer, a screwdriver, a saw, a bottle of wood glue — and strengthen the chair and table, perhaps replace the window at the back. The possibilities pleased him. He pictured himself labouring shirtless in the sunshine, his hands acquiring skills never needed in the capital where manual labour was plentiful and cheap. His father would have been amused, of course. One way in which he had measured his success in life was through his satisfaction in simply being able to call in a tradesman when a tap leaked, or a floorboard creaked, or the plumbing needed work.

As he took stock of the work to be done, of what could be achieved, Arun was brought up short by the cot. There was nothing to be done about it. His shoulders and back were still sore from the night. Surely there was a furniture dealer in town who could supply him with something less torturous?

He ran his palm along his cheek. He needed a shave and a change of clothing; then he would find some place to have breakfast before going in search of Mr Jaisaram, the closest thing, according to the ministry man, that the town had to a mayor. "No one wants the job," the man had added, slapping a strand of hair back into place. "Hardly surprising seeing that the last five had their throats slit."

The street was unpaved but, in the hard sun, few signs remained of the night's rain. On the roadway, ridges of mud had set like bricks in a kiln, and here and there a few puddles emitted final wisps of steam. High on their poles, the electric wires that paralleled the street glinted silver. There was no one about. His house was the second before last, meaning that he lived almost on the outskirts, the road and the bellying wires linking the electricity poles rutting on past grassed fields and, off to the right, the glassy ocean. It was, he knew, Omeara's only street. He headed in the other direction, towards the town centre.

The houses that lined the street to either side were of sturdy construction, of brick like his, and well maintained. Each one was painted a different, solid colour: this one moss green, that one canary yellow, then firetruck red, turquoise, midnight blue, lime green, sky blue. It was a child's rendering of a town, each building simple and stolid and securely shuttered. Only his house, the schoolteacher's quarters, had been left unfinished, the square of grey in a tin of watercolour paints. He was struck by the hush around him, as if the town were buildings and nothing more: no car horns, no blaring radios, not even a whimper from the stray dogs skulking around. He imagined that if he could peek into the houses he would see that the townspeople had all fallen asleep at their morning tasks, their animals also asleep beside them.

In the enchanted, unsettling silence, nothing moved, not even the air. As he walked along alert for any sign of activity, Arun thought that he would have to add a mirror to the list he intended to send to his sister. Already he was perspiring in the heat, his cheeks smarting from the many nicks he had inflicted on himself shaving blind.

Presently, the road was interrupted by a small asphalted square, beyond which, past the charred remains of a building, it continued, hedged by more houses as variously colourful as those behind him. The asphalt appeared fresh but was already seamed by cracks and crumbling at the edges. His soles pressed into the softened tar and onto what felt like loose sand beneath, a base so unstable he got the dizzying sense that the ground could suddenly give way and swallow him whole.

The square was bordered by a few business establishments, doors thrown open to darkened interiors: a bar hung with advertisements for beer and soft drinks, a café, a dry goods store, a textile store, others of less obvious purpose. They were not like establishments in the capital, had no glitz and glitter to them. They were made of wood and had the discretionary air of temporary stalls that could be quickly dismantled at the first sign of trouble. There were no customers to be seen, not even shopkeepers stocking shelves or twiddling their thumbs. To his left, an open expanse of sand led down to the ocean and a small wooden dock from which two men were setting out in a dinghy. For the second time that morning, Arun had the sense of being an interloper. His footsteps grew more cautious. He felt he would have to knock before entering a shop, ask permission.

He wandered across the hot asphalt, the heat radiating up through the sole of his shoe, towards the café. From the deep shadow of its overhanging roof a man emerged pushing a bicycle. A fedora sat low on his forehead, and a white dress shirt, the cuffs buttoned at his wrists, was tucked into baggy khaki trousers. He ignored Arun's nod of greeting.

Inside, in the sudden gloom, a waiter was dabbing a cloth at a tabletop. He looked up. "Help you?" He was not overjoyed at the sight of an unexpected client.

The café, like Arun's house, was basic: a dozen or so aluminium tables, metal chairs sprinkled with rust where they had shed their green paint. The walls were covered with faded posters for Bombay films, the bright lettering and smiling faces having long lost their lustre. "Breakfast?" Arun said.

THE UNYIELDING CLAMOUR OF THE NIGHT

The waiter gestured him to a table near the entrance and presently returned with a plate of fried bread and a mug of tea. Arun asked for some eggs. The waiter shrugged. "No eggs," he said, and returned unconcerned to wiping the tabletops. Arun ate quickly, swallowed his tea and, paying, asked where he could find Mr Jaisaram.

"You know Jaisaram?" the waiter said, carefully counting out the change. There was a note of suspicion in his voice.

"No, I was told to see him. I'm the new schoolteacher. I arrived last night."

"The schoolteacher," the man said, as if assessing the simple information. But if he drew any conclusion, his face betrayed no sign of it. "Three shops down," he said. "Meat. Just look for the flies."

Mr Jaisaram was the town's butcher. Arun had forgotten.

He paused at the entrance to the general store next door and peered into the gloom. Except for one spot on the rear wall occupied by a poster of James Dean, every wall was lined with shelves on which sat an astonishing variety of goods: canned foods, balls of string, bottles of soft drinks, mugs and plates, rolls of adhesive tape, knives, scissors, spools of thread, packets of coloured balloons, plastic clothespins, saws, chisels, hammers, manicure sets in bright pink plastic. From the ceiling dangled pots, pans, machetes in leather scabbards. In a corner sat a tower of plastic buckets, shovels and gardening forks, a few potbellied canisters of propane.

He called hello into the silence and, as the echo of his voice faded, a squat, dishevelled man appeared from behind a curtained door in the deeper shadows. He appeared to have just emerged from sleep.

"Good morning," Arun said, stepping inside. The shop smelled of kerosene and old flour.

"Morning." The man scratched at his grey hair cut spiky short and ran a plump hand down his unshaven cheeks. A hole in his sleeveless undershirt revealed a tuft of grey hair as thick as wild grass.

"I see you have propane."

The man's tired eyes darted to the white containers then back to Arun.

"I'm the new schoolmaster. I'm going to need one. And perhaps a new connection, too. The old hose doesn't look very trustworthy."

The man nodded vaguely, as if he had only half listened.

Arun reached into his back pocket for his wallet. "How much is it?"

"You need it right away, *Prahib*?"

The honorific surprised Arun, made him uneasy. It was brash testimony of the status he had suddenly acquired — status that was automatic and unearned. "I can't take it with me now," he said. "Later. This afternoon perhaps."

"You're staying at the schoolmaster's quarters?"

Arun nodded. Somewhere in the distance a dog barked.

"I live close by. I'll drop it off for you at the end of the day. Pay me then, *Prahib*."

Arun slid the wallet back into his pocket. "That's very kind of you, Mister ...?"

"If you're not there, you can pay me later," the man said, half turning and reaching a hand out to the curtain as if eager to return to his bed.

"And the children?" Arun said quickly. He was himself eager to establish a contact beyond the commercial. "What have they been doing? They haven't had a teacher for a long time."

"The children? They've been busy. Milking. Weeding. Tending the goats. There's a lot of work to do in life, *Prahib*. They don't have time to miss going to school." The man gave him a long sideways glance meant to remind him of his place in the scheme of things.

"Yes, well," Arun said after a moment. "I'm here now, so things can get back to normal for them."

"Normal?" The man pulled thoughtfully at his nose, then he laughed, a low tired growl that seemed to emerge from his belly.

"You know how to hook up the cylinder?" he said. "Do it carefully, or the first time you light your stove, boom!"

"I'll be careful," Arun said, turning to go.

The man stepped towards the curtained door, stopped. "My name is Madhu. But I don't want to know yours, *Prahib*. You won't be here long enough for it to matter."

Arun glanced back over his shoulder just as the curtain, billowing, swallowed Madhu. "Arun," he said loudly. "My name is Arun." From behind the curtain curled a growl of laughter but whether or not it was in response to his name he couldn't tell.

Arun found himself unaccountably aggravated by Madhu's laughter. He had long seen himself as being impervious to mockery — which was how he had survived the farewell dinner at his sister's, where, as the evening wore on, the food and drink had been increasingly accompanied by servings of ridicule marinated in humour. In the short walk to the butcher's — his eyes searching for flies, seeing none, seeing only an old woman crossing the square with a large cloth bundle clutched to her chest — he understood that his displeasure had been incurred by Madhu's unwillingness to learn his name, by his belief that he would not long fulfill his duty as teacher to the children of the town. It struck him as an undeserved judgement, and gratuitous: he knew his duty, had sought it out. Madhu didn't know that. The laughter had stung.

Arun strode across the asphalt and the soft sand on the other side, to the pebbled beach at the edge of the water. It was slightly cooler here. He took a deep breath of the salty air, dislodging some of the irritation Madhu had inspired. Far out on the water, the dinghy with the two men — reduced by distance to a shadow in the sunshine — was being approached by a larger, swifter boat with the sleek lines of a naval patrol craft. The vessel slowed and began circling the dinghy, its languorous movement suggesting suspicion. Arun recognised in its attitude the way police vehicles would drive slowly by him and his friends when they were out late in the streets of the capital, a way of serving notice of a surveillance reassuring only when directed at others. It circled the dinghy three times following the path of its own wake. Then, after making a close pass, it broke away and surged off towards the horizon, leaving the dinghy writhing as if unnerved on the disturbed water.

When the patrol boat could no longer be seen, Arun turned away from the ocean and walked back across the sand to the little square. Madhu had stifled his sense of well-being, and to what purpose? To make clear that he had no place here? Of course he didn't. Not yet. Or had he meant to ensure that the newcomer never would?

In the butcher's shop — there were no flies — a single bulb dangled on a cord from the ceiling, its light negligible, insufficient to alleviate the gloom. How curious it was that these shops were so sunken in darkness, that no one had thought to saw a hole in one of the wooden walls to invite in the light. The sunshine itself halted at the threshold as if having abruptly run into some invisible barrier. Standing at the door, he felt the sun prickling on his back while his face and chest were cast in shadow. The small room was filled with the low, reassuring hum of machinery and he saw that it was largely filled by the rectangular white bulk of a freezer. He stepped into the shop and above the squeak of a floorboard a female voice, rising as if in quiet interrogation, called, "Good morning?"

He didn't know where the voice had come from but by instinct he returned the greeting. A young woman rose from behind the freezer where evidently she had been sitting out of sight on a low chair or a stool. She had narrow, nervous eyes and the kind of face — bony, angular, with lines that defined her cheekbones before curving down to bracket her lips — he found appealing. Her wavy, black hair was pulled back tight on her head, but the style did not lend her the severity it might have to another. She was saved, he thought, by the soft rise of those cheekbones. All this he absorbed during the seconds it took her to ask what he required and to apologise for the meagre offerings in the freezer. The day was still early, she said, and if he wasn't in a hurry her father was even now seeing to the slaughter of a goat, and chickens would be available too within the hour.

"Actually," Arun said, "It's your father I want."

Her eyes fluttered in alarm.

"It's all right," he hastened to add, his palms rising in reassurance. "I'm the new schoolmaster. I was told to look up your father."

Her head jerked back slightly, her eyes narrowed further in scepticism. "The new schoolmaster," she said. "You look young enough to be in school yourself."

His jaws tightened: that sting again. She was hardly more than a year or two older than he. "Look here, Miss." Then the sting quickly gave way to a sense of foolishness. She had merely been teasing him, and he had confirmed her observation by reacting like a humourless adolescent. At that moment he realised that he wanted to be taken seriously here. It made him febrile in a way he hadn't been for very long time. He could think of no graceful way to retreat. "Look here, Miss," he repeated more softly but in the politely abrupt way his brother-in-law would describe as business-like, "I arrived very late last night to a house with no electricity and rusty water and as comfortable as a dog kennel. Moreover, the children of this town have had no schooling for weeks and I'd like to get classes organised as soon as possible. I'm told that your father can help me put things in place."

Her eyes lost all expression, all the playfulness he had misinterpreted as challenge. "One minute," she said. She turned, opened a door in the wall behind her and slipped out, pulling the door shut. Arun was left contemplating her eyes, the way they had hardened into disappointment. He would have to think of a way to put things right.

She was back very quickly. She motioned him through the door into a small yard enclosed by a wooden fence and with a floor of smooth concrete. It was open to the sky save for one corner that had been roofed in sheets of corrugated iron supported by sturdy wood beams. In its shade, before a counter composed of a thick cutting board on sawhorses, stood Mr Jaisaram. He was a large man wrapped in a long white apron spotted in blood both dried brown and freshly red. In front of him, suspended upside down from a roof beam by a length of rope knotted around its hind hooves, hung a goat. Its throat had been slit, the fur on its lower jaw matted dark by the blood that had coursed to its chin and into a bucket beneath. The chest had been sliced open, the cavity gutted. The viscera, a gleaming mass of vegetable colours, lay in a shallow aluminum pan beside the bucket. Mr Jaisaram, patiently skinning the goat with a small knife, paid no attention to Arun. He had removed the hide from the hind legs and was now stripping the chest, the freed skin hanging like a loose garment from the exposed, purplish flesh. The air was rancid with the smell of fresh blood. Arun felt his stomach rise and quickly turned his gaze away, so that he was looking not at Mr Jaisaram but just past him. Breathing through his mouth, he said, "Good morning." It was all he could manage.

Mr Jaisaram bent over and, with a grunt, tugged the hide sharply downward. There was a wet, ripping sound as it peeled from the forelegs. As if addressing the goat, he said, "You were supposed to be here two weeks ago." His tone was not friendly.

"Two weeks ago? There must be some mistake. They only offered me the job last week."

"Two weeks ago." With the knife, he severed the hide from the utterly revealed animal. "That's what they said."

"You must have misunderstood." Arun stopped himself, took a swift breath of air through his mouth. "You know what things are like these days. Someone got something wrong. Probably at the ministry. They're not the most organised people I've ever met."

Mr Jaisaram straightened up, tossed the knife onto the cutting board. "Well," he said more softly, "you're here now."

"Yes, I'm here now," Arun echoed, wishing the butcher would

34

step away from the purple and blue carcass that swung lazily around to reveal eyes as glazed as old marbles. "And eager to get started," he added.

Wiping his gleaming hands on his apron, Mr Jaisaram ambled over towards him. His was a light step for such a big man — a man with the build of a middleweight wrestler on the American fight spectacles so popular on television in the capital. His brother-in-law was a great fan of the programs, and had once declared, "Send a division of men like that to deal with the Boys in the south and all that nonsense'd be over in a week." Arun had never understood how Surein, of such keen mind and practical bent, could truly believe in the prowess of the costumed theatrical gorillas. He supposed that, like religious belief, it had something to do with unacknowledged fear and vulnerability seeking solace in fantasy.

"Yes, you're here now for better or worse," said Mr Jaisaram, settling his bulk close enough that Arun was forced to take a discreet step backwards from the odour of sweat and blood that rose from him. "They always send us the rejects."

Arun found himself at a loss for words. First the daughter, now the father. What kind of people were these? He saw immediately that he had asked himself the wrong question. The true question was, What kind of teachers had been sent here before him? Mr Jaisaram settled a frank gaze on him, expecting a reaction. In a quiet voice Arun said, "Not this time."

Mr Jaisaram let his eyes linger for some seconds before saying with a new animation, "Are you settled in, then? The last school-teacher didn't think much of his accommodations. He liked his comfort. Don't we all? But that's the way things are."

Arun thought briefly about the little house that was hardly larger than the butcher's shed, and about as charming. "I'll fix things up a bit," he said. "It'll be fine."

"Fix things up?" Mr Jaisaram cocked an eyebrow at him. "So you intend to stay for a while?"

"That's my intention."

The butcher kept a sceptical eye on him so long that the sun had time to move overhead. He could feel its heat spilling onto his shoulders, saw his shadow shortening and pooling around his feet. Once more he thought of the wrestlers and the way they pretended to intimidate each other with long and ferocious stares. Casting his gaze towards the entrance to the shop, he said, "I see you have electricity."

"Yes?"

"I don't."

"I know. We had it disconnected after the last teacher left. There was no point."

"Can you have it reconnected?"

"It can be done, but I warn you — keep oil in your lamp. They blow up the transformer every so often. The soldiers fix it then they blow it up again. Somehow. The soldiers've put mines in the ground a hundred feet around, they post guards, but still they manage to place bombs. It's like they have special powers, the Boys. That's what people around here think."

Arun knew of the rumours surrounding the Boys, rumours of supernatural abilities and divine protection. Such talk irritated him but it was, also, he knew, a sign of their success. "All those blackouts, it must be hard for you. The meat, I mean. Your freezer."

Mr Jaisaram waved Arun's concern away. "I have a small gen-erator. The army gave it to me, along with a monthly allotment of petrol. In return, I supply them with fresh meat. The general enjoys a generous table. Maybe you should talk to them about a generator for yourself. After all, you're a government employee too."

Arun shook his head in dismissal. "I don't think they'd agree."

"But you have army friends," Mr Jaisaram said with a small smile. "They drive you around."

"You mean last night?" Arun said. "Just someone I met on the train." But he was uneasy: how could Jaisaram possibly know about the lift Seth had offered him? Something his sister once said came back to him: a family was like a small town — both had secrets everyone knew.

Mr Jaisaram laced his fingers and, stretching his arms out, cracked his knuckles. "Have you seen the school?"

"Not yet."

"Go take a look." He would find it, he said, at the far end of the town, beside the playing field. "If you need anything, come back to me."

Arun nodded, turned to go.

"By the way, the cricket team could always use an extra player. Or are you more of a football man?"

Arun paused. "Neither actually. At least, not as a participant."

Mr Jaisaram threw up his hands in exasperation. "A reject! And lazy to boot!"

"It's not that. It's my leg." He leaned down and rapped his knuckles on the prosthesis. "Surely your cricket team isn't that desperate."

Mr Jaisaram looked stricken. "I'm sorry, I didn't know. You walk ..."

"Like a normal human being?"

"Well ... exactly."

"I'm used to it." Arun smiled. "I get around easily enough. Now, I've taken up enough of your time. I'd better go have a look at the school and let you get back to your goat." He suppressed his instinct to shake hands. Mr Jaisaram's hand was not one he wished to grasp just at this moment.

"Yes," Mr Jaisaram said, "in this heat meat doesn't last long." Then he put a finger to his lips. "You know, there's one advantage — to your leg, I mean."

"What's that?"

"If a dog tried to bite you he'd get a big surprise."

Arun laughed. "I guess I'd make him a rather unsatisfying lunch." He walked back to the door and was about to step into the shop to make his way out when the butcher, grasping a large carving knife, called to him. "Mr Arun, it's good you're here. The children need you."

His hand on the doorknob, Arun said, "How did you know my name?"

"It's my business to know things, that's not important. What's important is that you're here and you want to fix up your place. That's a good sign." Then he looked away, put the knife down on the cutting board. "You are looking, Mr Schoolteacher, at a man who cannot read or write. The children of Omeara must not be allowed to grow up like me. Ill-it-er-ate." He spoke the last word as if every syllable of it evoked his fury.

The admission astonished Arun. "You don't sound like an illiterate man to me, Mr Jaisaram."

"Oh, I know words, lots of words. But that's because my daughter reads to me. Every evening for years she has read to me. Newspapers, magazines, books — hundreds of books, some of them many times. What you hear when I speak, Mr Schoolteacher, are the sounds of words and sentences blown from the page by my daughter's breath."

He was relieved that the girl was not in the shop when he passed through and back to the asphalted square. His lingering sense of embarrassment, as if she had somehow caught him out, would have made him awkward with her. The sun was almost directly overhead, and the air over the water had grown hazy. The humidity coated his skin with warm vapour as he began the walk back, past the colourful houses and, in the distance, the mountains that had now acquired the look of wet moss. From one dark green slope rose a thick plume of smoke, white wreathed with grey, its form, as sturdy as a pillar, speaking to the absence of wind.

He spotted his house up ahead, a simple square with its roof sloping backwards, the only unpainted house. Its dark and stagnant interior came to him and he decided he would ask his sister to include a fan with the pictures and curtains he needed. As he approached, his eye was drawn to the weathered wood of the shutters, to the greyness of the brick, and he wondered what colour of paint would be appropriate to see between the pink of one neighbour and the blue of the other.

A female voice called out from behind him: "I see my father was right."

He turned around. The butcher's daughter was striding towards him. Her dress, cut just below her neckline, was of a light-brown cotton gathered in at the waist before flaring down below her knees. The fabric shaped itself to her supple movements so that, as she drew closer, he couldn't help noticing the suggestion of long and sturdy thighs and the light precision with which they moved. She gave the impression of being a woman who could walk forever, her feet barely touching the ground.

"My father sent me after you," she said, passing a palm along her gleaming forehead. "He forgot to tell you not to expect any students for a few days. They're very busy right now. He was sure you wouldn't find the school, even though it's the simplest thing in the world. He said you looked like the type who could get lost easily."

This woman seemed to have a talent for annoying him. "Well, he was wrong," Arun said, gesturing towards the final houses and the fields beyond. "As you can see."

She squinted at him in puzzlement. Then she snickered. "You think so?"

"He said it was here, at the far end of the town."

"Omeara's not a big town, but it does have two ends, you know."

"Oh." It occurred to him to say he'd decided to return to his house before visiting the school, but he saw little point. What difference could it make to her? He was not averse to lies, particularly harmless ones, but he did appreciate, as his brother-in-law held, that the worst lie was a transparent one. Transparent lies were bearers of contempt, while more significant lies, lies of careful construction, were prompted by far more complex motives. "Your father could have been a little clearer about which end he was talking about, don't you think?"

"Probably. Still, you're the only person who's ever got lost in Omeara as far as I know."

"I wasn't lost."

"I guess not. Just going in the wrong direction."

"It's not the same thing, you know."

"If you say so. You're the schoolteacher after all." She smiled, and what in the darkness of the shop had appeared to be beauty was revealed, in the stark daylight, to be the potential of beauty. Her attractive leanness was a step away from cadaverous, the liquid darkness of her eyes had leaked into the skin below them, and when she smiled he thought he saw the mechanics of her jaw, a kind of skeletal cantilevering too close to the surface, as if no flesh separated bone from skin. Arun found her as unsettling in the sun as she had been in the shadow, but for different reasons.

"Well?" she said with feigned impatience. "What are you waiting for? I haven't got all day."

"Of course," said Arun. "You've got to get back. You go on, I'll find my way."

"My father said to take you to the school. That's what I intend to do. Come on." With that, she turned and began striding away.

Those graceful movements, the sway of the dress: as if she were treading on eggs without fear of cracking them. He had no choice but to follow. "What's your name?" he said, taking a quick hop to fall into step with her.

"Anjani."

"Were you born here?"

"Yes."

"And you've lived here all your life?"

"Mostly. Apart from two years in the capital."

"When was that?"

"Six or seven years ago."

"What were you doing there?"

"My parents sent me to school there. Holy Faith Convent."

"Holy Faith? Really."

"You know it?"

"I went to St Alphonse-in-the-Fields. There were no fields, although there must have been once. We used to call it St Alphonse-in-the-Town."

Her narrowed eyes blinked at the road ahead. "There wasn't much holiness or faith at Holy Faith either."

"Why'd you come back? After the capital, Omeara must seem ..."

"Strange question from an Alphonsian. What are *you* doing here?"

He decided to ignore her question. "As a graduate of Holy Faith, you could've —"

"I never graduated."

"Why not?"

"I was expelled. Kicked out."

Her admission, the candour with which she had made it, startled him. He waited for her to continue.

"A couple of girls had been caught with a bag of *ganja*, so the nuns sprang a surprise inspection on the dorm rooms. They found a copy of *Playgirl* in my underwear drawer. I'd figured that they'd be too squeamish to touch my bras and panties. I figured wrong."

"How'd you get your hands on *Playgirl*? *Playboy* was worth several times its weight in gold at St Alphonse."

"Another girl had brought it back from a family vacation in California. Lord alone knows how she managed to slip it past her parents and the customs people. It was making the rounds. Anyway, the nuns gave me a choice. Confess where I got it or out on my tail. I've got a tough tail."

"Your parents must have been thrilled." At the square, the

surprising sounds of music drifted from the café. Two women, veils loosely draped on their heads, were leaving the general store with packages wrapped in newsprint. Calling good morning to them, Anjani said, "My father was disappointed, but he was okay after a while. As for my mother, she was glad to have me back. She doesn't trust the capital. Too many bad influences."

He laughed. "Funny. My family feels the same way about the south."

As they crossed the square and headed down the street on the other side, he indicated the charred ruins. "What happened here?"

"Somebody thought it would be a good idea to start up a little nightclub, mainly for the soldiers. The Boys didn't like the idea."

They walked on in silence for a while, past the houses on either side. Between them, in the fields, men, women, and children were hard at work, hoeing and weeding and watering the plants from buckets. At one point, he spotted several children with staves in their hands shepherding a flock of goats. "Will they be able to come to school?" he said.

"Some of them," she replied.

After the houses, the roadway grew stonier, more rutted, and up ahead the field of packed earth defined by bamboo goalposts came into view. Beside it stood the school, a simple building with a corrugated iron roof and walls of O-shaped ventilation brick painted lemon yellow. The large olive-green door added to its sturdy appearance.

Anjani said, "It's a gift from the army."

Arun grunted. He thought it prudent not to let on that he already knew that.

"We asked them for a thatched roof, it'd be cooler, but they like doing things their way."

They paused at the door, Arun reaching into his pants pocket for the key the man at the ministry had given him. As he withdrew it, Anjani reached out a hand and pushed the door open.

Arun held up the key. "It wasn't locked?"

"It never is. There's nothing to steal. What fool gave you a key?"

Before he could reply, a series of dull, distant thumps caught his attention. He glanced nervously at Anjani. She was unconcerned. "You'll get used to it," she said, stepping into the schoolhouse. "They don't usually come any closer than that."

He followed her into a cool, damp darkness pierced by hundreds of circles of light. Sunlight flooded in from behind him.

"You know," she said, "I'll bet those nuns have the centrefold pinned up in their refectory, right above the Reverend Mother. I kind of like the thought of them having two men hanging on the wall."

"Two men?" Then he understood what she meant and his face went warm.His gaze wandered around the schoolhouse: along the rough concrete floor, to the rows of vintage desks, each with two circular holes for ink pots, the dark wood of the benches burnished by decades of squirming students; to the teacher's table and chair — *his* table and chair — sitting stolid on a low dais before them; to the large chalkboard, its green paint abraded in spots but serviceable still, screwed to the wall behind the table. An open box of chalk sticks and a brand new felt eraser striped red, white and black sat on the tabletop.

Anjani said, "There's no electricity, so during the wet season — clouds, no sun — oil lamps would be useful." She slipped onto a desk in the front row.

Arun stepped onto the dais and eased back the chair, the rasp of wood on wood loud and strangely disorienting. Then, after a brief pause, he stepped into the space between chair and table — a deliberate claiming of duty — and sat.

Anjani, her beauty returned to her in the irresolute light, looked up at him and laughed.

"Do I look funny?" he said. Perhaps because he felt odd and slightly absurd, her laughter bore no sting.

"You look like a naughty student trying out the teacher's chair while he's gone. The table's too big for you."

He ran his palms slowly across the table top, feeling its unseen gouges, trying to divine if it would allow him to take possession; ran them without response to the edges where his fingers curled around the warm wood, gripped at it. *His* desk, *his* blackboard, *his* schoolroom. A disorder of pleasure fluttered through him.

He wished his parents could see him, especially his father. Wished they — he — could see him planted here making real the duty he had chosen for himself. He knew that his father had never believed in it, had never conceived that his son could shape for himself a serious life so unlike their own. Just before her marriage to Surein, Joy had asked him about what she had termed his stubbornness, and he had been obliged to explain — his dissatisfaction with the life their parents had constructed: this increasing sense of withdrawal, not quite into isolation but behind the walls of a family redoubt. And he had gone further, speaking of the path she and her soon-to-be husband had chosen, this filling of a need that brought the freedom previous generations had not enjoyed: he didn't condemn them for it, was even relieved that Surein would take up the business responsibilities he had disdained. But that life wasn't for him. He wanted, he said, to return to a more public life, even if that meant, as Joy had pointed out, being an employee of strangers rather than a man of independent means earned through a family business that had made their name a familiar one throughout the country. He wondered how it was that this was the only time he had put it into words for another, and he felt he had done an inadequate job. Joy couldn't grasp his meaning, couldn't understand what drove him to a duty that didn't serve the family. But, if they could see him now, he felt, in this modest schoolhouse, in the south — where they had never been, despite two visits to London, a package tour of the continent, a daring month in India — they might get it.

"So," Anjani said. "How does it look from up there? Do you feel all-powerful?"

All-powerful? Her question brought a smile to him. Not even in his idle moments had power, of any kind, been one of his ambitions.

"Look on the top edge of the blackboard," she said, a finger indicating the corner above him and to the left.

He half stood, reached up to the inch-wide frame, and found a slender switch about two feet long. It was smooth, with a knot towards one end, and had been darkened by varnish.

"It's your sceptre," she said, as he sat back down. "Your rod of authority. All the children know it. Everybody in town knows it. If you've been bad, Nawaal will get you."

"Nawaal?"

"The stick."

"It has a name?"

"Nawaal was a woodcutter from a village that used to be not far from here. It's gone now, wiped out during a battle soon after I returned from the capital. A few rockets from a helicopter. Nawaal lived in that village before I was born. Every morning he'd go into the forest with his axe and his ox cart, chop firewood all day, and return in the evening in time to make the rounds of the villages in the area. One day people started disappearing. Men, women, even children. They'd leave for the fields in the morning and never return. Somehow they discovered that Nawaal was the culprit. He'd tie up his victims in the oxcart, take them deep into the forest and whip them within an inch of their lives — then he'd go that extra inch with his axe. A dozen people disappeared before the army tracked him down. In fact, he was the reason the soldiers came here in the first place." She nodded at the whip. "Nawaal lives on. And the soldiers never left," she raised a baleful look at him, "as you well know."

Arun leaned forward, propping his elbows on the desk. "Tell me something, Anjani. How is it that everybody seems to know I got a lift in an army jeep last night? It was late, nobody was around."

"Madhu was there with his taxi. You didn't take it. Afterwards, well, who else drives around late at night? Do you think it's that hard to tell where they stop, just by the sound?" Her eyes narrowed at him, a half smile forming on her lips. "You think we've been spying on you since you stepped off the train, right?"

"Something like that. Omeara's a long way from the capital."

"Longer than you think. Things are different here."

"I've noticed."

"Have you? Remember this: there aren't any crowds to disappear into."

"I'm not looking to disappear." He grasped the whip at both ends, pulled them down, testing its flexibility. The tips touched; there was no hint of cracking. He let it straighten out then carefully placed it on the desktop. He looked up at Anjani. "It's time Nawaal retired, don't you think?" He couldn't imagine applying the whip to a pupil's flesh.

Anjani leaned back and folded her arms. "You can try, but it has a life of its own. It won't be sent away until it's ready to go. At least that's what people around here believe."

He nudged the stick to the centre of the desk. "That's another difference between the capital and Omeara," he said, reaching into his pocket for the Swiss Army knife he'd carried with him since high school. "There's less superstition in the capital. Or perhaps less resignation." He opened the larger blade and pressed the keen edge against Nawaal. It made little impression on the wood.

Anjani said, "Are you sure you know what you're doing?"

He pressed harder. Then, balling his left fist, delivered a swift blow to the top of the blade. The whip separated into two equal lengths, the knife edge nicking into the desktop. He flicked the knife shut. "Sometimes you just have to insist a little."

Anjani slid from her seat and approached his desk. She gazed down at the two pieces of stick, her face unreadable.

Arun wondered whether he had acted too hastily, too thoughtlessly, driven by his need to make a point. Had the whip, with its name and its mythological aura, represented more than a tool of corporal punishment to these people? He watched as she picked up a piece of the whip in each hand, holding them up the way a juggler grasped his pins before beginning his act. Then she whacked them down on the desktop one after the other: twice the whistling, twice the crack.

"Clever of you," she said without looking at him. "Now there are two of them."

THREE

Hᴇ ᴛʜᴏᴜɢʜᴛ ᴀᴛ first that the voices were shreds of a dream
that had strayed into his path as he awoke. But when he opened
his eyes to the stuffy darkness, the house already broiling under the
morning sun, he knew they were just outside, two, perhaps three
of them. The voices were low and indistinct, men speaking not in
whispers but in the relaxed tones of long-time friends. Had they
been trying to be discreet he wouldn't have heard them through
the closed shutters.

He sat up, pulled on a shirt, and quickly buckled on his
prosthesis. Buttoning his trousers, he trundled over to the door.
Outside three men were gathered at the corner of his house. One
was balanced on a rickety wooden ladder, another was steadying
the ladder with his hands, and the third was shepherding a homemade wheelbarrow riotous with electrical cables of various colour,

copper wire, rolls of tape, light switches, screwdrivers, pliers, and assorted bits of electrical paraphernalia as unfamiliar to him, and as vaguely unsettling, as medical equipment.

"Morning," Arun said hesitantly, smoothing his hair down with his palm.

The shirtless man perched on the ladder squinted down at him, while the one steadying it, his blue shirt untucked and unbuttoned, eyed him with the indifference he might have directed at a passing stray. The third man, dressed with greater care in a white short-sleeved shirt and old but serviceable dark pants, was pouring hot liquid from a thermos bottle into its lid. He said, "We're hooking up your electricity."

Arun nodded. "Thank you."

"The connection isn't good. We have to change it. It won't be long."

Arun nodded again. He saw that the men were staring at his feet. He had forgotten to put on his shoe. He was standing there with one foot shod and one bare.

The men glanced uneasily at one another, then back at Arun. The man in the white shirt, evidently the one in charge, proffered the thermos. "Tea?" A large gold watch dangled loose on his wrist.

"No, thank you."

"My name is Kumarsingh," the man said. When he smiled, yet more gold showed among his teeth. "President and sole proprietor of Kumarsingh Enterprises International Ink. It is my pleasure to welcome you to our fair town, *Prahib*, and if there is anything I can do to make your sojourn among us more agreeable, please do not hesitate to call on me." His voice rose and fell in pleasant waves.

The man in the blue shirt passed a screwdriver to the man on the ladder, who returned to his electrical tinkering.

"If I think of anything I'll let you know," Arun said.

"Perhaps a new table for your dining pleasure, *Prahib*. Or some bookshelves. Surely a teacher has need of many bookshelves." He had a thin, well-tended moustache.

"You're right," Arun said. "I'm sure teachers do. But not this one, not yet."

Kumarsingh considered this briefly, then he brightened. "But one day?"

"One day."

Kumarsingh dipped two fingers into his shirt pocket and extracted a card, which he handed to Arun with a flourish. "For when you're ready." On it, cursive print read:

Kumarsingh Enterprises International Ink.

P. Kumarsingh, Prop.-Pres.

Omeara Main Road, Omeara

Kumarsingh had acquired a filmic idea of style that Arun recognised, which suggested that he had spent time elsewhere, in some larger town. He was a man of nerves. Even standing still, he gave an impression of restlessness, of restrained frenzy, that might have made him untrustworthy. It was the film style that saved him. His assumption of it spoke of anxiety, and of ambition. It softened him.

"Sure about the tea?" Kumarsingh held up the thermos bottle. "It's the finest Burmese green tea. Good for the heart and —" his eyes and his grin grew wide in merriment "— for other parts of the body that require strong blood flow."

Burmese tea. It had been his mother's favourite. Arun hadn't had any in a long time. He remembered a woody, robust flavour, with an aftertaste of the mint leaves his mother placed on the bottom of the pot before sprinkling in three generous pinches of the tea leaves. "How do you brew it?" he said.

"Some people like to put in bougainvillaea flowers or even a few hibiscus petals. Orange rind too, believe it or not. Me, I like the traditional way. Mint."

"I'll have some."

Kumarsingh seemed pleased. "You have a cup?"

Arun ducked into the house, pausing to splash some water on his face and run his wet hands through his hair. He slipped his foot into his shoe before stepping back outside, cup in hand.

Kumarsingh was holding a square box of rusted metal with various wires sticking out of it. He glared at it. "Chinese junk," he said in disgust, before tossing it into the wheelbarrow. He appeared innocent of having made a pun.

Leaving the two men to their work, he led Arun through the ruined vegetable garden — the neighbour's shutter was closed — to the narrow backyard, a ribbon of beaten earth that gave way to wild grass and, a little farther out, the cultivated fields bordered by the mountains. Already immense labour was taking place among the furrows, men wielding hoes or rakes, women and children bending and squatting as they weeded or trundling along with shoulder braces from which swayed buckets heavy with water. Arun admired that labour, was awed by its sheer difficulty, but he understood none of it, knew none of the mechanics.

Kumarsingh filled his cup. The tea was strong, with a coarseness that signalled the leaves had been boiled and not steeped. And it had been sweetened with sugar, not honey. But that, Arun remembered, was the southern way. Their foods, like their manners, were not known for subtlety. It was part of what made them comical to northerners.

"Electricity, furniture." Arun tapped the cup with a fingernail. "Even aphrodisiacs! What else do you deal in, Mr Kumarsingh?"

"You name it, Kumarsingh can handle it, *Prahib*."

"Are you good at growing things?" He gestured at the fields with his cup. A bare-backed man was scooping water from a bucket with a gleaming tin can and dousing himself. The water fell from him in crystallised sheets and Arun imagined he could see steam rising from the man's close-cropped head and bony shoulders. A young boy stood in front of him, both hands gripping the handle of the bucket, his face screwed up either at the effort or at the brightness the sun, Arun couldn't tell which.

"I grew up like those children out there, *Prahib*," Kumarsingh said." With one pair of short pants and two jerseys. This became two pairs of short pants and four jerseys when my older brother died.

You had to be good at growing things. If not, well, you followed my brother on his journey before your time."

"Surely your brother didn't starve to death." There were many ways to die in this land, many of them unexpected and unnatural. But starvation, as far as he knew, was not one of them.

"No, *Prahib*. One night he got a pain in his side. By the morning he was hot and trembling and he couldn't stretch his legs out, he was wrapped up tight on the bed. By the afternoon he was hardly hearing my mother call his name. They tried to get a doctor but he lived two towns away and there was fighting and all the roads were blocked and the army was too busy to help. Then an officer rubbed his fingertips with his thumb and said that, even with the fighting, anything was possible. But he was just laughing at my father, *Prahib*. What he wanted we did not have and how could the officer not know that? By the evening my brother was dead."

He dipped his fingers into his other shirt pocket and plucked out a soft pack of Gold Standard. He extracted a cigarette, offered it to Arun and when it was refused clamped it between his lips. He lit it with a lighter he'd dug from his pants pocket.

"They burnt him the next day and I got his clothes. My mother thought bad food killed him. She said it was her fault and my father believed her. He never said a kind word to her after that. They lived out their lives that way."

"From what you describe, it sounds to me as if your brother had appendicitis."

"Seems like it to me too, *Prahib*. But we didn't know about this at the time. I found out about appen'citis only many years later." He sucked hard at the cigarette, so that the paper sizzled. "When the wind blows, *Prahib*, I can hear my brother groaning."

Arun took another sip of tea, found that it caused the inside of his cheeks to pucker, a not unpleasant sensation. "You must blame the army for his death, then. If they'd got a doctor, perhaps your brother —"

"The soldiers are my best customers, *Prahib*." He shrugged. "As for me, as soon as I was old enough, I went off to the capital." He turned towards Arun, eyes squinted against the smoke. "You are from the capital, if I am not mistaken?"

"Yes."

"It is a good place, the capital."

"Is it? For people like you, I mean."

"You mean two-percenters, *Prahib*? It is not a good place if you are a two-percenter, but I decided when my brother died that I would not be a two-percenter.I wanted to make my own way in the world, with my own mind and my own hands. A resting brain is a dead brain, I believe. My mind would come up with the dreams and my hands would make them real."

"You're what the Americans call a go-getter."

Kumarsingh considered the word. "A go-getter," he said. "Yah, I like that. I go and I get. I like that very much." He laughed, and a glint of gold showed through the smoke funnelling from his mouth.

Arun thought of the boy at the ministry, and of the brutality that was so casually dealt out throughout the north to people like him and Kumarsingh — especially Kumarsingh, who would have quickly earned a reputation for arrogance, for not knowing his place. "What was it like being a go-getter in the capital?"

"My idea was to find out what southerners like me needed, yah? And to supply it. I wasn't interested in going and getting from the others, they had their own go and getters. But it turned out that while the needs were many, the abilities to pay were few. There were people who wanted to help, people like ..."

He stopped himself, but Arun knew what he had been about to say. "People like me?"

"Yah, *Prahib*, people like you. From your community. Kind people."

His voice wavered, and Arun understood that Kumarsingh had once more given in to discretion. After the word *people* hovered the word *but*. So Arun said it for him.

Kumarsingh took a final puff of his cigarette, tossed the butt to the ground and crushed it under his shoe. "I don't want to sound

ungrateful, *Prahib*. They were good people. They worked *harred* —"
he pronounced it like a blend of *harried* and *hurried* "— to make
better how my people lived, to find them little jobs here and there.
But, with me, there was a little problem that grew into a big problem. My dreams seemed to them unrealist. My dreams made them
cranky. Here, they would say, take this job as office boy, take that
job as cleaner or that one as night watchman."

He was becoming agitated, his gestures — wrists and fingers
flicking like those of a man broadcasting grain — more spastic. His
language too, Arun noticed, was beginning to give him trouble.
He lit another cigarette and that seemed to calm him.

"The jobs weren't good jobs," Arun said, and he thought again
of the boy at the ministry.

"They were fine jobs, *Prahib*, for some people. But that was the
problem, you see. These good people looked at us and saw only
two-percenters. And they had their own ideas about us, ideas that
had nothing to do with being a go-getter. They spoke of us as
being the *real* people, *Prahib*, people —" he flung his arm at the
fields "— who spend their day working in the sun. Somehow this
back-breaking work made us real to them. They saw us the way
some people in rich countries see organic vegetables, *Prahib*."

Arun couldn't suppress a smile. "Organic vegetables?"

Kumarsingh stiffened, but only for a moment. "In the capital,
Prahib, I read the *Time* magazine every week. And the *Reader's
Digest*, *Prahib*, for improvement of my vocabulary."

"Very good, Mr Kumarsingh." Arun drained his teacup, and was
touched that Kumarsingh, with no hesitation, immediately filled
it again.

"If that is what is real, *Prahib*, then I don't want real." He flung
his arm again at the fields and the sweating bodies. "None of those
people want real! I saw that these good people in the capital
wanted me to live in a way that they did not have to, in a way that
they saw as real and true but only for two-percenters. I felt they
wanted me to be successful, yah, but a successful two-percenter.

They felt that if I tried to be a go-getter I was being pre-sump-tu-ous. That is the right pronunciation, yah, *Prahib?*"

Arun nodded.

Kumarsingh tapped out another cigarette. Pulling on the smoke, he squinted slyly at Arun. "That is what it was like, *Prahib*, being a go-getter in the capital." Smoke billowed from his nostrils. There was a smile on his lips, but his eyes were hard.

"So you came back here."

"So I came back here."

"And?"

"I am not a rich man yet, *Prahib*. But I am still a go-getter, yah!" A sparkle replaced the hardness in his eyes.

"Is it easier here, Mr Kumarsingh?"

"It is not easy anywhere. Many of our people have gone to other countries. Is it easier for them? Everywhere you must pay this way or that way." He turned his head, eyes sweeping across the fields, pausing on a woman who, from the swaying and flinging of her arms, was clearly berating a young girl.

On a hunch, Arun said, "The nightclub that was burnt down, that was yours, wasn't it?"

"It was mine." His lips tightened. "It is hard sometimes. You never know who will be unhappy with you, and why."

"I was told the insurgents burned it down."

He shrugged.

"What keeps you going?"

The tea in the thermos lid had gone cold. Kumarsingh tossed it aside, raised the thermos bottle in an offer of more — Arun waved it off with a smile — and refilled the lid. Leaning his head back, he chugged the hot liquid, clamped the lid onto the bottle and tightened it. "Dreams, *Prahib*," he said. "The man who does not dream is not alive, do you not agree? And the bigger you dream, the bigger you live. A resting brain is a dead brain, I believe. I read the *Time*, *Prahib*, and the *Reader's Digest*. And so I added International to Kumarsingh Contracting, because one day it will be."

"Mr Kumarsingh?"

"*Prahib?*"

"Please don't call me *Prahib*. It makes me uncomfortable."

"What do I call you, then?"

"Arun."

"I will call you Arun if you will call me Prakash."

"You've got a deal, Prakash."

Gold glinted in Kumarsingh's mouth. "Easiest deal I ever made," he said.

ON HIS THIRD morning in the town, Arun stood on the pebbly beach, at a certain remove from the townspeople, and watched a boat burning far out on the water. The sun was half risen, the sea calm and as solid as lead in the early light, its surface undisturbed by the cool, light breeze. Later, when he thought back to that moment, he would remember no sound, even though there had to have been the wash of water onto the wet stones. What he would remember was the detachment of the crowd: their unreadable faces, the blanket of soundlessness they had tossed around themselves.

It was a small boat, one of the river schooners that plied along the coast to trade with fishing villages in territory too remote or too dangerous to be supplied by truck. There was no flame, only the rising smoke, a dark and oily column that bisected the sun with geometric precision. Around the boat, two grey Navy patrol craft described relentless circles like hornets rounding on their prey. On the bow of each vessel — low and sleek, suggestive of swift deadliness — a helmeted figure in grey uniform clung to the handles of a heavy machine gun. The patrol craft were recent acquisitions. Arun recognised them from photographs he had seen in the newspaper not long before taking the train south from the capital. The government had high hopes for them. The army had been unable to dislodge the rebels. Perhaps the Navy could help starve them out.

He watched the circling craft, the burning boat, the curdled smoke, and ran his palm slowly up and down his left thigh. It was as if all his anxiety had gathered there, in a dull and growing ache. The southern dampness had irritated the skin around the stump, leaving him with the disagreeable impression that the knee and the shin and the foot were still there and were sore, perhaps from a rough game of football. A long burst of machine gun fire and the shouts of a fisherman preparing his nets on the beach had brought the townspeople out into the early morning, some from their beds, some from their breakfast tables. He had been the last to arrive — attaching the prosthesis, its pink plastic incongruous where it met his brown skin, had been difficult — and he had felt it prudent to keep his distance.

Out on the water, the boat continued to burn, the patrol craft continued to circle. He felt someone's eyes on him and again he glanced over at the crowd gathered in a knot some yards off. But he caught no one's gaze. He recognised many of the faces although he could not yet put names to most of them. At the front stood the butcher and his daughter, both as expressionless as disinterested witnesses. Several children of an age to be his students hung about in the crowd looking thin and malnourished, some with arms folded tight on their chests, some in the tighter embrace of their mothers. No one acknowledged him. This morning he felt a great deal older than his twenty-four years.

After a while, the ache in his thigh began to throb. He thought there would be nothing more to see. The boat would burn and sink, and the Navy men would point their prows elsewhere in search of smugglers bringing food and weapons to the rebels.

He had just decided he would leave when, with a thump hardly more dramatic than that of a door slammed in anger, the boat exploded. A fury of flame rose from surface of the water. A second or two later, a warm wind corded its way through the cool air. The column of smoke shuddered, thickened farther up, began to dissipate at its base, and he saw that the boat was no longer there, the water white and churning where it had been. Now the smoke had lost its illusion of solidity, black draining to grey then to a nothingness, which, following on the brief warmth, reached his nostrils with the slightly acrid smell of old fire.

Soon, the patrol boats broke their circle and began edging in, sailors peering down at the settling water, looking perhaps for survivors. But each helmeted man, he saw, had a rifle braced at his shoulder. If they were searching for survivors, it was not for rescue.

In ones and twos and family groups, the townspeople turned and began the short walk back to their houses. There was bread to be sliced, tea to be sipped. There were gardens to weed, fields to till, shops to open. No one greeted him, not even the children who, in time, would be sitting at their wooden desks with their faces turned to him in eagerness, in boredom, in puzzlement, in frequent consternation.

He turned back to the sea. The patrol craft had come to a standstill, and from each a man was using a long white pole to fish debris from the water while his comrades pointed their guns into the wet emptiness all around them.

A movement caught the corner of his eye. The butcher, already wrapped in his blood-stained apron, nodded gravely at him and gave a little wave. The daughter, striding along at his side, offered no greeting. Her dress, he noticed, was the colour of the sea.

FOUR

Gripped by a weariness that caused a gentle ache in his muscles, he took his chair around to the back of the house and sat in the fading light. The air smelled of baked earth. The sky, thickened to a royal blue, was still too bright for stars, but the mountains were already flat and black, drained of their bulk. The fields, dusky green, of a pleasing symmetry, were strewn with handfuls of shadow.

Arun stretched out his legs, clasped his hands behind his head. It was a time of day, this brief interlude between the dying of the light and the recrudescence of the night, which affected him in unpredictable ways. A time of day when a welling sadness sometimes brought thoughts of his parents. Or when a quiet hopefulness offered glimpses of satisfaction and optimism. A strange and unsettling time.

This evening, though, a new feeling came. At first he couldn't put words to it, could only feel it pulsing and elusive in his belly. Eventually, as he watched the shadows fatten in the fields, as he saw the sky darken and felt the air grow marginally less humid on his skin, he settled on the word "strangeness." That was it. An iridescent sense of strangeness was growing beneath his fatigue.

Nothing in this new place was truly unfamiliar, but little was quite familiar either. The air, the earth, the vegetation and its colours, even this ramshackle little house — they all had their reflections up north, less in the capital than in the outlying towns. And yet there was something to which he could put no name, an unseizable edge that was both unsettling and attractive. It was as if every familiar colour were shaded in a subtly different tone, as if every familiar leaf and flower were cast in a minutely different form. Even the shadows were somehow denser than those he had known at home. None of the differences was readily evident to the eye. He looked, focussing on the clumps of grass and wild flowers that dotted the ground just behind the house: green grass, yellow flowers, red flowers. Nothing extraordinary, but nothing quite ordinary to him either. Rather, the differences — undeniably there yet somehow not there — were made real only to the senses, as if this southern world encompassed elements that resisted the brain and revealed themselves only to the gut.

A light breeze began blowing down from the mountains and across the fields. It was one of the characteristics of this part of the island that hot breezes blew in from the sea one moment and cooler breezes down from the mountains the next, the narrow plain caught in the suffocating turmoil. The breeze was so slight that not a blade of grass stirred, but he could feel its movement on his skin.

"Mr Arun?"

He looked to his right, from where the female voice had come, and saw Anjani peering around the house at him, her face half shadowed. He leapt to his feet, feeling curiously as if he'd been caught in some vaguely disreputable activity.

"My father says you could join us for dinner if you want."

"That's very kind of him, but I don't want to impose." He quickly ran his splayed fingers through his hair, smoothed it down with his palms.

"Impose-shimpose," she said impatiently, stepping out from behind the house. "My father is inviting you. Are you hungry?"

Arun gave a nervous little laugh. "Yes."

"Well, come then," she said, turning and walking away.

He hooked his hands behind his back and followed her. "Is it far?"

She shook her head, glanced sceptically at him. "Don't you know that we're neighbours? You gave my mother a big shock that morning when you opened your shutters."

The woman with the silver hair fanned across her shoulders. Arun's neck and cheeks grew warm. And yet, as he recalled the moment, her face had registered no alarm, had registered nothing.

They walked in silence between their two houses to the road. Several barefoot boys were playing cricket in the last of the light, their wicket made of one cooking-oil can sitting on another. The butcher's house was a little longer than his and more than twice as wide. Anjani opened the front door and, expressionless, ushered him inside.

He found himself in a small living room brightly lit by two unshaded fluorescent bulbs and crowded with furniture: a red sofa with two matching armchairs; a round coffee table of gleaming mahogany in the middle of which a brass vase stood on a knitted white doily; a long, glass-fronted buffet along one wall. The walls, of raw brick like his, were painted a soft blue. They were covered in framed photographs and, hung between the photographs, were what appeared at a quick glance to be small wood carvings. Anjani gestured him towards the sofa just as her father entered the room.

Mr Jaisaram was freshly showered and shaved, his hair plastered flat on his head. In his white dress shirt, sleeves buttoned tight at the wrists, and the dark trousers belted high on his belly, he appeared a smaller, less imposing man than he had in his abattoir.

"Mr Schoolteacher," he said in a voice that filled the remaining space in the room the way, Arun thought, water insinuates itself into every unoccupied cranny, "I'm glad you could come."

"It's very kind of you to invite me."

"Sit, sit!" Mr Jaisaram said, motioning him down with his open palms and easing himself into one of the armchairs. He exuded the sharp tang of generous amounts of aftershave. "Make yourself at home. It's no secret your place is no paradise. My wife's cooked up a vegetable curry. You northerners, you like your food hot? Handfuls of red pepper?"

Arun nodded as Mr Jaisaram smacked his lips, the very thought of the dish evidently causing him to salivate.

"You must be thirsty," Mr Jaisaram continued, his tone suggesting that the contrary was simply not possible. "Something cold? Water, soft drink, juice? Or how about a real drink? Whisky, gin, vodka, tequila, beer, rum, vermouth, brandy, sherry. Name it, we probably have it."

"You're well supplied."

"The soldiers aren't very well paid, but their canteen is well stocked and they like good meat. Trade is brisk."

"Do you have tonic water?" Arun said.

"Of course," Anjani replied laconically. "Gin and tonic, I'll bet, right?"

Arun felt as if he'd been swatted, although he didn't know why. "If it's all right."

"It's all right. Beefeater or Bombay? Lemon or lime?"

"Ah, Beefeater. Lemon."

She turned to her father who, fingering his chin, was giving the question of his drink serious thought. "I think I'll have a soul kiss."

Arun looked quizzically at him.

Counting on his fingers, he said, "Orange juice, Dubonnet, vermouth and ... What else, Anji?"

"Bourbon," she said, leaving the room.

Mr Jaisaram sighed in contentment. "Anji's just like her

mother. They can put together this, that, and the other and take you completely by surprise. You name a dish, her mother can make it. You name a cocktail, Anji'll whip it up in two-twos. Don't take it wrong, but I think your G and T disappointed her. No challenge."

"Where'd she learn to be a bartender?"

"Right here, tending the shop. She has a lot of free time, just waiting. So she ordered a bartending book. Memorized the whole thing. Doesn't drink the stuff, though, doesn't like the taste."

"Why a bartending book, if she doesn't drink?"

Mr Jaisaram shrugged. "Why not? She likes to learn different things." He clasped his large hands on his belly. "So you're from the capital," he said, as if intrigued by the thought.

Arun nodded. "I was born there." He didn't know what else to add.

"I was there once, you know. Not a place for me. Too many streets, too many cars, too many people. Crowds and crowds of people, everywhere. Our little town must seem quiet to you."

"It's a change," Arun said.

Mr Jaisaram leaned forward, fingers interlocking. "They always send us teachers from the capital. They get bored after a few months and skedaddle back." His voice hardened. "Are you planning on skedaddling?"

Surprised by the question, Arun replied quickly: "I've only just got here. Ask me again in a few months."

Mr Jaisaram eyed him in silence for a moment. "An honest man?"

"I have no reason to lie. I'm here now. As for later, we'll see."

Mr Jaisaram shrugged, sat back in his chair. "Maybe you'll be different," he said pensively. "I was expecting the usual answer. Honesty is a virtue few men can afford these days."

Anjani returned with a platter bearing the drinks and a bowl of plantain chips. She placed the platter on the coffee table, passed a sweating tumbler to her father and one to Arun before perching on the sofa beside him. They raised their glasses to each other,

Mr Jaisaram taking a long and noisy swallow. Arun smiled thinly at Anjani — he wondered whether he should apologise for his choice — and took a mouthful of his drink. His throat immediately seized up. His eyes watered. He began to cough.

"Oh, I should have warned you," Anjani said in a tone less apologetic than amused. "We didn't have much tonic left, only about a thimbleful. The rest is gin."

Through his tears, he saw her father's face crumple in merriment.

"If it's too strong for you ..." Anjani said.

"No, no," Arun sputtered. "It's fine." Whatever it took, he would finish this drink. The melting ice cubes, he reasoned, would soon make it palatable.

Mr Jaisaram turned out to be full of questions about the capital, his life there, his schooling. Arun, made slightly drowsy by his fatigue, the heat, and the gin, found himself speaking with candour about his past, Mr Jaisaram laughing at his tales of high school pranks, nodding in approval of the strappings that followed.

Anjani followed the conversation closely but said nothing. She stirred only once, slipping out to get herself a glass of water.

As Arun spoke and sipped at the thinning drink, the occasional dull clanking of spoons and pots, the occasional splash of water, came from deeper in the house, and he pictured the woman with splayed silver hair busy at the stove and the sink. In response to a question, he found himself speaking about his parents and then, as if he couldn't summon just the memory of them alive, as if the end they'd come to were vital to his portrait of them, he spoke about their deaths. Pieces of plane tumbled into shadows multiplying in the crowded, little room. Mr Jaisaram grew indistinct, his features blurring above the startling whiteness of his shirt. Anjani, beside him on the soft sofa, became a presence felt rather than seen, an emanation of warmth and gentle breath.

He saw Mr Jaisaram glance at his daughter, saw him smile sadly, saw him wipe away a tear. There was something gratifying in that. So he continued talking — about the business, now, and his sister and brother-in-law. When he told of having signed away his inheritance, Mr Jaisaram declared himself impressed — Anjani squirming on the sofa, dropping a grunt of disapproval unleavened by discretion — but added that that he was unsure whether this was an act of bravery or foolishness, then concluded that the answer lay in the character of the one whose choice it was.

"In my case, neither," Arun said. "It was just ..." His voice trailed away. He knew what it wasn't, but he didn't know what it was. "... just the only thing ..."

Then, his lips barely parting, Mr Jaisaram said into the silence that Arun had constructed, "The problem with bombs is that they're so messy. As a butcher that offends me."

Arun's tongue curled backward into his mouth, his mind struggling to grasp the meaning of the strange words, and he felt rescued when Anjani signalled that it was time to eat.

The dining room, smaller than the living room and as crowded by the dining table and chairs, was at the back of the house, beside the kitchen. A shaded bulb, hanging from a cord braided in leafy gold foil, cast a yellowed light on the oilcloth across which a bullet train cut a swift path past an icy Mount Fuji. Before each chair stood an icy bottle of beer.

Mrs Jaisaram was standing in the doorway to the kitchen, her hair wound in a knot and pinned to the back of her head. She was a smaller woman than his glimpse of her at the window had led him to believe — shorter, with less bulk. When her husband perfunctorily introduced her, she merely nodded at him, and when he apologised for having startled her at the window, she gave a single twist of her head in acknowledgement. There was to her none of the friendliness he had found in her husband and daughter.

In silence, they took their places at the table, Mr Jaisaram across from him, Anjani to his left, the chair to his right kept free for Mrs Jaisaram. Through the open window behind him, the smells of earth from the fields now effaced by darkness billowed in on the light mountain breeze. As they settled in, Mrs Jaisaram emerged from the kitchen carrying plates heaped with rice and curried vegetables, from which rose with bracing insistence the biting aroma of fresh peppers.

Mr Jaisaram and Anjani immediately dug into their meals with their fingers, without waiting for Mrs Jaisaram to join them. Seeing Arun's hesitation, Mr Jaisaram said, "Eat up, eat up!" and scooped another mouthful of food. When his wife finally took her place a few minutes later, it was with a serving of meagre proportions, a few mouthfuls at best.

Arun, uncomfortable, asked for a fork.

Anjani, amused, said, "There aren't any."

Mr Jaisaram paused. "How about a spoon?"

They ate in silence, with concentration, at times even furiously. Mr Jaisaram sighed in contentment and occasionally swiped the back of his hand at his sweating forehead. Mrs Jaisaram rhythmically fed herself, seeming hardly to chew. Anjani fell somewhere between her father and mother, eating with relish, but distractedly, her mind elsewhere.

Observing them, feeling his skin grow damp from the assault of the peppery food, Arun thought that eating was serious business here in Omeara. Seeking to make conversation, he complimented Mrs Jaisaram on the curry. "I'll bet you do wonders with all that fresh meat from your husband's shop as well. I'm sure my sister would be grateful for any recipes —"

An outburst of laughter from Anjani cut off his words. "We're like shoemakers who go barefoot," she said, picking up her beer bottle. "Or writers who never read."

To Arun's look of puzzlement, Mr Jaisaram said, "We don't eat meat."

While Anjani and her mother washed the dishes, Mr Jaisaram took Arun by the arm and led him into the backyard to finish their second beers. It would be cooler outside, he said, although the difference was not immediately noticeable. They sat side by side on a bench of raw wood that had been planed smooth, staring out at a darkness that quickly swallowed the faint light emerging from the open window behind them. The breeze had fallen off and stars had emerged in the billions.

Neither spoke for a while, the only sounds those of Mr Jaisaram slurping at his beer followed by the hiss of a gentle belch.

Arun, stomach full, cocooned in satisfaction, stifled a yawn. "Well?" he said finally. "What else do you want to know?"

"What do you mean?"

"I thought you brought me out here to interrogate me."

"Why would I want to interrogate you?"

"Because I'm a stranger. And these are strange times."

Mr Jaisaram slurped at his beer, belched. "Is there anything else I should know about you?"

"No. No more than you already know."

"Well, then, there you are." He fell silent again.

Arun finished his beer, carefully put the empty bottle on the ground.

Some minutes later, Mr Jaisaram nudged him with his elbow. "Listen," he said. "What do you hear?"

Arun turned an ear to the night, held his breath. "Nothing."

"Are you sure?"

"What should I hear?"

"Exactly what you are hearing. The sound of nothing."

"I don't understand."

"You see," Mr Jaisaram said, his voice falling to a whisper, "before these strange times began, we would sit out here and you wouldn't be able to hear me speak in the way I'm speaking now. You couldn't whisper sweet nothings into the ear of your beloved because she could hardly hear you. The sounds of the jungle were too loud, you see. You'd have to shout out those sweet nothings, and then they wouldn't be so sweet anymore. Millions, billions of insects going about their business, the noises of their lovemaking

69

or whatever rumbling across the fields like a tidal wave of sound. You got used to it, of course, and it always fell off before midnight, like considerate neighbours. But, ever since these strange times began, the nights are full of what you hear. Nothing." His voice cracked. "Nothing left, nothing at all. Listen." He sniffled and fell silent. And when he sniffled again, Arun knew he was hearing the sound of a man undone by silence.

PAIN HAD ENAMELLED itself onto his father's face the afternoon four years before when Arun had announced — a great heat outside, the shutters of the shadowed living room half closed, the circling blades of the ceiling fan bringing barely a flutter to the potted ferns, Arun and his father seated in wicker armchairs facing each other — that he had no interest in taking over the print shop that had provided the family with a prosperous life.

"It's your inheritance," his father had said evenly. "We've decided to leave the house to Joy. We haven't got much else to give you, apart from some cash. Joy gets your mother's jewellery as well."

Later, Arun would remember the sound of his father's breathing — how it had suddenly turned raucous in the silent house. He would remember, too, his gratitude that his father never mentioned what seemed to him the greater betrayal: the image of his grandfather recently emerged from the paddies cranking out handbills and leaflets on an obsolete press, a labour that would leave him with a muscular arm and purple-stained fingers to the end of his days. In response to Arun's silence, his father had said, "So what do you plan to do with your life?" And Arun had said, the formulation surprising even himself, "I have my heart set on being a teacher."

Later, at the dinner table, his mother said, "It's all Mahadeo's fault." She spoke the words in a murmur but her breath caused the eight flames in the candelabra to shudder, shadows to sway on the dining room walls. She sat back against the high-backed chair and fanned herself with her napkin. She knew she was right. From the open windows, cutting through the moist air, came the unyielding clamour of the night, the shrill and rasp and whistle of insect convocation that every night calmed Arun and seduced him to sleep. His mother gazed expectantly at him between the candles. His father's knife scraped on his plate. Arun said nothing. He, too, knew she was right. Mahadeo, that scruffy man with a cigarette grafted onto his lips who was now the minister of government responsible for communications, had inspired his passion for books, for reading, for history.

His father reached for his glass of water, the ice cubes tinkling as he swirled them around, and he said in a voice that felt it held a winning hand that it was *their* printery that made the school books that were distributed to students around the country — *their* printery, which would be *his*, that assured education on a much larger scale than teaching a few minds to absorb their ABCs and their one-two-threes.

At that, Arun said, "It's not the same thing at all."

His mother said, "Of course not. Teaching's important but anybody can do it. Running the business on the other hand takes special skills."

His father took a long drink of water, and when he placed the glass back on the table it was as if he had swallowed his words too.

In the end they reached a compromise. After graduating from high school, he would give the printery a try — a good shot, his father said, at least two years, in return for a substantial salary. Then, if he still had his *heart set on teaching* — Arun searched the words for sarcasm, found none — they would not stand in his way. His mother, who knew him better than his father, gave only grudging assent.

Arun recognised the artifice in his father's proposal, heard the phantom echo of the phrase, left unstated but no doubt taking shape in his parents' minds, that his father would sigh in times of uncertainty: you can never tell how things'll work out. His father's offer was a silent bet, one he had made with many times with destiny in circumstances both personal and commercial. He had won more often than not.

The maid came to clear the table. Arun excused himself, he was meeting friends at the cinema. But, as he stepped out into the darkness of the gallery outside, the sound of his mother's unhappy voice caused him to pause. Among the nocturnal racket, he heard his father say in a tired, soothing tone, "Don't forget Joy." Then a chorus of frogs arose and their words were lost to him. He clattered down the stairs and across the gravelled driveway to the car and told himself the familiar story he knew his father was once more recalling to his mother: how Joy, having completed her advanced secretarial course, had been reluctant to assume the bookkeeping duties at the company, and if she hadn't been persuaded to do so, how would she have met the man she would marry? And what of Surein himself? Had he taken that sales job at the distillery, had they not managed to entice him into remaining at the printery, how would he have met Joy? Would he today be enjoying the fruits of being the boss's son-in-law?

The next morning after breakfast, as Arun was gathering up his school books in his room, his father came to him, embraced him, and said, "All I ask is that you stand by your duty." As if it were the easiest thing in the world. But then he had added, "Your duty to yourself, I mean. In the business or elsewhere."

Over time, Arun had come to recognise the truth of his brother-in-law's observation — offered one evening after several pre-wedding whiskies too many — that he had the bad habit of equivocating, of wrapping himself in layers of speculation that ended up binding him tight. Surein had said: think about things in both life and business, examine the angles, peer into the blinding light and into the dark corners, then make a decision, or decide not to — but stop spinning all these cobwebs around yourself! Be a man of considered action!

Right, Arun had thought at the time, be a comic strip hero. He wondered what his sister saw in Surein, this man whose singular passion was for sales figures. Still, it was Surein who had caused the company's annual revenues to leap by almost a third by securing contracts to print coffee table books for two major North American publishers — a scheme that had seemed farfetched to his father until Surein, who had spent many hours doing his homework, laid the figures out for him. Arun had been bored by all the talk of regional sources of high-quality paper, the intricacies of the new machinery required, the hiring and training of new personnel, the cost of shipping and all the other elements Surein had thought to include. His father had grown starry-eyed and, after a day of consideration, had announced that, despite the considerable financial outlay, he was prepared to take the risk because, although you never knew how things'd work out, Surein's plan was thorough and sensible and daring enough to work. He left in Surein's hands the task of weaning the publishers away from the Hong Kong and Singapore printers who enjoyed a reputation for inexpensive, high-quality work. Arun didn't know how his brother-in-law proceeded but was surprised when Surein returned from a two-week trip abroad — ten days in New York, the rest in Toronto — with two signed contracts and the possibility of several more. He had been appalled to find a wave of jealousy rising within himself and had hurried to suppress it under a show of enthusiasm.

THE HAND BELL was an object of great beauty. It was heavy, solid, weighty with authority. More than the schoolhouse itself, its machined oak handle, brass skirt and the lead clapper within made concrete his assumption of a responsibility that, for the first time, he felt to be beyond him. He hefted the bell, felt it tug on his arm, felt himself a bit of a fraud. There was a solemnity to the bell that brought to mind another moment when he had felt himself to be incidental to the proceedings, an interloper who would be exposed for what he was, humiliated, banished, even though no one else had seen him as such.

For the bell had released in his mind images of the commission of inquiry into the explosion of his parents' plane: the large, somnolent oak-panelled courtroom, large windows open to a painful brightness, slow fans stirring dust, the shuffle of papers, the sleepy growl of the judge coaxed out of retirement, the drone of witnesses and technical experts — all of it implying competence and impartiality and continuity in a courtroom where British judges once ordered some men incarcerated for their ideas and others hanged for their defiance. Sitting there, helpless, breathing mustiness, the sense came to him that he was out of place: he had had no role to play, no detail to add, no insight to offer. There, as here now, standing at the side of the unpaved road with the brass bell in his hand, he had felt himself the bearer of a responsibility — towards his parents then, towards the children now — that was beyond him. That sense of helplessness robbed him of the courage to swing his arm, to make the bell clang, to announce his presence, to demand attention, to assert his authority.

Yet, it was expected of him. Earlier that morning as he was about to leave for the schoolhouse, Mr Jaisaram had knocked at his door. He too was ready for work, dressed in a fraying white cotton undershirt and khaki shorts, a fresh apron strapped around his waist. On it could be seen, like the submerged traces of lost continents, the ineradicable stains of old blood. "You'll need this," he had said, extending his arm to show the bell grasped in his fist. "Ring it long and loud and they'll come running like grannies to gossip."

And here he was, standing in the sunshine before the schoolhouse, its door thrown open, his name and GOOD MORNING! printed on the chalkboard. He stared up the street towards the town, hoping to see hordes of children, neatly dressed but, he expected, barefoot, scurrying towards him. He knew that word of his arrival had spread quickly, that everyone had heard that classes would begin promptly at 8:30 on Monday morning. He hoped that that word would suffice, that he would be spared the effort of ringing the bell.

But the street remained empty save for a stray dog, its fur hanging ragged from its bony chest, ambling across it. He glanced at his watch. 8:40.

The first clang of the bell was clean and sharp and, in the morning stillness, as atrocious as a scream. He fought the urge to wrap his hands around the skirt, to stifle the sound before it ate more stringently into the calm that was left to him. He rang it again, swinging his stiffened right arm back and forth. After four clangs, the one blending into the other, the sound lost its edge of atrocity, became merely outrageous in the silence, its sharp tongue cutting cold through the warming air. A gentle vibration rose from the wooden handle into his palm, up his forearm and into his elbow, not an unpleasant sensation. He relaxed, letting his elbow bend a little, putting a discreet enthusiasm into the action. This reticence of his — it was something he had to get beyond.

He rang the bell for what felt like a long minute, then let it fall silent. The morning remained undisturbed, the road childless, the fields quiescent. Shadows hardened in the rising sun. He went wet under the arms. The bell's appeal had gone unheeded, its echoes dissipated like mocking laughter in the sunshine.

Still, he waited, scrutinizing the town in search of movement. And soon he began to feel foolish, a salesman hawking to an empty square. His resentment at that feeling of foolishness quickly gave way to pique: he rang the bell again, more stridently this time. He wanted to destroy that silence. He rang it again and again, as if his insistence alone would peel away their reticence and bring them to him.

He was about to give up, frustration tightening his throat, when a little girl appeared on the roadway. She was six, maybe seven, and walked awkwardly, leaning on a miniature crutch that took the place of her missing right leg, her progress slow and careful.

Just behind her came a boy, perhaps a year or two older. Even at a distance, Arun could see the scowl on his face.

He remained where he was, waiting for them, the bell hanging heavy and silent in his hand.

When they reached him, the girl raised her dark eyes towards his. Sweat glistened on her forehead and ran from her temples to her chin. "Good morning," she said in a light, high voice. "My name is Indira and I want to go to school."

"Good morning, Indira," Arun said. "Come inside and sit down." He led the way into the schoolhouse.

The boy said nothing. He followed Indira and sat beside her at the desk directly in front of Arun's table. He stared at the chalkboard, raised a finger towards the printed words. "Arun Bannerji. Good morning," he read before settling a gaze of impenetrable defiance on Arun.

"And good morning to you," Arun said. "What's your name?"

But the boy just looked away, towards the open door and the sunny day outside.

By lunchtime, five other children had drifted in, two girls and three boys, one of whom had been dragged in by his angry mother. She had lugged him into the schoolhouse, thrust him into a seat and, without a glance at Arun, stalked out, a hefty, harried woman with no time to waste. Left alone, the boy dried his eyes on his shirtsleeves and, blinking rapidly, looked around. Seeing other children seemed to calm him. He put his thumb into his mouth and kept it there for the rest of the morning.

Shanti, who had led her friend Radha to school by the hand, told Arun that the boy's name was Hari. His father, she added, had been taken away one night some months before by men with guns. He hadn't been seen since. It was also Shanti who — on the arrival with her friend, both of whom Arun guessed to be nine or ten years old — had responded when he asked their names. She had promptly declared hers, and when Radha replied with an open-mouthed grunt that gave the impression she had no tongue, had repeated her name for her, as if she were accustomed to acting as her friend's interpreter.

Later, during recess, after convincing Radha to turn a skipping rope for the other children, Shanti explained in a whisper to Arun that Radha had been left with what she called a lazy tongue after three men with guns had forced their way into their house one afternoon while their parents were in the fields and done bad things to Radha's older sister. The men had stuffed balls of cloth into the girls' mouths, she said, but Radha had tried to scream anyway. Shanti felt that, somehow, that useless effort had caused Radha's tongue to go dead.

When Arun asked, gently, whether Radha's sister would also be coming to school, Shanti replied that she couldn't, she didn't even have the time to play any more, she was too busy looking after her young baby. It was the only moment of feeling — a light impatience — in her dispassionate recounting of bad things done by men with guns.

The last to arrive were two boys who wandered shyly in within minutes of each other after the recess. Jai and Rai were plump eleven-year-olds. Jai's left hand had been severed at the wrist, Rai's right a little higher up. They were, Arun thought aghast, a matched pair.

Looking around the class, he understood that he had been sent the cripples, those who for the most part were incapable of physical labour. Many other children remained out there, tending animals, digging the soil, weeding and watering the plants beside their parents.

With stomach deflated, with intestines withered and roped, Arun managed to ascertain before lunch what each of his charges knew. It was not promising. Hari's attention could be brought to bear on nothing save the image of absence that occupied his head. Radha could write the alphabet but retained no spelling beyond her name. Jai and Rai read easily and with relish, but the peculiar nature of their handicap overwhelmed them with frustration: the right-hander had had his right hand excised, the left-hander his left. They knew how to write, but only with the missing hand. Indira proved assiduous, with a solid grasp of reading and writing and addition equal to Shanti's, but her friend — having established his ability to read — refused to participate, neither touching his chalk and slate board nor answering any questions. It was once more Shanti, revealing what elsewhere would have been a talent for journalism but which here could make her only Omeara's leading gossip, who explained that Roop came from a home where he was valued for his labour, his father made legless by a landmine, his mother — Arun remembered the harried woman — prone to depression that lasted for days. They now saw education as their son's only hope, so he would come to school, but there would be no time afterwards for homework. He still had to help his mother in the fields and spend Saturdays selling their produce at the market.

Arun spent that first lunchtime sitting at his table in the deserted schoolhouse, wondering how he could teach this class. He wasn't hungry, but his thirst eventually drove him to a quick walk over to Madhu's shop. He bought two ice-chilled bottles of lemonade. By the time he returned to the school, the chill had left the bottles and he was able to swallow only half a bottle of the thick, sweet drink whose colour alone justified its name. The children's needs were too diverse, their abilities too mismatched. And if, as he hoped, other children could be enticed into joining, the problem would only worsen.

When he rang the bell an hour later, only Indira and Roop returned. He decided he would teach them subtraction. Indira seized on the concept immediately. Roop, despite Arun's repeated attempts to engage him, remained stoic. At least he was following the scratching of the chalk on the board, evidence of interest in the simple sums. There was some comfort, some hope, to be found in that.

By three o'clock, the end of the school day, Arun was exhausted. He sent Indira and Roop home, lay his head on the table and fell into a doze.

The sunshine had turned dense in the late afternoon when Anjani woke him. As he blinked the sleep from his eyes, she said, "Now you know why the other teachers didn't stay. They couldn't bear the sight of the students. Too much damage." She brushed a lock of hair behind her ear. "Can you?"

FIVE

THE INCIDENT WITH the boat was never mentioned and when he sought to introduce it into conversation with Mr Jaisaram or Anjani, they pretended not to have heard him or, with a pointed clumsiness, remarked on the dryness of the soil or the humidity of the air. He decided after a while that it was one of those subjects best left unstirred.

His days fell into a pleasant rhythm, teaching from Monday to Friday, with one evening devoted to washing his clothes, another to ironing them, a third to composing a letter to his sister. He read every night before going to bed, Joy mailing him the latest bestsellers listed in *Time* magazine as well as paperback editions of the Russian classics that he requested. He suspected that *Lolita* was not unavailable, as she claimed, but that she didn't want to be seen buying it in the bookshop where she'd become well known. When, dipping into

American writing, he asked for *Portnoy's Complaint*, he described it to her as the story of a young boy growing up hard in America. It arrived with the next batch of books and weeks-old newspapers.

Friday evenings he spent with Mr Jaisaram and his family, enjoying the one meal he didn't cook for himself. Here, too, the routine varied little: the drink — a different cocktail each time — with Mr Jaisaram and Anjani before dinner, the silent Mrs Jaisaram at the table, sitting with Mr Jaisaram on the bench behind the house for a mostly silent vigil beneath the glittering sky, the only sound the almost imperceptible shaving of blade through wood.

One evening, as they sat on the bench enjoying the afterglow of a heavy meal, Mr Jaisaram appeared restless. He selected one knife, then another, then a third, weighing each in his palm, as if seeking a counterweight to the chunk of wood he held in the other. After plumbing each knife, hefting it, and wrapping its hilt in his palm, he would sigh and rummage around in his toolbox for another. Finally there were no more knives to be had. He held the piece of wood in both hands, turning it over and around, fingertips rubbing at it as if in search of some hidden clue, some unseen inscription. Then, with a soft belch, he reached beneath the bench and replaced the wood in the cardboard box in which he kept the oddly shaped ends of branches he'd picked up in the forest, on the roadsides, among the rocks on the beach. Then, clasping his hands together, he turned to Arun and asked if he would like to join him in being read to by Anjani. "Surely, as a teacher, you like books, Mr Arun."

They went to the living room, where Anjani was leafing through a bartending guide Joy had sent after learning of her propensity from one of Arun's letters. Mrs Jaisaram had already gone to bed. When Mr Jaisaram asked his daughter if she would read to them, she seemed unwilling. "It's late," she said, spreading her fingers on a colour photograph of a martini glass. But he insisted, gently, and she gave in, closing the book. "One chapter," she said. For the briefest moment — and Arun couldn't be sure that it wasn't just a trick of the light or his own fatigue — a look that resembled pity crossed her face.

She sat in the armchair, he and Mr Jaisaram on the sofa in front of her, and read to them from a paperback held carefully open so as not to crack the spine. The cover of *For the Sake of Love* showed a windswept Glorianna, long-haired, cloaked and buxom, astride a horse beneath a cloudy sky. Before beginning to read, Anjani had quickly shown it to Arun. She had avoided meeting his eyes.

She read well, in a soft and modulated voice, from the story of the beautiful and headstrong Glorianna, a hot-blooded Italian who, having forsaken her noble heritage, pursued her true love, the dashing Count of Lockley, through the nineteenth century Scottish highlands. In the chapter, Glorianna's faithful friend, the beautiful but cautious Sylvana, was killed in a furious battle with enemies of the Count. Glorianna, teary but determined, refused the help of her companions — Arun, having missed the previous chapters, was uncertain who they were — and buried her friend with her own hands under a stack of rocks. At the closing words of the chapter — Glorianna, addressing her dead friend, said something about her bones reposing for eternity, her soul flying to heaven — Arun saw Mr Jaisaram wipe at his eyes with the back of his hand.

When Anjani closed the book, Mr Jaisaram quickly got to his feet, mumbled goodnight and went off to bed.

Anjani saw Arun to the door. "Look," she whispered, "I should have warned you. My father's tastes run to —"

"Nothing that has anything to do with his reality?"

"Exactly."

She opened the door and, with a nod, he stepped out into the silence.

SOMEWHERE IN THE distance a dog barked a warning. Another took up the challenge, and for a few seconds their raucous exchange resonated through the schoolhouse. Arun looked up from the text-books spread before him, through the open door to the afternoon light sitting thick and heavy on the fields. His head felt heavy on a neck that had grown steadily brittle throughout the day.

His students had all gone, leaving him with their different needs. So many ages, so many levels. Each required a separate lesson, a separate exercise. It was impossible to plan a class, apart from the civics course he was required to teach explaining the role of the president, the prime minister, the army, the national assembly, and, especially, how their country was among the world's freest and most democratic. The obligatory text supplied by the ministry gave an impression of merry collegiality while avoiding any mention of the origins of the political system, so that students could be forgiven for assuming that it was one of their country's many gifts to the world.

The barking fell off as suddenly as it had begun and he could imagine the dogs, skeletal in their frayed coats, slinking away from each other with lolling tongues and glazed eyes. He flicked open the attendance record book and was about to pen a note beside Shashtri's name — after a month of intermittent attendance, she still couldn't grasp the alphabet — when the pitch of a shadow in the rectangle of soft light framed by the open door caught his eye. He looked up.

"Go on," Seth said, stepping into the shade of the schoolhouse. "Finish what you were doing. You look so engrossed." He removed his cap, glanced around the room. In his baggy, forest green uni-form that sprouted pockets everywhere, he appeared transformed — larger, bulkier than the last time Arun had seen him almost two months before. He was transformed, too, by the black holster cinched to his waist by a webbed belt. Flicking his cap at the fresco of shadow and light that threw itself across the floor and desks, he said, "It looks like a jigsaw puzzle."

Arun followed his gaze. He thought it strange that where Seth saw pieces he saw a whole. "How are you?" he said finally.

"Busy. There's a lot of activity out there these days. Our own little jigsaw puzzle. We spend our time trying to keep the pieces together."

"Is it working?"

"So far so good." His eyes were red with fatigue.

Arun stepped down from the dais and held out his hand. "Have a seat," he said, indicating a desk.

Seth perched on the desktop, folded the cap flat and slid it under an epaulette. "So how are things in the education business?"

"Slow. I'm afraid the children have grown used to not having a school. For the most part, they'd much rather be outside playing or even working in the fields."

"A sign of intelligence, wouldn't you say?" He wearily crossed his left leg over his right, his hand tugging the booted foot farther up the thigh as if it didn't have the strength to get there on its own. "Still, it must be discouraging for you."

Arun shrugged. "I'm a teacher."

Seth flicked a finger at the boot, circled a fingertip on the black leather as if to shine a spot sullied by a speck of dust. "In fact, that's why I'm here."

"There's a problem?"

"Relax. The general's got a proposition for you. He's got a special interest in education. He believes kids —"

Kids.

"— should have every possible chance."

"Even two-percenters?"

Seth glanced sharply at him. "We don't use that term in the military."

"What term *do* you use? *Rikshas?*"

Seth cupped a palm around his chin, brushed a finger across his lips. "Maybe I should come back some other time. When you're in a better mood."

Arun's temper flared in a rush of prickly heat through his chest and belly. "You know what the problem is with my mood, Seth?

The children don't want to come to school, and why should they? They learn how to read, they learn how to write, count, multiply, they learn how glorious and kind the government is and how their country is the envy of the world, and the only future they're looking at is a life in the fields like their parents or as some kind of hop-and-fetch-it for some useless bureaucrat in the capital. That's the problem with my mood, Seth."

The frown that had come to Seth during his outburst gave way to a slightly mocking smile. "I take it you don't think much of the two-percent program."

Arun, empty, gestured in frustration.

"But before that, they couldn't even get jobs as hop-and-fetch-its. That's progress. And the more they learn, the more things'll open up. They have to. Question of time."

"Tell that to the Boys. Time. Patience."

"The Boys are a whole other matter. They're my problem. The two-percenters, as you call them, are yours."

Arun shoved his hands into his pants pockets, turned away to the open door and the thickening light and the fields which held no answers. "You said the general had a proposition for me?"

"He's asked me to tell you that if you need anything, pencils, paper, textbooks, whatever, you're to let us know."

"What's the catch?"

"No catch. You have my word on that, Arun. No catch."

Arun turned to look around the deserted classroom again, and he saw now what Seth had seen. Pieces. He had a baker's dozen of children between the ages of five and twelve. Some could read haltingly, many needed to learn the alphabet. Some could count to ten, some to a hundred, a few could manage rudimentary addition and subtraction. They knew little of the wider world, not even enough to be curious about it; beyond their town and the fields there was only the capital, enticing, menacing, mythic. As for subjects such as history or science or literature: they were as alien to them as computers and microscopes. Besides, he thought once more, what use could they ever hope to make of such knowledge? Seth's idea of time and patience and the changes they would bring was not hope or optimism; it was merely fantasy.

"I don't know that we need anything as such," he said finally, turning towards Seth. "Unless you can manage other schoolrooms, more teachers."

"We can't go quite that far, I'm afraid. But we can get books, for instance. Do you need textbooks?"

"No. My sister sends me what I need. Primers. Math exercise books. *Dick and Jane*. We, that is, my family, we print them at our plant."

"I know."

"You know?"

"We did some checking. That doesn't surprise you, does it?"

"No, I guess not." But the news did disturb him. Even if he had led a blameless life, it was unsettling to think that the authorities had rummaged through his past, pulling open its drawers, peering into its corners, riffling through whatever papers they found there.

"The general was pleased to find out you were who you are."

"Who am I?"

"Reliable. At least your family is." Seth glanced at the watch strapped tightly to his wrist. "So what can we supply you with?"

Arun perched on the desk beside him, ran his eyes over the blackboard: A B C D ... "Look, there's only so much I can teach these children. Basic reading, basic writing, basic math. Beyond that there isn't much point."

"I won't tell the general you said that. He'd have you teach them calculus, physics, chemistry."

"What in the world for?"

"For the world. He'd like to see us sending our own spaceship to Mars one day."

Arun stiffened in astonishment. "And what planet does he come from?"

"Don't be too quick to judge him. He's a kind of visionary, I guess. We sure can use a few of those — people who can see beyond our present situation, even if it seems like fantasy."

"For God's sake, Seth, you can't —"

"That's another thing. He doesn't like hearing the Lord's name taken in vain. He's sensitive on that point."

"He's a Christian?"

"One of the first things he did on taking command was to issue a standing order banning swearing."

"That couldn't be easy for soldiers."

"The men are well disciplined." Seth gave a low laugh. "And not even the general can read their thoughts." He uncrossed his legs and eased himself to his feet, adjusting the gun belt as he did so. "If you think of anything you need, let me know."

"How do I do that?"

"Come up to the camp and give the sentries my name." He slid the cap from his shoulder, flapped it open and pulled it down tight on his head.

Arun followed him to the doorway. Outside, a jeep sat idling; the driver, cap visor lowered over his eyes, appeared to be in a doze. Across the street in the grassy field beyond the open sewer, a small group of boys — some of them his students — stood in a cluster gazing at the jeep. Their eyes were blank, their faces unreadable. Even their gestures — a hand reaching into an unbuttoned shirt to scratch at an itching chest, a dusty foot rubbing at a bony shin — seemed noncommittal. Arun wondered what was on their minds.

Seth nodded towards the boys. "It's very important that your students learn to read," he said. "They have to know what they stand to lose. Those guys in the mountains —"

Guys.

"— they're becoming bolder. We think they might be aiming to take the town. We won't let them, of course."

Arun felt a laugh swell in his throat. Repressing it, he said, "You won't let them? But they've pulled that off before." Farther south, huge swatches of land and several towns were firmly under control of the insurgents, what they referred to as the liberated territories. The navy was obliged to maintain permanent blockades of two small ports to stem the flow of arms.

"We're going to have to mine the edge of the forest," Seth said. "To protect the town. We'll warn the people, we'll post warning signs. Discreet signs, no death's head or anything. Just little signs with the word 'mines' printed on them. You must teach your students how to recognize the word."

Arun looked at the boys gathered around the jeep, at the glittery eyes, the ragged clothes, the bare feet rubbing bony shins. An ache ran through his thigh. "But why not put up big signs? Put up the death's head, whatever. Surely that would deter the children and keep the Boys away."

Seth looked away towards the distant forest — in irritation, Arun thought. "The general doesn't just want to warn them off, your Boys. He'd prefer to blow up a few of them, too. A more dramatic statement. We'd prefer not to blow up any of the townspeople, though."

"That's kind of you."

"Sarcasm doesn't become you, Arun."

"I wasn't being sarcastic."

"Liar. By the way, have you heard about the attack in the capital? Another suicide bomber. She walked into the middle of central market on Saturday morning and pressed the button. Took ten people with her and sent another dozen to hospital."

Arun tried to summon the scene. The ramshackle stalls knocked together from cast-off wood and bits of corrugated iron, the mounds of fruit and vegetables, tables laden with carved "handicrafts." The wood and metal would have shredded, the produce reduced to pulp. Like the people. God, the people. A Saturday morning.

Seth strode off towards the jeep. Across the street, the children took several tentative steps backwards, as if to preserve the space that separated them from the objects of their fascination. Without looking back, Seth called over his shoulder, "Sarcasm doesn't have a place here, Arun. Sarcasm's a sign of helplessness. We can't afford that, any of us."

SATURDAY MORNINGS LEFT him feeling bereft. He awoke early but, with no classes to teach, remained in bed, cocooned in the accommodation the thin mattress afforded his body. He was growing accustomed to its toughness, enjoyed awaking to muscles that felt taut and well rested. He could hear people passing in the street: the low grumble of voices, a chuckle, a trundling cart, a mother calling to a child, a child calling to another, hands clapping attention.

The sounds, merry, irresistible, rescued him, promised purpose to the day. He eased himself from bed, washed, went out.

It began early every Saturday morning, this influx of people to Omeara. They arrived from miles around, from up and down the coast, from cleared patches in the jungle, men pushing wooden carts or bicycles laden with bundles of articles to sell, women and children trudging along behind them with more bundles bending their backs and stretching their arms. They set up shop in the asphalted square, offering woven baskets and home-sewn clothes, mats of colourful weave, hands of bananas and mounds of cashews and peanuts, candied papaya, sugared coconut, roasted corn. At a little stall, a man displayed reading glasses, sunglasses, and a basket of second-hand dentures, the dark pink gums and shiny teeth wired in silver. They sold to and bought from each other. Occasionally they bartered. Once, Arun saw a soldier accept a leather machete scabbard in exchange for a surreptitiously surrendered military flashlight. Then he traded the batteries for a belt. Happily stringing the scabbard on the belt, he went off whistling.

It was Madhu's busiest day. Short lines formed outside his shop all morning, customers emerging with sacks of flour and sugar, cans of pears in sweet syrup, lamps and wicks and kerosene, flashlights and batteries, lengths of cloth, bottles of sugared drinks. Little excitements broke out. One commotion began when a black spider the size of a wicketkeeper's glove darted from a hand of bananas and scampered across the asphalt, a posse of children darting gleefully after it only to be robbed of their prize — What in the world would they have done with it? Turned it into a household pet? — by a hungry stray which seized the struggling spider in its jaws and ran off. The dusty-footed children gave up the chase and returned to the centre of the square to gawk at the itinerant circus of twin brothers who juggled coloured balls, swallowed gobs of flame, flung knives at each other, vaulted from the ground onto each other's heads. Arun tossed a coin onto the red scarf they'd placed on the ground and, realising that their takings were probably meagre, tossed another. All around, the static of greetings and conversation flared through the dusty air.

A little past eleven o'clock the coastal bus, an ancient red coach swathed in rust and festooned with gold-coloured tassels, rattled to a stop at the edge of the square and blared its horn twice. Passengers surged towards it, tossing their bundles to the conductor who had clambered onto the roof, already a jagged mountain chain of roped down baggage. At the door, Arun saw Kumarsingh, dressed as nattily as ever, selling tickets to the rowdy, clawing, cawing crowd. On Wednesdays and Saturdays — Kumarsingh had explained that what had begun as a daily service had had to be scaled back for lack of passengers — the bus made the run along the Omeara Road, from village to village then back again. It was his most lucrative venture and he was considering adding another day to its schedule.

Wandering aimless through the crowd, pausing here and there to eye the stacks of goods and fruit and clothing, Arun found himself in front of the butcher's shop. There was no line up, no flow of people toting packages of freshly slaughtered meat. Meat was the one thing they could not buy in quantity. Saturday, for Mr Jaisaram, was just an ordinary business day. He went in. A man and woman were standing at the large freezer, Anjani behind it, a slab of dark red meat on top of it.

In a combative voice, the woman said, "Is it fresh?"

Anjani, in an equally combative voice, said, "Of course it's fresh. What do you think? You think we —"

At that moment the back door swung open and Mr Jaisaram, wringing his hands on a towel, hustled in. He smiled like a man pleasantly surprised. "Good morning, *Prahiba*, good morning, *Prahib*, how are you this morning? Life is being kind?"

The man nodded his bald head vigorously. "Greetings, *Prahib*."

The woman said, "*Prahib*." She jerked her chin towards the meat. "The girl says this is fresh. Looks dry to me. I must have fresh. My daughter's future in-laws are coming to dinner. I cannot serve them tough meat, they have very few teeth left."

Anjani opened her mouth to respond but her father, never taking his eyes off the man and woman, cut her off by tossing the towel at her. She caught it and immediately began twisting it in her hands as if wringing the neck of a chicken.

"*Prahiba*," Mr Jaisaram said, inclining his head in a gesture of sincerity. "I assure you, if this meat was any fresher it would be walking around on four legs and chewing grass. Your daughter's future in-laws will be most impressed, especially after you have prepared it. After all, everyone knows that in the kitchen you have a magical touch."

Arun saw the woman's cheek twitch in pleasure. "And you have a golden tongue, Jaisaram. Everybody knows that too." She cast another suspicious glance at the meat. "All right, then, we'll take it. But if my guests go away hungry, I'll be back and I will stuff every piece down your ear."

"Ahh, Sona, you will be back. But only to thank me." Mr Jaisaram swept the meat off the freezer top and swiftly wrapped it in paper. Tying the parcel with string, he said, "So Rana is to marry. It seems she was born only yesterday."

"She's sixteen already," Sona replied. "It's time. We were lucky to find Vishnu."

"Your daughter is very fortunate."

"Yes. He's a good worker, he'll provide well. Not all young women are so ..."

Arun saw Anjani's jaws tighten.

Sona, flustered, said, "I mean, men like Vishnu are not easy to find."

Mr Jaisaram put the parcel into Sona's hands, accepted payment from her husband. "Please give my best wishes to Rana. May heaven shower her with more happiness than she can handle."

"Never mind happiness," Sona said as she led her husband past Arun out of the shop. "Sons and money will do. Good day, *Prahib*."

Arun, amused, nodded at Anjani and Mr Jaisaram. "Good morning."

Mr Jaisaram smiled wanly. "Good morning to you."

Anjani, unleashing her fury, said, "What a stupid woman!" She tossed the towel back at her father.

"Now, now, Anji."

"Don't now-now me! Is the meat fresh? Is the meat fresh? What does she think I'm going to say? No, it's as old as dry coconut? I want to sell the meat, of course I'm going to say it's fresh!"

Mr Jaisaram flung the towel over his shoulder. "Anjani, we have company."

"And what was that nonsense about her magical touch in the kitchen? She has a magical touch, all right. Everyone knows that woman could turn cotton into stone."

"I wanted to sell the meat too. And I didn't lie, did I?"

"As for that daughter of hers, she better start using her womb because she's never used her brain. I've known goats more intelligent."

Mr Jaisaram said, "Anjani, enough."

Anjani stormed out.

Mr Jaisaram sighed and a smile came to him. "She's right, you know," he said. "About Sona and Rana. But still."

"She says what she thinks, doesn't she."

Mr Jaisaram went thoughtful. Then he nodded. "It's a fine quality, wouldn't you say?"

"Not good for business, though."

"No," Mr Jaisaram said with an amused grunt. "Not good for business at all."

Sitting in the shade of the café hours later, Arun watched in stupefaction as the square emptied, the market disappearing, taking with it children whose bare feet would never cross the threshold of the schoolhouse.

He'd had a relaxing morning, mingling with the crowd, wandering among the goods on offer, joining the queue at Madhu's to buy a box of matches and extra light bulbs. He'd spent an hour drinking tea at the café and trying without success to write a letter to his sister. He'd eaten an early lunch — curried eggs on rice — while the waiter went from table to table slapping desultorily at flies with a damp cloth. Afterwards, pen and paper having once more failed him, that early-morning sense of being somehow bereft returned to him. The well-being he'd enjoyed earlier began leaking away, yielding to an awareness that, in some subtle and ungraspable way, things were not quite right. The curry had contained some unidentifiable spice, its flavour nagging his tongue. The hot and gritty air bore scents which, he now noticed, were not just different but *unknown* and, so, vaguely unsettling.

As one o'clock approached, after a brief flurry of buying and trading, the unsold goods were methodically bundled and wrapped, trays were emptied, spoiled fruit and vegetables discarded, the remaining cones of cotton candy sold off for a penny to children who had waited all morning just for this moment. Hoisting their stock, vendors, singly, in groups, in families, began retracing the paths they had taken hours before in the early morning darkness, some along the road, some across the fields towards the jungle, some on board the boat that would take them to their villages farther up the coast. They were quiet now as they trudged off in the leaden heat. Backs seemed a little more bent, the pace less vigorous. Children who had spent the morning in hectic activity began dawdling in the grip of afternoon drowsiness, their parents, patience thinned, giving them the occasional push or tug to hurry them along.

He looked again at the people left in the square — a market-day crowd, at ease, the women brightly dressed, the men more restrained — and he realised that he couldn't imagine their more intimate lives: the look of their houses, the smell of their food, the games they played. Even the sunshine showering them appeared all at once to be underlaid by shadow.

He paid for his meal, the waiter absentmindedly plucking his change from a can with one hand and shaking dead flies from his cloth with the other. As the last of the people wandered off, the stretch of asphalt returned to its habitual somnolence.

The butcher shop was still open. As he approached the open door, a man he had seen meandering through the crowds mounted the bicycle he'd left leaning on the wall outside and rode away. Arun had seen him before, on his first day in town and a few times after that. He was wearing, as always, a fedora, a white dress shirt buttoned at the wrists and baggy khaki trousers.

Mr Jaisaram motioned to Arun to wait for him and continued quietly adding up the morning's takings, stacking the bills according to denomination, separating the coins according to their value and, lips moving silently as he counted, spooning them with his cupped palm into cloth bags. When each set of coins was done, he secured the mouth of the bag with a string and noted the total on a pad. Between two bags of coins, Mr Jaisaram informed him that Anjani had gone home early. "Sona gave her a *meegrain*," he said. "That's one of her fancy words from the capital but it's still just a headache. Wait for me, if you like. We will begin the weekend with a cold drink."

At precisely one o'clock, Mr Jaisaram, having checked that the freezer was working to his satisfaction, switched off the light bulb, pulled the heavy door into place and locked it at the top and the bottom. Then he placed a thick wooden bar across the middle and secured it at each end with a lock and bolt.

Arun said, "That man who just left, who is he? He's not from Omeara."

Mr Jaisaram, looking uncomfortable, said, "No, he doesn't live here. He just comes on market days."

"Who is he?"

"He's just a man," Mr Jaisaram said with dismissive vagueness.

"It's just that there's something about him. He doesn't seem like the others ..."

"He's not from here." He tugged at the locks, checking their sturdiness. "I don't know him by name." He dropped the key ring into the larger bag in which he had placed the money and, grasping the bag in his fist, wrapped its long drawstring around his forearm. With a smile and a nod of his head, "You are my body-guard, my secret service. You will give your life to protect me and my money, yes?"

"And what do I get in exchange? It sounds like dangerous duty."

"It is. But you get the satisfaction of knowing that you have preserved the life and well-being of the best butcher in the country."

"Is that all? Seems like meagre compensation for such grand responsibility."

"I will give you a bonus, then. Perhaps one of Anji's cocktails, something you have never had before, something green or blue or orange with a little umbrella floating on it."

"You drive a hard bargain, Mr Jaisaram. How can I refuse?" Arun could feel his mood lifting, could feel himself growing lighter.

They sat out back on Mr Jaisaram's bench, gazing at the fields shimmering in the afternoon heat, at the light clouds gathered low behind the mountains. Mr Jaisaram had not been able to keep his promise. Anjani, locked in her bedroom battling her migraine, had refused to come out to prepare cocktails. Mr Jaisaram, sighing, had filled two tall glasses with ice and then to the brim with whisky and a dribble of soda. The ice melted quickly and Arun found himself taking generous sips to prevent the liquid from spilling. Somewhere high above, unseen in the blue expanse of sky, an army spotter plane whined like an airborne lawnmower.

Arun imagined that from the plane — which he had seen many times on television, a small, single-engine craft painted olive green, its shape and colour bringing to mind a grasshopper in flight — the town must have appeared like an inexplicable growth on the straight stem of the coastal road. There was no obvious reason for its existence. But Omeara, he learned from the loquacious Mr Jaisaram, had come first, beginning as a homestead when a few itinerant families staked out the land and cleared it of forest.

"They cleared a lot of land," he said, sipping from his drink. "But they couldn't grow much. It wasn't the soil's fault. They were not very good farmers, but some of them were good sailors. So they became fishermen instead and, soon, smugglers. They could make a round trip across the gulf to the mainland in a single night. Food, radios, household goods of every kind. And guns of course, lots of guns. They grew very rich and eventually those first families left this place. Some moved to the capital. Some went abroad. At least one of their descendants now sits in the House of Lords in London; another one, I am told, is an important businessman in Canada, and so on."

Others had followed them, attracted by the rich soil and land free for the taking. In time, the road, which had begun as a trail cut through the jungle to the settlement and then a path for the contraband to the capital, was widened and flattened, taking shape as a real road. The railway had come much later, in the early days of the move towards independence. The autonomous colonial government had understood that its new army would need increased mobility and a secure means of transport when the rains turned many roads impassable for weeks on end. The British had understood these needs and agreed to pay for the construction of the railway and to donate used locomotives and wagons. "But all the talk at the time was of uniting the country and bringing the people together, one nice big happy family." He examined the amber liquid slowly diluting in his glass. "Perhaps they believed it, too, some of them."

"Do you really think so?"

"Why not?" Mr Jaisaram turned a sorrowful gaze on him, a look, Arun felt, that was full of reprimand. In the silence that followed, he understood that deep within the butcher was an optimist, an idealist of a kind, whom he had wounded with his simple question.

Mr Jaisaram turned his gaze back to the fields and the shimmering air above them. "Our houses, *these* houses," he continued, having chosen to ignore Arun's gaffe, "came much later. The army had a small outpost here and when the Boys appeared, the outpost became a camp. Then one day the soldiers offered to tear down our houses — the old-time houses, you know, wood and straw, with coconut branch roofs that leaked in a thousand places — and put up new houses for us. They strung electricity lines. Omeara was transformed."

"It sounds like a fairy tale," Arun said.

"Maybe that's what it is." Mr Jaisaram laughed, swallowed a long draught from his glass. "Maybe that's all it is. After all, this town began as place where people could make a living through their own labour, legal, illegal, it didn't matter, and suddenly a kind of magic comes and changes things. Brick houses, electricity, a new schoolhouse. Even a teacher! The only thing is, Mr Arun, you never know what kind of ending a fairy tale's going to have. The ugly duckling could have turned out to be a vulture, not so?"

Somewhere high above, the spotter plane whined its way through the sultry air. Mr Jaisaram, peering up, pointed a finger at the sky. Arun saw a dark speck heading for the mountains. He said, "So the army has been good for you."

"A solid house, lights, paying customers, enough liquor to pickle a thousand livers. You could say so."

"And what about the others? The Boys, as people call them."

Mr Jaisaram, glass perched on his lower lip, squinted sideways at him. "What do you know about the Boys?"

The Boys — the freedom-fighters, the guerrillas, the revolutionaries, the subversives, the outlaws, the terrorists — were a band of fighters who had been sent from the rebel stronghold farther south to take the war to the army. "I know they're very good at what they do." Their goal, as explained in army communiqués, was to secure a base in the mountains, then a second and then a third, gradually expanding what they called their "liberated" territory, a strategy army spokesmen swore was doomed to failure. "But they also have a reputation for viciousness."

Mr Jaisaram shrugged. "War is war."

"Yes. War is war. But they sever the heads of their enemies and leave them on stakes. They cut off the hands of children whose parents don't cooperate. They blow up innocent women and children."

"Perhaps yes, perhaps no. No doubt, they are hard people, Mr Arun."

"Doesn't that bother you?"

Mr Jaisaram said, "You live your life, Mr Arun, and you hope that things don't come too close to you or your family. You carry on and you try not to think about things too much so you don't go crazy."

"How do people in Omeara feel about them? They say they're fighting to liberate you."

"What from?"

"From — and please pardon the expression — from being two-percenters."

"And the soldiers say they are fighting to protect us. So many people killing on our behalf."

Arun sipped carefully at the whisky, watery now at the surface. He had hoped to learn something useful from Mr Jaisaram, something that would help him position himself in this new place. But Mr Jaisaram's answers offered no direction. You carry on, you hope. Wasn't that a kind of despair? Then he said, "Their leader ..."

"Ahhh." Mr Jaisaram leaned forward, elbows on his knees, glass grasped lightly in both hands. "Their leader, you've heard about him. His reputation has reached the capital, then?"

"They say he's a foreigner."

"A foreigner!" He snorted. "We like to blame foreigners for all our troubles, Mr Arun. For a long time — and I'm old enough to remember this — for a long time everybody hated the British. Everything that was wrong with our lives was their fault. But the British left a long time ago, their time is already like ancient history. But an even more ancient history, our history, has survived them." He flicked a finger at the rim of his glass. "A foreigner, you say. Where from?"

"Nobody seems to know."

"Well, I'll tell you what people around here believe, Mr Arun. They say that he is a young boy, eleven, twelve. Some say he's really a girl. They say he has yellow hair and green eyes and is the son of a mountain gorilla and a village woman. They say he smokes cigars and has banned pork, alcohol, even eggs. He and his people live off the land — wild vegetables, lizards, monkeys. Some believe he has mystical powers. No bullet can harm him or those close to him. He has gifts, he can foresee danger. They claim that when his followers step on landmines, the mines don't explode. They claim that when his people set off bombs strapped around their waists or in their bags, they walk away unharmed." He grimaced, sceptical. "They say he has no name."

"And you, Mr Jaisaram? What do you believe?"

"I believe I am a two-percenter in your country, Mr Arun." He spoke dispassionately, merely stating the obvious.

The door beside them opened and Anjani stepped out, blinking, into the sunshine. She was barefoot, her eyes red, the skin beneath them swollen and dark. She looked depleted. "Headache's gone," she said, "but you!" She blinked at her father. "You're going to give me another one. What are you doing telling him all those fairy tales? Yellow hair and green eyes! Son of a mountain gorilla, my ass!" She turned her blinking eyes on Arun. "And as for you, sitting there listening to this crap, you should be ashamed of yourself."

Arun's lips trembled with a rising grin. "I am," he said. "Deeply ashamed." He clapped his hand on Mr Jaisaram's shoulder. "And so is he."

"Yes, yes," Mr Jaisaram said. "Deeply ashamed."

Anjani tightened her lips, blinking hard at them both. She had been outdone and she knew it. "What are you drinking?" she said. "One of my father's whisky and sodas?"

Arun nodded.

"What a waste of good whisky. Get rid of it. Let me make you a real drink."

"What about me?" Mr Jaisaram said.

She considered him for a moment. "You too."

Mr Jaisaram immediately emptied his glass onto the ground. Arun followed his lead.

"Come," Anjani said, turning back to the open door. "I'll give you your choice even though you don't deserve it."

As he rose unsteadily — the drink had been unexpectedly potent — Arun saw the speck of the spotter plane soaring over the mountains. They would know before long whether the pilot had seen anything worthy of a visit from the helicopter gunships.

SIX

Except for the most basic of needs — I am hungry therefore I eat, I am thirsty therefore I drink — motivation, Arun believed, was rarely crystal clear. Most people fell into things, the way his grandfather fell into the printing business through a fascination with machinery — a broken hand-cranked press found half submerged in a stream, the challenge of understanding and repairing the unfamiliar, a request to print a handbill, then another, then political posters, and finding himself drawn out of the fields by what had begun as simple tinkering. Or the way his sister fell into marriage through happenstance and a desire to avoid work, not because of laziness — although as a housewife she would be surrounded by the maid, the cook, the laundress, the gardener — but because of a certain idea of herself she had grown up with, as mother, as matron, as matriarch. It was as if his grandfather's potential had befallen him, while his sister — no fool — had snubbed hers. Just as their grandfather had come across the printing press in the water, so she had come across Surein in the printery. His grandfather had never thought that the junked machinery coaxed back to life would bring wealth to him and his descendants. Joy had never expected she would encounter her future husband while performing a job she was not eager to do. Each had simply drifted down roads that appeared before them.

As, he felt, had he. He could never adequately explain, to himself or to anyone else, his desire to teach — and to teach *rikshas* at that. At best, he had his suspicions. His mother had been right, it had to do with Mahadeo, his old teacher turned government minister. It had to do with Mahadeo's passion, his inspiration. And it had to do with his intransigence, which Arun was a long time in recognising as ruthlessness.

Mahadeo should not have been teaching at St Alphonse-in-the-Fields. There was something perverse in his wishing to join the staff of a school that was seen as a training ground for the privileged. His occasional newspaper article and to a lesser extent his books had given him a certain notoriety. He'd published two collections of historical essays that purported to be reinterpretations of the nation's past — essays which, in their unabashed triumphalism, in a language that eschewed the academic for the popular, had attracted a good deal of attention despite what traditional historians had denounced as a mishmash of rumour, unsubstantiated assertion, blind interpretation, and selective deployment of facts. One essay, "Aryadasha: A Man with Balls," had been printed up by the Ministry of Education and distributed free to all primary schoolchildren.

When it was announced that Mahadeo would be joining the school as a history teacher for the upper forms, many parents had expressed concern, their letters and phone calls to the principal couched in language less virulent that what they felt: the fit was so obviously awkward that parents were made cautious. The principal's reply in each case was simple: "Our new history teacher has been hired on the personal recommendation of the Minister of Education." Everyone understood that the matter was best dropped.

Arun, puzzled at first, then intrigued, purchased a copy of Mahadeo's social criticism, a salad of his newspaper writing "expanded and updated." It was a slender volume bound in cheap paper and written in the blustery style of propaganda leaflets. The book roared criticism at the softness, the flabbiness, the moral weakness that northerners had acquired. It spoke of a debasement of the culture. It proposed a return to the martial values of Aryadasha and urged that his methods be used to extirpate the cancer that was destroying their civilisation. He had no need to identify the cancer. After ten embarrassing pages, Arun quietly put the book away. But — and this surprised him — he found he could not dismiss Mahadeo. Something in his passion excited him, this sense of commitment to something larger than himself. He remained intrigued.

A grumbling cough and a surge of smoke from the corridor had heralded Mahadeo's arrival in the classroom. Arun, standing at his desk like the rest of the boys, saw a tall, skinny shadow amble in, as nonchalant as a tourist wandering along a beach. His hair was short and uncombed, as grey as the rumpled T-shirt he wore beneath the light black jacket that matched his trousers. He was unshaven and shadows of exhaustion seemed to lurk beneath his skin. He took a last drag of his cigarette, squinted at it, flicked the butt in a high arc back out through the door. Then, venting smoke, he turned towards the boys, considered them for a moment and growled, "Do I look like some fucking general? Sit, sit. At your desk, on your desk, on the floor, I don't give a shit. Just don't ever do that again, understand?"

One boy raised his hand. "Do what, sir?"

Mahadeo threw his hands into the air and snorted in exasperation. "Somebody, quick," he barked, revealing crooked teeth. "Help out that genius."

Laughter shuddered through the classroom. Arun, nervous, sat at his desk like most of the boys; then he changed his mind and sat on it as a few had done.

"History!" Mahadeo declaimed. He strode from one side of the classroom to the other. "What is history?" He glared around the classroom. "What. Is. History!"

A few tentative hands went up. Arun's was not among them. Instead, in contravention of yet another school regulation, he simply blurted out: "History is what happened yesterday."

Mahadeo's eyes curled towards him. "Bullshit," he said. "Julius Caesar was a great man? Ask the people whose villages the bastard burnt down how great he was. Churchill? That motherfucker thought Indians were too stupid to run their own country. Gandhi? Reminds me of a friend I had when I was little. You know the kind: I'm going to hold my breath till you do what I want and if I die it'll be your fault! That was Gandhi for you." He raised a hand to the class and counted on his fingers. "A killer. A racist. A blackmailer. Heroes or assholes?" He dug a hand into the pocket of his jacket and extracted a pack of cigarettes. His thumb rapped at the bottom of the pack, launching a single cigarette like a miniature missile. With a twist of his head, Mahadeo caught it between his lips like a seal seizing a tossed fish and lit it with a match that had materialised in his fingers.

Arun saw his friends exchanging glances — some impressed, some amused, some outraged. He found himself admiring the theatre.

"Most historians," Mahadeo said, blowing a gust of smoke towards the door, "are yesterday's men. What's the bloody point? History must be used to shape today and change tomorrow. History is a weapon. It is a dangerous, unstable element, handle with care. No way you can ever make those musty bastards understand that. But this historian —" he thumped his index finger on his chest "— believes that history must be made politically useful and socially relevant. History must not just be some airy-fairy story. It must have a point. And it is the historian who gives it a point."

He sucked hard at the cigarette, chuffed smoke, sucked hard at it again. "So. Once more. What. Is. History."

Arun, looking straight at him, said, "History is whatever you or I make of yesterday, whatever is most useful for us."

Mahadeo gestured at him with his cigarette. "Not so stupid after all, I guess," he said with a grin.

In the weeks and months to come, Mahadeo would, like all the teachers, acquire a nickname. Astonished that he was allowed to continue smoking in the classroom, the boys took to referring to him as Smoky. It was known that the name pleased him and, once he had made it clear that he would respond to neither "sir" nor "mister," they took to addressing him as Sir Smoky. His desk in the masters' common room — a mess of books and papers, spilled ashes and crumpled cigarette boxes — enhanced his popularity. Few boys were repelled by his scratching of his neck or his crotch, only a few more by his habit of occasionally striding from the classroom into the corridor, pressing an index finger to a nostril and sending a string of phlegm spinning from the other into the garden below. He was, they thought with a certain awe, a man whose mind mattered more to him than his body. He revealed no interest in cricket or football. They could not imagine him relaxing at the beach. Everything Mahadeo did or said seemed calculated to thumb his nose at authority. He oozed defiance. Mahadeo played at being the commonest of men, all the while building a reputation as an intellectual speaker-of-truths slightly embarrassed by his learning. His passion for history, his ability to stir the dusty past into a cauldron of heroic achievement and lively resentment, carried the day. Southerners, he argued, had to be made to bend to the will of the majority, for their own good, for the good of the country.

History became Arun's favourite subject.

THE KITCHEN GARDEN, squeezed between his house and Mr Jaisaram's, seemed a lost cause. There was, to his eye, nothing to be done. He had no experience with soil and plants — his parents had employed a gardener, a skinny old man grateful for the money and the food packages his mother made up — and while he could admire a trimmed and ordered garden, the soil tilled and weeded, so unlike the chaos of the forests, he had little idea of how to go about achieving such harmony.

Lying on the ground beside the house were a rusted hoe and a garden fork with one prong missing. They might have been abandoned there — he could imagine the frustration of the previous occupant faced with the same crusty earth, the desiccated tomato plants, the weeds that grew strong and tall — but they had been placed neatly side by side, like some ancient but devoted couple. He picked up the hoe, weighed it in his hand, enjoyed the smooth warmth of the handle in his grip.

Then suddenly he felt foolish, let out a little laugh as he remembered the scene from *Anna Karenina* where the intellectual decided to toil in the fields along with the peasants. There had been something slightly embarrassing about that scene, the aristocrat playing at labour. For Levin, and for Tolstoy too, it had been a game — they both returned to their comfortable homes at the end of the day while the peasants trudged back to their hovels. He had to admit to himself that for him, too, it was a bit of a game, this thought of reviving the kitchen garden. It seemed a good thing to do, a useful way of passing his free time. And then, too, so many of his students sacrificed school days to work in the fields, surely it was a good idea to experience a little bit of ... He shook his head, laughed again at himself. Wasn't that what lay behind Tolstoy's fantasy of physical labour? Getting closer to the peasants, who surely would have thought that the Count had gone a little off his rocker?

Still, as he stood there feeling the weight of the hoe, his muscles seemed to anticipate the work, the new experience. He let the blade fall tentatively to the ground, watched it bite into the soil. Then he struck a more powerful blow, putting his arms and back into the effort. This time the blade hit something hard and bounced away, the shock travelling up his forearms to his elbow.

Laughter erupted behind him.

Stung, he turned around. "Were you spying on me, Anjani?"

"You have no idea what you're doing, do you?"

"None."

Her lips twitching in amusement, she said, "I'm sorry, I shouldn't have laughed."

"Why not? You do it all the time. You seem to find me entertaining."

"Well." She put two fingers to her lips, struck a thoughtful pose. "You are. Would you rather be boring?"

Arun felt disarmed. He let the hoe fall from his hand. "It doesn't seem to work properly," he said.

Casting a critical eye at the garden, Anjani gathered up her skirt around her legs so that it was transformed into baggy trousers and squatted before the profusion of weeds and dead plants. She glanced up at him. "What are you waiting for?"

He stepped over to her and carefully lowered himself in precarious balance onto his haunches, the strap of his prosthesis tightening into his thigh. Almost immediately, his shin began to burn from the effort of the unaccustomed posture and it was only by slinging his arms over his knees in what felt like the attitude of a chimpanzee that he was able to save himself from toppling over onto his back.

"Now," she said, her hand surging into a clump of weeds, "you grasp them hard at the base and you give a sharp pull so all the roots come out." She held up a fistful of uprooted weed. "You never learnt how to do this?"

"Weeding was not part of my upbringing."

"So you're about to enter a whole new world, aren't you? Go on, give it a try."

Arun followed her instructions, was surprised at how tenacious the roots were. After he had successfully pulled his second clump,

Anjani, humming to herself, returned to the weeding. Arun followed her lead, but it wasn't long before he found himself drenched in sweat, his fingers green with chlorophyll, his muscles — from his neck, down his back, along his arms, through his thighs — pulsing in agony. His pile of weeds, he saw, was barely a third the size of Anjani's. At this rate, it would take him better part of a week just to weed the garden. Anjani herself had only the slightest sheen on her skin. She didn't look to be in any discomfort, her hands plucking and tugging with a tireless, metronomic rapidity. There was something relentless in the way she attacked the work.

He tossed a weed onto his pitiful pile and, unable to maintain the crouch any longer, slowly straightened up.

Without breaking the rhythm of her hands, Anjani said, "Try kneeling, you might find it easier."

"I'm not used to squatting like that," he said, his arms stretching overhead, his hands clawing spasmodically at the sky. The blood seemed to be lurching through his body, through crinkled veins and past constricted muscle, with the uneasy languor of water in a silted-up river.

"You don't have to apologise. When you grow up in the city, there's no need, I guess."

"I'm not apologising, just explaining."

Anjani smiled at the weeds.

Arun let his hands fall, mopped his brow with the back of his forearm. "Look," he said, "it's kind of you lend a hand but I don't want to take up any more of your time. I can get the rest done myself."

"I'm sure you could." Her hands never paused in their busyness. "It'd get done a lot faster if we both did it, though. I find it relaxing."

Arun reflected that Anjani didn't seem to do much besides relax, but he kept the thought to himself. He was being unkind, and he really was grateful for her help, even for her company. He fetched a square of cardboard from the house and put it on the ground. Kneeling was a great deal more comfortable for him and he was almost able to match Anjani's rate of weeding.

As his pile of weeds grew, she cast a quick glance his way. "You're a fast learner."

"Weeding doesn't take great skill, does it. Grab, pull. I'll bet even Holy Faith Convent could teach it in a single semester."

"You have more faith in the nuns than I do."

Soon a respectable swatch of the garden had been cleared of weeds. Anjani rose and, muttering to herself, examined the anemic tomato plants one after the other, deciding as she went which would be worth preserving. Those judged not hopeless were pruned of unhealthy leaves — a pinch of the fingers, a twist of the wrist — while the others were wrenched from the soil as unceremoniously as the weeds.

Arun sat back on the piece of cardboard, watching. "You look as if you know what you're doing." He balanced his forearms on his knees.

"It's called common sense," she replied, snapping a dry stalk in two. "Any fool could do it. Or almost any fool."

"Who'd you inherit your frankness from?"

"My mother."

"You're joking, right?"

"She's the most direct person I know. You always know exactly how she feels."

"I'll say."

"What does that mean?" She gazed askance at him, her face grim.

"Well, she clearly doesn't like me much. Is it because I'm from the north?"

She ripped a tomato plant from the soil. "What makes you think my mother doesn't like you?"

"She's never said a word to me."

"I see." She turned her attention to another plant.

"Well?"

"Arun, I ..." She bent the plant this way and that, examining its leaves.

"Well?" Arun repeated.

"My father says we shouldn't speak to you about these things."

"What things?"

"Just ... things." She released the plant, deciding it would stay.

"Are you the kind of woman who does everything her father says?"

"Of course I am. I'm a good girl, I went to convent school, can't you tell?" She pulled a leaf from the next plant, crumbling it between her fingertips.

"I never said you weren't. But only you'd know how true that is."

She looked away, across the fields to the mountains. Arun saw the rise and fall of her chest, found himself admiring the fine shape of her collarbone. Then she turned her gaze back to him. "My mother doesn't talk to anyone, not just you."

"She doesn't or she can't?"

Anjani sighed, her eyes leaving his and falling to the ground, to the wounds left in the weeded earth. "My father says we shouldn't speak to you about these things," she repeated, with even less conviction.

"Anjani," Arun said, "it's your business, I don't mean to —"

"I used to have a brother. He was older than me. I won't tell you his name because I promised my mother his name would never again pass my lips. I won't break my word to her."

"Not to your mother at any rate. To your father?"

"Not to my father either. He said we shouldn't talk to you about these things. I never promised I wouldn't."

"I'm sorry, I just assumed —"

"Don't bother. You should just be careful about making assumptions. They could lead you off cliffs."

"I'll be more careful."

She looked away again, eyes once more seeking the mountains, with intensity now, as if she were trying to see through them. In the strong sunlight, he saw her jaw shudder, saw the muscles in her neck ripple as she swallowed a mouthful of words. He saw how those muscles and tendons skirted into her thin shoulders where they were subsumed into a shapeliness that camouflaged their power.

"Your brother was killed in the war, is that it?"

"My brother knew that's what would've happened to him eventually, most likely. So he stole money from my father and ran away to the capital. There he found a man who would hide him in a shipping container with a dozen others. That container was shipped to Hong Kong and then to Canada. It was supposed to continue to New York City, which was the place my brother dreamed of. The man promised, but they were discovered. Three of them were already dead, another died a few hours later. My brother survived. He said he was a refugee. The Canadians believed him. He spent a few weeks in Vancouver, then he moved to Toronto. Thousands of our people live there, you know. They say there are little villages of them scattered around the big city."

Her voice trailed off in what sounded to him like wistfulness, her gaze wavering, losing itself in the section of the garden not yet weeded. She had related the story in the simplest way, with a dispassion that left her feelings about her brother's flight unreadable. The story had been washed clean of its inherent drama — the fear, the dreams, the flight to the capital, the weeks locked in a dark and airless metal container. It had become, in Anjani's retelling, just another story.

"Are you in touch with him?"

"We know what happened to him because others told us. News travels back and forth over the ocean as if it was just a wide river — news and lots of other things. But my brother's never tried to contact us, not as far as we know. We know he's alive, we know he's well. But, for us, especially for my mother, he might as well be dead."

"Maybe he's ashamed he stole the money?"

"I hope so."

"He could be your way out of here, you know."

Her jaw tightened. "What makes you think I want a way out of here?"

"Your parents, then. Surely they want to see their son again."

"You don't understand. I told you. My mother's banned me from saying his name. She cut him out of all the family photos. Everything that was his — his clothes, his books, his shoes, even his toothbrush — she took to the jungle one morning and buried. Nothing remains of him in our house."

Arun thought of his parents, of their bedroom left undisturbed in the large house, now locked and shuttered, in which he had continued to live with the maid and the cook, despite his sister's entreaties that he move in with her and her husband. The day would come when he and Joy would decide to sell the house. Surein had pointed out that the land alone was of immense value. On that day they would have to gather up their parents' belongings — their clothes, their books, their shoes, yes, even their toothbrushes — and ... And then what? He couldn't imagine what would be done with it all.

"His memory remains, though," he said. "His ghost, in a way."

"Does a memory exist if no one recalls it? One day we will all be dead and then the last fumes of his existence will be blown away. As far as my parents are concerned, they have no son. That's why my mother doesn't speak anymore. Burying his things and banishing his name — it's turned out to be, well, not enough. She tells herself she has no son but her womb has a more powerful memory. For weeks after she found out what he'd done she raged at having given birth to a coward. Then one day, well after she'd got rid of his belongings, well after she'd banned the mention of his name, she announced that she would not speak again until he returned and atoned — or until he was dead. That was six years ago. She's kept her word." She bent over, scooped up a handful of earth and frittered it to dust between her fingers. "They like having me back here from the capital. To make sure I wouldn't try to follow him."

Arun stepped closer to her. "And would you?"

The skin around her eyes darkened. "Not once in all these years have I resented my mother's silence. Not once have I tried to make her go back on her vow. My father has, it's very hard on him. But me? Never. Does that answer your question?" She turned wearily towards him. "The war didn't kill my brother, but he let it turn him into a ghost."

"Your mother, she would've been happier if he'd stayed here and got blown to pieces?"

"Yes."

Something froze for an instant within Arun. It was the way in which she had pronounced the word — simply, without hesitation, without emotion. Coldly. He understood that Anjani, too, would have been happier had her brother chosen a fate from which there might be no return.

"Enough chatter," she said, summoning a new energy and stepping firmly around the surviving tomato plants to where the weeds still grew in profusion. "There's work to be done."

Light, Arun thought, sometimes transforms a place, lifts its weight, makes its air more breathable. Mr Jaisaram's living room, only a touch brighter during the day than during the evening, was not one of those places. Here, the new light simply made details clearer without altering their essence. The raw-brick walls were painted a soft blue — a shade Arun's mother would have dubbed baby blue for the hint of powder it carried — but the furniture would have been as weighty, as cumbersome, even if placed in an open field under the midday sun.

In the kitchen, Anjani knocked ice cubes from a metal tray for the iced water they both craved.

The photographs on the walls had all been mounted in the black plastic frames Madhu sold at the general store. They were an assortment of family arrangements: mother, father, and daughter holding themselves in rigid suspension before the lens. Even those photos meant to convey spontaneity suggested a guiding hand, directing Mrs Jaisaram to raise her glass halfway to her mouth, instructing Mr Jaisaram to ignore the camera as he drew a file along a knife blade. They had been taken mainly in and around Omeara, but some showed Anjani standing in school uniform before the formidable, fortress-like convent in the capital. In several, Mrs Jaisaram, younger, was smiling, but only with her lips; her eyes, full of suspicion or uncertainty, reflected another state of mind, as if the smile were a concession to the moment. In the more recent photos — Anjani with face and body more defined, Mr Jaisaram with a touch less grey in his hair — Mrs Jaisaram offered no smile, her face blank except when stitched by the hint of a grimace, with a hardness in the eyes and a jaw-clenched firmness around the mouth.

Anjani, in her nose, her cheekbones, her chin, was clearly her father's daughter, but the photographs revealed the more subtle resemblance between mother and daughter, a resemblance that proceeded from the eyes: a blatant determination that would make no concession to the demands of convention. If the photographer had asked them to say "Cheese!" in the moment before the release of the shutter, they would not have submitted to the theatre.

Many of the photographs appeared to suggest moments of bizarre spatial distortion, with ill-fitting vertical joints up the middle or off to one side showing a tree that appeared to have been cleaved neatly in two and one half carted away, a truncated house with a doorway too narrow to allow passage to any human, background landscape that looked like pieces of a jigsaw puzzle forced together despite a missing chunk. Here and there a hand or an elbow or a sliver of clothing infringed on the remaining image, fleeting glimpses of the ghost.

"Who's the photographer?" he asked when Anjani appeared with a jug of water and two glasses.

"Whoever happens to be holding the camera," she said dryly,

placing the glasses on the coffee table and jostling the ice cubes as she filled them.

"Right." Arun decided he would turn his attention to the fist-sized carvings that occupied the spaces between the photographs. They were of birds, dogs, goats, and creatures of the imagination spouting wings and horns and talons, all finely carved in minute detail. "Do I dare ask who the sculptor is?"

She joined him at the wall, handed him a glass of water. "My father. It's sort of his hobby."

He remembered the bench out back, the pieces of wood, the knives. Mr Jaisaram had deflected his curiosity by saying that he had restless hands, that he liked to keep them busy. Arun peered more closely at the carvings, saw a suggestion of flight and breeze in the birds' wings, an illusion of movement in a goat's raised hoof, the finely detailed fur on the dogs. He was astonished that such large hands could shape such delicate objects, that so large and powerful a body could harbour such finesse.

"My father wanted to be a shakir when he was young," Anjani said. "You know what a shakir is?"

Shakir, he knew, were self-taught folk artisans but his knowledge of them was meagre, vague notions acquired at an arts-and-crafts show his mother had dragged him to some years before. They had hustled past acres of coconut shells carved into piggy banks with fanciful faces, forests of necklaces made from beads and seashells, empty cans stripped of labels and sliced into candle holders. She had shown him a series of watercolours — bucolic scenes of the northern peninsula, sea and sand and huts emerging from vegetation — which had been done by a quadriplegic who had only limited movement in his right foot; he had gripped the paint brushes in his toes. She had bought several of the paintings, her impulse less artistic than charitable. Arun had admired that act and was glad that he had come. The art hadn't moved him, but his mother had.

When he mentioned this to Anjani, she scoffed. "Real shakir," she said, "spend their lives carving gods for temples. You've seen our temples? All those carvings, thousands of them, they don't come from Hong Kong, you know. At least, they didn't, before. The shakir made them, working only at night, sometimes by fire-light, more often just by touch, in total darkness. The gods should never be revealed to direct sunlight, that's why our temples are so dark. The temples used to give the shakir employment for life. Food, lodging, clothes — all their material needs were provided for. On the other hand, they weren't allowed to take wives or have children, and their movements were quite restricted. Friendship outside the temple community was discouraged. Their devotion to the gods had to be absolute. They were seeing the gods in their heads, you see, and they were giving shape to them. The priests were their superiors, but in every way they were less important than the shakir. The priests were the servants of the gods, but the shakir were their makers. Without the shakir, the gods would exist only as an idea."

Arun ran his eyes along the wall. "I don't see any gods."

"Of course not. My father's not a shakir, and this sure as hell isn't a temple."

"It's hard to imagine Mr Jaisaram living that kind of life, cloistered in some temple."

"He was attracted to it. But he wanted a wife and children too. He decided in the end that he didn't have enough devotion, so he apprenticed himself to a butcher and found that the work appealed to him. But he still has the impulse to make things. He says he has restless hands. So most evenings he sits out back on his bench with his knives and lets his hands shape wood."

"And then he hangs them here."

"What else is he to do with them? Sell them at some arts-and-crafts fair in the capital?"

STANDING AT THE chalkboard, Arun stifled one yawn but was not quick enough for the second. Behind him, the children laughed, bringing a smile to his lips. He finished writing out the sentences they would copy for penmanship practice, put down the chalk and dusted his fingers. "Take your time," he said, lowering himself onto his chair. "When you've finished bring me your slates." He tapped the tin of chocolates he'd placed in the middle of his table, one of a small consignment Madhu had recently got in. "Those who do a good job will get one of these."

Rai, breaking into a grin, licked his lips.

Eyeing the boy's plump cheeks, Arun said, "And those who don't will get a piece of chalk."

At his words — meant to be funny — Rai seemed to deflate, his eyes losing the sparkle of greed. While Jai had adapted well to switching his writing hand, Rai was having more trouble convincing his left hand to do what did not come naturally: it was not the quality of his penmanship that would earn him a square of chocolate.

Arun added, "Of course, effort counts as well."

Rai, picking up his chalk, appeared only a little soothed. Perspiration slicked his forehead.

Shanti raised her hand. "What about those who yawn?" she said. "What do they get?"

"If they're lucky they get to sleep," Arun said, enjoying Shanti's laugh, even a little relieved by it following his awkward attempt at humour. "Now, enough talk, get to work."

Shanti snatched up her chalk. Rai took what sounded like a breath of resignation.

A restless night had left Arun irritable. Behind the shuttered windows, the air in the house had grown close. Opening the window above his bed hadn't helped. There was no breeze and the air that had drifted in was sluggish with humidity.

The air in the school was only slightly better. The sun had dried out the air a little but his walk to school had left him feeling uncomfortable. The children themselves seemed not quite awake, even the usually vibrant Indrani, always so eager to learn, was constantly rubbing sleep from her eyes. Rai and Jai were unusually subdued. Only Shanti sat alert at her desk, her eyes bright, her hair freshly washed, Radha somnolent beside her. Roop sat in his usual spot, off by himself, thumb stuck in his mouth, eyes distant. Arun had been unable to evoke any response from him; the promise of chocolates or candy failed to rouse him. Arun had learnt from Mr Jaisaram that his parents sent him to school mostly as a way of relieving them-selves of his presence. Hari hadn't been to school for several days. There were rumours, so far unconfirmed, that a body found in a shallow grave by an army patrol might be that of his missing father.

The scratching of chalk sticks on slate filled the schoolhouse — some fluid and confident, others unsure, stopping and starting. Rai, crouched over his slate, sighed, sniffled.

Arun stretched, took a deep breath of the boiled air. He was beginning to get a sense of some of the children, beginning in idle moments to sketch possible futures for them. He could see Rai working for Kumarsingh one day — he had the salesman person-ality it would take. Jai, on the other hand, was quick with figures and a bit more placid. There was, Arun felt, something of the shopkeeper to him; he might eventually take over Madhu's store. Indira was bright but curiously bereft of imagination, something of a plodder. Were she not a southerner, she might have found a job as a receptionist or typist As it was, she was more likely to end up at some hairdressing and nail-care salon in one of the larger towns. Shanti — the gossip, the chatterbox, the one who always knew everyone else's story — was just as bright, just as avid, but she had a quality the others did not: she seemed, in her childish way, to be more aware of her world, knew how to *see* it and, more impor-tantly, how to react to it. While the other children grew impatient with Radha's inability to express herself clearly, Shanti accepted her role as translator with a natural ease. In some ways, she reminded Arun of his sister who, when young, could be combative — but only when the need arose. Joy had lost that edge as she grew. He didn't think Shanti would. When he tried to imagine a future for her, his imagination failed him, not because the possibilities were so limited but because they were so great. She would need help, of course — sponsorship to a good school in the capital, a certain degree of guidance, help eventually in finding a job with potential.

Rai emitted another sigh of frustration, more pronounced this time, almost a lament. He was bent inches over his slate, the chalk clutched in the fingers of his left hand barely moving.

Arun shook off his speculation. He was getting ahead of himself. For now his job was to ensure a solid grounding. The rest would come in its own good time. Then a movement of light swifter than a shooting star drew his eye: a spark that appeared to dart from Rai's face to his slate. Arun looked more closely. Another spark faster than a blink. Except that it wasn't just light that he'd seen, and it wasn't perspiration either. It was light licking at tears. The sight — this glimpse of a hidden pain — froze him for a moment.

At her desk, Shanti leaned forward and eyed Rai with concern.

Before anyone else could see what was happening, Arun said, "All right, that's enough for today. Stop now, bring me your slates."

As the children dusted their fingers and cast last looks at their work, Arun wished he had a solution to offer Rai but all that came to him were words that would be, at this moment, useless and irritating: the effort would pay off, one day writing with the wrong hand would seem easy and natural to him — almost as easy and natural as it had been with his severed hand. He knew it was not a time for reassurances, which, no matter how true, would resemble platitudes. But that meant that all he was left with was a sense of helplessness.

When it came time to distribute the chocolates, he gave Rai two squares. "For the effort," he said, discomfited by the knowledge that he was trying to compensate for his inability to help.

THE NEXT DAY, Rai arrived at school with what appeared to be some kind of homemade toy strapped to his attenuated right forearm.

A strip of wood the size of a ruler had been secured along the top of the forearm with three strips of red gift ribbon, its tip extending a couple of inches beyond the stump. He sat at his desk and carefully inserted his chalk stick into a hole that had been cut into the tip. The fit, Arun could see, was snug. Holding the slate in his left hand, he described a series of fluid flourishes with his right. He held up the slate up for Arun to see. He had written his name in large, confident letters.

Arun examined the contraption. It was simple but clever. "What gave you the idea?" he said.

"It wasn't me, Mr Arun." Rai lifted his forearm and pointed at Shanti. "She gave it to me."

Arun turned towards Shanti.

She shrugged. "Now we won't have to put up with his sighing and moaning all the time. It's better for everybody, yes?"

"Yes," Arun said. He smiled. "No doubt."

SEVEN

A<small>T FIRST, HE</small> thought the rains that had been predicted for weeks had at last come with the crackle of thunder that had snapped him into wakefulness. It had resonated with all the authority of a math master's ruler cracking in anger onto a desktop: steel on wood that chased away the afternoon drowsiness of his charges and caused their blood to race.

For weeks, a heat more intense than he'd ever known had gripped the town. Not even the capital, where the hot months usually occasioned a rise in heat prostration and heart attacks, had been prone to this curious, suffocating quality. This was like inhaling liquid fire. If, in the capital, the heat threatened to roast the flesh on your bones, here in Omeara, where the greenery turned so dark and rich it seemed as if the trees and the grass were oozing chlorophyll, it held out the threat of death by steaming. In the greatest heat, just after midday, Arun could picture the marrow bubbling within the casement of his bones. More than once the vision had grown intense enough that, after school, he had rushed to the shower stall behind his house and let the water flow endlessly over him. It smelled of rust and was so heated it was like standing under a cascade of warm tea, but if he closed his eyes and summoned images of coolness — a tall, frosted glass with passion fruit juice bubbling down through crushed ice; a flute of the champagne his father used to open once a year on his parents' wedding anniversary, the lively golden liquid so chilled that the first sip was like placing your tongue on a chunk of dry ice; standing in the tumble of a spring-fed waterfall, the water so cold it hurt — he could convince himself for a few delicious seconds that he wasn't being consumed by heat. His body, tricked, would actually shiver.

So when the crackle and boom of lighting and thunder yanked him from his drugged, exhausted sleep just in time to hear its final echoes, he welcomed it with a silent exultation. Now the rains would come, they would crash down for days and nights with drops as fat as plums, washing away the heat, churning up the soil, slamming like bullets into the sea, spreading a relief that would be as sweet and gratifying as cold beer flowing down a parched throat. The sounds were like promises of survival.

Arun clasped a palm to his neck and rode it slowly down to his chest, wiping away the sweat. His breathing eased. Then there was another crack, followed closely by a second, and then a third. He sat up in the bed, his heart thrumming like a panicked bird trapped in his chest. *Not thunder.* Then came the chatter of what he knew to be several heavy machine guns, their staccato screams superimposed on one another, running into each other, blending. Three heavy explosions rose behind them, the sharp crackle that had awoken him slicing like a buzz saw through their majestic bass.

He swung his foot out of bed and placed it squarely on the warm concrete floor. It was not the sounds of weather that had awoken him. It was the sounds of battle. He reached for his leg.

Outside, the night sky was clear despite the crushing humidity. The air was sluggish, as viscous as that inside his house. There was no moon. His eyes, burning, flickered in discomfort at the starlight. Somehow, out here, perhaps because he had identified the sounds, the roar of battle seemed more distant, the individual voices of the rocket fire, artillery bursts, and machine guns melding into a chaotic mosaic. He glanced up and down the street, squared blocks of shadow in the blue gleam of the stars. Not a light showed, though he was certain that everyone had to be awake listening to the roar flowing down from the mountains, hoping and perhaps praying that it would creep no closer.

Treading carefully, letting his fingers guide him along the wall of the house, he picked his way around to the back. The darkness had swallowed the fields and, for a moment, he felt it was on the verge of swallowing him up too. He grew dizzy as he felt his body slip from his grasp, felt it somehow begin to merge with the dark bulk of the mountains far away.

A flare saved him. It was suddenly there in the sky above the conical silhouette of a mountaintop, hovering above the rumble of activity — furious, bone-crushing activity — taking place below it among the trees and the undergrowth as dense as fibre. Above the battleground that emitted no light, the flare shone with painful brilliance — perhaps, he thought, like the star that hung over Bethlehem in the Christian legend — displaying itself and lighting the way. Its glare anchored him, made him once more aware of the hot air and his body and the sweat coursing down his torso. Its descent was languorous, as if some mysterious force had slowed a shooting star. Or a falling aircraft.

The sounds of battle subtly changed as the light drifted lower, its brightness now obscuring the conical tip of the mountain. A lighter gunfire arose, grew quickly intense — a distant and swelling cacophony that lingered for several long minutes until the flare, falling into the trees or behind a lower mountain indistinguishable in the darkness, suddenly winked out. Then, in the renewed totality of the night, the gunfire fell off, became ragged and stopped altogether.

He realised in the silence that he had not taken a breath in too long. His mouth fell open and he found himself gulping as if famished at air so thick it was like swallowing chunks of the night. Dizzy again, he found the rear wall of the house and let his fingers guide him back to the front door. Only once inside, when he had turned on the light, did he see that dragging his fingertips along the rough brick had rubbed them raw.

He washed his fingers in the warm water of the kitchen sink, peeling away loose bits of skin. There was little blood. Then he stretched out on the bed. He couldn't bring himself to turn off the light. He felt that he would evaporate without the weak bulb there to show him the reality of himself.

He knew it was dawn when he heard the thump of his neighbours' wooden shutters being flung open. He knew that Mrs Jaisaram would be there, framed in the window as she had been that first morning, her hair falling silver around her shoulders, her mind wrapped around the concerns of her day. He wondered whether she missed speaking, whether she muttered in her sleep or whispered a few words to herself when she was alone. Surely, after all these years, she must have been tempted to hear the sound of her own voice, or to check that her vocal cords had not atrophied. Yet, even as he thought this, he knew that it wasn't so. There was, he had come to see, a tranquility to Mrs Jaisaram's strictness that suggested a woman at peace with her decision. She radiated a firmness of will that was inflexible, decorous, and immune to frivolity. He would never, he was sure, learn the tones of her voice.

He eased himself from the cot, tension coiling itself in his shoulders and arms and legs and even in the prosthesis that he hadn't unstrapped, as if the strain had communicated itself to the very plastic. He padded over to the rear window, hesitated. The noises of the night were constraining him, resounding yet in his head like faded but insistent echoes. There was a slight burning in his fingertips. He made a fist and, with his knuckles, unbarred the shutters and punched them open. The sunlight startled him. He had expected cloud and drizzle and a greyness appropriate to the taking of life.

The blue sky and the dazzling sunshine made him feel foolish. Often in books the weather mirrored the lives of the characters, anguish prompting rain clouds, anger prompting storms. Somehow he had come to expect this of real life, had come to expect the atmosphere to shape itself to the events of human destiny. Yet, hadn't his parents' plane exploded on a morning of great beauty, a morning made for plunging heedlessly into the sea?

The distant mountains, so green they looked as if they would begin at any moment leaking rivers of colour onto the tilled and planted plain, revealed no sign of the previous night's events. Not a tree appeared to have been disturbed, no trace of smoke drifted across the sky. He couldn't even be sure which of the mountains had provided the conical silhouette. It was often said that a man could disappear forever into those forests. Many had. None of the victims of the legendary Nawaal had ever been found. Examining the greenery that remained apparently undisturbed, he thought that hordes of men with tons of equipment could enter there and never be seen again. Legions swallowed whole.

He shuddered in the mounting heat of the morning — shuddered at the menace that lay beneath the tranquility. Or perhaps, he said to himself, embarrassed at his puerile gravity, perhaps he had shuddered just from fatigue.

Later that morning, a knock at his door roused him from sleep. His watch showed it was past ten o'clock. He couldn't remember sitting at the table, or laying his head on it. He felt as if he were emerging from a well so deep that it admitted no light, no sound, no image — from utter nothingness to a world in which solidity hadn't yet been fully restored.

At the door he found Kumarsingh. He was uncharacteristically well groomed in an ironed white shirt — the cuffs buttoned at the wrist, the gold watch hanging loose around the hand — and pleated grey trousers secured by the new belt he had boasted about some days before. Arun recognised the large silver buckle imprinted with an eagle's head motif and the shiny strap made of "the best quality plastic."

Kumarsingh said, "You're sleeping at this time of the morning?" He was subdued, his natural high spirits seemed defused. "This is not a good thing, you know. A resting brain is a dead brain."

Arun ran a hand through his uncombed hair. "I didn't get much sleep last night."

"Ahh! The thunder kept you awake?"

"Thunder?"

Kumarsingh hooked his thumbs into the belt. His eyes widened with amusement. "You know what thunder is, yah? Thunder is the sound of demons fighting for control of the sky. Last night, we heard thunder. Recognise it for what it was, my friend. When demons fight, it is best to lock your doors and secure your windows and remain inside and pray that none of their thunderbolts find you."

Arun circled his neck. Bones cracked. He could feel a headache coming on. "What can I do for you, Kumarsingh?"

"Jaisaram asked me to tell you that school's cancelled for this afternoon."

"I can't say I'm disappointed." This was not an unusual occurrence. School hours were tailored to the availability of the children, with classes sometimes held all day, sometimes only in the mornings, sometimes only in the afternoons. Cancellations were so frequent he was no longer bothered by them. "I need to catch up on my sleep anyway."

"That wouldn't be a good idea. You're expected."

"Expected where? What are you talking about?"

"This afternoon. At the cremation ground, across the road from the football field."

"Someone's died?"

"You heard the thunder last night. Someone always dies."

"But what does that have to do with me?"

Kumarsingh licked his lips, glanced nervously over his shoulder. "At some point this afternoon," he said, his voice almost a whisper, "the trucks will arrive, the army trucks. There will be a ceremony. Everybody is expected to attend."

"What kind of ceremony?"

"A victory ceremony, of course."

"A victory ceremony, at the cremation ground."

Kumarsingh nodded.

"What time?

"You'll know when it's time."

"How?"

"You'll know. Make sure to be there. They take note of who is not. They look for certain people. Jaisaram, Madhu, the café owner, the notary, and, of course, the schoolteacher. Dress well. A tie, if you have one. Make sure they see you. Understand?"

Arun, though perplexed, nodded. He was still a little groggy. With a thin smile, Kumarsingh turned and walked away.

He obtained two eggs from Mrs Jaisaram. She was, as usual, tight-lipped and watchful, as if she had treasures buttoned up inside her and suspected him of coveting them. He fried the eggs his favourite way, in a generous amount of butter and heavily sprinkled with salt, black pepper, and dollops of red pepper sauce. Then he fried two thick slices of bread in the singed, leftover butter. Standing before the open rear window, looking out occasionally until the fields and mountains once more became ordinary, he slowly consumed it all with a glass of water that he wished cold and a large mug of milky, sweetened coffee that he wished stronger. The food restored him.

After he had dressed, opting to button his sleeves as Kumarsingh had done rather than roll them to his elbows as he usually did, he sat at his table and tried to read. The Conrad had remained untouched since his arrival here, the closeness and suffocations of its world more accessible, even attractive in a grotesque way, when entered amidst the houses and office buildings and tended gardens of the capital. To read of jungle and menace while surrounded by it held little appeal for him and Marlow's voice struck him not as intermediary showing the way but as interpreter requiring too great a measure of confidence: what he told was important but he could not know all there was to tell. What before had struck him as an appalled voice of reason, applying notions of civilisation to extremities of decadence, now came to him merely as that of one white man dismayed at the depths to which other white men could sink when relieved of social constraint. Marlow — and perhaps his creator — now appeared to him merely as the upholder of ideals that arose not from within but that had been imposed from without. Arun believed that ideals imposed by circumstance were not ideals at all but merely ideology; the one timeless, the other false and changeable. Was the novel, as one high school English teacher had claimed, merely a warning to the white race that it trafficked with blacks at its own peril — an argument in favour of the separation of races? Or was it a novel, as another teacher had insisted, that underlined the essential frailty of human society — that all human beings, freed from the constraints of hard-won notions much grander than any single man, risked tumbling into the abyss that finally swallowed Kurtz?

He glanced at his watch. It was well after noon. He wondered what lay ahead. A ceremony, at the cremation ground. Victory. At the *cremation* ground? He would know when it was time. There was no point in thinking about it. He got out a pad of paper and a pen and began writing a letter to his sister.

Some time later, he had written only *Dear Joy & Surein, I am fine*. He hadn't been able to go beyond that. He sat at the table for a long time, his leg jumping nervously, one palm resting flat on the paper, the fingers of his other hand twirling the pen.

He was beginning to sweat once more in the thickening heat

when he heard the rumble, distant but growing steadily louder, of many heavy vehicles closing in on the town. He capped the pen and pushed the paper aside.

The earth shook as the army convoy — half-ton trucks, jeeps with towering antennae, armoured personnel carriers, brief glimpses of helmets and gun barrels — thundered past his house in a cloud of dust so thick he could feel the grit powdering his skin and crusting in his nostrils. He held the front door open just a crack, the wood vibrating into his fingers, watching what appeared to be almost a moving wall of olive green.

When they had gone by, the rumble growing fainter, he stepped outside into a world whitened by dust, the sky and houses and trees scrubbed by a seething mass so thick it dimmed the sun. Ahead of him, treading in silence through the mist, he saw figures following in the wake of the convoy. They were indistinct, somehow formless, fashioned from steam and dust. Suggestions of bodies, simulacra of human shapes: his neighbours. It was as if he were seeing clear through them.

As he caught up to them, their forms acquired substance and colour, a filter being steadily erased from the blues and reds and yellows of their clothes. Some walked on their own, others in family clusters, their faces solemn and joyless. He recognised several of his students. Their eyes blinked against the dust. None returned his nodded greeting. Overhead, the sky hardened into a crusty blue.

A hand touched his elbow. Kumarsingh. His face was dusted white, his skin had gone waxy in the heat. He appeared to have been made up by an undertaker. "I told you you'd know when it was time, yah?" he said. He took Arun lightly by the arm and urged him to match his quicker pace.

By the time they reached the field, Kumarsingh still grasping Arun's arm, the crowd thickening around them, the dust had settled. The army vehicles had formed a semicircle — trucks, armoured personnel carriers, three jeeps spouting an array of antennae. They were mounted with heavy machine guns attached to metal frames, two-man teams on alert at each of them, one man gripping the weapon's handles, the other with an ammunition belt drooping in his hand, both with their eyes trained beyond the mouth of the black barrel on the fields and the dark tree line. Kumarsingh whispered that inside the trucks, hidden from view by the canvas coverings that were rolled discreetly to the top of the metal trays, other riflemen surveyed the jungle through their gun sights.

Kumarsingh cleared a path through the crowd for Arun and himself and when they had come to the front rank, Arun saw that in the space between the townspeople and the army vehicles a low, wooden dais had been set up. At each corner a short flagpole held a limp flag: two of the country's flags, one of the army, and the fourth, he assumed, of the regiment. On the dais, six officers in dress uniform sat fanning themselves and whispering into each other's ears. The shadow of their cap visors obscured their faces with all the efficacy of midnight. Arun found his gaze drawn to their uniforms, blue-grey tunics flecked with brass buttons and silver insignia, a snippet of red ribbon here, a snippet of blue there, shoulder tabs and chests crawling with the pretty hieroglyphs of brotherhood.

To the left of the dais a small military band, also in dress uniform, stood at attention with drums and trumpets. At a signal from the band leader — a man so thin that his tunic gathered in big folds around his vermilion waistband — the musicians launched into a vigorous if somewhat metallic rendition of the national anthem. At the opening note, the six officers snapped to attention and saluted. The crowd, already subdued, seemed to retreat into an even greater pocket of silence. Arun found himself slipping into the posture drilled into him at school: back stiffened, arms hanging loose, chin slightly raised. But this was not like the flag-raising, anthem-singing ceremonies that marked the first day of the term or that preceded prize-giving on the last. This was a martial ceremony, there was nothing benign about it, and he noticed halfway through the song that his fingertips were plucking at his trouser seams. Kumarsingh, he saw, had folded his arms across his chest.

As the final note soared into the heavy air, the thump of a lone drum arose from somewhere off to the right, a steady and mournful cadence that quickly displaced the livelier airs of nation-building. There was a stirring in the crowd — a swaying, a giving way — and presently there appeared four coffins, each borne by six military pallbearers in combat fatigues. The coffins, industrial containers of dull aluminum, were draped in the national flag, the red, green, brown and white oddly rich in the sunshine. At that moment, a thick odour filled Arun's nostrils, a pungent mixture of dust and earth and steamy jungle. It caused him to gag.

Slowly, in obedience to the cadence of the drum, the cortege made its way to the centre of the circle, lining up side by side before the dais and its saluting officers. The drum fell silent. Then an order was shouted, a brief bark that held meaning for the initiated. The pallbearers immediately eased their charges to the dusty ground. Another bark sent them marching off to the left where, in a crisp choreography, they formed themselves into four ranks of six. As the last man took his place, two of the officers made their way down from the dais. The first, Arun assumed, was the general. He couldn't help noting the swell in his tunic that was suggestive of pregnancy. The other officer followed a respectful step behind, a red velvet cushion balanced in his hands. Arun didn't recognise Seth at first. The dress uniform had transformed him, had made him indistinguishable. He moved differently in it. The general approached the closest coffin, paused before it, placed his fingertips on the lid as if in a moment of private meditation. He took a medal from Seth's cushion, pinned it to the flag, saluted, and moved on to the next, where he repeated the gestures. He seemed to Arun a man straining to lend solemnity to his actions. There

was a dispatch in the way he moved from coffin to coffin, a restive-
ness in his legs that belied the display of reverence, that suggested
theatre barely tolerated.

When he was done, he led the way back to the dais. As he
mounted it, the other officers rose. The general, with Seth behind
him, turned to face the coffins. An order was barked, and instantly,
the painful stridency of a single bagpipe rose from behind the band.
The officers saluted. The pallbearers marched back in, took up
their positions beside the coffins and retrieved their charges. As the
dirge of the bagpipe rose to a wail — Arun could put no name to
the tune — they marched off to the left, the crowd parting at their
progress. The officers unsnapped their salutes, the general leaning
over to Seth and whispering into his ear.

Arun found himself chilled from within, not from the beauty of
the music — the instrument always reminded him of the first time
he heard the nocturnal caterwauling of felines in heat — but from
a sense that he'd just witnessed a ceremony rife with undertones of
the macabre. He rubbed at his nose with the back of his hand. The
smell of dust and earth and jungle was lighter now, but it would,
he knew, be a while leaving him. From somewhere in the silent
crowd came the sounds of someone sniffling.

Kumarsingh leaned in close to him. His right forearm still lay
across his chest, but his left palm now cupped his chin. Speaking
low past fingers that crossed his lips, he said, "Notice anything
strange?"

Arun frowned in puzzlement. What was *not* strange?

Kumarsingh, reading Arun's expression, let a smile show
through his fingers. "Let me tell you what you're seeing, apart from
the obvious of course. Take the bagpipes. In the highlands of
Scotland, okay, but here ..."

"They're still part of our military tradition," Arun grumbled.

"And the weapons," Kumarsingh continued, undeterred. "Czech.
Israeli. The uniforms from Thailand, the boots from Germany, the
jeeps from the Americans, and the APCs from the Russians, via

India." The rise and fall of his voice gave the list the cadence of song lyrics. "The medals are made in China, of course, they're good at the gaudy stuff."

The pallbearers made their slow way to the rear of the crowd, the screech of the bagpipe softening in the rumble of truck engines coming to life.

"The world sends us its goods," Kumarsingh said. "Most of it second-hand, of course, but still ... Aren't we a lucky little country?"

"I suppose we are," Arun said without irony.

Kumarsingh was silent for a moment. Then, reverting to a more neutral tone, he explained that the bodies would be driven back to the base before being flown by supply helicopter to the capital for delivery to their families. All around them the crowd was stirring, a rising out of torpor made manifest in a gentle rustling. Here and there, urgent whispers called children to order. Arun asked if the ceremony was over.

"Not yet." Kumarsingh gestured grim-faced towards the far edge of the field. Already the crowd was moving in that direction like a slow but inexorable tide. On the dais, the military officers clustered like crows in secret conference. As Arun walked past, he saw Seth's face turn towards him, saw his hand rise in an almost surreptitious greeting. He nodded but did not break his stride. The surge of the crowd was quickening in the way of an undertow, an innocuous tug that suddenly grew irresistible.

Kumarsingh said, "Now they will show us the spoils of their victory."

"How do we know it was a victory?"

"It always is."

The march across the field was accomplished in silence. This was an exercise the townspeople were accustomed to, as if choreographed and rehearsed, and Arun followed the flow, let himself be led. If he closed his eyes, he might have been walking alone, his shoes pressing into earth that felt softer with every other step. Up ahead, the crowd was congregating at a corner of the field where the earth was moist and dank, where ferns grew among the trees.

As before, Arun found himself ushered to the front rank. Kumarsingh remained behind him. To his left Mr Jaisaram stood stiff-backed and unhappy in a worn grey suit that clasped him so tightly — it was at least three sizes too small — that Arun had a flash of his wife stitching him into it. To his right Madhu blinked rapidly at the forest gloom not far away, as if trying to penetrate it with fogged vision. They were gathered, he saw, like some kind of unofficial committee. He nodded at Mr Jaisaram but received only a baleful stare in return. The notary, too absorbed to notice Arun's greeting, swept his palm at the runnels of sweat creeping down his bald head. He was a small, neat man with anxious eyes whose business had been turned itinerant by the habits of the region. It was said that in every town he had a widow or a spinster willing to offer him a bed, food, and, no doubt, other bodily pleasures. It was his bad luck to have been caught in Omeara on this day.

A backhoe had scooped out a large hole in the ground, the extracted earth piled wet like a mound of fresh excrement beside it. The machine had withdrawn some distance away, its green-painted body almost blending with the trees, its articulated arm crooked down to the ground, suggestive of homage. An army transport truck was reversing up to the pit under the gestured directions of a military policeman. He waved it to a halt when the edge of the tray was aligned with the edge of the pit. In the cab, the driver swept a restless gaze through the crowd — worried, old-man's eyes in a young, plump-cheeked face. His muscled arm hung from the window, fingers drumming on the regimental crest decorating the door.

Kumarsingh edged closer to Arun. He tapped a cigarette from a soft pack and placed it between his lips. He offered one to Arun. Arun refused but Kumarsingh insisted, handing him one the way he might a pen. Taking a plastic lighter from his pants pocket, he mumbled, "You don't have to swallow the smoke. Just puff hard. Cigars would be better but you must make do with what you have."

"Is this part of the ceremony?" Arun leaned the tip of his cigarette into the offered flame. The taste of the tobacco made him grimace; it was bitter on the tongue.

"You could say so."

All around them tobacco smoke began rising like fog. Men, women, even children were sucking at cigarettes and expelling the smoke at each other in mushrooming streams. The notary pinched a slim cigarillo from his jacket pocket, tightened his lips around the plastic tip as he would at a straw, and attempted with shaking hands to light it. Two sticks of matches burned to his fingertips before he succeeded. Arun's eyes began to smart.

At that moment, the military policeman raised a white gloved hand into the air and pumped his fist. The truck driver's attention turned inward. Seconds later, the tray of the truck began to rise, machined steadily upward until its rear flap swayed open. For some seconds nothing happened. Smoke billowed and curled past Arun's head, filled his nostrils with its acrid smell, reminded him of the dust raised earlier by the army convoy. Then a dark mass appeared at the edge of the tray. It hesitated there, as if reluctant to emerge. The truck shuddered once. The mass, dense and lumpy, a blend of grey, black, some green perhaps, slid with viscous sluggishness from the tray, balanced briefly at the edge, then tumbled in leaden slow motion into the pit.

It was some seconds before Arun understood what he'd seen, some seconds before his mind would accept the arms and legs and faces, bodies and body parts so interlaced, so intertwined, they were blended into one, all but a single head which bounced along at the very end with all the alacrity of a soccer ball, as if eager to rejoin the body from which it had been severed.

His head rocked back in shock, time slowed in the way that it had the first time he smoked *ganja*: his brain registering the images he saw only a full second after his eyes had seen them, well after his gaze had already moved on.

There was no sound from the pit when the bodies hit, no rise of dust, no turbulence in the air: simply a kind of swallowing, an absorption. A rustle of wind and whispers filled his head. His heart thudded tumultuous against his chest like a fist punching meat.

The tray thumped back into place and the truck moved slowly off. With a growl, the backhoe began advancing towards the pit. The cigarette smoke thickened, turning the air milky and acrid. Mr Jaisaram coughed, his reddened eyes focused intently on the pit and the mound of exposed earth and the machine creeping towards them. He wasn't just looking, Arun realised. He was watching, observing. Witnessing.

Then, faintly at first, another smell infiltrated the cigarette smoke, a sweetish smell not immediately identifiable but familiar in some distant way. There was a density to it, a moistness, that caused it cut through the tobacco cloud like floodwaters through a field. Quickly it invaded Arun's nostrils and his mouth, poured down his throat and into his stomach. He retched. He knew this smell, knew its essence. Many years before. A rat problem at home. His father had hired professional exterminators. They had distributed handfuls of a granular poison throughout the house, had sprayed a white toxic mist outside, its odour cloying and persistent. But no, that wasn't it. It was later, days later, as the rats began to die, their long, grey bodies curled up on the kitchen counters, on the dining table, on the living room and bathroom floors, when they began to die between walls and under the floorboards, that the smell had begun. The smell of suppurating flesh, of swollen bodies splitting open and spilling sickly-sweet gases and maggoty guts.

A sharp pain bit at his fingertips. His cigarette, long forgotten, had burned down to the filter. He flung it away. Now he understood the barrage of smoke. He leaned over, his stomach heaving. He felt Kumarsingh seize him at the waist and propel him away.

A few minutes later, as Arun spat the bitter taste of vomit from his mouth and wiped his shoes clean on the grass as best he could, Kumarsingh explained in an apologetic voice that, in the heat and humidity of the jungle where they had fallen, bodies ripened quickly. Being dumped into the pit caused them to split open, releasing their bodily fluids and pent-up gases. "Maybe I should have warned you," he said, holding out a neatly folded handkerchief.

Arun thought again of the rats. He wiped his chin with the handkerchief. "Maybe you should have," he said.

That evening he gave way to impulse.

The fan his sister had sent him — a large, tabletop Japanese model painted lime green — whirred warm air at him in the quiet of his shuttered house. He sat once more at the table, picked up the pen, and drew the pad of paper towards him. *Dear Joy, Thank you so much for the whirling samurai. As I write this, its blades are helping immensely to keep me comfortable in the unimaginably hot south.* His pen stopped moving, its point fixed to the period inked in at the end of the sentence, as if the pen itself recognised the falseness of the words it had just written. Words meant to reassure his sister rather than reveal his reality. The fan didn't keep him comfortable. It couldn't in this suppurating air; the best it could do was keep him dry, causing his sweat to evaporate the moment it broke through his skin.

He laid the pen down across the paper. He couldn't write what he wanted to write. Not to her. She wouldn't know what to do with the images he had to offer, the scents and the sights of the day that flowed from his head, down through his arm to his finger-tips, where they remained dammed only because, by releasing the pen, he had forbidden them from escaping onto the paper, refusing to allow their horror to take shape in ink and letters.

He had always been frank with Joy. She viewed him, as their mother had often fondly recalled, as a living doll. One day, when he was no more than six months old, the maid had found Joy with her arms stuck through the bars of his crib, holding her doll's bottle to his lips. He had awoken from his afternoon nap, gurgling contentedly as he sucked at the water meant for her doll.

That was the way it had been as they grew, his sister as solicitous of him as their mother. He would never forget — with shame shadowed by pride — a morning at school when they were both very young. For days a bully had been following him around the schoolyard during recreation. *Hey, mummy's boy! You afraid of me, little girl? You're a two-percenter, aren't you? You and your whole family. You stink like two-percenters.* Arun, each time, had tried to flee him and his words of aggression. He found himself speechless, without defence, and the one time he had managed to respond — *Go away, leave me alone!* — his voice had betrayed him, emerging cramped and high-pitched, *girly-voiced.* His tormentor, taller, more muscular, held in general awe for his ability to thread sewing needles through the membrane between his thumb and forefinger, cackled in response. His fingers reached out for Arun's shirt. Arun leaned backward, out of reach. His breath seized in his throat, his hands tightened into fists. It was at that moment that someone tackled his tormentor and shoved him to the ground. Arun, startled, saw arms and legs flailing through a cloud of dust. Saw Joy straddling his prostrate tormentor and swinging at him with fists full of rage. Her hair was whitened, her dress bedraggled. He had no memory of how the battle ended, but the boy had kept his distance after that. That evening at the dinner table, after the head teacher, a family friend, had stopped by for a private chat with his father, he was, with humour, told to thank his sister. He'd thanked her as their father reached out and tousled her hair. But he didn't know if he could ever forgive her and, when they were alone, he told her so. She looked puzzled, but said nothing. For a long time afterwards, lying in bed at night or wandering aimlessly through the bush behind their house, Arun replayed the fight in his mind, he the one lunging at the boy, his the thighs pinning him, his the fists crunching into his face. His fantasies left him saddened, his only consolation the knowledge that he had readied himself mentally to strike back.

He picked up the pen once more. He should tell Joy about Omeara and the forested mountains that surrounded it, and the people he had met who seemed to live so much within themselves, swallowing the sounds that came to them at night and the sights that came to them by day. Those very sounds and sights he could not bring himself to offer his sister as elements of the life he found himself living. In the capital, they knew about the battles, of course. The newspapers faithfully printed government and army communiqués. Television and radio faithfully broadcast statements by government and army spokesmen. But the news media had never printed a photograph or run film of bodies being dumped from a truck, there had never been mention of southerners forced to endure humiliating, hastily arranged victory ceremonies by the army. There had been no reports of dozens of people spewing bile as the stench of rotting corpses enveloped them. Should he write about this to his sister, so proud, despite her anxiety, of the little brother who had accepted a life of hardship in order to help children in need? They had talked it out one night while Surein was reading a bedtime story to their daughter, and he had understood that she viewed his coming hardship — as, to some extent, did he — in idyllic terms: the lushness of the south, the refreshing simplicity of the life. She had heard somewhere that mangoes from the south were fleshier and juicier and sweeter than those from the north.

Sitting at his table with pen poised, he wondered what would be the point of disabusing her. He was afraid, too, that if she learned how things really were, she would insist on his leaving. She and Surein knew people; they could have him recalled to the capital without apology or explanation. More than that, though, he feared that if she appealed to him to leave — *I've already lost mummy and daddy, I don't want to lose you, too* — he would be tempted.

Mummy's boy.

The pen fell from his fingers and as it rapped onto the paper he saw that, in the hours he had been sitting there, he had somehow bitten his fingernails to the edge of blood. He put the pen and paper away, their very sight a rebuke, reminders of failure.

Restless, he wandered around the house, following the walls: twelve short steps lengthways, ten along its breadth, eyeing the rise and fall and inflated disjointedness of his shadow on the brick. At six steps along the rear wall, he stopped and opened the window. The darkness outside was as hard as stone. Clouds had heaved in late in the afternoon, thick, off-white, edged in grey and henna, as if their own shadows were on the verge of enveloping them. They held portents of rain — not now, but soon. He, like his neighbours, had begun longing for the relief the rains would bring, their drops shattering the heat, but now the thought of water thundering onto the ground, soaking through the earth and worming its way among the folds of decaying flesh removed all anticipation of the pleasure. Now he hoped the rains would hold off to give the bodies time to decompose fully, to blend with the soil and become indistinguishable from it.

His stomach was still unsettled and an acrid taste coated his tongue. He reached into his shirt pocket for a few of the mint leaves he'd picked in Mr Jaisaram's garden, nibbled at their edges then folded them into his mouth. But even their brisk, peppery flavour failed to cleanse the bile that had impregnated the surface of his tongue and the inner walls of his cheeks. He spat the wad of mint leaves into the night, broke a chunk from the loaf of bread that had been sitting for days on his kitchen counter, and chewed on it. The crust was hard, the interior dry and powdery. Soon he began to feel better. As his fingers cracked another piece from the loaf, there came a knock at the door.

Seth entered with neither word nor nod of greeting. He was draped in an olive-green rain poncho with the hood drawn up around his head — a disguise perhaps, a simple camouflage. He shut the door behind him with a deliberation that elicited a sound that was like a drawbridge thudding discreetly shut. Then he pushed the hood back. Dark bags hung beneath his eyes, but the eyes themselves were clear.

Arun said, "How's your wife?"

Seth frowned. "My wife? She's fine. Why?"

"I know how important having a baby is to you. That's all. I just wondered."

Seth glanced around. "As charming as I remember." He tugged the poncho off over his head, slung it on his shoulder. "All the discomforts of home."

"It's not as bad as it looks."

"I've seen monks' cells that were more inviting." He reached into the side pocket of his camouflage jacket, held up a metal flask. "Whisky," he said. "A few drops of the general's stock. Couldn't manage ice or soda, but you don't mind it neat, do you?"

"No." The thought of alcohol was, at that very moment, pleasing. He fetched two glasses and put them on the table. Seth unscrewed the flask as he strode over to the table. He filled both glasses almost to the brim with a dark, amber liquid. Picking up a glass, he said, "So, what did you make of our little show today?"

"I threw up." Arun picked up his glass, sniffed at its contents. He thought of sweetened turpentine.

Seth snickered. "I know. I saw you. Don't worry, you'll get used to it." He clinked his glass on Arun's. "Drink up. It's better than liver salts for settling the stomach."

Arun took a sip, inhaling deeply. The fumes alone made his head swim.

"Go on, drink up. You'll see." Eyeing him, Seth took a large gulp of the whisky.

Arun hazarded another sip, hardly more than a dampening of the tongue, then another, more generous one. The whisky singed and soothed his throat at the same time, quickly showering through his chest and unleashing a shudder that ran through the very marrow of his bones. His eyes watered.

Seth smiled. "Better?"

Arun nodded. He could feel his body welcoming the alcohol.

"You know what I'd really like to know," Seth said, walking slowly around the room examining all that he saw: the sink, the tap, the stove, the cot, the swirling blades of the fan. "What'd I'd like to know is what our Polish friend would make of all this." He tossed the poncho onto the bed.

"Our Polish friend?"

"Korzeniovski. The Konrad with a K who became Conrad with a C."

Arun thought that, now, at this moment, he could write a letter to his sister. Another sip of the whisky had made him wistful. He could write many pages mendacious with wit and description, selling the place and the people and never speaking — at least not directly — about himself. A sense of peace followed yet another sip. Finally he said, "I don't know about the Pole, I don't know what ..." Then a smile came to him although he didn't know why. His eyelids grew heavy. "Perhaps, 'the horror, the horror?'"

Seth brought the glass to his lips. His eyes skittered from Arun to the open window behind him, to that square of perfect darkness. "It's been done, *he* did it. Who knows what he'd say. But I'm pretty damn sure he'd recognise us."

Arun found his smile widening, was surprised at the gurgle of laughter that rose from his throat. "Have a seat," he said, indicating first the chair then the cot.

Seth lowered himself heavily to the cot, leaning his back against the wall, stretching his legs out before him and hooking one black combat boot over the other. He patted the thin mattress. "One of ours," he said. "I'd recognise the feel anywhere. No doubt liberated by some enterprising soldier."

Arun sat on the chair. "Just like your whisky?"

"Just like my whisky."

Arun crossed his legs. He was glad Seth had come. He was grateful for the company. Earlier, he'd thought of going next door to Mr Jaisaram's, but the afternoon had left him with a curious sense of shame. He felt it would be a while before he could comfortably look his neighbours in the eyes again. He would find no solace there, but why this should be so — why he should feel himself judged and soiled in ways that they were not — he couldn't fathom. Why he should not feel so in Seth's presence was even more puzzling. He put it down to the whisky.

A long moment of silence descended between them, a kind of wordless stock-taking. Arun relaxed. It was like sitting alone with his sister — companionable, undemanding, a silence into which no words had to be shovelled. Seth drained his glass, refilled it. Finally Arun said, "What are you doing in this place, Seth?"

"I'm a military man. I'm posted here."

"But you don't have to be. Your general would have you transferred if you wanted, wouldn't he?"

"He would."

"He knows about your wife?"

"Yes."

"So why hasn't he had you transferred?"

"I haven't asked him."

Arun looked up in surprise. "Are you going to?"

"If I did, I might as well just resign my commission and find something else to do."

"And your wife? Surely she'd like to see you do something else."

"She's accustomed to army life. She knows what it's all about."

"Still, surely she must ... Living alone, I mean, she ..."

"She gets lonely, yes, but she's with my parents."

"She lives with them?"

"Well, hers are kind of far away. She comes from America. Did I mention that?"

"No, you didn't."

"We met in North Carolina. I was there for an officers' training course. Her father was one of the instructors. An amazing man. He had stories from Korea and Vietnam that'd peel the eyelids from your face."

Arun winced, saw again the languid tumble of bodies into the pit.

"Anyway, she came home on vacation from college —"

Vacation, not holidays, *college*, not university: Arun envied Seth the experiences that had given him a new vocabulary.

"— and came to a reception our hosts threw for us, to mark our independence day, which was thoughtful of them when you think about it. That's where we met. I remember seeing this tall, thin woman with the most extraordinary face and dark brown hair cut short standing in a corner of the officers' mess. I wondered who she was and the next thing you know, John — Colonel Barnes, her dad —"

Dad.

"— was introducing her around the room. Felicia. The following week John and Meg had a few of us over for a barbecue, and a few days later Felicia and I went to see the new Woody Allen movie."

Woody Allen. Arun had only read about him and his films. Here, they would find no market among the Bombay romances and the Hong Kong martial arts intrigues. And this strange word, movie. *Movie.* It embarrassed him, somehow. He knew he could never bring himself to use it. It was like saying *pop* rather than soft drink, or *Mom* rather than Mummy. To his ear, there was something pretentious about such words — or, at least, he felt that he hadn't earned the right to say them. They were words that belonged to some American suburb, as in those television serials that filled the evening hours in the capital, nicely dressed teenagers obsessing over their love lives and roaring off to college in shiny new cars. *Mummy* and *Daddy* and *holidays*, even if coated in a kind of mustiness, were more appropriate to his tongue. But these other words — suggestive of a world only vaguely familiar to him, and so seductive and intimidating — came easily to Seth.

"Felicia wasn't like our girls here," Seth continued, twirling the glass of whisky before his eyes. "She was so open, so direct. She loved flirting. I was a little uncomfortable at first but, believe me, I got used to it real fast. There was nothing coy about her, no sense that — you know what the girls are like here — no sense that she was trying to spin marriage webs around you. What you saw was what you got, and I liked what I saw.

"I didn't dare make the first move, of course. I convinced myself she was just being kind to a foreigner. Then one evening while we were out for a stroll along the banks of a river that wound its way through the town — a quiet, peaceful spot — she suddenly said, 'So how come you don't find me attractive?' Just like that. She kind of blurted it out. I was so stunned it took me a minute to find my voice and when I did it came out like some whiny five-year-old's. '*But I do!*' 'Oh, yeah,' she said, 'so how come you haven't tried to kiss me?' And the next thing you know, of course, I was. Or she was. Or we were. She's the first woman I slept with without paying for the privilege. We've been together ever since. It took a couple of years to finally put things in place. She needed to finish her doctorate in anthropology and I had to fulfill some obligations here, but everything worked out in the end, especially after John got the army to pull some strings. We've been here for almost two years now. She teaches at the university."

"Does she find it hard, being away from America?"

"She misses her parents, but she's a resilient girl, Felicia. Given a choice, she'd rather live alone, she's very independent, but my mother would die of shame. Her daughter-in-law living on her own. What a scandal! So Felicia gave in and agreed to live with them so long as my responsibilities keep me down here. I think that's the hardest part for her: not being able to come and go as she pleases without someone asking where she's going and when she'll be back."

"It's hard to imagine," Arun said. "An American woman choosing to live here."

"She didn't choose this place. She chose me."

"Lucky man."

Seth leaned his head backward and poured the remaining whisky into his open mouth. "I know."

"Any news about a baby?"

"It's promising. The general had me give her his personal phone number, the one he uses to communicate with the high command and the prime minister — and his wife. So the moment she's got news ..."

"The general sounds like a kind man."

"He is. Very thoughtful. Not your gung-ho type, not like John. I doubt he's ever been in a firefight. But that's not his strength. His genius is up here." He tapped a finger at his temple. "He could be PM one day."

Arun shifted in his chair. He thought of the man he'd seen at the ceremony earlier in the day, the man who had made a formalistic show of saying goodbye to his dead soldiers, and he found himself confused between his own impressions and Seth's words. He said, "Seth, about this afternoon."

Seth sat up, waved the empty glass at him. "Not a word," he said. "This afternoon. The ceremony. That has nothing to do with anything." He glanced at his watch. "I've *gotta go.*"

He pulled himself heavily to his feet, shook the flask, tossed it to Arun. "It's about half full," he said, snatching up his poncho. "Enjoy." He stepped over to the open window, stared out into the darkness for a moment, then slammed the shutters into place. "You have a lot to learn, Arun."

"Like what?"

"Like how not to let the darkness in." He pulled the poncho down over his head, adjusted the hood, and let himself out with a purposeful stride into the unyielding night.

EIGHT

THE JEEP ARRIVED, as promised on the invitation delivered by a soldier, promptly at six p.m. The sun was gone, the clatter of night insects filling the ripening darkness. Arun was asked to take a seat in the back, beneath the low awning. The battered leather cushion was thin. He could feel the metal frame through it. There were two armed guards, one beside the driver, one beside Arun, each cradling a submachine gun between his legs. Like the driver, they wore green helmets and, in the enclosed space, smelled of sweat.

"How long to the camp?" Arun said, addressing the question to no one in particular.

"About twenty minutes," the driver replied, putting the jeep into gear and slowly pulling away from his house.

Night came on quickly as they headed out of the town, filling the jeep like a surge of liquid so that, soon, he was barely aware of the guard beside him, could see only the shadowed backs of the driver and the other guard against the faint glow of the headlights. Up ahead, there was only darkness, a darkness that was deeper to either side and lighter up above. The growl of the engine filled his head. It seemed to him that he could hear every one of its internal sounds, the meshing of every cog, the spinning of every shaft, the gasp of every piston. Beyond that labour, the rugged bite of tires into the hardened earth. Wind swirled around the jeep, and the smell of jungle — a burgeoning of moist earth and mildewed wood, decaying leaves and the musty ripeness of damp fur — washed away the smell of sweat.

The jeep lurched up a small rise, throwing Arun back against the seat. The man beside him raised his weapon from between his legs, braced it on his lap and lowered the barrel into the darkness. The guard beside the driver did the same, to the other side. The jeep surged forward. Arun could feel the pulse of the men's tension. It suffused the jeep, enmeshed him in a sudden chill, and he wondered whether the greater darkness to either side of them concealed other armed men eyeing their progress and awaiting the moment when they would turn the jeep from vehicle into target. An ache ran through his thigh and it seemed to him that he could now hear the internal sounds of his own body: the quickened thrumming of his heart, the agonised passage of breath, the rush of blood. His head went light and he grasped at the top of the seat in front of him but the thin cushion offered little purchase to his fingers. The jeep was now bouncing and rattling through the darkness, its engine sawing out a raucous scream. At moments it seemed to hurtle briefly through the air. Like an airplane, Arun thought, fighting to stay aloft. Up ahead, the beams of the headlights danced wildly against shadows with no shape.

The surrounding darkness softened, gave way to a sense of openness. The jeep slowed. The air grew lighter. In the distance, across fields razed of all obstruction, the lights of the camp glowed like a giant flare brought to earth, electric white fringed in electric blue. As they drew closer, the glow revealed rows of razor wire curled like breaking waves across the fields. In the flat ground between the glinting wire and the chain-link fence of the camp, dark mounds rose at regular intervals. Well beyond the fence punctuated by squat watch towers was what appeared to be a tranquil, well-lit, well-ordered town.

They slowed at one of the dark mounds set beside the road, a sentry materialising as if out of the earth, and Arun saw that the mounds were machine gun emplacements, waist-deep pits hemmed in by walls of sandbags. The sentry, weapon dangling from his shoulder by a strap, shone a flashlight into the jeep — the beam briefly illuminating each man, flicking back and forth between Arun's identification card and, blindingly, his face — then waved them on.

At the gate, Arun was once more asked for his identification card, once more blinded by the brazen phosphorescence of a flashlight. He had seen silhouetted men, hanging back, angling weapons at the jeep. He had never before been targeted by guns and he found the sight — his awareness of them ballooning within him as the light effaced the men, the gate, the camp beyond — impossible to push aside. His body tightened, contracted, as if the muscles were retreating into themselves. He hoped, when he reached out to retrieve his papers, that the guard didn't notice the shaking of his hand.

The gate swung open, the jeep eased forward between a salute of weapons rising towards the night sky. Beside him, the guard removed his helmet and sighed like a man reprieved.

As he was escorted through the camp, through an unwavering artificial twilight, the sense came to him that he was being led through a maze to the mess, where he was expected. He had the sense of doubling back on some paths and criss-crossing others. Twice he thought he recognized the same wire-mesh window, but then all the windows were the same, as were the doors, the buildings differing only in size. By the time his escort — another soldier in anonymous green wrapped in a silence that discouraged questions or the smallest of talk — ushered him almost surreptitiously through a door, he had lost all sense of direction. All that was left to him were up and down. He would be at a loss to find his way out on his own.

The room was filled with light and the murmur of low conversation from clusters of uniformed men holding drinks. The cream-coloured walls were unadorned save for blinds stretched tight over the windows; the blinds were printed with what he assumed to be the regimental crest. In one corner, three flags hung from a cluster of poles. Behind him the door clicked as his escort let himself out.

Seth looked up, disengaged himself from the group he was with, and strode over to him. "Arun, how was the ride?"

"Unnerving."

"Welcome to my world," he said, his breath heavy with whisky. He gestured towards a group in the far corner. "Come meet the general."

At that moment a portly man with greying hair and silver-framed glasses broke away from the group and came towards them, his hand extended in greeting. Arun took the proffered hand. "Pleased to meet you, General." Arun would not have recognised him. Like the others, he was in informal dress: light grey short-sleeved shirt tucked into dark grey trousers, distinguished from a school uniform only by the military insignia and campaign ribbons pinned to the shoulder tabs and chest He had tired eyes, appeared less formidable, less forbidding, than he had on that day at the cremation ground.

"Come, come, let's not stand on formality," the general said, squeezing Arun's hand in the way a friendly uncle might. "Call me Ashok. May I call you Arun?"

"Ah, yes, by all means." Arun, expecting a certain formality, could think of nothing else to say.

The general took him by the arm and, with Seth following a step or two behind, led him to a table congested with glasses, tubs of ice cubes, bottles of beer, and alcohol. "Help yourself," he said, holding up his glass for Seth to refill it from a whisky bottle.

Arun selected a beer. The general took his arm again and led him to a corner where several armchairs had been arranged around a low table. He lowered himself into one armchair, gestured Arun into the one beside him. Glancing up at Seth, he said, "Run along, Captain, go enjoy yourself. I'll have a little chat with our new friend here."

Seth, his face betraying a brief uncertainty, nodded, turned, and wandered away.

"It's good to see someone new," the general said, sipping at his drink. "You can get to feeling a little isolated down here, always seeing the same people, talking about the same things." He held up his glass, peered at the dark liquid. "Always drinking the same whisky." He turned to Arun. "You know what I mean?"

Arun shifted in his seat. "Well, actually, it's still all quite new to me, the school keeps me busy. I haven't really had the time to ..."

"If you don't mind my saying so," the general said briskly, "you seem rather young to be a schoolteacher."

"I suppose. But it's what I want to do."

"You come from a well-off family." His eyes had lost their fatigue, appeared now sharp and attentive.

Arun nodded, raised the bottle to his lips, enjoyed the coldness of the beer coating his tongue. He wondered how much the general had been told about him.

"So well-off in fact," the general continued, "that some people might say you don't belong here."

Arun was taken aback. "Then some people would be wrong. I mean, this is my country, too."

"Are you sure? Up north, the capital, yes. The beaches, the resorts. That is your country. It is mine. But down here ... Even the air smells different, have you noticed?"

"Yes, it does," Arun said, making an effort to restrain his irritation. He looked across the room, saw Seth standing at the periphery of a group of men, met his wary gaze. "But, you see, General —"

"Ashok."

"— I was brought up to think of the entire country as mine. With its different landscapes, its geography that goes from mountains to plains to water. With its different people in the north and the —"

"You had good teachers. They inspired you to be like them."

"Perhaps."

Suddenly the general's face appeared to sag, fatigue gathering once more in his eyes. His jowls grew puffy. "I had good teachers, too," he said. "They taught me the same things. I feel the same way you do. This land, all of it, is mine. And, yes, the people, too. They are part of me. That's why I'm here. I am serving my country. Trying to stop those who claim to speak, and kill, in the name of their people — their people who are my people, too. And yours. And his and his and his." The general's index finger stabbed around the room, but he had not spoken with great passion, had spoken instead with resignation.

Encouraged, Arun said, "So why did you say I don't belong here, then?"

"What I meant was, perhaps it's not the proper time for people like you to be here. What do you know about this place, about what is happening here?"

"I know what I've read in the newspapers, seen on TV."

"So you know about the attacks on my men, on the populace? About the bombs."

"As I've said —"

"My friend, you know nothing. You see? That's what I mean. Of course, you as a teacher have a place here, a very important place, but you have brought a satchel of ignorance with you. Do you appreciate what we face? An implacable foe, who is willing to do anything to achieve his ends. Anything. And not only with rifles and bombs, but with the most outrageous lies. Not even reality will stop them. They believe they have history on their side, and that's what makes them implacable. They are working in the service of destiny, you see. Tell me, my friend, do you know anything about these people?"

"No more than I know about you, General."

"Me?" He smiled in amusement. This time, Arun noted, he didn't insist on the use of his first name. "I'm an open book. A career military man. My service record's not a state secret. I have nothing to hide, not personally, I mean. There are military secrets, but that's another matter. With me, what you see is what you get, as one of our advisors from North Carolina liked to say."

"Sometimes, General, I'm not sure of what I'm seeing."

The general slapped his thigh and laughed. "That's a serious problem, you know, particularly in this neck of the woods."

This neck of the woods.

Arun leaned forward, elbows on his thighs, both hands wrapped around the beer bottle. "General, do you remember, about three years ago, an airplane exploded over the Northern Straits?"

"Of course I do. The deputy minister's wife was on board. She and my wife were close friends." The general sighed, gulped at his drink. "He's utterly destroyed, you know. He dreams of Madri blowing apart, into little pieces." The tips of his fingers rubbed dryly together: a dissipation, a grounding up. "As if the bomb had —" his fingers suddenly splayed "— exploded within her. Fragments of bone and flesh, an eye, her fingers, all those bits of her flying apart inside the aircraft and then the aircraft itself hurtling to the water. Poor fellow. He spends all his time locked away in his house now. He can't stand the sight of the sky or the sea. The sound of an aircraft drives him mad."

"My parents were on that plane."

"Oh, I ..." The general paused, his eyes blinking rapidly. "I'm so sorry. I recall members of the Bannerji family were on the plane but I didn't know they were your parents." He leaned forward, hunching into himself. "It must be terribly hard for you." But his voice had lost its feeling.

"So you see, General," Arun continued, "I'm not a total stranger to reality. But, as you must know, there's no conclusive proof as to who set the bomb. No one's ever claimed responsibility."

The general sat back in the chair, his brow furrowing. "There's enough proof for those who wish to see it. My friend has no doubt as to who put it there, and why. They couldn't get to him any other way, he was too well protected. He must try to live with that burden."

"Some people think that those who wanted to get him came from his own circles. They say he was pushing for peace talks with the rebels. And, well, you know what our politics are like. Let's face it, the bomb was good propaganda, too. Two birds with one stone."

"Proverbs notwithstanding, my young friend, I wouldn't pay much heed to crazy rumours if I were you. It's a bad habit. And like a lot of bad habits, it could be dangerous."

"Dangerous? How?"

"For your mental health. All that uncertainty. The heart doesn't like confusion. Believe me, I know." He tapped at his chest. "Triple bypass, two years ago."

"This doesn't seem like the best job for someone with a heart condition."

The general peered over his glasses at him. A bleary, haunted stare. "Some things take precedence over personal concerns. Duty, for instance. The prime minister asked. He thought I was the best man for the job. Of course I said yes."

There it was again. That word — duty — that seemed to emerge like a spider from a crack.

"You understand that, don't you?" the general continued. "You don't belong here, but that's what it's all about, isn't it. That's why you've come. Duty to the children, duty to your country, perhaps even duty to yourself. Isn't that so?"

Arun didn't know what to reply. He could have easily found a comfortable position in the capital, at one of the private schools, but he had discounted the possibility without much thought. It simply hadn't appealed to him. He had taken this job because it was far away. Far from the shuttered house his sister would one day sell, far from the business left to him but now signed over to his brother-in-law, and most of all far from debris raining out of a clear blue sky. He raised the bottle to his lips and found that he couldn't drink.

The general swiped the back of his hand along his forehead. "Captain!" he called. "Check the air conditioner, will you? It's bloody hot in here." Seth immediately handed his drink to another officer and strode over to the air conditioning unit protruding from the wall. As he fiddled with the buttons, holding his palm up to check the flow of air, the general said in a weary voice, "Don't you see, my friend? These bombs, they all explode inside of us. That's why I'm here. Trying to do what I can to save us all from being blown to bits." The general sat heavily back in his chair, raised his glass and emptied it into his yawning mouth.

The image he'd been given flashed through Arun's mind: the disintegrating cabin, his father's arm, his mother's jaw, his finger, her leg ... His fingers trembled, lost their grip on his bottle. Hurriedly he reached down to the floor, seized the pouring bottle and saw only then, to his astonishment, that the general was shod in furry black bedroom slippers.

Dinner was a sombre affair in an adjoining dining room, the walls painted a dusky olive and hung with banners and trophy cases. They sat, about twenty of them, at a long table draped in a white cloth embroidered in the middle with the regimental crest — the work, the general said, of his wife, who had occupied her months of solitary evenings during his many absences with this labour. He planned to bequeath it to the regiment upon his retirement.

Arun was seated beside the general and directly across from Seth — a place of honour, Seth had mumbled to him as they drifted in to dinner.

The first two courses were eaten in silence, the subdued cama-raderie left behind in the lounge. Two soldiers in white shirts and black trousers served shrimp cocktails, then lamb chops with a mound of fragrant rice and spiced papaya. Accompanied by the scratching of cutlery on china, the sounds of vigorous chewing, and the occasional sigh, they kept glasses full of chilled red wine.

At one point, the general was brought a note which he peered at through his glasses. Dismissing the message with a curt "No reply," he said to his plate, "Lieutenant Anand's patrol made brief contact, but the bastards melted away as usual. They won't stand and fight like men! He's going in pursuit, but ... Oh well." Forking a mouthful of rice into his mouth, he turned to Arun and said, "You'll agree with me that nothing justifies terrorism. If these fellows want to take us on, let them come. That's our job. But to kill innocents — that I can't forgive." He signalled a waiter to take away his plate, his meal half finished.

Arun, chewing at his last piece of lamb, sat back and pushed his plate away. He took a gulp of the wine, relishing its crispness and the way it soothed his tongue and throat. It was the best meal he'd had since arriving here, but he'd eaten too quickly. His stomach felt bloated, as if it were no longer accustomed to such quantity.

"Would you like some more?" the general said.

Arun demurred with a smile and a wave of his hand. "Thank you, it was very good."

The general reached for his wine. "You must keep your strength up, young man. You're bony enough as it is. You'll need your energy for all that lies ahead."

"Teaching isn't really that strenuous, you know. You've got to be on your toes all the time, that's all."

"Just like soldiering," Seth said. "Only you've got no heavy equipment to lug around, just books."

"True, Captain," the general said, "but what he's doing is vital to the country. It's vital to all of us sitting here at this table." All eyes were now on him.

"To the children, yes," Arun said. "But to you? How?"

Around them, the waiters were busy clearing the table.

The general raised a fist to his lips to greet a gentle burp. Peering at Seth above the frame of his glasses, he said, "Do you remember what Mao said about terrorists?"

"That they're like fish," Seth replied.

"They need a sea to swim around in," said someone else from farther down the table. "They look like all the other fish until they —"

"Exactly, Major," the general said, his tone mellower now than in the lounge. "And that sea is?"

Arun found himself relaxing, his body settling into the comfort of the chair, the general's voice recalling that of his favourite teachers and the way they nudged rather than hectored.

"The populace," said an eager voice from the other end of the table. "They disappear among them, they find sustenance."

"And so, you've got a choice." The general impatiently signalled a waiter to refill the glasses. "Either you drain the sea ..." He drank the last of his wine, licked his lips. "... and you kill all the fish. Or you make the sea inhospitable. The only way to do that, in the long run, is through education. Help the populace to see what it is they have and what they have to lose." He twisted his head around, looked behind him. "Where's that damned wine?"

"It's coming, sir," Seth said quickly, pushing back his chair. At that moment the door to the kitchen opened and the waiters hurried out, each grasping two wine bottles. Seth settled back, his glare never leaving the waiter as he filled the general's glass.

The general turned back to Arun. "And that, my friend, is why your work is so vital. It is also why you, too, are a soldier in this war."

Arun, startled, said, "General, I —"

"What do you teach the children? Reading, writing, grammar? Mathematics?"

"Essentially. But —"

"How about civics?"

"Once they know the alphabet and how to count to —"

"They don't need to read to learn civics. The art of being a good citizen. No littering, no loitering, no laziness. No cheating, no stealing. No blowing up people."

Arun, fetching for a response, glanced at Seth, but saw that his eyes were on the general.

"You could teach them some history. How good this country has been to them."

"General," Arun said, circling his fingertip on the rim of his wine glass, "you want me to teach propaganda."

"Don't you believe that good citizenship should be taught? Don't you think this country has been good to them?"

To two percent of them, perhaps, Arun thought. He said, "As a teacher, I'm uneasy with opinion. If I'm to teach history, I must use facts."

"Facts? You want facts? The world is full of facts. I can give you facts by the barrelful. But facts, my friend, are just raw material. They're like diamonds extracted from the earth. They must be cleaned and polished and cut to yield their beauty. Those are highly refined skills. Make a wrong cut, for instance, and the entire thing's spoiled, it's no use to anyone. You see what I'm driving at? You're a diamond cutter, and you can offer jewels to your country if you do your job conscientiously."

Arun once again sought out Seth, and saw that he, like the general, was awaiting his reaction. A nervous laugh escaped him. "A soldier. A diamond cutter. I'd be happy if they learned how to write their names and count to a hundred."

Seth frowned. As Arun's mind raced in search of words of redemption, a crackle of laughter from the general brought smiles and uneasy glances to the solemn faces ranged across the table from him. Even Seth, absorbed still by unhappy thoughts, managed to twitch his lips in a semblance of amusement.

"Good," the general said. "One step at a time, easy does it. Smart man." He leaned forward, looked up and down the table. "You see, gentlemen, he really is one of us. If we went crashing through the jungle like some elephant on a rampage, we'd fall into one ambush after another. He does the same thing we do: one step at a time, easy does it." All along the table heads nodded in agreement.

"You're a natural soldier," Seth said, taking a sip of his wine. "Who would've guessed? Maybe you'd like to come along on a patrol some time."

"I'll leave the soldiering to you," Arun said, "if you'll leave the teaching to me."

Seth raised his glass in agreement. "You bet."

You bet.

The general clapped his hands and rubbed them together in satisfaction. "Time for cigars and brandy," he said.

At Seth's signal the waiters began passing around with silver platters on which were generously filled brandy snifters and wooden cigar boxes. Arun accepted the brandy, refused the cigar. Beside him, the general's cheeks inflated and deflated, his eyes squinting, as he noisily sucked fire into his cigar from a lighter held by a waiter. Seth tucked the cigar into the corner of his mouth, waved off the offered flame. For the next moments, lighters rasped and sparked in a series of miniature explosions and soon clouds of bittersweet smoke were roiling through the room.

The general shifted in his seat towards Arun. "There's one more thing I'd like to ask you."

Arun raised the snifter to his lips, breathed deeply of the sharp fumes rising from the brandy.

"Many of our men can't read and write, or at least only minimally. They're country boys, like your students. Conscripts. I believe good works should start at home, and the army's my home. Would you agree to give them literacy classes?"

Arun thought of the unsettling drive to the camp earlier in the evening, of the narrow road and the forest that would trap its darkness even on bright days. "Getting here would be difficult," he said. "Could they come to the school?"

"No, you'd have to come here. The school's too exposed.

Security, you know. I'm sure you understand. We'll arrange transport, and a stipend, of course. Provide any supplies you might need. What do you say? Will you do it?"

Refusal, Arun knew, was out of the question. "Of course."

"Good!" The general slapped the table, smoke billowing from his mouth. "The captain here will see to the arrangements."

Seth said, "I'll come by in a few days. This could be the start of something big, you know."

"How so?" Arun said, but before Seth could answer, the general rose abruptly, the others at the table snapping to their feet in crisp unison. Clapping Arun on the shoulder, he mumbled good night and ambled from the room, cigar smoke trailing on his left and Seth on his right.

Less than a minute later, Arun was informed that his jeep was waiting.

THE DAY HIS parents' plane blew up over the ocean, Arun had gone snorkelling. His final examinations were over and he was looking forward to a few carefree weeks before assuming his duties at the printery.

Their flight had been an early one. The plane — a twin-engine commuter aircraft that held twenty passengers and a crew of three — was well suited to the short-haul flights that linked the capital to the towns and resorts on the north coast, where his parents planned to take their vacation. It was an unprepossessing machine, its high wings and propellers vaguely reminiscent of Sopwith Camels, but it had earned a reputation for sturdiness; it could hold its own through the most ferocious of storms and would be able — when the troubles in the south abated enough to permit safe travel — to negotiate the treacherous winds among the mountains.

It was because of this reputation that his father had been relaxed and happy that morning. Flying made him anxious. Frequent breakdowns at the printery had taught him to be distrustful of machinery, and there was an indecisiveness to his laughter at the old joke that he always requested a window seat so that he could, if need be, stick out an arm and flap it. But he was looking forward to this vacation, a week at a small guest house at the tip of the northeastern peninsula. Whatever anxiety his father displayed — a certain quickness in his step, the way he fidgeted with their tickets — Arun had explained as his eagerness to see the house itself.

When his father was a child, he and his family had spent the August holidays there in a region that was cooler, less stifling than in the capital, the house on loan from a cousin of Arun's grandfather. Eventually the house had been sold and had disappeared from his father's consciousness. Then, leafing through the newspaper after breakfast one Saturday morning, his father had been startled to see the house in a holiday advertisement. His cry of surprise caused Arun's mother to look up in alarm from her fingernails, which were half cleaned of old polish. Arun, wandering sleepily into the dining room in search of the coffee percolator, found his way blocked by a photograph of a large wooden house of the type — gables, carved filigree, wraparound porch — colonial administrators seeking retreat from the rigours of the climate used to have built. The house, his father said, was unchanged from what he could remember. Rustling the newspaper away from under Arun's nose, he read the advertisement. "Ah," he said, "it's been renovated. Rajah Guest House. All the modern conveniences. Which surely means electricity and flush toilets." Taking his first sip of fragrant coffee, Arun exchanged a smile with his mother. In his father's scheme of things, flush toilets ranked near the top of technological achievement, an advance that had revolutionised sanitation without receiving its fair share of recognition. Within an hour, he had booked a room and airplane tickets.

The night before they left, his father had scribbled last-minute instructions for his son-in-law on the fine points of a new government contract. The maid and the cook having been given a few days off — Arun was relieved: he wouldn't be responsible for keeping an eye on his parents' valuables — his mother wrote out in her neat hand all the instructions she had already rattled off about unfreezing his meals and warming them up, double checking the locks on the doors and windows at night, watering the house plants and picking the tomatoes in the vegetable garden out back — her little hobby, growing foreign varieties — because they would be ready in two or three days and if he didn't pick them at the very right moment, they would spoil within half a day. She had wanted him to stay with his sister during their absence but he had insisted that, at eighteen, he was quite capable of looking after himself. At a nod of assent from his father, she had agreed, but she would leave him with a written constitution of obligations.

And so they had awoken early, breakfasted on buttered toast and milky tea — the remains would still be sitting like relics on the dining table at the end of the day — and prepared for the ride to the airport through the pre-dawn darkness. The sound of Surein's car crunching across the gravelled driveway woke him. His mother came to the door softly calling his name. Through the darkness, he felt for his leg, which was standing beside the bed.

When he emerged from his room some minutes later, his father and Surein were competing to see who could tote more suitcases and bags from the living room to the car trunk. His parents had packed voluminously for their trip to his father's past, as if they wished to take as much of the present with them as they could manage. His mother stood at the front door, holding it wide open with one hand, clutching their airline tickets in the other as if in evidence that they hadn't been forgotten. Arun could see his father's excitement in his bustle and he wondered what the older man expected to find at the guest house at the edge of the sea: whispers of himself, shards of a distant youth?

His mother was wearing her face of tolerance, the face she assumed when Arun or his father latched on to an enthusiasm, her husband's sudden interest in whisky, for instance, triggered by a magazine spread, which led to the acquisition of a large teak cabinet whose intricately carved doors opened to reveal pigeon-holes which he filled over the years with bottles of the finest whiskies he could find. He drank sparingly, the first sips cautious, enjoyment seeming to come only after a studied approval. It was Joy who had explained to Arun that their mother's tolerance arose from her understanding that his consuming interest arose not from an incipient alcoholism but from his astonishment that he could afford to indulge this rare thing, and indulge it fully. His mother's face that morning told him that she held this trip in similar esteem: the quick decision, the guest house reservation, the airline bookings. Joy's explanation caused Arun to glimpse his father's insecurity, to see that, even coming from a family that had long enjoyed a certain measure of ease, he had been unsure of himself and his ability to make a success of his life. Perhaps that was what had driven him. That early anxiety ensured that, no longer a young man but not yet old, he could still astonish himself with the audacity of possibility.

Standing there dishevelled in the living room, his eyes full of sleep, seeing his father's contentment, Arun recognised his own anxiety as a version of the one his father had felt as a young man. And he hoped at that moment that he was glimpsing a version of himself as he would be three decades on: whispers of the future, shards of tomorrow.

He followed his mother out to the porch. The air was cool. He hugged himself, watching his father and Surein struggle with the suitcases towards the open trunk of the car. In the sky, the very earliest glimmer of dawn was tossing a hint of blue at the dark night. The stars were undiminished, but within minutes they would be gone, swallowed up in sunlight.

His mother turned to him. "You'll remember, now. Water the plants in two days, check the tomatoes in three."

"Of course I'll remember." He would remember her face half in shadow.

The trunk thudded shut. Surein got into the car and turned on the engine. The headlights shot out, revealing the whiteness of the gravel and the sparkle of dew-drenched greenery off to the side of the house. His father called impatiently to his mother.

"I'm coming." She reached over and gave Arun a light kiss on the cheek. "See you in a week."

"Have a good time," he said as she clattered down the stairs. His father, waiting at the open car door, took her hand and ushered her into the car. Then he made his way around to the front passenger seat and waved once at Arun before getting in himself. His door slapped shut and the car eased away, two red and yellow tail lights retreating into the darkness to the low growl of the engine and the bite of tires on gravel. Above them, the sky paled into dawn.

He returned to bed, but sleep would not come. The house felt different in his parents' absence, somehow unencumbered. He grew keenly aware of the silence, and the slivers of sunlight hardening around the windows, and the lavender smell of the sheets. His skin felt dry and smooth against the cotton, his muscles taut and relaxed beneath the skin. Presently his penis stiffened. He slipped off his pyjama bottoms and caressed the erection with his hand. Afterwards he broke out in a light sweat.

He prepared the percolator and, as it bubbled and spat, the sight of his schoolbooks stacked on the kitchen counter gave him the idea of going to the beach. His final exams were over, the books were now part of his past. He could do as he wished and going to the beach alone early on a weekday morning was oddly appealing. No one did that. He quickly gathered his snorkelling gear and, hunger satiated by two cups of coffee, caught the bus to the beach.

By the time he climbed down from the bus forty-five minutes later, his parents had already been at the airport for a couple of hours. They would be waiting nervously at the exit doors of the small departure lounge for the dash across the tarmac to the waiting aircraft. The plane would be overbooked — it always was — with no seats assigned. To sit together his parents would have to arrive before the horde and stake their claim.

The sun was not yet high, the sky cloudless. He was alone. He sat on the sand for some minutes, the sunshine warming his back and turning the water turquoise. The waves broke gently in the low tide. When perspiration gathered at his collarbone, when it broke free and coursed down his chest, he unstrapped his leg and pulled on the swimming fins, one of which had been adapted for his stump. By the time he had waded in, the rubber fin splashing behind him, the water and sand tugging gently at his knees, the first delay of his parents' flight had been announced — ten minutes, which everyone knew would last twice as long. As he adjusted his face mask and blew through the snorkel to ensure the passage was clear, they would probably have sighed and unshouldered their bags.

Their second delay would have been announced as he was paddling out beyond the first breakers, eyes following the shafts of sunlight piercing the surface, diffusing deep in water so clear it was like peering through liquid air to the sandy bed fifteen feet below. He looked for rocks, seeing at first just a few strewn about, then clusters of them that signalled the rise in the seabed. It was there, at the shelf that stretched for a mile or so to either side and half a mile farther out to sea, that he would explore, paddling along the surface or, with a gulp of air through the tube, plunging to the rocks — to their chaotic world of dips and rises animated with strands of swaying seaweed and the flutter and glide of countless fish that accepted his presence but darted away at the reach of his hand, their round eyes glaring sideways at him in reproach.

He would have been out there paddling and diving, propelling himself along the seabed by tugging at the rocks, trying to seize with his eye the colours of the fish — scarlet and vermilion, green and yellow and flashes of white and black — that seemed to exist only at the bottom of the sea, when the boarding announcement was finally made. Perhaps he had been chasing the school of transparent fish that had cut across his path, eager for a closer look at the skeletons that showed clearly through their translucence, when they fell into their seats, stuffing carry-on bags beneath the seats in front of them and buckling their seat belts, his father's cinched tight.

Take off, he knew, had been without incident. He wondered later whether, had he been looking up rather than down, he might have seen their plane fly by high overhead, heading on its flight path northeast over the ocean, a less direct route to the northern peninsula.

He was probably taking a final turn among the rocks and boulders and fish forty-five minutes later when the captain announced the beginning of the final approach and asked that their trays be fastened into place and that their seat belts be buckled. Perhaps he had already completed the turn or had just begun to paddle his way back to shore when the bomb hidden in a suitcase stowed in the luggage hold at the rear of the plane exploded. The tail broke off immediately while the rest of the fuselage full of passengers spun into a nose dive. The drag was too great. One wing ripped off, taking with it the wheel assembly that had already been deployed. The rest began to corkscrew, bits and pieces flaking off and spinning through the sunlight.

When the aircraft and the bodies — or what was left of them, for some would have been dismembered — hit the water many, many miles from where he was, he had probably passed back through the first breakers and slipped under the water to let himself be dragged along by the tug towards the beach. It was almost as if by being submerged at that moment he had been there to greet them. The light, the warmth, the water. The shock. Like a birth into another world.

Later, he would mark that moment — painstakingly recreated through a combination of imagination and the detailed report of the government enquiry — as the moment he began believing in the existence of forces too large to comprehend, imperatives too powerful to resist.

When he got off the bus not far from his home two hours later, he was hungry. He stopped at a nearby Lebanese restaurant and bought a falafel sandwich from the old woman and her even older husband, people who had fled ruined Beirut many years before and had never managed to return. He was a frequent enough customer that he didn't have to ask the woman to spoon extra hot sauce onto the filling before rolling it up. He walked to the house at a brisk pace, anticipating a cold beer to go with his sandwich. Only as he clambered up the stairs did he realise that Surein was sitting on a chair on the porch. He paused in surprise. Surein half rose, his eyes vermilion, his face so tight and swollen he appeared to be on the point of shattering.

NINE

"Right," Arun said, suppressing a shudder of anxiety. "Let's get down to business. Let me hear you say the alphabet. All together now."

Silence. The twelve men arrayed at the lacquered table in front of him returned gazes that were sceptical, pained, embarrassed. Some looked away, a few closed their eyes. They were freshly barbered, their field uniforms clean but rumpled. The windows in the room designated as his classroom were small, the wire mesh leeching brightness from the little sunshine they admitted.

Arun grasped the back of the chair that had been provided for him, glanced down at the small desk on which lay unopened the reading primers he'd brought along. "Come now, gentlemen," he said in a gentler voice. "ABC anyone?"

Eyes reached for the ceiling, for the tabletop. Blinked hard, trying to banish some unwelcome apparition.

Arun turned to the portable chalk board behind him, wrote out the letters with bold strokes, pointed to the first with his index finger. "A."

"A!" they chorused.

He pointed to the second.

"B!" came the answer with diminished but still vigorous assurance.

He pointed to the third.

"C!"

Using his hands like a conductor, he encouraged them to continue, glad to see a grin breaking out here and there, a few at least getting into the spirit of the thing. They dug deeper into the alphabet, voices beginning to fall away, until X, Y and Z straggled in on perhaps two or three ragged tones.

"Very good," Arun said, struggling with a rising sense of despair. "Now, how many can write their names?"

Eight hands went up in response.

"Read a newspaper?"

Five hands this time, one hesitating before deciding to affirm his ability.

"Easily?"

Two of the hands disappeared.

"Right," Arun said. "Now, all of you can stay in the army for the rest of your lives and never have to read and write. You won't get promoted, but you'll be guaranteed a job. Why do you want to take this class? Were you ordered to?"

One man, one of those who could read a newspaper easily, raised his hand. He had round cheeks, large, matte-black eyes. His shaved head marked him as a member of the Special Operations Unit of the Aryadasha Regiment — a unit whose exploits had achieved such celebrity that Arun knew of young boys who dreamt of being a member either of the SOU or of the national cricket team.

Arun nodded at him, asked for his name.

"Private Mukherjee, sir."

"Yes, Private Mukherjee?"

"I don't want to stay in the army all my life, sir," he said. "I want to learn bookkeeping so I can support my family."

"You plan to have children?"

"I have children, sir. My wife lives in our village with my three sons. It is hard for her, sir."

Other hands rose. Some spoke, like Private Mukherjee, of seeking another kind of life, modest ambitions — office clerk, bank teller, warehouse manager — that Arun found strangely moving in their unstated wish for the ordinary, the uncomplicated. One soldier, so young that the fuzz on his upper lip had never been shaved, said that he would like to be able to write to his parents, letters which their neighbour, an educated man, could read to them. Another said shyly — to the amiable taunting of his comrades — that his future wife already knew how to read and write, and so he wanted to also.

After a few minutes, all had spoken except a young man in his early twenties with a face pared to the skull and eyes that glittered with a private humour. He, too, sported a shaved head.

"What about you?" Arun said. "What's your name?"

A stillness suddenly came over the others.

"Mangal Pande." The young man smiled, baring teeth and gums.

Arun, thinking he was being played with, said, "Are you sure?" The name, as he knew from his reading of history, had belonged to a famous sepoy rebel during the mutiny against the British in mid-nineteenth-century India. He had put up a good fight, and when the battle was lost had turned his rifle on himself. His attempt to take his own life had failed, but some weeks later the British completed the job and appropriated his name as epithet for all those they viewed as vicious and uncontrollable, as mutineers.

"It's the name I've given myself," the young man said, relishing the effect his name had had. "It's the only one I have. I'm a private.

173

For now. I don't want to leave the army. I want to stay. But I'm tired of taking orders. I want to give them. I want to be an officer. A lieutenant, a captain, a general someday. Maybe commander-in-chief." He spoke without arrogance.

"You know that Pande was defeated," Arun said, "because his comrades wouldn't follow him."

"He should have used his tulwar on one or two of them." Pande smiled again. "Send a couple of heads rolling. That would've got them moving. I would never make a mistake like that. It would have been easy to change things, no? Everything would have been different. Maybe you and me wouldn't be here. Maybe we'd be sitting in some rich palace, surrounded by beautiful women, eating and drinking and enjoying life." His eyes, alive with that private humour, met Arun's.

Arun held the gaze for a long moment, the silence in the room growing taut. Then he turned away, picked up the reading primers and distributed them to the class.

That evening, from among the small selection of books he'd brought with him, he got out the slender volume by his old teacher Mahadeo, whom his mother had seen as a font of waywardness. Cleaning up his room before his departure, he'd almost thrown it out with his old textbooks and the yellowed collection of Biggles adventures he'd read as a young teenager, but Mahadeo had signed it for him, had inscribed his hope that Arun would devote his life to ideals larger than the making of money. At the last minute he'd tossed it onto the pile with Tolstoy and Conrad and Mishima.

Chewing at a bread and cheese sandwich — it was dry, he had forgotten to buy a can of butter at Madhu's — he turned to the section where Mahadeo's public lectures and radio texts had been reprinted verbatim. He quickly found the text he was looking for.

In a talk to the History Society, Mahadeo had argued that their land was one that Europeans had taken possession of, even fought over, not because it held any intrinsic value but simply because it was there, just there, sitting in the middle of the ocean. They came across it on their way to or from more important places. They'd go to the mainland, load up on spices and jewels and textiles and then stop by on their way back to Europe. They would top up their food and water, admire the landscape and the temples and the women, help themselves to anything that caught their fancy and then move on. "Those bastards didn't need us," Mahadeo had declared, Arun recognising his habit of growing increasingly vulgar as his passion rose. "When they fought sea battles over us, it was only because of their own greed, like some spoiled brat who sees a shiny marble in a shop and must have it even if he has no need of it. More often, we were just part of the booty of European wars. We were traded or surrendered like some crappy piece of real estate. They didn't give a shit about us, the people. And as for us, well, we postponed our local hatred for a hundred and fifty years, that's all. Inevitably the time came when the bastards didn't want to put up with us anymore, we were becoming too troublesome. So they *gave* us our independence, which wasn't theirs to give because they'd never really taken it away. They'd *ignored* us. They just kind of went away with their flag, and the moment they left we got our knives and swords and guns and bombs and went after each other again as we've always done, unfinished business from a century and a half before. The Dutch, the British, the Indians — they were just hiccups in our history. Our real history just went underground for a while and then sprang back up again in fountains of blood. And don't talk to me about the so-called heroes of independence. Those shitfaces, from one community or the other, from the north and the south, were just more impatient than most. They wanted the Brits out so they could go at each others' fucking throats. That's where we are now, going after each other. The Indians thought they could step in and impose order and they learned fast enough what their interference would get them — a prime minister whose remains they could cremate in a coal pot. Make no mistake, that's the way it's always been and you have to choose your side. Leave, go away if you want. Go to England or Canada or America but don't fool yourself, our history will always haunt you. As for all those young idealists who insist it has to stop, that we can't go on like this, well, I love young people. They're so bright, so full of goodness. But our history has them by the balls too and it won't let them go. It'll squeeze all that goodness out of them until we, by ourselves, have a winner. Remember, today is in our hands, tomorrow is in our hearts." When he entered active politics, that phrase, slightly amended — "our" became "your" — would become his mantra.

Arun put aside the sandwich, took a sip of water. He wondered whether Pande had ever attended one of Mahadeo's talks.

HE AWOKE WITH the mail on his mind. Three weeks before, Joy had posted a box of books and magazines and it still hadn't been delivered. Kumarsingh, who ran the local post office from the cubbyhole that housed Kumarsingh Enterprises International Ink, had promised to keep an eye out for the parcel. The mail business was, to this point, the international arm of his business since he handled letters and parcels to and from abroad. It was through Kumarsingh that Arun's salary came to him. The day before, he'd mentioned to Arun, "confidentially, just between you and me and the deep blue sea," that he'd had a "communication" from the postal authorities in the capital that a transport truck with mail destined for the south had experienced technical problems resulting in the loss of its entire cargo. "Maybe your parcel was on that truck," Kumarsingh had said, businesslike.

Arun was curious to know what kind of technical truck problem could have caused such a loss.

Kumarsingh had shrugged. "All I can tell you is that I heard, unofficially of course, that several lives were lost in the incident along with many bags of mail."

"An accident?" They happened all the time, nasty collisions on the narrow roads, cans of extra fuel exploding on impact, instant cremation.

"Perhaps."

As he lay in bed stretching, Arun had a vision of *The Hunchback of Notre Dame*, *Midnight's Children*, *One Hundred Years of Solitude*, and *Love's Tender Harvest*, which Joy had selected for Mr Jaisaram, burning crisply in some overturned cab made bright by flames. He saw pages being flipped by fiery fingers, letters and entire words peeling from the paper and flitting away ablaze. It was somehow better, more comforting, than imagining the books and the brick of magazines lost somewhere, in some warehouse perhaps, or buried under a mountain of unclaimed mail, left to age, to yellow, to moulder, useless.

From outside came the tinkle of a bicycle bell, and friendly voices calling greetings. Saturday morning. Market day. He needed new shirts, some socks, and he'd been thinking that he might try on a few hats, to help ward off the sun. Few people in the capital wore hats — they were seen as an affectation, suggested a certain untrustworthiness — and Arun would have felt foolish wearing one, but here in Omeara they were not unusual. Mr Jaisaram occasionally sported a slightly battered fedora. Kumarsingh, when obliged to spend long hours in the hot sun tending to a job for one of his businesses, favoured a cap that had been sent to him by a cousin in Toronto that featured a sharp-beaked bird and the words "Blue Jays," which, he explained to Arun, was the name of the Canadian national ice hockey team.

Sitting up in the bed, Arun wondered idly what kind of hat might best suit him.

Kumarsingh kept glancing at his watch. He was growing more agitated with each passing minute, sucking at his cigarette like a thirsty man trying to draw ice through a straw. The bus was late and Kumarsingh prided himself on providing a service that was dependable and on time. He threw the butt to the asphalt, ground it beneath his shoe. "Seventeen minutes late," he said to Arun, spittle flying from his mouth. "Seventeen minutes, soon to be eighteen. In six months, soon to be seven, he has never been this late. For his sake I hope he got a flat, although the tires are new, or else seven months will not become eight." He paused for breath.

Arun said, "Take it easy, Kumarsingh. You'll give yourself a heart attack. A bus is a machine. Anything can go wrong at any time."

"There you are wrong, my friend. You are judging the book by the cover. My Rainbow doesn't have the prettiest body in the world but inside she is in top shape, number one. Every week she gets checked from top to bottom. One day I will give her a new coat of red paint. She deserves it, my Rainbow."

"Why Rainbow?"

"Don't you think it's a pretty name?"

"Very. But still, it's unusual."

"A rainbow appears after a storm, yah? It tells of better times to come. It's the name I will give to my daughter, when I have a daughter. No one will forget it." He glanced at his watch, peered down the still empty road. "No, the problem is not with her but with that *pourri* of a driver. I should never have hired him in the first place."

"He's never been late before?"

"Not this late."

"So he's probably got a good reason."

"Tell that to my customers." He stuck a thumb towards a group of people a few yards away waiting patiently with their bundles. Among them, Shanti was standing with her parents, a small book of fairy tales Arun had given her tightly clutched in her hand. She had told him proudly that they were going to visit her aunt in the next town for the weekend. She was excited about taking the bus, about the new dress her mother had bought her for the occasion

— a frilly thing, Arun now saw, in egg-yolk yellow. It was strange to see her without Radha. She looked somehow incomplete, as if she had lost her shadow. He waved to her but she was looking away and didn't see him.

Kumarsingh slapped his palms together in irritation. "Where is that *pourri*? If he's put a dent in my Rainbow, I'll put a dent in him."

Arun pretended to scratch his upper lip so Kumarsingh wouldn't see his smile. If Rainbow were in a collision, he thought, she wouldn't be dented. All that rust would simply crumble like a dry biscuit.

"Eighteen minutes, soon to be nineteen," Kumarsingh said in a mixture of sadness and desperation.

"Kumarsingh, about the hats."

Suddenly Kumarsingh's right arm flew up, his finger pointing. "There she is! There's my Rainbow! She's all right!"

And there was the bus, trundling past the schoolhouse towards them, looking top-heavy with its roped-down luggage, tassels leaping and jerking, white dust billowing in its wake.

Kumarsingh clapped Arun on the shoulder. "I must go, my friend. If you want the best hats, go see Lakhan." He was already trotting off, hand digging into his pants pocket for the roll of bus tickets. "His hats are made in Singapore. Best quality. Tell him I sent you, yah, he will give you a good price."

Up ahead, the waiting passengers were stirring, hefting bags and parcels, already waving money at the approaching Kumarsingh. Children, too, were converging on the group, hastening to witness the arrival of the bus. The screeching, the rattling, the rumble of the engine, the squeal of the brakes: it was spectacle for them in the same way that the materialisation of a rainbow was spectacle, as innocent, as awe-inspiring.

Arun turned back to the crowded square, the sun-softened asphalt giving way slightly under the pressure of his foot. Lakhan wouldn't be difficult to find. Few vendors sold hats, and those that did offered cast-off military berets, ill-woven straw hats, and caps garish with advertisements. Wandering through the crowd, his eye fell on a display of shirts. They weren't of the finest quality — the cloth looked coarse, the colours bright but uncertain. Still, the simple style — roomy and buttonless, so they would have to be pulled on like a jersey, the wide collars forming a V — appealed to him.

The vendor, an emaciated old man with rheumy eyes and toothless gums, encouraged him to feel the fabric, to examine the seams. "Top quality, *Prahib*, top quality." His wife had woven and dyed the cloth, his daughter had designed and sewn the shirts. He offered him a price, an outrageous price, and when Arun, shaking his head, made to move on, cut the price in half. "Special price for you, *Prahib*. Very special, only for you." There was now a note of desperation in the man's voice: he needed a sale.

Still, Arun hesitated. If the first price had been far too high, the second was far too low — and here he was, caught in a familiar bind. He heard his brother-in-law's mocking chuckle coming at him out of the low rumble of surrounding voices. Such a simple decision: pay the too-high price and feel stupid, or pay the too-low price and feel reprehensible. He could, of course, simply walk away, but that would be vile.

He fingered the fabric again. It was thick but loosely woven; it would be cool. He tapped a blue shirt with his finger and reached into his back pocket for his wallet. He would pay what he considered to be fair, somewhere between the two prices the man had mentioned. Behind him, the bus was slowly making its way through the square, grumbling and creaking, Kumarsingh preceding it on foot and yelling at people to clear a passage. The crowd closed in on Arun as the bus trundled by, a gaggle of children trotting along beside and behind it. As Arun counted out the notes, the vendor carefully folded the shirt in stiff brown paper. Arun handed over the money and, taking his package, turned to leave.

"Your change, *Prahib*," the man called, clutching Arun's money in one hand and digging into his pants pocket with the other.

"It's all right," Arun replied. "It's a nice shirt."

"No, *Prahib*, we agreed on the price. I must give you change."

"Instead of change," Arun said, "give me some information."

A wary look crossed the man's face. "If I can, *Prahib*."

"Perhaps you know where I can find a man named Lakhan. He sells hats. I need a hat."

"Lakhan? I know no Lakhan." He turned to the vendor beside him, a younger man whose tray and forearm were covered in cheap wristwatches. "You know a Lakhan? He sells hats."

The crowd eddied and flowed, the crush thinning as the bus moved on, Kumarsingh's ritualistic cajoling rising and falling in an antagonistic plea. He had been asked not to sound the horn in town; it was loud enough to leave people's ears ringing, a source of pride to Kumarsingh, who said, "She has a big voice, my Rainbow." By the time the bus was firmly on its way on the far side of the town, he would be hoarse and in need of a shot of whisky to soothe the burning in his throat.

The man with the watches shook his head. He'd never heard of Lakhan either, but one of the customers crowded around his tray said that the hat-seller was on the other side of the square, closer to the road. He raised a hand to indicate the direction, then pointed at a watch on the tray and said, "How much?"

Arun, cradling the package in his left arm, meandered through the crowd, his eyes scrutinizing the displays of goods for the tell-tale hats. A gaggle of children jostled past him, "police" in pursuit of the "thief." Two growling strays conjoined at the muzzle by a scrap of meat wrenched and heaved at each other, their legs twitching and quivering. At a sweets stand — stacks of braided crisps golden with honey, pyramids of coconut squares, ranks of chocolate and nut clusters, clouds of pink cotton candy in paper cones — a crowd looked on in amusement as the vendor, a plump young woman with muscular arms, vigorously twisted a boy's ear with one hand and slapped him about the head with the other. Then another, older woman, evidently the boy's mother, surged angrily from the crowd and lashed out at the vendor. Protesting voices yelled out the details of the attempted larceny. The mother hesitated, then turned swiftly on the boy and began wringing his other ear, her free hand now thumping at his backside. Arun found himself staring in dismay at the spectacle of the bedraggled boy, almost suspended in mid-air by the ears, his toes barely touching the ground, being pummeled by the two women.

"They're not from here," a voiced rasped beside him. Kumarsingh. He looked sweaty and happy. "People in Omeara don't carry on that way, at least not in public."

Arun, turning to face him, said, "You know about Nawaal?"

"The man or the stick?"

"The stick."

"I heard about what you did to it."

"And?"

"Children have to be disciplined. Only not like that, in public."

The vendor released the boy. Hardly had his soles touched the ground before they were wrenched up again as his mother clutched him by the scruff of the neck and marched him off on the balls of his feet. Scattered applause accompanied them as they disappeared into the crowd.

Kumarsingh said, "Have you found Lakhan?"

"I was just on my way to see him."

"Come," he said, taking Arun by the arm. "I'll show you. Lakhan usually has a bottle of throat medicine handy."

They had hardly taken six steps when Arun received a tremendous shove from the right. It was so powerful he didn't stumble, simply found himself toppling over, eyes wide open, the asphalt rushing up to meet him. Just before his head cracked painfully onto the ground, just before he felt something heavy and pliant crash on top of him, he heard a massive, hissing roar, the sound of two freight trains converging at full speed. He was engulfed by a wave of heat and then, face pressed against the asphalt, pinned under some unknown weight, was pelted by a flurry of small, hard objects. They seemed to be falling out of the sky. One landed, burning, on the back of his hand. He shook it off and saw what looked to be a fragment of smoking metal. All around him people were sprawled on the ground, helpless beneath a shower of small, shapeless particles. He gulped at air, struggling to fill his emptied lungs.

Then the metallic rain stopped and the weight rose from him. He looked around, his head heavy. Kumarsingh was sitting beside him, his face in his hands, a trickle of blood running between his fingers and down his arm, a red stain spreading through the sleeve of his white shirt.

Arun sat up, his skull ringing. The air was ripped in places, battered in others. Shock waves' invisible hands thumped at his chest from outside and inside. He reached an arm out. "Kumarsingh? Kumarsingh? You all right?" His head swirled, he felt himself swaying, and he had to steady himself on his outstretched arms. "Kumarsingh?"

Kumarsingh's hands fell from his head and he looked bleary-eyed at Arun. Blood leaked from a small gash on his forehead, dripped from his eyebrow, channelled itself along his temple and down his chin.

"You've got a cut," Arun said. His head was beginning to throb.

Kumarsingh, in a daze, raised a hand to his forehead, felt the blood. "Yah," he said in a voice full of curiosity. "I have a cut."

Around them people were beginning to stir, rising to their knees, unsteadily to their feet. Someone shrieked. A baby wailed. Another shriek joined the first. A tumult of voices rose: "The bus! The bus!"

Kumarsingh's eyes widened on Arun. "Rainbow?" He leapt to his feet, seizing Arun's arm as he did so and tugging him up. Arun's head spun and he braced himself on Kumarsingh's shoulder. People were scurrying in all directions now, some fleeing with children clutched in their arms, others — most — surging towards the Omeara Road on the far side of the square. Together they turned and saw that the bus had not proceeded far down the road. It had come to a halt. Smoke was funnelling from its windows. It had spilled its cargo of baggage and looked strangely bald. Around it the only movement was the strands of smoke braiding themselves together against the blue sky.

Kumarsingh yelped. He shoved Arun away and joined the rush towards the bus. Arun staggered but succeeded in maintaining his balance. His legs were unsteady and he'd fallen hard on his left shoulder and hip — they were beginning to ache — but he managed to work up a vigorous pace towards the bus. Ahead of him, beside him, people were walking along more slowly, bloodied handkerchiefs pressed to their cheeks and mouths, bloodied shirts wrapped around their heads or arms or thighs. Quickly, he checked himself for blood, found none.

By the time he got to the bus, it was already spilling smoke less furiously and several young men — Arun recognised them as members of the town's cricket team — were urging people to keep back. Still, the crowd pressed forward, its stunned hush disturbed by an occasional gush of sobs, an occasional searing ululation. The bus looked as if it had been seared from the inside, its frame intact except for a panel of metal siding that had been peeled back in the middle, exposing metal struts. Every window had been blown out. In the seat just behind the driver, a grey-haired man was leaning out the window as if to chat with someone, his arm dangling, his chin resting on his chest turned ruby red. Beside him, a young woman, clothes shredded, face streaked in blood, appeared to be addressing a frozen scream to the heavens. Behind her, a balding man with a face turned to raw meat and, behind him, two young women — one untouched except for a missing left arm, the other with a smudge of blood on her cheek — all seemed to have joined her in that final, silenced protest. And there were more, one in every seat: men, women, none moving. The bus would have been packed, it always was, with passengers standing squeezed into every available space.

Arun saw Kumarsingh in the bus, one of half a dozen men picking their way along the aisle. From the back of the crowd came a scream and a flurry of activity. Arun glanced back to see a woman being restrained. Suddenly, through the fog of unreality that held him in its grip, he remembered.

Shanti. The visit to her aunt.

He began shoving his way through the crowd. Voices growled in protest. He ignored them. When he got to the front, one of the cricketers raised a restraining hand. Then he lowered it. He'd recognised Arun. The schoolteacher had status, even here.

Arun took two quick steps towards the bus and then he saw what he hadn't been able to see before. On the ground, scattered among the bundles and boxes and suitcases spilled from the roof of the bus and showered with broken glass, were pieces of human bodies: a bare leg ripped whole from its torso, a hand severed at the wrist still clutching a handbag, a foot here, a gruel of intestines there, chunks of red flesh, seared flesh that brought to mind with a rise of bile the piece of meat the strays had been fighting over earlier, a head — male? female? — face down in the dirt, its cranium sheared off, its brain spilled grey beside it. And ... At first he didn't know what it was. It was red and raw and round, and there was movement in it, a steady pulsing. His stomach wrenched. He had seen it in magazine photographs. He'd seen it in television documentaries. And so, after a moment, he knew it for what it was. A human heart, still beating.

And he knew, after another moment, what he had to do. Somehow, through it all, his new shirt had remained squeezed tight under his left arm. His heart pounding into his throat, he knelt beside the orphaned heart. It appeared, from his memory of the images, to have been ripped intact from its owner's chest, appeared undamaged, fit for transplantation. With hands that neither hesitated nor shook, with gestures that were precise and knowing, he unwrapped the shirt and, when the heart no longer pulsed, draped it over its lustrous stillness.

He knew then, kneeling there, that there was no point in searching for Shanti, that whatever more lay strewn or splattered in the bus was beyond his comfort.

PART TWO

ONE

THE MAN STOOD before his table, lips stirring, priming his mouth to speak. His eyes were moist and so large he appeared to be staring in alarm past Arun's shoulder at the chalkboard. His shirt, faded colourless, was frayed at the collar. Several missing buttons revealed a bony, concave chest.

He said, "We ..."

He stopped, embarrassed, switched a heavy paper bag from one hand to the other. There was something physically awkward about him, as if his face were sheathed in a thin layer of cracked clay, a pronounced droop on the left side causing it to seem ill-matched to the right. His shoulders sloped like the sides of an equilateral triangle, so that his neck ran into his wiry arms.

"We, that is, his mother, my wife, and me, we hopes that he can go to higher studies." He spoke in a deliberate manner, each word

189

seeming to require preparation before leaving his tongue, his voice emerging as if from behind several layers of cobweb. Arun looked past the man's sloping shoulder to the doorway where his son's silhouette suggested a stunted tree — the withered trunk, four forlorn boughs incapable of supporting the weight of leaves.

"We know of a good school in the capital where they give bursies to people like my son, people who cannot pay. But he must learn to read and write and count before he can go there, and for this we must depend on you, *Prahib*. We cannot help him."

"What's his name?"

"Saman."

Arun sighed. Hope had never struck him as an ugly thing, but in the weeks since the bombing of the bus it had come to seem orphaned, foolish even. A silence had settled on the town like an invisible shroud, stifling all sound except for the wind and the sea. The work in the fields had gone on undeterred either by the tragedy or the great heat, but Radha had not returned to school, nor for a while had Hari and Roop. Jai, Rai, and Indira had come back, and then only for the mornings. They had, Arun noticed, avoided even looking at Shanti's desk.

Within twenty minutes of the explosion, army trucks had arrived, disgorging heavily armed soldiers who quickly pushed Arun and the cricketers into the crowd and imposed a cordon of bayonets. Kumarsingh and the other men in the bus were ejected. As they were led away, Arun saw that their hands and clothes were bloody. The crowd turned restive: their tragedy was being taken from them. A nervous order was given, a few shots fired into the air. Silence returned. Some people began drifting away, mostly women with children in tow. Arun, in the front ranks of the crowd, began to tremble. His muscles fluttered and twitched, his head shuddered on his neck, his teeth clattered against each other like collapsing dominoes. The soldiers began moving forward, shouting at the crowd to return to their homes and stay indoors for the next two hours. At first no one stirred. The soldiers became aggressive and the people, sullen, reluctant, turned away and did as ordered. In the days to come, Arun would have no memory of his opening his door, entering his house, collapsing on his bed. He would remember only awakening to stiffened muscles and a racing heart.

The man's eyes went watery. "My life, *Prahib*, is like my father's life. And my father's life was like his father's life. It is a good life, but hard. My son is a little weak. My wife says he has thin bones. We give him milk and meat but it makes no difference. His muscles can't grow solid on those weak bones. My wife ..."

The army took possession of the truck and the dead. The next day bodies were returned to families. Shanti and her parents, the only victims from Omeara, were claimed by her aunt. Arun had seen Kumarsingh only once. He had responded to his handshake and words of condolence with a stunned, wild-eyed look. Arun was not quite sure that Kumarsingh had recognised him. Mr Jaisaram said he'd been running around town falling in and out of despair. "Not to worry, though," he'd added. "I know Kumarsingh. He will pull himself up by his bootstraps — whatever bootstraps are, I've never understood that expression — and he will find himself another Rainbow. You know what they say, there's a lot of rainbows in the sky."

"Isn't that fish in the sea?" Arun had said.

"Yes, but we're talking abut Kumarsingh here. He doesn't care for fish." He'd let fall a tight little laugh, a sound without merriment, as if he were trying out some difficult foreign vowel.

"Your wife is a smart woman. That is a fine dream that she has — that you have — for your son." Arun's shoulder blades tightened. They had been hard words to pronounce, because they were only the beginning and he had no wish to pursue them to the end. Not before those pleading, watery eyes, not before the boy whose frailty against the light suggested he might wink out at any moment. This boy, this Saman, who would be lucky to acquire the basic skills he would need to perhaps run a little shop like Madhu's; who, even if by some miracle were tapped by an angel and given

brilliance and wisdom, would be hard pressed, with no connec-
tions, no mentor, no money, to secure one of the few places in the
college system reserved for his kind.

An army communiqué a week later announced that the bus
had been the target of a bomb smuggled on board by a man — his
body, or parts of it, had not been claimed — who had been caught
up in its blast when, they further believed, it had gone off either
too early or too late. The authorities hoped that the ongoing
investigation would reveal whether the intended target had been
the market or the army base where the bus always made a brief
stop. Nothing more had been heard since.

The man smiled, a wan, submissive smile, and placed his paper
bag on Arun's desk. He opened it, invited Arun to look inside.
Oranges, mangoes, okra, a ripe papaya.

Arun shook his head. "Thank you, but I cannot accept this. It's
too much, it's not necessary."

The man backed away. "No, no." He gestured at the bag. "For the
teacher." Then he turned and walked off, hardly glancing at his son
standing still like some wayward shadow in the blinding doorway.

"Come in, Saman," Arun said. "Sit down."

Saman raised his head and after a brief hesitation crept to the
desk nearest the door. Arun reached for a reading primer, slipped
into the desk beside him. At that moment he became aware of the
weight of the food he'd eaten earlier. The fried bread and curried
chick peas sat heavy in his stomach. He swallowed, opened the
book, pointed to the letter A. Saman's dark eyes blinked in
puzzlement first at the letter, then at him.

He was young then, ten perhaps, and he dreamed of adventure,
of heading off on his own into the wilderness. One Saturday afternoon during the long holidays, when the sky had cleared after the
rains and the sun shone hot and hard between the dissipating
clouds, he'd wandered away from the country house his parents
had rented for a month into the forest at the back, a forest tamed

by locals and holiday visitors, a forest crisscrossed by footpaths beaten through the bush and without danger.

He walked for a long time through the steamy forest gloom, the interlaced branches of the trees forming a canopy through which leaked shafts and starbursts of light, his bare foot squishing into the muddy ground. He got pleasure from watching the mud gurgle and rise between his toes, rise up against the sides of his shoe. When the path branched he let instinct guide him. He was not worried about getting lost. He trusted that when he was ready to return, that same instinct would guide him back to the house. He took pride in his sense of direction. His sister had once said that this ability of his proved only that he had a bird's brain. No, he had retorted, he had a strong homing instinct, which was a good thing to have for he always knew where safety lay.

Peering ahead, he saw what appeared to be footprints in the mud. They began suddenly, as if their maker had materialised in the middle of the path or had sprung down from the trees. They had no beginning, then, but strode off ahead along the path. Were they his? Had he somehow walked in a circle? But the prints had been made by two large feet, not a foot and a shoe; the feet were larger than his, longer, wider, adult feet, and the third toe on the right foot seemed to be missing. He grew uneasy, but his curiosity was piqued. Adventure, heading off into the unknown: he followed the prints, stepping beside them, refusing to put his own feet into their wet moulds, so that his own feet marked a path parallel to the bigger ones.

He followed them for some time along the meandering trail, working his way deeper and deeper into the forest. Then, abruptly, without explanation, the tracks stopped. There was the final footprint and then there were no more. It was as if their maker had evaporated or had sprung back into the trees. Or, it suddenly occurred to him, had leapt away from the path into the surrounding bush.

That was when fear seized his throat, like a hand squeezing his windpipe from within and throttling him. He looked to the right, then the left. The bush was still, heavy, a breathless presence. He looked above. The light had diminished, the shafts dissipated, the starbursts now dull and distant. It was getting late. He should have turned back before now, fled the approaching darkness. The footsteps had ended, *just like that.*

Then he did something that he could not, afterwards, explain to himself. He shut his eyes tight, tensed his arms and legs, and launched himself off the path. He fell hard into the thick bush, twigs scratching at his skin. He banged his shoulder into a mossy tree trunk. As he lay there stunned, his nostrils thick with the smells of dank earth and crushed vegetation, he wondered what had prompted him to leap blindly from the path. No answer came to him but he knew, with certainty, that it had been the right thing to do.

He picked himself up, stepped out of the bush onto the path, and, bleeding from his cuts and bruises, let his instinct set him back on the way home.

Sitting at his table, his shirt sticking wet to him, Saman hunched at a desk working laboriously with chalk and slate at the first six letters of the alphabet, Arun remembered his mother had been unhappy with him that evening. She had cleansed his bruises, bandaged his cuts, leaving his arms and legs dotted red with mercurochrome, and then sent him off to clean and polish his shoe. It had never been quite the same afterwards, that shoe. The mud had irritated the leather, so that it never again acquired quite the brilliance of its mate. Sitting out back in the dim light of a bare bulb, the forest blending seamlessly with the night, his eyes had fallen on his feet, the brown, bony toes of the one, the smooth, dull, pink plastic of the other, and he had wondered whether it would be possible to paint in toes, nails, brown the leg. He'd swiped his cloth into a can of brown shoe polish and smeared it on the plastic shin, spreading it as evenly as he could. The result was not pleasing — it looked like a mud stain — and he'd quickly wiped it off. The failure had left him slightly saddened. That pair of shoes, like the prosthesis that was replaced as he grew taller, was still carefully stored away somewhere in his parents' house.

Saman held the slate at arm's length, examined his work, replaced it on his desk, thumbed out a letter and wrote it in again. Then he looked up expectantly at Arun.

"Bring it to me," Arun said.

Saman held out the slate.

"Bring it here," Arun said.

Saman continued holding out the slate, as if he'd failed to understand.

Arun motioned at him with a finger, tapped the top of his table. "Please bring me the slate, Saman."

Still Saman did not move, but his fragile jaws tightened against each other. Arun, puzzled, waited. Surely the boy understood what was required of him. He looked carefully at Saman, took note of the steady hands proffering the slate, the jaw bones so tightly clenched that his cheeks were striated, the eyes that were hard and unblinking, and understood, without knowing the reason for the game, that they boy required that he leave his table and come to him. He leaned back in his chair, said, "I can wait all day, Saman, all evening and all night, too. Please bring me the slate. You've worked very hard."

Saman lowered his arm and deposited the slate on the desk. Without a glance at Arun, he got stiffly to his feet, turned, and walked out of the schoolhouse.

Arun watched him go and felt a stirring of anger deep within him. It wasn't, he was aware, Saman's refusal to bring him the slate that bothered him. Nor was it his leaving. It was rather something in his posture, something in his gait. A challenge? No, not quite. Rejection, disapproval: they were perhaps closer. Hard to put a name to it, but whatever it was, it had touched Arun to the quick. From beneath the enervation that had settled in him after the bombing there rose something that he recognised as being sharper than anger, more vibrant, less temporary, something that only the word *wrath* could adequately describe. Why this thin and fragile boy should have been the one to trigger it he couldn't say, but he knew, as surely as he knew his own name, that had Saman known where Shanti had sat, he would have taken the seat with an arrogance meant to send a message.

JUST AFTER MIDDAY, grey clouds scudded across the sky, emerging from the horizon like ink tumbling through fresh water. The sun winked out. The sea turned dark. Arun could see webs of night folding beneath the curls of the breakers. He said, "Looks like a storm. Maybe we should head back."

Anjani folded her arms across her chest. Not raising her eyes from the pebbled beach, placing her bare feet carefully so as to avoid jagged stones, she said, "It won't rain. But we can go back if you want."

The town lay unseen behind them, tucked into a bend in the coast that formed a shallow bay. They had been walking, slowly, for almost an hour. In the silvered light, the dense vegetation that ended where the beach began appeared liquefied by shadow, too dark ink leaking from some undetected fracture.

"Let's push on," Arun said.

Anjani hadn't waited for him to announce his decision. She had walked on, letting the wash of a wave engulf her feet. Arun climbed higher up the beach to avoid the water. She had urged him to roll up his pant legs, to remove his shoe so he could feel the warmth of the sea, but that was impossible. The shoe on his prosthesis would have been soaked, and using his prosthesis alone on wet rock would have been risky.

"So what happened to your leg?" Anjani called out as the water rushed back past her ankles into the sea. She turned, carefully picked her way towards him. Some distance back, she had slipped her shoes off and perched them on a large rock. She would retrieve them on their way back.

"How come you haven't asked me before?"

"We learn discretion in Omeara. Haven't you noticed?"

"How come you're asking me now?"

"Because, in the long run, discretion and I don't get along very well."

Her answer made him laugh. He relished the thought of her swallowing the question that must have come to her countless times like an irritation on the tongue. He said, "Nothing happened to it."

"Were you born without it?"

"No."

"Are my questions making you uncomfortable? It's no big deal, you know. My great grandmother had a fake leg. Not like yours, of course. I don't know if they even had plastic back then."

Arun slid his hands into his pants pockets, glanced away towards the sharp, black line of the horizon. Her questions *were* making him uncomfortable. Everyone was curious about his leg — he would see the hesitation in strangers' eyes when they found out about it — but, if they asked, they would direct their question to his parents or his sister, never to him. It was as if they didn't dare, believing that he would be offended or wounded in some way. And now, here was Anjani asking about his missing leg as she might ask about a cut on his thumb and he wasn't quite sure how to respond.

"You don't have to tell me if you don't want to," she said, flicking a spray of hair from her eyes. "If it makes you uneasy. If you feel sorry for yourself. But I'd have thought that seeing the children in your class, you'd feel a little more at home here."

"That's a cruel thing to say." Out on the water, a flash of silver caught his eye, a fish leaping through the air, perhaps, and re-entering the water with no splash.

"There's nothing cruel about it, and if you don't see that you'll never be able to help the children. It's a fact of life, of yours and theirs. Nothing more. But if you want to turn it into something dramatic, go ahead, no one will stop you."

She bent over, fingers reaching down to the ground, shuffling the dark pebbles aside. Then she straightened up, brushing sand from something she had picked up. She handed it to him and he saw that she had found a natural crystal, a rectangular stone of transparent milkiness worn to smooth perfection by the abrasion of water and sand. He closed his fist around it, felt the warmth it had absorbed from the sun earlier in the day.

"I was born without it," he said. "Or almost."

"Almost?"

"It was withered from the knee down, as if it had started growing normally like the rest of me then stopped for some reason. My parents hoped it would catch up eventually but the doctors told them there was no chance. They recommended that it be excised. So that's what happened."

"You mean they just cut it off?"

"Well, surgically, of course. They didn't exactly take an axe to it." She grimaced. "I'm not stupid, you know."

Arun glanced sharply at her, at the frown that still tightened her forehead and temples. "I'm sorry, I didn't mean to imply —"

"Do you remember what it was like or were you too young?" Her frown persisted, and he saw how translucent the skin was on her face, thought he could see threaded veins and the spread of fine muscle.

"I was about six months old, so I don't remember a thing. I guess it's kind of like when a baby gets circumcised. Snip, it's gone and you never even knew it was there, at least you never feel its absence."

"A leg isn't a foreskin," she said in a flat voice. "It haunts you still, doesn't it?"

"I wonder sometimes if my life would've been different with the leg — the whole leg, I mean. And not in the small ways — I can't play football or cricket but I can swim. I mean in the bigger ways. If I'd been born with a normal leg, would I have experienced the world differently? Would I have seen or felt things I didn't?"

"Those are stupid questions. Even if you found the answers, what would they give you, except for sadness?"

Arun felt his eyes burn, and he turned away quickly, the dark sky and dark sea dissolving before him. He knew that, knew it even as the questions pressed themselves in on him. But the knowledge of their futility had always proved less persuasive than the enticement of where the questions might lead.

Anjani smiled thinly. "There's no need to go looking for sadness, Arun. The world's already full of it. That's what I meant about the children."

He returned her smile, with effort at first and then, as a sense of lightness came to him, with warmth.

Anjani turned and began stepping carefully away, her toes splaying as the balls of her feet found purchase on the stones. The purr of an engine caused them both to look up. Out on the water, a Navy patrol boat was cutting a steady path along the coast. On its prow, beside a manned machine gun, a helmeted sailor stood splay-legged surveying the shoreline through binoculars. As it drew parallel to them, the boat slowed. Arun could feel the reach of the lenses, could see them as the sailor was seeing them. He found himself suddenly assessing his posture, wondering whether the lenses could detect nervousness, wondering what to do with his hands. At that moment, Anjani reached her hand out, slipped it into his, drew him close. "Just walk," she said. They walked, hand in hand, the crystal between their fingers, and a tableau was created. The engine growled then fell back as the boat resumed its previous speed and left them behind.

The beach was growing rocky, the stones larger. Farther on, a fall of large boulders had tumbled out from the vegetation across the beach and into the sea. They continued on in silence for a while. Eventually, Anjani said, "They're gone now." But out on the water the trail of the boat was still visible, as if it had been etched into the surface. She let go of his hand, and Arun was surprised to find himself feeling a tinge of regret. He slid the crystal into his pants pocket.

When they got to the boulders, Anjani gathered up the skirt of her dress in her fist, clambered to the top. Arun followed her up more carefully, with less agility, using his hands to brace himself should his prosthesis slip under him. She sat facing the sea. He sat beside her. On the other side, the vegetation crept closer to the water, the strip of beach strewn with boulders and rocks.

Anjani said, "This is my favourite spot. It's about as far as you can get from Holy Faith Convent. When I first came back from the capital I used to spend hours here every day."

"Doing what?"

"Looking."

"Looking for what?"

"Just looking."

"It must have been hard. Unfair. I mean, *Playgirl*. It hardly seems cause for expulsion."

Anjani drew her legs up, encircled them with her arms. "Actually," she said after a moment, "it was a little more complicated than that." Her eyes skimmed the water, rose towards a break in the clouds, towards the shaft of sunshine that drove down as hard as a searchlight onto the surface. "I think the phrase they used was *behaviour inconsistent with the moral standards of Holy Faith Convent.*"

Arun was amused. Her impatience with discretion applied not only to him. He said, "Not hard to see how that would include hiding pictures of naked men in your room."

"I've already told you, it was a little more complicated than that."

The window in the clouds closed, the column of light dissipated. Arun said, "So the story about the *ganja* and the search of the rooms and the *Playgirl* ..." Just above the horizon there was a brightening as the cloud thinned.

"Isn't quite the whole story." Her eyes remained fixed on that distant brightening: a breach opening up, cloud shredding around a blue lozenge.

"Are you going to tell me the rest or is it another one of those stories it's better not to share with me? Not that it's any of my business, of course."

"No, it isn't. It isn't even my parents' business, which is why they don't know about it."

"So why are you telling me?"

"That's what I'm wondering. Perhaps it's because I'm not like my mother and can't keep my mouth shut year after year. Perhaps because you're a stranger and one day you'll be gone." She gestured in impatience, as if chasing away a fly. "Perhaps, perhaps, perhaps. Maybe because you're safe somehow, and what happened at the convent doesn't have anything to do with anything anymore."

"You sound as if you need to make some kind of confession. Perhaps — another perhaps — perhaps the convent had more of an effect on you than you realise."

"The Catholics all went looking for absolution. I'm not looking for any kind of forgiveness for, Father, I haven't sinned. Sin is in the eye of the beholder."

"Is that what they taught you?"

"It's what I learned from living with them."

The brightness was rising from the horizon, blue steadily taking possession of the sky, pushing the dark clouds farther north.

"So what did happen there?" Arun said. "What was true in what you told me? The *ganja?*"

"True."

"The *Playgirl?*"

"True. Except they found it in my roommate's dresser, not mine."

"So how come you got expelled?"

Anjani screwed up her face, as if she were about to spit. "She wasn't a two-percenter."

A shudder ran through Arun's belly. He could feel a dry thumping in his chest. "So they made you the scapegoat." Still, part of him remained sceptical: had it really been as simple as that?

"You decide." She tightened the clutch of her arms, crushing her thighs against her chest, and suddenly it was as if she were sitting in her own shadow. "When the nuns barged into the room, they found me in my roommate's bed. With my roommate."

"You weren't just talking."

She shook her head. "*Behaviour inconsistent with the moral standards of Holy Faith Convent.*"

"So it was hardly because you were a southerner that they —"

Anjani laughed, but without humour. "Typical northern response. Even you. Damned two-percenters. Always complaining."

Arun, stung, said, "That's not what I meant and you know it."

Anjani shrugged. "Still, I was the one who got thrown out."

"And your roommate?"

"Her parents were generous benefactors of the school, pillars of the community as she was always saying. She herself wanted to prove how cool she was by rooming with me. What do *you* think happened to her? The nuns used the magazine to send me packing and hushed everything else up. They said they were doing me a favour, saving my reputation. They never mentioned the school's reputation, or my roommate's, or her family's. They said they had to protect the school's two-percent program, because they were just as cool as my roommate was, you know? Other parents would've used me as an excuse to throw out all the other southerners, to save their little princesses from our perversity. All in all, a typical northern response."

Arun could understand her anger, but he couldn't share it. He was not naive about the way things were. The nuns were astute. Others would have paid the price had the story got out. But he kept his thoughts to himself. Then he remembered the warmth and softness of her hand, the firm way she had gripped his, and he couldn't resist the question that came to him. "So, your roommate. Is that why you haven't married?"

"My former roommate has nothing to do with it. It's a matter of all this marriage stuff, the way my parents live, working, keeping house, washing clothes, cooking." She made a face. "Not to mention promising to make love to only one person for the rest of my life. I can't promise that."

"But most people do."

"People make all kinds of promises, but have you ever noticed that the word promise is just compromise without the first three letters? For me, it's simple. Take you and me, for instance. We go for a walk together. We talk, we laugh, we give each other pleasure. Tomorrow I might do the same thing with Kumarsingh or one of the cricket players. No one gives it a second thought, no one says anything. Why should sex be any different?"

"But having sex with someone isn't just like playing cards or laughing at a good joke. It's more fundamental than that."

"Why do you like to complicate things?"

"It's not me. Life is complicated, don't you think?"

"We make it complicated. I mean, if I got married, why shouldn't I be free to have sex with someone else like I'm free to have a good conversation with someone else? So long as I know where I'm going afterwards, who I'll be making dinner for, who I'll be taking care of when he's sick or unhappy."

"You have an elastic idea of loyalty."

"What's loyalty, Arun? So I have fun with one person and go home to my husband and have fun with him too. Where's the disloyalty?"

"And what if your husband and the other person had a dis-agreement that had nothing to do with you, some kind of business conflict, say?"

"Then I'd have to decide who was right, wouldn't I? Depending on the situation, I mean. If my husband was wrong I'd have to tell him so. It would be wrong to take his side just because he was my husband, don't you think? Isn't that a kind of loyalty, too?"

Suddenly, Arun despaired for her. She would, he felt, never find a comfortable place here, not in this town, not in this country, where ideas of loyalty were set hard and fast.

"The only loyalty that counts," she said, "is the one to yourself."

"Isn't that selfish?"

"You don't understand. Loyalty to yourself is what makes you loyal to others. That's where it all begins."

"You're a strange person, Anjani."

"Everybody's strange. Even you. Being strange, being inexplicable — that's what makes us human."

"But don't you ever feel lonely? Surely marriage to the right person would allow us to —"

"Arun, look around you." She peered up at the sky, gave a bitter laugh. "There's nobody in Omeara worth marrying."

"Would you, if there were?"

"Why don't you just come right out and ask what you want to ask, Arun?"

His neck and shoulders grew warm. "Let me put it like this. If you could get a subscription to *Playboy* or *Playgirl*, which would you choose?"

"Both," she said, with a grin. "Feel better now?"

But she didn't wait for his answer. She leapt lithely to her feet and skipped down the stack of boulders to the beach. Arun, clambering down with care, sought an answer to her question. He couldn't find one. He was grateful, when he had caught up with her, that she asked what his sister was like and whether he got along with his brother-in-law.

TWO

S*HRRR SHRRR SHRRR*

"Corporal Pande," Arun said.

"Sor." The ceiling light reflected off his freshly oiled pate.

"If it's not too much trouble, corporal, would you mind putting your tools aside?"

"Begging your pardon, sor, you ask me that every class, sor, and every class I must give the same answer, sor." Pande had the knack of being politely insolent. "So if I may, sor, I will repeat. You have to prepare for your classes. I have to prepare for my patrols. If you don't prepare, we have a boring class. If I don't prepare, I lose my life. Thank you, sor."

Shrrr

The same request had been made, the same reply given, many times over the past weeks. Arun said, "I will continue to ask, corporal."

"I understand, sor."

Shrrr

"Perhaps from now on, sor, we can simply consider your question asked and my answer given."

Shrrr

The sound began the moment he'd walked into the room and the soldiers took their seats. They were always waiting for him, standing before their chairs, uniforms clean, boots shined, books and pencils placed neatly on the table in front of them. They were a disciplined group, each ambitious in his own way. Their progress was swift. Some of them were working through simple novels, dictionary at hand. Sherlock Holmes was a favourite and they enjoyed reading aloud in class, frequently adding clumsy theatricals to their performance. Private Ramlakhan, whose wife already knew how to read and write, regularly brought to Arun short letters he'd written to her. He would stand at Arun's shoulder, anxious eyes planted on the paper, chubby cheeks glistening, while Arun corrected the spelling and sorted out his more mangled phrases. Occasionally, too, he would bring to Arun his wife's reply, when a word or a sentence gave him trouble. "She has very bad handwriting," he once said, not without a certain satisfaction.

Only Mangal Pande maintained a cool reserve. He remained unmoved by the others' antics. He read, when it was his turn to read, in a toneless voice. His assignments were letter perfect. He responded, when asked a question, in a crisp, dismissive manner. He took few notes. Instead, he sat there, from the beginning of the class to the end, drawing a file back and forth along the blade of his machete, the soft, metallic rasp as if marking time. Arun had asked him to leave his equipment in his quarters and his request had given rise to the exchange that had become ritual. Arun had mentioned the problem to Seth. "He's an unusual one, that Pande," Seth had said. "Is it such a big problem?" Arun knew then that Pande would do as he wished. Like Saman.

Arun said, "You're suggesting I pretend to ask you and you pretend to answer?"

"Not pretend, sor. Just not bother to pronounce the words. It would save time, sor."

Shrrr

Shrrr

Arun disguised his rush of anger by clenching his fist at his lips and coughing.

Throughout the exchange, the others remained passive and distant, simply looking straight ahead at the blank chalkboard, as if fiddling with their pencils or flicking through their books would somehow implicate them in an affair they wished to avoid.

The room shook as a succession of heavy vehicles rumbled by outside.

At the end of the class, Pande was the first to leave, the others filing quietly out of the room after him, their books tucked under their arms. Arun wearily gathered up his manuals and the small stack of homework to be marked. As he plopped them into his briefcase, Seth ambled in, hands tucked into the pants pockets of his camouflage battledress. "Cup of coffee?" he said. The belly above his web belt appeared newly rounded.

"Tea would go down better."

"I got used to coffee in the States, but tea's better for you. Tea it is, then."

Arun snapped the locks shut on the briefcase. "Can I show you something? Your Corporal Pande's full of tricks."

"What's he done now?"

Arun stepped over to Pande's seat. On the table were two sheets of paper. He picked them up. "When class was over, he ripped a page from his notebook. He turned the blade of his machete up towards the ceiling and balanced the page on it. Within seconds, the page was cut in two, as if the blade had melted through it. It was like magic, Seth. The page had been cut in two by its own weight. Its own weight! Can you imagine how sharp that thing is?"

Seth smiled. "He's a commando. They like doing things like that, those guys. He's one of our best, if not the best. Loves being in the thick of things."

"He's a little scary, if you ask me." Arun held up the two pieces of paper, examined the edges where they had been sliced.

"Of course he is. Like anybody who's the best at what he does. That kind of mastery, the kind that goes beyond training, the kind that comes from somewhere inside, is always a little scary."

"The other men seem intimidated by him too."

"But they wouldn't want anyone else beside them in a fight, I promise you."

Arun crumpled up the sheets and tossed them into the waste-paper basket beside his table. "I should let Kumarsingh know I'm going to be a while." Kumarsingh had managed to buy Madhu's taxi and planned to use it to fill the gap left by Rainbow's destruction. The army had hired him to drive Arun to the camp for his classes and to pick him up afterwards. He would be waiting as usual outside the gates.

"I'll take care of that. I'll have someone bring him a drink and something to eat. How's he doing, by the way? Shame about his bus. Total write-off."

"He's still spinning schemes. If anyone can make this taxi busi-ness work, it's him. And he's got an idea about putting on cinema evenings. You know, a TV, a VCR, pirated tapes. He's even got a contact in America who's going to tape soap operas and mail him the cassettes. It's hard to kill a man's dreams."

"Easier to kill a man," Seth said.

The parade ground was deserted, the air moist and still. They walked over to the officers' mess, the bare earth packed as hard as concrete.

Arun said, "How's your wife?"

"She's fine. A little tired. The doctor's ordered bed rest, but there's no problem. She works too hard and the heat makes things more difficult. My mother's looking after her hand and foot. She's almost six months along now, so the most dangerous time's past. She's thinking of going home to have the baby."

"America?"

"Yes. She'd stay with her parents."

"And you?"

"I'd prefer it if she stayed here. She's got top-class care at the military hospital. But still, I guess it isn't the States." His brow furrowed.

Across the parade ground, the main gate swung open and two mud-splattered trucks rumbled in.

"She'll be all right," Seth said as if to convince himself. "The general's arranged to have her room air-conditioned so she'll be more comfortable."

"When do you get to see her next?"

"In a couple of weeks. We talk almost every day." He chuckled. "She's spending her time eating chocolates and reading novels, which is a damn sight better than what I spend my time doing."

The officer's mess, where the dinner had been held the evening of Arun's first visit to the camp, was full of shadows, the air sultry and sharp with disinfectant. The floor was still damp from a recent mopping. It was deserted save for a sleepy-eyed waiter eager to be of service and two men huddled over bottles of beer. Seth nodded at the men, ordered a pot of tea and a plate of pastries and steered Arun towards the corner where he had sat that first night with the general.

Arun said, "So how's the war going?"

"We're winning."

"You are?"

Seth flicked an eyebrow at him. "*We* are."

Arun laughed. "We've been hearing that for years."

"Yes, well. Things have changed. We've grown up. You've seen the gunships. Did you know that in the old days we had to improvise bombs with grenades? You pulled the pin and put the grenade into a wine glass, so that the lever would stay depressed. Then you dropped them from a civilian helicopter. Imagine all those wine glasses falling through the air, sunlight glinting off them. When they hit the ground, the glass would shatter, the lever would activate and boom." He smiled. "It took some ingenuity to fight a war in those days. Now instead of wine glasses tumbling merrily down, we've got streams of tracer bullets at night. Have you ever seen that? It's a beautiful sight, but I miss the wine glasses."

"So tracer bullets are more effective than wine glasses at winning wars?"

"The body count favours us by fifty to one."

"Fifty! I didn't realise there were so many of them."

"That's not the conclusion you're supposed to draw, Arun"

"What is the conclusion I'm supposed to draw?"

"That we're winning."

"I'll remember that." From deeper in the room, the air conditioner coughed and rattled and settled into a hum.

"Smart man. There are some things that are worth remembering. A penny saved is a penny earned. A stitch in time saves nine. All work and no play makes Jack a dull boy."

"My, aren't you the font of wisdom today."

"Proverbs offer good, solid advice, if incomplete."

"Meaning?"

"Meaning that a penny doesn't get you very far in life. Meaning that sometimes it's easier to buy a new garment than to mend an old one. Meaning that Jack should be careful who he plays with."

Arun sat forward in his chair. "What are you saying, Seth?"

The waiter returned trundling a wooden tea cart which he manoeuvred beside them: teacups on saucers, silver spoons, dessert plates, neatly ironed green napkins embroidered with the regiment's crest, a silver sugar bowl, a silver milk cup. Beside the steaming teapot — white porcelain with the regimental crest in gold — a silver platter held a variety of little cakes. As the waiter busied himself snapping open the napkins, straining the tea, offering sugar, milk, Arun wondered about the meaning of Seth's comment, his curiosity rising with the impression that Seth, spooning sugar into his cup, stirring, sipping, adding more sugar then a splash of milk, was making a show of being occupied. The waiter served them their choice of cake — chocolate topped by a single blanched almond for Arun, spongy lemon topped by shredded coconut for Seth — and withdrew to the kitchen.

"So," Arun said, nicking the cake with his fork. "What's this about Jack and his playmates?"

Seth picked up his cake between thumb and forefinger and took a large bite from it. Chewing, he brushed a few yellow crumbs from his chin. He said, "Did you enjoy your walk with the butcher's daughter on the beach the other day?"

Arun, startled, watched wordless as Seth consumed the second half of his cake and reached for another. Questions crowded in, crowded out any simple answer. Across the room, the two men laughed and clinked bottles.

Seth took a sip of tea. "The patrol boat."

The patrol boat. Of course. "Yes," Arun said finally. "It was a relaxing walk. Ever since the bus, it's been difficult to, you know ..."

Seth leaned forward. "You should be careful, Arun. You don't want to get into a, well, let's say a dicey situation."

"What do you mean?"

"I'm telling you this as a friend. That girl doesn't exactly dig guys."

Dig?

"We're just friends, nothing more." Arun put the dessert plate and cake on the tea cart. He raised his cup to his lips but couldn't drink.

"Not hungry?" Seth said. "You mustn't be upset. Life's like that."

"I told you, we're just friends." He wondered whether he should tell Seth that Anjani had already revealed to him the circumstances of her expulsion, but he thought better of it.

"Still, she's not unattractive. She's just not for you, is all I'm saying. Not for any man."

"Thanks for the warning," Arun said, "but no cause for worry."

Seth took a bite of his second piece of cake, chewed, swallowed. "You were holding hands." His tone was prosecutorial.

"What business is that of yours?"

"Don't be upset." His tone softened. "This is a friend talking, a friend concerned for your well-being."

Arun felt a hollow carve itself within him, an excavation so profound he could imagine the empty, echoing space. He had felt it only once before but he knew it for what it was: the almost physical excision of trust. "She was concerned for my well-being, too. She wanted to make sure I wouldn't slip on the stones. My leg, you see."

Seth smiled with one corner of his mouth. "How touching."

Arun, irritated, said, "You don't sound like a friend. Why are you being sarcastic? What aren't you telling me?"

Seth slouched in his seat, stretching out his legs and crossing his combat boots over one another. He nibbled at the cake. "Has she told you about her brother?"

"Yes, she has."

"She has!" Surprise quickly gave way to scepticism. "And what has she told you?"

"You know the story."

"Yes, but do you?"

"You don't trust her."

"Arun, we can't afford to trust anybody. Somebody makes those bombs that go off, somebody made that bomb that went off in Kumarsingh's bus. It's a specialised art, we know there's a master bomb maker out there somewhere. Only we don't know where and we don't know who. Not yet. And until we do, trust can prove deadly."

"Surely you don't suspect Anjani."

"We suspect everybody."

"Even me?"

"The bombs have been going off since long before you got here. Then there's your parents. Plus — let me be blunt — you're no *riksha*. I doubt you'd be in the business of wiring up explosives."

Arun nodded, knowing that it would be interpreted as assent and not the simple acknowledgement that he meant it as.

Seth drained his teacup, filled it again. "Now, what'd she tell you about her brother?"

"She told me about the trip in the container, about Canada, his disappearance. They've banned his name from their house, you know."

Seth began to laugh. His lips stretched tight against his teeth, his belly jiggled, his teacup rattled on its saucer. He put the cup on the cart to avoid spilling the tea on himself. "And you bought that fairy tale!"

"Are you saying it's not true?"

Seth reached for his cup, gulped down the tea. "I'm sorry, Arun. I shouldn't laugh. You had no way of knowing. It's not funny, really. Just that — I think I told you this on the train — just that in Omeara, throughout the south actually, nothing is ever quite what it seems. Take Kumarsingh. Is he a businessman or a hustler? And Jaisaram — is he a butcher or a sculptor, a shakir?"

"People are never just one thing or another, Seth, you know that. You, for instance. Husband, father, book lover, soldier. A bunch of contradictions, on the face of it."

"I'm not that simple-minded, Arun. What I'm talking about goes way beyond that kind of thing. I'm talking about how something can appear to be one way, while it's actually quite another."

"Is that the nature of the south or of the entire country? Don't you remember the last general elections? There were more votes cast than there were voters. What do you call that?"

"There was no truth to it, just the kind of rumour people start when they lose. It's part of the same problem I'm talking about.

But enough about the country, that's not our problem. I'm talking about the south, I'm talking about Omeara, I'm talking about the butcher's son."

"So, what about the butcher's son?"

"He's not hiding somewhere in Toronto or Vancouver like they claim. We have reason to believe that pieces of him were picked up and eventually cremated after a train bombing a few years ago. He was carrying it in a bag and set it off in a crowded compartment. He took seventeen others with him."

Arun was silent for a moment, the voices of the men and the rattle of more beers being delivered seeming to retreat before his thoughts as he set Seth's version beside Anjani's. "But his mother," he said finally. "She doesn't speak anymore, and she cut him out of all the family photos. Her disappointment — a mother's disappointment — at being abandoned, at the betrayal. I don't see how that fits with what you say."

Seth pulled himself up in the chair, fingers interlacing on his belly. "Or perhaps a mother's grief, a grief so searing it ties your tongue in knots, so agonising that either you kill yourself or do everything you can to pretend that the person never existed. I feel sorry for the old people. Jaisaram's a character and his wife, well, she's had a rough life, what with the son blown to smithereens and the daughter who ... Grandchildren are important to people here, and they're not likely to have any."

"So why invent that story about Canada?"

"Suicide bombing is a military tactic and nothing more. We try to keep things calm, normal, and they come along, kill a bunch of people, and keep everyone on edge. A hell of a tactic, and very effective. No crap about express trains to paradise and herds of dancing virgins as a reward. These are hard-nosed people. It's about serving the cause, hardly different from conventional soldiers who throw themselves at machine guns knowing they're going to die. Think of the thousands who went over the top during World War I, or the Japanese Banzai charges, or the waves of Chinese troops in Korea. Hundreds were slaughtered within minutes but they did it time and again. Here, even those who support the insurgents, and there are some, know it's obscene. They're awed by the suicide bomber, but they don't admire him. They suspect that someone who throws his life away, for whatever reason, has got to be a bit of a nut case. As far as Jaisaram and family are concerned, it's better to have an ingrate for a son than a madman. Everyone can commiserate with parents whose son runs off, but insanity attaches to the family, as if they're all infected."

Arun found it increasingly difficult to breathe. Seth's explanation made sense, as much sense as Anjani's explanation of her mother's strange behaviour. He took a deep breath, found it unsatisfying, took another.

Seth said, "Look, Arun, I'm not trying to choose your friends for you. What I'm saying is, there are lots of reasons to be careful."

"I appreciate your thoughtfulness."

"We aren't at home in this place, you and me. We have to look out for each other, if you get my meaning."

Arun didn't know what to say. It seemed an invitation to betrayal. And yet perhaps Anjani had told him, too, a story as fanciful as those she read to her father on quiet evenings.

Seth waved his hand at the tea cart. "Your cake?" he said.

Arun shook his head. No amount of cake would fill the space that Seth's concern had excavated within him.

From behind them, the men's voices rose in a drunken squabble. Seth leaned in close to Arun. "We live in a country," he said, "where alcohol isn't a thing to be savoured. It's merely a means to temporary amnesia. We have a long way to go before beer or wine or whisky can signify pleasure and not escape."

WHEN MAHADEO WAS named to the cabinet, Surein led the mumbled outrage. He questioned the prime minister's right to appoint ministers unelected to parliament, but Arun's father reminded him that the emergency regulations permitted a host of unorthodox measures. Surein had argued in favour of them around the dinner table, so how could he now call them into question?

Surein, unchastened, then declared that Mahadeo was like a magician who, with a flick of the tongue, could turn an innocent "How are you this morning?" into an excuse for a lecture on why the so-called social graces were merely a means of oppressing "our people" — by whom he meant northerners, all northerners, but particularly the hallowed poor — and exploiting them even further. What could a man like that bring to government deliberations?

Arun listened. He expressed no opinion. He understood that Sir Smoky, as uncouth as he was, had a talent for stating what many believed but would never declare, in language they would use only when muttering to themselves. Little more than veneer separated Mahadeo from Surein, but neither would countenance dining with the other. They had both come out of poverty but while Surein, aided by Joy, made constant efforts to distance himself from that past, Mahadeo, with his rumpled grey and black outfits and his coarseness and his cultivated scruffiness, had chosen to billboard it. Arun's father had once said that Mahadeo's radio pronouncements were like a man gargling on the airwaves but that didn't explain why he, like so many others, paid attention. This ambiguity — a figure of ridicule and, at the same time, a figure of admiration — gave Mahadeo his influence. He had a constituency of a kind. It made him handy. The prime minister, his father said without conviction, had seated him at the cabinet table in order to control him. People wanted him around, but at arm's length.

Like a toilet bowl, Surein said.

Like a latrine, Arun's mother echoed.

That was why he'd been appointed minister of procurement and supply. A nothing job. He would spend his days ordering toilet paper for the government.

But Arun knew the man. It was only a beginning. Mahadeo would know how to manoeuvre himself over time into more influential portfolios. His buffoonish style was his greatest weapon. People found him amusing and so underestimated him. It explained how a simple high school teacher had come to exercise power.

THREE

SHE HAD SAID she would come when she had some spare time. When he said, "You spend most of your day doing crossword puzzles and dreaming up new cocktails, spare time is all you have," she had frowned at him in displeasure before turning away and making a show of dusting the shop. He'd stood there for perhaps a minute watching her flick a cloth at the freezer top, at the walls, at the low stool in the corner. Amused, he'd said, "And all that dusting, of course. I'd forgotten about that." But she paid him no attention and it dawned on him that his teasing truly had offended her. "Look, Anjani, I'm sorry, I was just ..." Wiping down the sides of the freezer, she began humming. He turned to go. "Anyway, if you can, he could really use some help. I don't know what to do next."

And now here she was, two days later, striding into the school-house without a glance at him, eyes sweeping over the children working at their desks. She made directly for Saman. The boy was hunched over his slate, bravely copying out the list of simple words Arun had given to him mainly as a way of keeping him occupied.

Saman's frailty, it had become clear, went beyond the physical to a mind that reminded Arun of his vegetable garden, with its crumbly and infertile soil. Weeks of effort had yielded little reward. Saman could write his name but he had trouble getting through the alphabet. He sometimes managed to count to ten but was defeated by the numbers that followed. Arun had tried everything he could think of, inventing games, rhymes — *one pebble, two pebbles, three* — but by the following class Saman would have forgotten it all. Some of the other children — the eager Indira, Rai — had tried to help, to no avail. They began giggling at his inability, whispering to each other that he was too stupid to understand.

Anjani sat with Saman in a far corner of the room. She examined the word list with interest, nodded approval at his efforts on the slate, pointed to a mistake which Saman effaced with his thumb and then rewrote. She smiled, whispered encouragement, pointed to another mistake. Saman, Arun saw, was taken with her.

Occasionally, one of the other students would glance around at them, exchange whispers with a neighbour before Arun's eyes, rising from the book open on his desk, sent them back to the additions he had written on the board.

Rai raised his right arm, Shanti's contraption secured to it. Arun sighed. Rai was always full of questions rarely connected to the work at hand.

"Yes, Rai?"

"Mr Arun, sir, Jai and me were wondering —"

"Not me, just you," Jai said, punching him in the shoulder with the stump of his wrist.

Fending him off, Rai said, "Is it true what they say about girls in the capital?"

Indira looked up, blinking her eyes. Roop, behind her, sucked more avidly at his thumb.

Arun leaned forward, elbow on the table, chin cupped in his palm. "What do they say about girls in the capital, Rai?"

He went shy. "You know."

"No, tell me."

"Well, they say that girls in the capital ..."

Beside him, Jai giggled, eyes falling to the desk to avoid Arun's. "Go on."

"They say ..." Rai's left hand rose to his lips as if to prevent the words from escaping.

"Well, if you can't tell me what they say, I can't tell you if it's true, can I?"

Rai shifted uneasily in his seat. "It's okay," he whispered.

"Fine, then. If you ever want to ask me, I'll answer. Until then, back to your work."

Some time later, Anjani rose from the desk, tousled Saman's hair, and, paying no attention to Arun, strode towards the door. Then she paused, turned back, and walked up to him. She leaned in close. "What they say is that girls in the capital are wanton sluts. If he ever asks again, you'll know what he's getting at. Remember, that's nothing compared to what your people say about *rikshas*. Now if you'll excuse me, I've got a crossword puzzle to do." She turned around and walked out.

When she returned three days later, Arun took her off to the side and apologised. "I didn't mean to imply you were lazy," he said. "It was just a bad joke, that's all."

She considered his words, biting at her lower lip, tossing in her palm the little bag of coins she had brought to teach arithmetic to Saman. "All right," she said, but her flat tone suggested that she had merely heard him.

"All right?"

"All right," she repeated, her tone no less neutral than the first time. Turning away from him, she said, "Saman's waiting for me."

She was there for about an hour, sitting with Saman in the corner, whispering to him as she laid out the coins one by one, removed them one by one. Once in a while, Arun would steal a glance at them: Saman's puzzlement evident on his tightened face, the growing tension in Anjani's jaw. And, despite his irritation with her, he couldn't help but admire the tenacity she brought to the enterprise, the way her neck undulated when she swallowed her exasperation, the way her hands moved as she swept up the coins to begin again.

Before leaving she gave the bag of coins to Saman. Arun stopped her on her way out. "Why are you giving him money?"

"It's homework," she said. "Chalk marks mean nothing to a boy like that. Money's real."

"He'll spend it."

"We'll see, won't we."

When Anjani returned after the weekend, she came up to him and, with a thin smile, said, "Your sense of humour is forgiven."

"And me?"

"You come with it, don't you?"

Arun derived only a little satisfaction when he turned out to have been right. At the Saturday market Saman had bought himself a cone of cotton candy.

Her lips pursed, Anjani took two sticks of chalk and snapped them into pieces. Arun watched from his table as she laid out the pieces one by one on the desk before Saman. Saw her cock her head into her palm in discouragement. Saw her remove the pieces one by one. Saw her rub her forehead, pinch the bridge of her nose, her throat palpitating as if forcing down a rock. Her palm tightened around the pieces of chalk. The index finger of her other hand stabbing the air in front of Saman's face, she spoke rapidly to him in what reached Arun's ears as an unsteady hiss.

Indira, Jai, and Rai glanced wide-eyed over their shoulders, chalk sticks held in suspension above their slates. Roop and Hari — the one caring only for his thumb, the other hermetic with images of his lost father — failed to react.

In the corner, Anjani sat up straight. With great deliberation, she dipped into her now open palm, extracted a piece of chalk and placed it on the desk. She whispered to Saman. Hesitant, he mumbled a response. She picked up the chalk and rapped it back down. Whispered again. Saman did not react. She rapped a second piece of chalk down beside the first. Another whisper. Saman appeared to be staring at the chalk with something resembling fear. She rapped down a third piece and this time there was no whisper. A fourth piece. A fifth.

As she reached for the sixth piece of chalk, Saman suddenly bared his teeth and, keening like an animal in pain, began pummelling the desk with his fists.

The other children started in fear, Rai and Jai half rising until Arun, hurrying from his table towards the corner, motioned them to remain still. "Saman," he said in as authoritative a voice as he could muster, "stop that now. Now, do you hear me?"

Abruptly the keening fell off, his fists pumping to a halt with the cadence of a slowing train.

Anjani, unperturbed, simply sat there and stared at Saman. When he had calmed down, his chest heaving, his fists between his legs, she put the handful of chalk bits on the desktop, stood, and stepped over to Arun. "The children are right, you know," she whispered. "He's stupid. Sometimes there's nothing you can do."

They were words Arun didn't want to hear. He had tried, as had she with the same results. But still — she was being hasty, impatient, surely there was something ...

"Just tell his parents there's no point, Arun. You're not God, you can't change nature."

For the rest of the day, Arun couldn't decide whether he admired the finality with which she had spoken or disliked the harshness with which she had judged. Still, he envied her the ability to know with such certainty what she believed.

THE EXPLOSIONS HAD been echoing down from the mountains for hours, a distant percussion rent occasionally by a sharp crack like a block of iron shattering. The noise — this peculiar, atonal music of what Seth referred to as *ordnance* — had awoken him like a rude hand joggling the scruff of his neck. He'd opened his eyes to a raging darkness, to thoughts of storm unleashed, a raucous deluge seared by lighting and flailed by thunder, only to be jolted again moments later when he grasped the true source of the commotion. Nature's ferocity bore no responsibility for its consequences. Some poor butterfly in Brazil flapped its wings and thousands of kilometres away and days later villages were flattened, plains flooded, lives lost. But man's ferocity was the consequence of will — an order given, an order obeyed. No order could stop the wind, but a whispered word could create a firestorm. He lay in bed grasping the terrifying thought to his chest, his heartbeat thudding into his tightened knuckles.

He awoke again to silence. No, not quite silence. Something had awoken him, something that had announced its presence then withdrawn. Something discreet that had remained in his memory like an echo.

The hands of his watch glowed close to his eyes. Five-thirty. Dawn. He listened, found it curious that no cocks were crowing, no dogs yapping; he understood that they, too, like the night insects, had been hushed by the clamour from the mountains.

Then — a rustle at his door. He sat up, the sheet falling away from his chest. He strapped on his leg. Another rustle, more extended this time, as if some wayward branch were nudging at his door. But that could not be, there were no trees close by.

At the sound of a rap — a definite rap now — he stepped out of bed and groped his way to the door. Outside, dawn had thinned the nocturnal darkness and it was in a grey and uncertain light that he saw Mr Jaisaram standing at his door. His hair was dishevelled and he was still in his pyjamas, a white undershirt tucked into striped cotton pants held up by a drawstring. "Mr Jaisaram? Is something wrong?"

Mr Jaisaram raised a hand and gestured for him to step outside.

"I'm not dressed," Arun said. He was wearing only his shorts. "Let me get a shirt." He felt for the light switch beside the door, flicked on the light.

"No!" Mr Jaisaram's hand flew up to the switch and plunged the house back into darkness.

"What's going on?"

"Hurry up."

Quickly Arun slipped on his shoe, pulled on a shirt. At the door, Mr Jaisaram grasped his arm and tugged him out into the steadily brightening morning.

"What is it?"

Mr Jaisaram's grip tightened painfully on his bicep. With his other arm, he pointed upwards, towards the sky, towards the nearest electricity pole. Something was hanging by a rope from the crossbar at the very top, its silhouette suggesting a slender, elongated duffel bag. Then Mr Jaisaram pointed at the next pole. There too something was hanging from the crossbar. Then, as the light reached the next pole and the one after that, Arun saw that something was hanging from each.

"What are they?" Hardly had the whisper left him than he had his answer. A ray of sunshine hit the object hanging from the nearest pole and he saw that it was a dog. On the next pole too and the one after that and on every pole that he could see: dogs hanging by the neck from tightened nooses.

From houses all along the street, people were emerging in their nightclothes, staring wordlessly up at the gruesome sight revealed by the dawn. Suddenly, farther along, a child screamed. The crowd began running, converging on a pole at the edge of the town square. Arun and Mr Jaisaram joined the rush, Arun limping beside the butcher. From a distance, they could see that the thing hanging from the pole was too big to be a dog.

They pushed their way through the crowd. Some men — Arun recognised the cricketers — had already placed a ladder against the pole and one of them was halfway up towards the man, whose neck had been squeezed tight by the noose and elongated by the weight of his own body. The cricketer, grasping a higher rung with his left hand and resting his chest on the ladder, leaned out towards the body as if to check for signs of life. Suddenly he recoiled, knees buckling. He flung his arms around the wobbling ladder. Voices shouted up words of caution. The crowd, fearing he would fall onto them, pulled back. At that moment the man hacked and choked and vomited into the crystalline light.

Mr Jaisaram took charge. He dispatched Kumarsingh to alert the army, then, with Arun's help, shooed people back to their homes. "Go, go," he said, gently nudging people away. "Nothing to do here. Go home, have breakfast."

Arun gave him a baleful look, shook his head: breakfast was perhaps not the timeliest of suggestions.

An hour later a dozen soldiers arrived in a truck. Six stood guard while six worked out the logistics of lowering the man's corpse. A soldier with a length of rope looped around his shoulder removed his helmet and, with great agility, scaled the ladder.

Arun, standing on the far side of the road with Mr Jaisaram, recognised Pande.

He swiftly knotted the rope around the man's waist and tossed the other end over the crossbar. When the soldiers on the ground had taken firm hold of the loose rope end, Pande severed the noose with his machete. The body doubled over, the face slapping onto the shins, the arms dangling towards the ground. Something snapped and Arun, with a sudden sick feeling, imagined that it was the man's spine.

Mr Jaisaram said in an angry whisper, "I slaughter animals with greater kindness."

The body was loaded into the truck, the soldiers scrambling in as it drove off. The dogs, which had held only an amused interest for them, were left where they were.

Arun said, "Is that all? I'd have expected questions or something."

"They're not policemen," Mr Jaisaram said. "They're used to finding bodies all over the place. But, never you mind, we'll be hearing from them when they're good and ready."

By mid-morning, the cricketers had cut down and buried all the dogs. Few of the strays had escaped and it was only around midday that two, suspicious-eyed and furtive, padded back into town in search of food. Mr Jaisaram took pity on them and, breaking his own rule, tossed them some scraps of meat from his shop.

Arun, perched on a stool just inside the door, said, "There was something familiar about that man. Did you recognise him?" No one had come to school that morning and after a fitful hour of waiting, he had locked the door and wandered over to the butcher's.

Mr Jaisaram shrugged. He was leaning against the freezer, his arms folded on his chest.

"It's the clothes. The white shirt, the khaki pants. I've seen him before here in Omeara. He was always pushing a bicycle. I've seen him leaving your shop."

"Maybe yes, maybe no."

"Surely you know your customers?"

"Not all. Maybe he came in once, maybe Anji served him, who knows?"

"Mr Jaisaram, I don't mean any disrespect but I think you're being ..."

He unfolded his arms, clapped his palms against his thighs.

"Well, if you must know," he said with slight exasperation, "he's called the Collector. Or was."

"What did he collect?"

He pursed his lips, rocked his head back and forth. "There are many words for what he collected. Some call it taxes, others ..." He shrugged again.

"He worked for the government?"

"No, not for the government."

Anjani, bent over a crossword puzzle at the counter, said, "What's an eight-letter word for tergiversator?"

"Mr Arun, some things it's better not to get too close to." He turned to Anjani. "Ter-what?"

"Tergiversator."

"Mr Schoolteacher?" he said.

Arun shook his head. "How can you concentrate on a cross-word puzzle at a time like this, Anjani?"

"You heard my father," she said without raising her head. "Some things it's better not to get too close to."

But he noticed that the pencil was trembling lightly in her hand.

Mr Jaisaram said, "Are you hungry, Mr Arun? Some lunch perhaps."

"No, I don't think I could keep anything down."

Mr Jaisaram sighed. "Me neither," he said.

That afternoon he tried weeding his garden but the heat soon defeated him. He took a long shower and, without drying off, sat in front of the fan. The relief was short-lived. He tried reading but found himself re-reading sentences in search of their meaning. The words had been emptied of sense, the letters of the alphabet elegant hieroglyphs drained of implication. In his mind, the corpse was lowered time and again from the top of the pole, corkscrewing slowly like the concluding act of some high-wire contortionist, folded in two. Over and over, the dogs cut loose fell from the sky into the canvas sheet held like a net by half the cricket team.

First the bus, now this. Arun had the sense that something was closing in on Omeara, closing in on him. Something. *Some thing*. The words, he realised with a shudder, had taken control of his day. This morning, he had seen *some thing* dangling from the top of the pole but he hadn't known precisely what. Then he had tried to distract himself — with gardening, with reading, with *some thing* — but had failed to find it. And now here it was again, *some thing*, bigger somehow, more present yet more nebulous, impossible to define. He could give it no shape, no weight. It had a sound, though it was yet inaudible, a sound that could be felt on the skin like the cryptic precursors of an approaching storm.

He stepped over to the radio his sister had sent for his birthday, the dust on its black plastic casing reminding him that he hadn't cleaned the place in weeks. It was a cheap, robust Japanese model but the location of Omeara — the mountains, the sea — made reception difficult. Sometimes a station from the mainland would drift weakly in over the water with snatches of music, advertising jingles, a word or two of chatter. Twice he got the beginning of the BBC World Service news, just enough to inspire longing.

He turned the dial, the radio spitting static, offering no promise until at the very end of the spectrum a well-modulated voice pushed back the crackling with news of a stunning rise in the country's Gross National Product. Most often, when the weather conditions permitted, he picked up the government station, its powerful transmitter broadcasting earnest announcements of bountiful harvests, burgeoning exports, great military victories, rising standards of living, lessening rates of poverty, rising rates of literacy. In these reports, the nation was enjoying a golden time, the rest of the world was sinking into an abyss of decadence. At home in the capital, Arun had been among those who treated the station with contempt. He and his school friends would tune into it sometimes for its comedic potential; they joked that its news director deserved the Nobel Prize for his imaginative fictions. It was considered so untrustworthy that even its weather forecasts were ignored. Here in Omeara, it had become his only choice. He played with the dial until the announcer's voice no longer wavered.

He learned that the UN General Assembly had sat enthralled as the prime minister delivered an address castigating the rich for ignoring the poor, that national rice production had attained record levels, that the national cricket team had performed valiantly against the Indians and the Pakistanis in the regional champion-ship, that the national football team would be a strong contender at the next World Cup, and that the national push-up champion was a candidate for the *Guinness Book of World Records*.

Anjani said, "What were you up to? When you opened your door, I almost changed my mind about inviting you over. You weren't brooding about this morning, were you? It'll get you nowhere."

The lights were on in the Jaisarams' living room but shadows still congregated around them. The carvings and photos were vaguely unsettling splotches on the walls.

"No, not about this morning." Arun accepted the cocktail she'd made for him — a Peter Pan, a simple but heady concoction of orange juice, dry vermouth, and gin. "That's the last thing I wanted to dwell on. I was thinking about my days at school."

Mr Jaisaram sipped at his Thunderclap. "Nostalgia's an old man's pastime," he said. "You're too young."

"I don't feel as young as I did when I got on the train to come to Omeara," he said. "I feel I've aged a great deal in a short time."

"That's not good." Mr Jaisaram took another sip and raised an inquisitive eyebrow at Anjani. "The whisky and brandy are there, but perhaps you went a little light on the gin?"

Anjani looked sharply at the glass in her father's hand. "Oh my god, I forgot the gin."

"You forgot the gin?" Mr Jaisaram said, astonished. "But you never forget anything."

Anjani leapt to her feet and pulled the glass from his hand. She ran to the kitchen as if to hide some terrible secret.

Mr Jaisaram leaned in closer to Arun. "Who can blame her? It's the day. She likes to pretend none of this bothers her but, between you and me, it disturbs her terribly. How can it not? She is young, she is making her life here. This morning — I think for Anjani it was like looking at the future."

"And what about for you, Mr Jaisaram?"

He shrugged. "It's the way things are." He lowered his voice. "Tell me, last night, did you hear nothing?"

"Not a thing."

"Me neither. And you know, I have asked many people. No one heard anything. Not a bark, not a rattle. Is that not strange? Whoever did this had to capture a dozen dogs, throttle them, string them up, all of that in total silence. How is that possible? People are saying it's a sign of the magic, the powers that the —"

"Stop it," Anjani said, returning from the kitchen with her father's drink. "All this talk about magic powers is for fools."

Mr Jaisaram took his drink in both hands. "Please, Anji, they are good people."

"Good people can be fools too," she said.

"It's just that they don't know how —"

She braced her hands on her hips. "You think it's magic too, don't you?" She turned to Arun. "You see, even my father. And how about you, do you think it's magic?"

"I think it's a mystery," Arun said.

"Magic. Mystery. What's the difference? Crossword puzzles are harder. Whoever did that last night only had one problem — to prevent the dogs from barking. Schoolboys could do the rest."

"That's just it," Mr Jaisaram said, taking a sip of his drink and nodding his approval.

"When you fed those surviving dogs this morning," she said, "did they bark and make a fuss?"

"No, there was enough meat for each of them. They just picked up the pieces in their mouths and —"

"Right," Anjani said. "That's why you have to be careful when someone gives you a gift. An electric generator, a new school-house, Kumarsingh's contract to drive Arun here to the camp, free meat. Any one of them could turn out to be poisoned in one way or another."

Arun said, "Mystery solved." He took another sip of his Peter Pan. "Are you saying the army did this?"

"I'm just saying gifts can be dangerous, that's all."

Mr Jaisaram, voice tightened, said, "There's no harm in the generator. They were doing themselves a favour. They like fresh meat."

"Of course. But not everybody might see it that way."

"What? I should give it back?"

"Don't be silly. But don't be naive either."

Mr Jaisaram guffawed. "Look at this!" he said, appealing to Arun. "This young girl telling her father not to be naive! Oh, the wisdom of her years!"

"You know what I mean, papa."

"I know what you mean, Anji, but we must live, no?"

"Yes," she said. "It's just that sometimes it's hard to know how to do that."

Arun started in recognition. Classes had become sporadic in recent weeks, attendance meagre and unpredictable. He had wondered — but had refused to entertain the thought — what good he was managing to achieve when, increasingly, his role was simply that of an army teacher. His desire had been to teach the children, to help them make the best of their meagre chances, but if the children would not be taught, where did his duty lie? Was he to wait around, hoping that one morning he would enter a schoolhouse full of curious eyes? Or was he to pack his suitcase? He had not yet allowed himself to pursue the thought but had been unable to prevent an image forming in his mind of a train heading north.

Mr Jaisaram smiled. "Ahh, Anji, I know just the thing."

Anjani sighed. "No, not this evening. I'm not in the mood."

"Please, Anji. It will help us all." He turned to Arun. "What do you say? Anji could read to us."

Anjani said, "Really, papa, I —"

"It's a wonderful idea," Arun said. Perhaps some simple fantasy of faraway lands would help keep the shadows of the spinning corpse and the hanging dogs where he had consigned them, just out of reach.

She let her shoulders droop, turned an exaggerated glare of disapproval on him, as if he had let her down. Then she turned and stalked from the living room, shadows seeming to flow in her wake. When she returned a moment later, she was holding a book and it seemed to Arun that the shadows that had left with her had not come back.

"Sir Richard's heart pounded in his chest as he tiptoed down the cold stone corridor of the chateau ..."

From the kitchen, like background accompaniment to Anjani's soft voice, came the sizzle of hot oil and the scents of frying dough. All this time, Mrs Jaisaram had been there, kneading and slicing and dicing, her silence stifling the sounds of her labour.

"Suddenly someone jumped him from behind! Coldhart! A forearm locked around his neck ..."

A pot clattered in the kitchen. Something metallic, a spoon perhaps, rattled into the sink. Mr Jaisaram glanced quickly over his shoulder.

It's the day, Arun thought. *Even the unflappable Mrs Jaisaram ...*

Anjani, undeterred, continued reading. "... last ounce of strength, Sir Richard grasped at the forearm ..." She licked her fingertip and turned the page, a smooth elegant gesture that caused Arun's eyes to remain fastened to her hand: the slender fingers splayed on the paper, the gentle rise of her knuckles, the back of the hand lightly scored by the fan of fine bones that lay just below the skin.

"Sir Richard dropped the dagger and ripped away the mask. It was true! Here, swooning in his arms, was Rosalinda, his one true love!"

A smile came to Mr Jaisaram. Arun drowned a laugh with a gulp of his Peter Pan. Her lips and chin trembling lightly, Anjani said, "End of chapter."

Mr Jaisaram reached out and rested his palm on her forearm. "One more, Anji?"

"Not tonight. Dinner should be ready soon."

As if on cue, Mrs Jaisaram emerged from the kitchen, her hair wrapped in a green bandana, but instead of motioning them to the dining room, she raised a finger to her lips.

Anjani, frowning in puzzlement, said, "Mama?"

Mr Jaisaram turned around, "What's wrong?"

Mrs Jaisaram batted the finger against her chin, then jabbed it towards the ceiling, her urgency unleashing a silence so intense Arun thought for a long moment that he had gone deaf. Across from him, Mr Jaisaram searched the ceiling. Anjani, eyes unfocussed, cocked her ear this way and that, an antenna searching for a frequency.

They all heard it at the same time, a muffled, rhythmic thumping, still far off but approaching quickly.

Mr Jaisaram's eyes ceased their meandering. Anjani's head locked in the attitude of an alerted animal. Arun, body tensed, half rose from his chair.

Mr Jaisaram said, "I told you we'd be ..."

He mouthed the rest of the words but they went unheard, effaced by the helicopter already roaring above the house.

He was engulfed in a brilliant cacophony.

Through the chatter and thump of the hovering helicopters — two of them, he thought, although he could not be certain as there were spotlights blaring down with a bracing white light — angry men screamed orders, voices duelling to repeat the same warning: *Stay down! Don't move! Keep your hands where they are! Stay down don't move keep your hands where they are. Staydowdon'mokeep yourhandsstay ...*

The wind from the helicopter blades drummed at his back. He worked his tongue around his teeth, spat. It made little difference. His mouth remained gritty with sand. If only he could probe with a finger, but that was not permitted, his fingers had to remain interlaced on the back of his head, pressing his cheek into the ground. He had managed to blink away the grains from his eyes, although they still stung.

Stay down! Don't move! Keep your hands where they are! Stay down don't move keep your hands where they are. Staydowdon'mokeepyour handsstay ...

Mr Jaisaram lay beside him — they'd been shoved to the ground together, hands wrenched into position — but he had no idea where Mrs Jaisaram and Anjani were. Soldiers had burst into the house, screaming at the women to fall back and bundling him and Mr Jaisaram outside at gunpoint. The street was filled with a harsh light and, as he fell hard onto his chest, he'd seen a blur of army vehicles, soldiers with weapons at the ready, neighbours lying face down on the ground, others being wrenched out of their homes. Then the sand had rushed into his eyes and mouth and the noises had filled his head: the thumping of rotor blades, the *staydowdon'mokeepyourhandsstaydow don'mokeepyourhandsstay ...*

A hand touched his elbow. A voice said, "Get up, come with me."

Slowly Arun got to his feet. Through gritty eyes, he saw what struck him as an underwater tableau, a school of fish caught immobile in a diffused white light, fishermen arrayed around them poised to pounce.

Shouting above the thump of the rotor blades, Corporal Ramlakhan said, "Captain Jamadar sent me to look for you. Are you all right, sor?"

Arun nodded vaguely. "What's going on?"

"Please come with me, sor." The corporal took him by the arm, not ungently, and led him along a winding path past the townsmen lying like beached sea creatures in rigor mortis on the sand. As they made their way past the prone bodies, Arun was glad no eyes dared rise from the ground to follow their passage. He felt exposed, vulnerable. And he felt, through his receding fear, the stirrings of shame.

At their approach, Seth removed his helmet and placed it, upturned, on the hood of the jeep parked outside Madhu's shop. He shrugged the strap of his weapon higher onto his shoulder. Soldiers with guns held high meandered among the military vehicles parked in neat rows along the edges of the square. A few men were clustered on the other side of the jeep talking in urgent whispers. Somewhere a radio crackled and an electric voice blurted something incomprehensible.

Seth said, "Sorry about that. I thought you'd be home. The troops had orders not to touch you."

"I was at Jaisaram's. We were about to have dinner." The air smelled of warm tar and exhaust fumes.

Seth batted dust from the front of Arun's shirt. "No harm done, right?"

Arun seized his wrist, pushed his hand away. "What the fuck is this all about, Seth? What d'you people think you're doing?"

"We got a tip. The Boys are planning something. There's a chance we'll find the bomb maker tonight. It was too good a chance to pass up."

"After this morning? You storm in here and treat people like that?" He stuck his thumb over his shoulder, glancing back from where he had come: the road lit by the helicopter searchlights, the townsmen prone and motionless. Two-man teams of soldiers were now walking among them, ripping them from the ground, searching them. Arun jerked his head around when he saw Mr Jaisaram being led away by one of the teams.

Seth grabbed his arm. "Stop, Arun. Everybody'll be searched and then their houses too. One by one. It's going to take a while."

"What have you done with the women?"

"They're in their homes, under guard. It's better to separate the men from the women. The uncertainty keeps everyone docile."

"Are they being searched too?"

"I'm afraid so. Can't be helped."

"Not by your men!"

"They're professionals. If they do anything ... well, you know what I mean. The general is unforgiving. Things like that fire up his religious zeal. Any trooper whose hand wanders where it shouldn't is likely to lose it. They know that."

"Literally?"

"Literally."

"My god, Seth."

"They're a disciplined bunch, Arun. Nothing to worry about."

"This won't win you any friends."

"And this morning? Who won friends with that? Sometimes fists have to take precedence over hearts and minds. Did you see what they did to that guy? Not that it breaks my heart."

"I didn't exactly go in for a close-up look."

"Well, just so that you know," Seth said in a hard whisper, "they gave him exquisite treatment. His ankles were chafed and skinless, which meant they'd hung him upside down before tracing patterns on his skin with a red hot iron. That's traditional. Then they thrust sewing needles clean through each of his fingernails, one by one and probably slowly. Imported, that one. A refinement. Then they finished him off by pounding a railway stake through his heart. Around here, that's an innovation. They strung him up so everyone would get the message: This is what we do to dogs."

Arun shuddered. "Who was he?"

"A bagman for the insurgents. His job was to go from town to town collecting dues from the merchants, protection money. It all went into their coffers. Your friend Kumarsingh lost his nightclub when he balked at paying."

"Why didn't you arrest him?"

"We hoped we could follow his trail, catch some bigger fish. But he was too good. We never got anywhere. So finally the general decided it was time to get rid of him."

"*You* did that to him?"

"No, no, it was his own people. But we helped."

"What do you mean you helped?"

"We picked him up, held him for a week, locked him in a room, fed him well. Then we sent him off. Never touched a hair on his head. We put out the word that he'd sung like a bird. All we had to do after that was sit back and wait. This morning we got the results, slightly more dramatically than we'd expected."

Arun shuddered again. "Why are you telling me all this, Seth?"

"You asked. And, frankly, because a little knowledge is a dangerous thing. You know that. By the way, we won't be searching your house."

"You son of a bitch."

Seth looked away. "I know you're upset, Arun, but it's for your own good. Just do your job and don't forget why you're here."

"My job is to teach the children and only the children."

"Don't be stupid."

One of the men on the other side of the jeep looked over at them. "Captain Jamadar?" he called.

"See you at the camp next week," Seth said. He picked up his helmet, unshouldered his weapon and walked around the jeep to join the group.

Arun turned to face the street still littered with prone men, with men being frisked, men being led off to their homes.

Staydowdon'mokeepyourhandsstaydowdon'mokeepyourhands stay …

Beyond the thump of the rotor blades and the hysteria of the chant, he discovered a terrible silence. Where was he to go?

FOUR

THE SEA WAS calm, the breeze light and salty, the horizon hazy
with afternoon cloud which, as evening approached, would grow
and thicken, covering half the sky. Early that morning, a soldier
had delivered to him a typed note from Seth. Classes at the camp
were suspended until further notice. Beneath his official signature,
Seth had added in a hasty hand that two of his students, including
Private Mukherjee, he of the modest ambitions, had been killed,
confirming in this way the rumours that had been going around
town of a battle in the mountains.

Anjani spread the fingers of her left hand. "They say there were
big needles stuck through all of his fingernails."

"Needles?" Arun remembered only at the last moment to add a
question mark to the word.

"And there was a big nail through his heart." She picked up a loose pebble and flung it from the rock pile into the water. "That's what Ashok said."

Ashok was the captain of the cricket team, the man who had climbed the ladder and nearly showered the crowd with his vomit.

Arun reached down and brushed wet sand from his shoes. "I don't understand. The needles, the nail."

The clouds would disappear overnight but return the following afternoon, harbingers of the rains that were soon to come. It had been like this for almost two weeks now, the townspeople questioning the darkening sky, interpreting its shades of grey like soothsayers trolling for omens.

"Today is in your hands. Tomorrow is in your heart. Sound familiar?"

"You're joking."

"You see another explanation? The Boys have a sense of humour."

"Oh, they're a riot all right. Laughing all the way to the crema-tion ground." They hadn't talked since the army raid. Arun had avoided talking about that night with anyone. A little knowledge made him uncomfortable, but pretending ignorance had grown easier. It allowed him to ask the question that had been gnawing at him. "Did they search you?"

"Yes."

"How did they ..." He didn't know how to put the question. "I mean, were they ..."

"They didn't touch me."

Arun took a deep breath. The air was thick, humid. It was like breathing in steam. "I don't understand."

"They never laid a hand on me. That's what you're wondering, isn't it?"

"But how did they search you?"

"Only with their eyes."

"So they just looked you over." He was relieved.

"Yes. But they made me strip first." The words seemed to be strangling her. "Completely." She rubbed her chin on her shoulder. "I could see their erections. I might almost have preferred their hands, that patting down they gave the men."

"And your mother — did they make her ...?"

"No, just me. But they made her watch. And they made sure she saw everything."

Arun thought: Seth didn't say anything about gouging out their eyes.

Anjani shrugged, the sway of her shoulders suggesting a nudging away of memory. She said, "Sometimes it feels as if time has stopped here in Omeara. Like there's no morning or evening, it's always afternoon. You know what I mean?"

Arun thought of afternoons in Omeara: heat and humidity, drowsiness. The languid approach of stasis.

"There's no beginning," she said. "There's no end. Just a kind of endless middle."

After a moment he said, "Everything comes to an end eventually." History had taught him that: that every idea, every monument, was doomed to dust one day. This, in the end, was what Mahadeo had failed to understand, what had rendered futile so much of his passion. The difficulty was to find value in the transitory, to recognise a duty that was worthwhile anyway.

Anjani gave a sharp, dry laugh. "Maybe you find that comforting. We can't afford to."

"It's just that you can't let the past strangle you. You have to learn to master it." He thought of Mangal Pande, of Mahadeo, and he saw them as caught in a vortex they couldn't escape.

Anjani laughed again. "The past is all we have, don't you understand that? You've seen our present —"

"Whose fault is that? The kinds of things the Boys do — it's really what boys do. Useless destruction. Mindless. It's like setting a cat's tail on fire."

Anjani turned so sharply towards him her neck crackled. "You think so? Then you haven't been here long enough. What's our future, Arun? Tell me! Think about that, because it's all you need understand the Boys."

"Are you defending them?"

"I'm not defending anybody. But I'm tired of living in a country that pretends we hardly exist. If you hardly exist, you hardly matter, unless you make yourself matter in any way you can. If that means setting a cat's tail on fire, there are a lot of people with matches."

"That's dangerous talk."

"Are you going to tell your army friends?"

"I haven't got any army friends."

"It took my mother and me the best part of a day to clean up our house after they searched it. How long did it take you?"

"That's not my fault."

She stared at him for a long time. Finally, softening, she said, "Know what I think, Arun?"

"What?"

"I think you're one of us at heart." She leaned her head on his shoulder and slid her arm around his waist.

Arun wondered whether, somewhere out there on the vast expanse of sea, lost perhaps in the gathering clouds, powerful binoculars were trained on them, watching her hand caress his thigh, watching her lips climb his neck. Could they see her nose tracing his jaw line, her nostrils quiver as she drew breath? How would they read his lowering eyelids, the rearward sway of his head? Her hand slid up his spine, folded warm and moist around the back of his neck. He turned to meet her lips.

She slid the mattress off the thin metal frame and spread it on the floor. He hadn't cleaned the house in weeks. The smell of dust spread through the webby darkness. The door and windows were shut; she had said no to the light.

He stood at the door and watched the sheet billowing in her hands, watched her kneel as it fluttered down onto the mattress, her arms spreading like a swimmer's as she smoothed it into place: a shadow play of domesticity. Still on her knees, she crooked her left arm high on her back and drew down the zipper of her dress in a surreptitious rasp. She drew the dress up over her head and tossed it onto the metal frame. Her hands met in the middle of her back; then her arms reached out, one then the other luring the brassiere away from her chest. She eased herself onto the mattress, drew her legs in and wrapped her arms around them.

He could feel her watching him in the dark.

"Well?" she said. She had whispered but had somehow shaped the word with a rich fusion of uncertainty and enticement, query and challenge. It came to him with a clarity that seemed to enter his pores. He stepped over to the mattress and sat beside her.

She released her legs and pressed herself to him, one hand on his lower back, the other above his heart. Her hair smelled of the sun. Her lips sought out his, offered the light saltiness of the sea. A rattle rose in her throat, her eyelids flickered. She grasped the back of his head and fit her lips firmly to his. When he felt her tongue, an overwhelming wish rose within him: to savour her body, to feel her bones tremble and her skin sweat, to hear a clamorous pleasure rising raucous from her throat.

She unbuttoned his shirt, tugged it off, her palm drawing like a feather across his chest. She seemed to be whispering, not words, but sounds like those of a light breeze through leaves. She pressed him onto his back and he felt himself soothed. Her hand swirled over his ribs, over his belly, sharpening his yearning. He was full of desire. Still, he was startled — was that the word? — when she undid his pants and slid her hand under the waistband of his shorts. He couldn't suppress a gasp when her fingers found his hardness.

Suddenly, in a voice tinged with surprise, she said, "It's your first time, isn't it."

He swallowed, nodded against her breast.

Gently she began easing his pants down his hips, but when the waistband reached the tight strap around his thigh, he seized her hand. "My leg," he said. "Don't ..."

Her fingers traced the strap through the thick fabric, found the metal band, slid farther down his thigh to where it was without feeling. "It's all right, Arun," she said.

"I don't want you to ..."

She paid no attention to him and he closed his eyes as she withdrew the pants. Then she removed his shorts. He felt himself diminish.

The first time: he had often wondered what it would be like, had always imagined himself remaining clothed from the waist down. The prosthesis was as much part of him as his real leg, but the picture that came to him of him naked with a woman, the prosthesis revealed, seemed ludicrous. There had been opportunities — with the daughter of one of his mother's friends, with a young maid at home who had taken to playing secret afternoon games with him and would have gone further had he not panicked at the thought of removing his pants. Once he had thought of a single pant leg, elasticised at the top, which he would wear at such moments, but that too seemed ludicrous. Younger, he had despaired until he learnt to put it out of his mind. Now, that despair, that sense of the ridiculous, returned.

Anjani leaned over him, brushed his lips lightly with hers as she threw a leg over his thighs, straddling him. Her hair ticked his forehead, his eyelids, slid liquid along his cheeks. Her hands travelled slowly down his arms, raised them, stretched them out behind his head. Then she lowered herself, hands travelling now up along the inside of his arms, soft breast offering a stiffened nipple to his mouth. As her hands approached his wrists, his flesh prickled, first on his arms and then elsewhere. And when their palms met, her fingers bonding with his as if drawn by a plush electricity, all notion of time and place and fear fell away, his body, tautened, febrile, surrendering to what felt like a fitting inevitability.

When she drew her hips back, her fingers tightening on his, her breath falling warm and moist on his neck, he was neither eager nor anxious. He was simply ready.

He didn't know whether his eyes were open or shut. He was hovering weightless in a place beyond gravity, a place unlit and unbordered, with no shape, no colour, where words were without meaning and logic pointless. He didn't know how long it was before thought returned.

Anjani lay on top of him, her face buried in his shoulder.

He raised a hand, placed it on her sweaty back, and her body twitched, as if brushed by electricity.

"No," she whispered into his ear. "Don't touch me. Not yet."

The rush of anguish that came to him was disarmed only by the word *yet.*

As he lay still beneath her, he remembered how, sitting on him, she had stirred the darkness with the rhythmic spasm of her hips, one hand pressed to his ribcage for balance, the other between her legs at the spot where they were joined in a tight, wet embrace. His fingers had reached up to clasp her face, tracing the contours of her cheeks and her nose. He was startled by the palpitation at her temples. Her breath had begun to grow shorter and deeper, her movements more emphatic, his own arousal beginning to escape him as she seemed to draw him deeper and deeper into her, pushing him towards the edges of some vast and unavoidable chasm. His body tightened, as if his skin were contracting, every muscle, every organ inside beginning to tingle and roil. Anjani's head fell backwards and a low keening arose from her throat, a keening that seemed to reach into the recesses of his brain, turning him inside out, slipping him away from his body. And then, that tumble into the chasm, that incoherence.

But there was more than that. There was something else ... a sensation that had marked itself out in the maelstrom. It was as if the prosthesis had somehow acquired flesh and sinew and nerves, as if it had participated fully in the surge of raw feeling. He had for the briefest moment felt *whole*.

Anjani stirred, rolled off him onto the mattress, drew the back of her hand across her forehead, as if to wipe away sweat.

Arun took a big breath of the stuffy air, rolled onto his side. As he slid his arm across her belly, she pushed it away and rose to her feet. She stepped into her panties, ran her arms through the straps of the brassiere.

He said, "You'll come back?"

She reached for her dress, draped herself soundlessly in it.

"Anjani?"

She was already at the door when he said her name. She paused, hand on the doorknob. "Look, Arun, don't make more of this —"

"What is it? Do you regret —"

"Not for a moment." Her hand fell away from the doorknob. "But —"

He sat up. "But this isn't the start of anything more serious."

"Exactly. You understand, don't you?"

"I thought you liked me."

"I do."

"So why ..." He clasped his shin in his hand. "I feel good when I'm with you."

"Isn't that enough?"

"I guess it'll have to be."

"Don't go weird on me, Arun. Nothing says I have to be in love with the person I have sex with, I thought you understood that. Sex is like thirst. Love is like magic. You didn't believe me when I told you I'm not looking for marriage or children or any of that."

She was right. Part of him hadn't believed her. "What are you looking for?"

"Why do I have to be looking for anything? I have needs. I like satisfying them."

"But everybody wants —"

"Stop it. Who are you to talk for everybody? I don't want to hear those stupid ideas anymore. Find a man, cook his food, wash his clothes, produce his children. I grew up with them and you know what? I don't see any difference between those foolish dreams and my father's ridiculous novels. I wanted to go to school in the capital to get away from all that, and all it got me was back here."

"Yes, and so you'll live your life that way? Making cocktails and doing crossword puzzles and reading to your father?"

"You talk as if you know everything about my life, Arun." She snuffled dismissively. "How long have you been in Omeara? You think you know everything that goes on here?" She snuffled again. Then, quickly, she opened the door and slipped out through the sliver of afternoon sunshine.

Arun sat on his mattress for a long time in confusion. He could smell her still in a faint suggestion of coconut oil, could detect her warmth on his skin. But he was troubled, in part by the sudden extinction of an equally sudden discovery, in part by all that she had said. How could she not want what it was normal to want? What could she be dreaming of that she would not share with him? But most of all, he was bothered by her reminder, her assertion, that there were parts of her life that remained unknown to him. She was right, and the thought left him uneasy. It was the kind of thing Seth would want to know.

Finally he rose, dressed, went out back to wash. The day was almost gone. When he closed the door on the shower stall, he had to feel for the tap in darkness.

FIVE

THE RAIN, WHEN it came, arrived without preamble. It came with violence, with what sounded like the crash of metal pellets on the galvanized iron sheets above his head. The light bulb swayed, flickered, but held, light licking dully at the beach crystal that sat on a corner of the table. All around him, shadows came alive, lurching from one side to the other as if the house were being tossed around on a raging sea. For a moment he felt queasy, light-headed, and had to steady himself by laying his palms on the table beside the small stack of essays he'd been marking. On the paper, the shadow of his head swung from left to right and back again.

On his way home from school earlier in the afternoon, he'd stopped at the butcher's to buy himself a piece of meat. Anjani was leaning on the freezer absorbed in a crossword puzzle. She looked up when he entered, put down her pencil, and, leaning on her elbows, cupped her chin in her palms. She appeared amused to see him. "You've been avoiding me," she said. "Not an easy thing to do in a town this size."

"I've been busy."

"Nobody's that busy in Omeara. It's been over two weeks. Do you make sure the coast is clear before you leave home in the morning?"

"Don't be silly." But his face grew warm. "I've had a lot of marking to do. And I'm trying to get through some reading."

"If you say so." She straightened up. "Is this a social visit?"

"I thought I might get some meat for dinner. Goat perhaps, or some chicken."

She folded her arms. "Being ambitious, aren't we? I'd have thought that a few cans from Madhu's would be about all you could handle in the kitchen."

"My sister's sent me some recipes."

"That's like a heart surgeon sending me a how-to manual. I still wouldn't know how to do it."

"Cooking couldn't be that hard."

She shrugged. "You're the one who'll have to eat it."

Just then the back door opened and Mr Jaisaram stepped into the shop. "Ah," he said. "I thought I heard your voice. You've been as scarce as firewood in the desert! I see you go to school, I see you come home, but I don't see you. Too much work?" A few chicken feathers were caught in his hair. Hands on his hips, he scrutinised Arun. "You've lost weight, and you didn't have much to begin with. Are you unwell?"

Anjani said, "He's been doing his own cooking."

"That explains it."

He hadn't in fact done any cooking but had — how did she know? — been alternating between cans from Madhu's meagre stock. A mushy spaghetti one day, a mushy vegetable stew another day, a chicken soup that tasted as if some scrawny animal had been drowned in a vat of salt. Desperation had driven him to the recipes his sister had included in a chatty letter that went on at length about all the weight Surein had put on recently.

Mr Jaisaram looked shyly at him. "Look, Mr Arun, everybody knows about the army search. So they didn't touch your house — is that your fault? Yes, some people find it suspicious, but not everybody." He paused, smiled, but his eyes were unsure. "It's no reason to starve yourself. Come to dinner this evening. Kumarsingh will be there. Anjani will make her new cocktail, something to do with pineapples."

It seemed to Arun that this was why he'd been avoiding the Jaisarams. The consideration the army had shown him, his shame at that consideration. Nothing to do with Anjani. He glanced at her.

With challenge in her eyes she said, "Pineapple and coconut and a few other things, too."

Relieved that he would be spared the ordeal of deciphering his sister's recipes, and pleased at the thought of being close to Anjani again, he accepted.

"See you later," Mr Jaisaram said. "I must return to my chickens, I still have four to pluck and the rains will be here soon."

"How soon?" Arun said.

"Hours. I can smell it."

Kumarsingh was already there, sitting in the living room with Mr Jaisaram, when he arrived. Each held a glass half filled with a milky liquid. A third glass, full, sat on the round table between them. Mr Jaisaram gestured at it. "Yours," he said. "Anji's not happy with you. You're late. It's getting watery."

Arun sat, nodded at Kumarsingh, sipped from his glass. From behind the pineapple and coconut flavours, the pungent blend of alcohols brought tears to his eyes. Flecks of fruit slipped between his teeth, tickled the back of his throat. He coughed. "Quite the drink," he said. "What's it called?"

Mr Jaisaram said, "It's her own invention. She hasn't found a name for it yet."

Kumarsingh said, "I think she should call it Tropical Lava, don't you?"

Mr Jaisaram said, "Lava's hot. This drink is cold."

"It's a good name," Kumarsingh insisted. "The marketing would be easy. Posters showing bottles of Tropical Lava exploding from a volcano or —"

"Marketing?" Mr Jaisaram said. "What's this about marketing?"

Arun laughed. "I think it's the birth of a new arm of Kumarsingh Enterprises International Ink."

Kumarsingh said, "We would split the profits fifty-fifty, export to the continent, then America and Europe. Imagine the possibilities."

"Kumarsingh, you're a dreamer," Mr Jaisaram said.

"Big ideas always start small, Jai. Like a big tree that grows from a small mango seed."

"I am not criticising, Kumarsingh. It is a good thing. I admire your fortitude. First the night club, then the bus. But you carry on."

Anjani, drying a plate with a kitchen towel, stepped into the living room. Arun had glimpsed her shuttling back and forth between the kitchen and the dining room. "Here at last," she said. "What do you think of the drink?"

Arun raised the glass. "Tropical Lava is delicious," he said.

"Tropical Lava? What a stupid name."

Kumarsingh's lips seemed to collapse into his mouth.

Mr Jaisaram laughed. "Back to the drawing board, my friend. There'll be no bottles spouting from volcanoes."

"In any case," said Arun, "it seems to me like a rather infelicitous image, considering."

Kumarsingh said, "But Miss Anjani, this drink of yours, it is full of commercial possibility. Do you have a name in mind, may I ask?"

"A few," she said, turning back to the dining room.

Kumarsingh leapt to his feet. "May I know them?" He hurried after her.

Mr Jaisaram leaned in to Arun. In a low voice he said, "He will make a fine son-in-law, don't you think?"

"Son-in-law?" Arun heard himself repeat the word and was aware of the white void following in its wake.

Mr Jaisaram took a gulp of the drink, tongued a fleck of coconut from his lower lip. "Perhaps. One day. He and Anji don't know anything yet, so shhh! But if they get to know each other better, who knows? It is a capital idea, no? Every father wants to see his girl-children happily settled. Kumarsingh is a good man, a hard worker, a thinker. Of course, when she gets married she will move to her husband's home and she will not be able to read to me as much, but it is a small price to pay for her happiness."

Arun got a hold of himself, clicked his glass on Mr Jaisaram's. "You're a good man, too, Mr Jaisaram, a dreamer, just like Kumarsingh."

Mr Jaisaram smiled proudly. "What is a man without dreams, Mr Arun? I thank you for the compliment."

But he hadn't meant it as a compliment, not inside. For he realised that, to Mr Jaisaram as well, parts of his daughter's life were unknown and this dream he had for her — a dream not so different, perhaps, from the dreams his parents had had for him, dreams born of their own idea of happiness — was destined to fail before her private imperatives.

From the dining room, Anjani called, "What are you two whispering about? Come, it's time to eat."

Arun looked up, beyond Mr Jaisaram's shoulder. Kumarsingh was already seated at the table, at the place where Arun usually sat. Anjani stood behind him. Mrs Jaisaram emerged briefly from the kitchen, handed her a dish heaped with steaming food. It was as if he were glimpsing a future that would never be.

At dinner, the talk was animated, Kumarsingh's natural volubility filling the silence that usually attended the Jaisarams' table. He had emerged from the loss of the bus with his enthusiasm undiminished. He talked about his plans for the travelling cinema. Tapes were being made by his contacts in America, the television and VCR were awaiting shipment from New Delhi. He was having a difficult time locating a portable generator to power them, though. He had a line on one in Colombo but the import duties were high — some government minister was starting up a factory for generators and wanted to protect his investment from foreign competition — and he would have to find a way to smuggle it into the country. He imagined an outdoor cinema during the dry months but would have to find indoor locations for the rainy season. Would Arun lend him the school? Arun nodded. And perhaps Mr Jaisaram would like to have "an exclusive" to sell snacks? And why not a stand where Anjani could dispense her cocktails?

The more he talked, the more he ate, as if the exhaling of words required the inhaling of food. Arun wasn't sure that anyone was really listening to him. Mr Jaisaram would nod from time to time. Anjani fed herself slowly, chewing behind pursed lips, her gaze lost somewhere in the middle of the table. Mrs Jaisaram concentrated as usual on her plate. The skin beneath her eyes was dark and her cheeks seemed swollen by fatigue. Weariness softened her, Arun thought, camouflaging the glower she habitually offered the world. He wondered what she was thinking as Kumarsingh prattled on, this woman whose life was even more camouflaged than her daughter's. He imagined she spent much time contemplating the face whose name she had banished.

Kumarsingh held up his emptied plate to accept another help-ing from Mrs Jaisaram. "So, Jai," he said, "what do you think? I offer an exclusive and a sixty-forty split. Same for Anjani."

Mr Jaisaram ripped off a piece of bread and swirled it in the oily curry sauce. "If I get your meaning, we split the profits."

"Yah, sixty for you, forty for me."

Holding the soaked bread before his lips, Mr Jaisaram said, "Explain to me why it should not be 100-nought. It would be my food, my work, my sales."

"But my cinema, Jai."

Mr Jaisaram contemplated this. "Eighty-twenty."

"Seventy-thirty."

Mr Jaisaram placed the bread on his tongue, chewed. "When you have your cinema, we will talk again."

"So is it a go?" Kumarsingh said in a surge of enthusiasm.

Mr Jaisaram, chewing with vigour, circled his open palm in the air, as if to indicate agreement in principle.

"And what about Miss Anjani?" Kumarsingh said, addressing her.

"My father can do what he wants," Anjani said, affecting boredom.

"Seventy-thirty for you, too."

Arun said, "That's better than the fifty-fifty he talked about earlier."

Anjani hardened her eyes at him. Beneath the table, a foot kicked at his prosthesis. She said, "My cocktails aren't for making money. They're for having fun. I like putting different things together to see how they work."

"But Miss Anjani —"

"That's all, Kumarsingh. I'm not interested in your scheme, thank you."

Kumarsingh's lips stirred but, warned off by her tone, he thought better of pursuing it.

"And what about our schoolteacher friend, here?" Mr Jaisaram jumped in. "Don't you have something he could do to make a little money?"

Arun was about to protest when he saw thought creasing Kumarsingh's forehead like an accordion.

"Maybe he could sell the tickets, yah?" Kumarsingh said. "But on a commission basis, say five percent."

Quickly, Arun said, "Fifty-fifty. Take it or leave it."

Kumarsingh, unfazed, caressed his chin. "If you can get the soldiers to buy tickets, I'll raise your commission to seven percent general, ten percent army."

"Fifty-fifty," Arun repeated.

Kumarsingh sighed. "Arun, you are a very good teacher, but I must tell you that you are a very bad businessman, very bad. This is not how you negotiate. You are talking yourself out of a lucrative sideline."

"Those are my terms," Arun said, reaching for his glass of water. Across the table Anjani offered him a smile so fleeting he'd have missed it had his eyes not been on her that very moment.

"Sorry, my friend," Kumarsingh said, "but it's out of the question." He paused briefly, the accordion returning to his forehead. "But of course, if you want to invest, to become a partner in the cinema, then we can consider another arrangement."

Arun shook his head and laughed. "Does your brain ever rest, Kumarsingh?"

"You know what I believe. A resting brain is a —" His face suddenly went sombre, his eyes fell to the table. "I mean ..."

Arun reached a hand out and clasped Kumarsingh's shoulder. "It's all right."

"It's not an easy word for me to say yet," Kumarsingh said.

Arun knew that they were all sharing the vision that had severed Kumarsingh's words: the carnage in the bus, the cadavers hanging from the posts. *A resting brain is a dead brain.* It would be a while before Kumarsingh would again be able to state his mantra.

Anjani, elbows on the table, chin resting on her interlaced fingers, stared blankly past Arun's shoulder. Then, following her mother's lead, she rose to clear the table.

Mr Jaisaram cleared his throat. "So, Kumarsingh, tell me more about this cinema idea. It is very original. Where did you get it from?"

"It is not so original," Kumarsingh said reluctantly. He began to speak, with growing animation, about a trip he'd made to Bombay some years before, of seeing a travelling cinema that had been set up on the outskirts of the city. "There used to be very many of them but they are almost gone now. I thought it would be a good idea for us here." Encouraged by Mr Jaisaram's new and too-vibrant interest, he launched into the evolution of the idea in his mind, from projector to VCR, from cinema screen to television screen, which led him to the wondrous possibilities of one technology after another.

Arun grew drowsy. Kumarsingh's voice — cellular phones, personal computers, car manufacturing plants, something about jet engines? — morphed into a low and increasingly distant drone punctuated by Mr Jaisaram's occasional grunt, beyond them the gush of water, the clink of plates.

Anjani came to the kitchen door, offered tea. Kumarsingh and Mr Jaisaram both accepted. Arun pushed back his chair and got to his feet. "Not for me thanks. I've got some marking to do."

Mr Jaisaram rose to accompany him out, but Anjani gently pushed him back into his seat. "It's okay, papa, I'll lock the door behind him."

Arun said goodnight, looking into the kitchen to thank Mrs Jaisaram. Intent on putting the dishes away, she paid him no attention. Anjani walked him to the door. As he stepped outside into the heavy darkness, she grasped at his shirt sleeve. "Don't go to sleep too early," she said.

"Why not?"

"I can come over later."

"Your parents?"

"I'll wait until they're asleep." She searched his face. "Don't you want me to?"

"I'll be waiting," he said.

He'd been waiting for almost two hours. Time for his marking, fitfully accomplished, to be long done. Time for the rain predicted by Mr Jaisaram to begin crashing down. Time for the agitation she'd aroused to subside into a vague dissatisfaction.

The drumming overhead had grown into a constant roar, the billions of raindrops acting in concert. A damp chill grew in the room. He fetched a T-shirt from his suitcase and pulled it on over his shirt. If Anjani could see him, he thought, she would laugh and make some derisive comment about his sense of style, but there was little chance of her coming now. He filled a saucepan with water and put it on the stove. He'd just picked up the box of matches when three thumps resounded on his door, followed quickly by three more. Astonished, the image of a soaked Anjani standing in the night banishing every other thought, he hurried over to the door and tugged it open. "It's pouring," he said. "I didn't think you'd —"

Then his breath left him. He took a step backwards, away from the door swinging fully open under its own weight, back into the unstable shadows, away from the doorway. He stepped backwards once more, bumping into the table, when Mr Jaisaram stumbled into the house, his hair plastered to his head, his skin showing through the white undershirt turned transparent by the rain. Forearms tightened around his belly, the hems of his pyjama pants hugging his muddy feet, Mr Jaisaram said between gasps, "They've taken her."

Dawn was glowing wan and thin, the sky hanging low like a rumple of oil-stained rags, when Arun left the Jaisarams to return to his house. The rain, ended only a few minutes before, had left the air close and steamy, a pungent stew of rotting vegetation and the fresh tang of snake. A thin curtain of water was falling from the roof of every house, the last of the rain running down the galvanised iron sheeting and landing hard on the softened surface of the road. With each step his shoes sank deep into mud, emerging with a fleshy sucking sound that put him in mind of leeches. By the time he got to his door, left wide open in the rush to Mr Jaisaram's house, the hems of his pants, too, were slathered in mud.

He stood for a minute inside the door, hands on his hips, trying to get his bearings. The light bulb, burning as dully as the dawn, now hung unmoving at the end of its cord, its light revealing that rain had blown in through the unbarred doorway and soaked the floor almost up to his table. Some of the essays lay on the floor, fingered from the table by the errant wind. He picked them up, replaced them on the stack, and recalled not for the first time Mr Jaisaram's observation about words and sentences blown from the page by Anjani's breath.

He looked around, feeling a little lost, sensing — at the sight of the rickety cot, the rusted stove, the fan now dusted in grime, the books piled in a corner, the cold bare cinderblock walls — that he had been camping here, that he had failed to compose even the vaguest reference of permanence. He saw himself, then, as others might have seen him: professing one thing, practising quite another. It had been easy, till now. Doggedly teaching whomever would come, forming undemanding friendships with people like Mr Jaisaram and Kumarsingh, even Seth, tasting with Anjani unexpected pleasures free from expectation or consequence. Now, all of a sudden, he felt like fleeing.

In the shame that buffeted him like waves of heat spreading from his belly to his chest, he began forcing himself to think coldly and logically. What first? A shower, perhaps, followed by a cup of tea. He would need a clear head in the hours to come. He knew he should eat, but putting food into his mouth, chewing, swallowing were, for the moment, beyond him. The tiniest piece of bread would stick in his throat. Besides, Kumarsingh would soon be here with the car. Despite Mr Jaisaram's pleas, he had wisely insisted on waiting for first light to drive to the army camp to report Anjani's abduction. To drive along that lonely road at night was perilous enough.

They had waited together in the living room through the long, slow hours, Mr Jaisaram clutching his face in his hands and rocking back and forth in his chair, a low moan escaping him once in a while, as if his body couldn't contain his anguish, Arun and Kumarsingh glancing helplessly at each other, then looking away as if unable to bear the shame of that helplessness. In the bedroom, two neighbours tended to Mrs Jaisaram, applying bay rum and coconut oil and cold compresses and, Arun imagined, whatever words of comfort they could find.

When the sky began to lighten, Mr Jaisaram announced that he would accompany them to the camp. He would go crazy, he declared, if he had to continue sitting there doing nothing. Arun, with Kumarsingh's help, attempted to dissuade him. It would be best, they argued, if Arun spoke to the army people alone. They knew him, they would listen to him, and because of who he was they would be confident they weren't being lured into an ambush. The matter was settled when the two neighbours emerged from the bedroom to announce that Mrs Jaisaram had finally fallen asleep and that they had to see to their own families but would be back later. Kumarsingh left with them, Arun a few minutes later, after having convinced Mr Jaisaram that he, too, should try to get some sleep.

In the chill damp of the morning, he couldn't face the thought of a shower. He went over to the stove and lit the burner under the pot of water he'd prepared the night before. Waiting for it to boil, he stripped off his clothes and, with a rag and water, washed the mud from his shoes at the kitchen sink. Then he removed his socks, his toes already wrinkled and greyish, the foot of his prosthesis gleaming pink again after a few swipes of the rag. The water boiled. Waiting for the tea to steep, drying his shoes with another rag, he ran over in his mind what he could report to Seth.

Not long after he'd left, Kumarsingh, too, with a little persuasion, had said goodnight. Mrs Jaisaram had gone to bed immediately but Mr Jaisaram, finding that the fatigue that had caused him to begin yawning had eased upon Kumarsingh's departure, prevailed upon Anjani to read to him. She hadn't wanted to and had read badly, without the usual melodiousness that caused the sentences to take wing. She seemed distracted, he'd said, her tongue pronouncing words her mind was not absorbing and when he'd remarked on this she'd snapped at him in irritation. He'd put it down to, as he put it, her "monthly." Halfway through the chapter she'd declared she was too tired to continue and promised to finish tomorrow. They turned off the lights and went to bed as the rains were beginning.

Sometime later, he wasn't sure how much later, he'd been awoken by a loud crash, thunder he'd assumed. But then he heard the tramp of footfalls, many of them — soft-soled shoes, not boots. He flung back the blanket when their bedroom door crashed open, flashlight beams, three, four perhaps, slicing through the darkness, blinding him. A kind of physical helplessness over-whelmed him: a rugged punch to his chest that jolted his heart, another to his belly that reached up inside him and seized hold of his windpipe pinching it tight, many hands rolling him over on the bed, a cloth bag being tugged down over his head, his ears hearing as if from far away the sounds of his wife scuffling, his wrists being quickly bound behind his back, his ankles being lashed together in the way he tied up goats before opening their veins. And then, all of a sudden, silence, the only sound that of his open mouth pulling hard at air through the thick cloth. He wasn't sure but he thought that, at one point, his heart began to race and he passed out.

Eventually his wife managed to work her hands free. She pulled the hood from her head, pulled the hood from his, and untied his hands. Then, lying head to foot, they unbound each other's ankles. On feet numb and prickly, Mr Jaisaram ran to Anjani's room, his wife following close behind. The door was open, the mattress askew on the bed, the sheet and blanket missing, as was Anjani. That was when, his lungs still braided together, Mr Jaisaram had launched himself into the rain to pound on Arun's door. Later, sitting with Arun and Kumarsingh in the living room, Mr Jaisaram had speculated that the men had wrapped her in the bedding and carted her away.

The tea had steeped for too long. At first taste, it was thick and bitter, and it wasn't scalding, the way he liked it. He drank quickly, felt the liquid moving down into him with the warm insistence of alcohol, soothing the tensions within, fortifying him. So that when, a few minutes later, Kumarsingh opened the door without knocking and said, "Ready?" he was. Arun snatched up the beach crystal from the corner of the table, slipped it into the pocket of his pants and followed him outside.

The going was slow, at times excruciatingly so as Kumarsingh nursed the car through sections of road liquefied into muddy pools. Arun sat in the passenger seat beside him, the fabric so worn he could feel the springs beneath him as the car lumbered into holes and over hidden rocks. He had never sat here before. Seth had been categorical. "Always sit in the back seat," he had said. "Let the men see you being chauffeured. You'll have an easier time with them that way. These are soldiers, remember. They respect authority." The way ahead was still dark, dawn's light too fragile yet to penetrate the canopy of trees. The weak headlights jostled with the captured night, offering through a veil of mist snatches of wet vegetation and darkened tree trunks washed by shadow. The narrow road, its rutted surface riddled with puddles of dark water, unrolled slowly before them.

Frequently the tires threatened to bog down and Kumarsingh would change gears, wrestling the mechanism from one to another in a pandemonium of screeching and grinding. The engine wheezed with the effort of pulling the car along ground that seemed to suck at it with the insistence of quicksand.

Arun said, "Where do you get the petrol for your car, Kumarsingh?"

"The same place Jaisaram gets his alcohol." Kumarsingh, his chin held high above the steering wheel, peered into the darkness. "The soldiers are very accommodating."

"You do a lot of business with them?"

Kumarsingh concentrated on steering the car. He appeared to be driving as much by feel as by sight. "I provide some services," he said. "Unofficial ones."

"What do you mean unofficial ones?"

He bit at his lower lip. "I provide services that the men need."

"Such as?"

"Listen to me carefully. Services that the men need but that the army cannot provide. The general is a religious man. There are some things that religious men do not admit to needing." He twisted the steering wheel, causing the car to lurch to the left, then he pulled it carefully back on course. "The general can get home any time he wants, to visit his wife when his needs become too great. The ordinary soldiers have no such luck."

"My god, Kumarsingh, are you saying you're a pimp?"

"I do not like the word, Arun. I am a facilitator. Sometimes a few men get a weekend pass, not enough time to go home, and there's nothing to do in Omeara. The idea for the nightclub came to me but, well, you know what happened. And then some customers asked if I could help them find some women, they had money, yah. I arranged a party with some girls from villages farther up the coast. It wasn't too hard. One thing led to another. It provides Kumarsingh Enterprises Ink with cash flow from time to time, but it is too irregular to make me rich."

Arun's stomach churned. He didn't know what to say.

"You are upset, Arun. I shouldn't have told you."

"I would have preferred not to know," Arun replied, glancing away through his window at the night. He thought of Anjani, out there somewhere, and a ripple of loneliness suddenly twisted its way through him.

"Business is business, Arun. When times are hard, you do what you must to survive."

"How far would you go, Kumarsingh?"

"You are saying I have gone too far."

"Only you can say that."

Kumarsingh grasped the stick shift, trundled it from second to third. "I hope I never have to answer that question, Arun."

They drove on in silence for a while, Kumarsingh manoeuvring the car with greater assuredness as the darkness began to thin, the jungle beyond the reach of the headlights now hinting at silhouettes, a darkness greater than that of the night. Up above, the leaves offered the occasional flash of grey sky. One of the head-lights winked out and the greater darkness surged back at them like a wave. Arun flinched. There was almost something physical to it, as if he had suddenly gone blind in one eye.

Kumarsingh said, "Shit!" and slammed a palm against the curve of the steering wheel. "That damned Madhu and his fucking Chinese light bulbs! Top quality, he said! Last forever, he said! I will make him eat that bulb. I want to hear glass crunching between his teeth!"

It was at that moment, in the heat of Kumarsingh's anger, that Arun's anxiety came rushing back at him, as if the darkness had breached his composure and was pumping into his veins, bringing with it all those useless questions, questions with no answers, which he had not dared entertain during the long wait for dawn at Mr Jaisaram's, shoving brutally at him the shard of an image he could not bear: Anjani's hair loose and flinging wildly about, her arms seized in some unknown fist, the ripping of nightclothes ...

Kumarsingh said, "What do you think they've done with her?"

Arun struggled with his voice. "I don't even know who they are, Kumarsingh. It's better not to speculate, I think."

The darkness suddenly gave way to grey sky and a dank, misty field. Up ahead, the lights of the camp glowed phosphorescent beyond the fence not yet visible and the watchtowers still drained to silhouette.

Kumarsingh sounded his horn twice. "To warn them we're coming," he said. "It would be stupid to get shot now, yah?"

Arun reached for the steaming mug of coffee the waiter had set before him. The general, forking a last piece of scrambled egg into his mouth, waved his knife towards the silver bowls of milk and sugar. Seth, hair still damp from his morning shower, cheeks freshly shaven, drew a napkin along his lips. "You're sure you won't eat something?" he said. At tables around them, each elegantly set with white tablecloths and silver cutlery, officers were having breakfast, some conversing quietly, others shuffling through papers or peering at maps.

Arun shook his head, took a sip of coffee rich with the flavours of roasted nuts. During the half-hour wait he and Kumarsingh had had to endure at the gate, a damp chill had filled the car, penetrating his clothes and causing his skin to go clammy. Kumarsingh, carefully averting his gaze from the pointed weapons of the guards, had muttered, "The army doesn't like unexpected visitors." At the sandbags, Corporal Ramlakhan, sheathed in a rain poncho, pressed a field telephone to his left ear and a flattened palm to his right. In his last letter home, he had sent news of his promotion and of the small increase in salary his wife was to expect. After several minutes, he'd hung up and come over to the car. "I'm sorry, sor," he'd said to Arun through the rolled-down window. "The captain is with the general. He cannot be disturbed. They will tell him you are here wanting to see him when he is finished, sor."

"It's an emergency, Corporal Ramlakhan. Did you tell them that?"

"Yes, sor. I'm sorry, sor."

"But they must —"

"The captain will be informed, sor. It is all I can do."

"Can we at least go wait for him somewhere?"

"Only the captain can give permission for you to enter the camp, sor. I'm sorry."

In a spurt of anger, Arun began rolling up the window. Corporal Ramlakhan grabbed the edge of the glass. "Please do not do anything foolish, sor. I have much respect for you. Please wait. The captain will not be long."

And so, they had waited, he and Kumarsingh, through a gradual darkening of the sky, through a light shower that began and ended as if by the twisting of a tap, and which caused the soldiers to raise the hoods of their ponchos, through a renewal of the light which slowly gave depth and colour to the watchtowers. When the camp lights began to lose their brilliance, Arun heard the muffled ring of Corporal Ramlakhan's telephone. He waited for the corporal to rap at the window with his knuckle before rolling it halfway down. A hand-rolled cigarette was clamped between his lips and when he opened his mouth to speak the musty stench of *ganja* — a smell that always brought to Arun's mind the image of a badly decayed tooth — surged into the car.

"The captain will see you now, sor."

Kumarsingh pressed the clutch and reached to turn the key in the ignition.

"Only you, sor," Corporal Ramlakhan said.

"And what about Mr Kumarsingh?"

"He must wait here, sor. With us."

"Out of the question, Corporal. We're here together."

"Only you, sor. The captain said."

Kumarsingh released the clutch, sat back in his seat. "Go, go. I'll wait for you." Then he peered past Arun at the Corporal. "Hey, Ramlakhan, corporal now, yah? Making more money? Time for another party soon?"

Ramlakhan stared stone-faced back at him. He wrenched open Arun's door and stood aside to let him out.

Now here he was — annoyed at having been made to wait, his nostrils stinging still from the bite of the corporal's cigarette, uneasy from a dampness that seemed to have slid under his skin — having morning coffee with Seth and the general. He told the whole story, blurting it out with what struck him, even as he spoke, as a kind of incoherence. Anjani's reading to her father, her irritability, the door smashing open, the flashlights, the hood, and the binding of Mr and Mrs Jaisaram: none of it, he realized, had any meaning, any relevance, to what had happened to Anjani. None of the details he had so carefully rehearsed while waiting for Kumarsingh to pick him up offered any clue as to her fate. He saw with a growing sense of helplessness that the story he had to tell was as dramatic and as inconsequential as those that so moved Mr Jaisaram.

After listening to him, the general turned to Seth and said, "Jaisaram. He's the butcher, isn't he?"

"Yes, sir. The butcher."

"Ahh," the general said, buttering a slice of toast. "So the girl, this Anjani. She's his daughter." He glanced again at Seth for confirmation of shared knowledge before turning to Arun. "Young man, do you know what we are about here? We're fighting a war where no heroes are made. A war with no front lines, no trenches to conquer, no pillboxes to storm. You stare into the dark, you shoot, and you hope no one shoots back. You are determined to win but you don't know how you will. All you know is that you can't give up — and that there will be many victims along the way, some innocent, some less so. This Anjani may be one of those, and that is terrible for Jaisaram, another tragedy, but against the larger picture, her disappearance is of little consequence. It's like the dogs. In fifty years — we must take the long view — no one will remember that incident, no matter how gruesome it was." He took a bite of his toast, grimaced, reached for a jar of jam.

Seth's eyes danced away from the table. Arun's breath left him and in a voice unsteady with disbelief he said, "General, how can you compare Anjani to —"

"Do you think I enjoy being here?" He spooned jam onto his toast, spread it around with his finger, licked his finger clean. "I'd much rather be at home bouncing my grandson on my knees than out here killing these fellows. Not that I mind killing them, of course, not at all, that's part of my job, and any career man who gets upset at having to kill — well, he's just a damned fool. Suffers from terminal naïveté. The truth? You're not a military man until you've blown someone away, because then you *know* you can. Till then you're just a bloody Boy Scout." He spooned more jam onto the toast. "Young man, stick to what you know and do it as well as you can and accept the consequences. You see what I mean? If someone breaks into your house and steals your money, you call the police and you let them do their job. Sometimes the police can help, sometimes they can't, but you wouldn't go running around playing detective now, would you? You accept your loss and you move on."

"Accept the loss? General, we're not talking about rupees here."

The general took a bite of his toast. He might as well have shrugged.

Arun took a gulp of air. "I have no intention of looking for her. I wouldn't know where to start, but I thought you might —"

"Good. You spoke so passionately about the girl, I was beginning to fear more personal motives."

"I'm a rational man, General. Of course I'm upset. I know these people, I see them almost every day. But I like to believe that reason always trumps passion."

"Yes, but usually only after the passion has worn itself out. And sometimes it's not easy to distinguish reason from passion. That's the way it is with religious belief, for instance. Tell me, do you believe in god?"

"No. Sometimes I wish I could. But as a teacher of mine once said, religious faith is just fear soothed by magic and superstition."

"You believe that?"

Around them, officers were rising from their tables and shuffling out. Whenever the door was opened, the sound of gruff chanting wafted in, the platoons at their morning calisthenics raising the spectre of warrior priests arousing bloodlust. Arun leaned forward and rested his forearms on the table. "I'm not here for a theological debate, General. I haven't slept all night and I'm very tired. All I want to know is what you're going to do about Miss Jaisaram."

Waiters were beginning to clear the tables, their movements brisk and precise. Although neither Seth nor the general gave a hint of it, he sensed that the time they had afforded him was drawing to an end.

"To do? What do you expect me to do?" He set his palm on a book bound in dull gold that lay beside his plate. He picked it up, held it in both hands. On the cover, large brown letters declared HOLY BIBLE. Lower down, beneath the image of what appeared to be an amphora or an oil lamp, smaller letters attested that it had been "Placed by THE GIDEONS". "I could pray for her but, frankly, my friend, there is not much more that I can do. When the insurgents take people, they take them for good. Sometimes they return, mostly not; sometimes alive, mostly not."

"What makes you say they're the ones who took her? We don't know who took her."

"If not the insurgents, then who? Surely you're not implying that this is our doing? It isn't our policy to kidnap people. Not that it hasn't occurred to us. There are some troublemakers who might be better dealt with in, shall we say, an unorthodox manner. But that is the rule and, as a teacher, you surely know that a rule weathered by exception is not a rule." He glanced at Seth. "You were warned, I believe, not to get too close to this family. We deal with the butcher, we do what we can to help him, but who knows who else the butcher deals with?"

Seth cleared his throat into the napkin crumpled in his hand. "Arun, we have reason to believe that there's some bad feeling between the Jaisarams and the Boys, as you call them. It has to do with the son and what happened to him. The parents aren't happy with them, it's hardly surprising."

"Seth, I know these people. There's never been any hint —"

"You know what they want you to know. Do you think they'd let you in on their unhappiness? You think they trust you?"

The general glanced at his watch, drained his coffee, and patted his lips with his napkin. He pushed back his chair, and rose, immediately mimicked by Seth. "Thank you for letting us know," he said, already turning away from Arun. "Give the butcher my condolences, will you?"

"Condolences?"

But neither the general nor Seth, walking away together, seemed to hear him.

He was escorted back to the camp gate past formations of men stripped to the waist labouring through their choreography of physical training, hundreds of arms and legs scissoring simultaneously in the grey morning light, hundreds of hoarse voices roaring the indistinct words of a chant. The sound, out here, unfiltered by distance and walls, was less melodious, more strident, menacing in its cadenced communal growl. It reminded him of the night of the raid on the town. *Staydowdon'mokeepyourhandsstaydon'mokeepyourhandsstay.* He quickened his pace.

The guard had been changed. Ramlakhan was no longer there. Kumarsingh was still sitting at the steering wheel, his hands clasped to his face. When Arun got in, Kumarsingh turned only his eyes towards him. Then he lowered his clasped hands and Arun saw that they held a bloodied handkerchief. "What happened to you?"

"I got out to take a stretch," Kumarsingh said in a nasal voice. "I slipped in the mud and hit my nose on the ground." He dabbed the kerchief carefully at his discoloured nose. "That's what Ramlakhan tells me happened and I have no reason to doubt him."

"Is it broken?"

"It'll be fine. What about Miss Anjani?"

Arun shook his head. "Let's get back to Omeara," he said.

SIX

The shriek of rain on the metal roof yanked him awake. Outside, he knew, there was no moon, there were no stars, there was only night tightly drawn. Blinded by the darkness, he imagined the drops slicing down through the night, shimmering ribbons of quicksilver exploding on impact with the eclipsed earth. He peered at the luminescent hands of his watch. He had been asleep for hours. He lay back again, palms beneath his head, listening to the cadenced hammering of the rain, imagining that it was doing what it could to wash the world clean.

When the rain eased — a sudden falling off to a reluctant clatter — he threw back his blanket to air that was thick and damp and cool enough to cause him to shiver. He strapped on his leg, filled the kettle, and lit the burner. The drizzle was already so light that it couldn't be heard above the hiss of the propane flame. He leaned over the sink, cupping his palms beneath the rush of tap water and scooping it onto his face and hair. Droplets ran down the back of his neck, causing him to shiver again. Beside him, the pot began to rattle beneath spouting steam.

He shaved as his tea steeped, the rasping of the razor's edge through his overnight bristle almost alarming in the silence that now surrounded him. He wondered how many children would turn up for school today. He had no idea how the rains affected the rhythm of their lives. The fields would not need watering, but might there still be weeding to be done, tasks unknown to him that still required performing? And then he wondered how he would manage to teach them, much of his mind waiting with Mr Jaisaram for news. When he had told him of the army's unwillingness to help, Mr Jaisaram had just nodded numbly, as if he had all along expected nothing more. Kumarsingh, fingering his throbbing nose, had offered to assemble the cricket team and begin a search, but they all knew it was pointless and Mr Jaisaram had waved him off. Then he'd sent them both home to get some rest. "There's nothing to be done," he'd said. The flesh on his face appeared slack, as if the anxiety eating at him had unfastened it from his skull. He had aged a decade. "Now we can only wait and see what happens."

Arun hadn't expected to sleep but he did, despite his own anxiety, despite the resentment that had slowly come to him during the drive back to Omeara. He had invested much hope in Seth and the general, had expected that they — *his* people so intent on sending messages of goodwill — would seize the opportunity to display their concern. He had expected not only that they would know what to do but that they would do it with alacrity, had imagined a mobilization of troops: officers yelling orders and strapping on revolvers, soldiers buckling helmets and checking weapons as they dashed through the mud to trucks, engines growling with impatience to launch the search. Instead, a kind of silence had invested him and it was into that silence that he had descended until he was wrenched from it by the rain.

He quickly finished shaving and gulped at his tea while getting dressed. Struggling with a sense of futility, he gathered up his books and steeled himself for the hours to come. Only the thought that no class was scheduled today for the army camp consoled him, or at least made the hours to come seem bearable.

On impulse, he opened the window above the disordered cot, the shutters exposing him to grey light, to his garden washed to ruin, to — and this gave him a jolt of surprise — a woman's face framed by the Jaisarams' open kitchen window. For the briefest moment, his vision reeled and he thought that it was Mrs Jaisaram. When he saw that it wasn't Mrs Jaisaram, he thought that it must be Anjani. And when he saw that it wasn't Anjani, he felt a stab of despair.

The woman, Sona, was one of the neighbours who had cared for Mrs Jaisaram the previous evening. She gazed back at him without surprise.

With a rising of his hands and a twisting of his head, Arun gestured a request for news.

Sona shook her head and shrugged.

Arun pulled the shutters in. They were heavier than usual, the wood so swollen with moisture that he had to bang the latch into place with the heel of his palm before it would hold them fast.

His shoes were muddy and his socks soaked by the time he arrived at the schoolhouse. No one was waiting at the door. He had trodden carefully along the deserted street, his shoes sinking into its glutinous paste, past darkened walls and galvanised iron roofs without sparkle. Once he thought he smelled hot oil and fried dough, but the odour was gone as quickly as it had come, intensifying the mingled mustiness of earth and the tang of salt water. Far off in the waterlogged fields, a man lumbered shin-deep through the muck, leading a reluctant cow by a leash of rope. Arun was reminded of the morning he'd first seen the town, the vibrant colour photograph in his mind cast now almost in negative. Off to his right, the mountains crouched stolid and inert, like a massive shadow battened down by the rain. Walking through the square, he glimpsed the sea. It was as grey as the sky but less luminous, and ridged like a field of badly poured concrete.

He tapped his shoes against the wall of the school, knocking off some of the mud. Halfway up, the cinder blocks had turned a darker shade of grey. The rain hadn't washed the world clean. It had merely washed it of colour.

He had just finished wringing out his socks when Saman wandered in. In the thin grey light, he appeared more fragile than ever. He held a paper bag, which he put on Arun's table without meeting his eyes, before turning away to his desk.

Arun pulled on his socks. "Thank you, Saman."

Every week, the boy brought an offering from his parents: fruit, vegetables, coconut sweets concocted by his mother. This week, the offering was smaller than before, two stunted mangoes, one too green to be of use — a symbolic gift. Arun had tried to refuse the weekly offering at first but had eventually understood it to be a matter of pride. Later on, he saw that the parents were people of little illusion. They knew that Saman was hardly a future candidate for scholarships to the capital. But Arun remembered Saman's father too well, remembered the hope he had for his son. How could he kill that hope?

Every day that Saman came to school, Arun felt a surge of despair and admiration. By the end of the day, all that remained was the despair and he began steeling himself to talk to Saman's father. He had grown to hate the paper bag the boy deposited every week on his table.

Outside, the world darkened further. Fat raindrops began splashing onto the ground. Within seconds, it turned ferocious and a sonorous thrumming filled the schoolhouse. No other students would be coming today. Arun felt Saman's dark, skittish eyes on him. The boy — *this two-percenter*, he thought bitterly — was awaiting another session of futility. His stomach began to burn. He saw the mangoes sitting on the table before him and he suddenly found them ugly and offensive, a bribe from the parents meant as compensation for their son's stupidity.

Slowly he pushed back his chair and got to his feet. If Saman wouldn't learn, it was time for a change in tactics. He turned towards the chalkboard, reached his fingers to its upper edge and felt around. At first there was only dust but he soon found what he was looking for, the two halves of the stick, Nawaal, precisely where he had put them on his first morning here with Anjani so long ago.

When he turned around to face Saman, the rage of the rain seemed to retreat even though its intensity hadn't diminished. It was as if some thin membrane had woven itself around him, separating him ever so slightly from the world, from Saman, from what he knew he was about to do. He sat once more at his table, one half of Nawaal loosely gripped in his right fist. "Saman," he said. "Come here." With the stick, he indicated that the boy should stand across the table from him.

Saman, eyes fluttering in panic, did not move.

"Saman. I said, come here. Now." His own voice sounded distanced from him, as if it weren't issuing from his own throat but from outside, from somewhere in the raucous deluge.

He is in his father's car, his driver's permit tucked into the wallet he can feel under him in his back pocket. The permit, a rectangle of blue cardboard still stiff with newness, bears a black-and-white photograph of himself that makes him look like a thug. Ahead, the two-lane highway runs straight and flat and dry through forest cleared a hundred feet to either side. There are no cars in front of him, or behind. He thinks: Let's see what it's like. His foot steadily increases its pressure on the accelerator. As steadily, the needle rises past eighty miles an hour, to ninety, ninety-three, nine-four, ninety-five ...

Slowly Saman got to his feet, hesitated. Shoulders hunched, he stepped over to Arun's table.

"Put your hands on the table. Palms up."

The boy's eyes filled with tears but he obeyed, fingers curled back.

"Open your palms."

The fingers splayed open.

"Why are you here, Saman?"

"To learn, *Prahib*," he whispered.

"To learn. And do you learn, Saman?"

"Yes, *Prahib*. I learn."

"You learn. What do you learn?"

"To read and count, *Prahib*."

"Is that so? Say the alphabet for me."

Saman's lower lip fluttered, his mouth opened, closed.

Without warning and without removing his eyes from the boy's, Arun flicked the stick down hard onto his left palm.

Ninety-six, ninety-seven, ninety-eight ... He senses the car, hurtling forward, lose contact with the asphalt. It is as if he is driving on a cushion of air, or flying rather an inch above the earth, the steering wheel trembling lightly against his fingertips, the cleared ground to either side blurring in the corner of his eyes, the long road peeling back beneath him. Ninety-nine ...

Saman shrieked, withdrew the hand.

"Put it back."

Trembling, he did as ordered. A dark welt rose along the middle finger, across the palm and into the wrist.

Arun, unaffected, said, "Count for me then. To twenty."

Saman swallowed, his forehead crinkling with effort. "Wan ..."

"Good. One. Then what?"

"Wan ..."

Arun brought the stick down on the other palm. Saman yelped again and his hand curled into a tight fist. His eyes reddened and a tear ran down each cheek.

"Look here, Saman." With the rain trammelling in the distance, with his own voice flowing in through the door, Arun marvelled at the reasonable tone with which he spoke. "Every week your parents send me these gifts." He prodded at the mangoes with the point of the stick, rolled them to the edge of the table, nudged them off. They fell with dull thuds to the ground. "And every week, every day, I try to teach you. But you won't learn. What am I supposed to tell your poor parents?"

Saman, tears flowing freely, said, "Wan, fife, t'ree."

A sudden rage. Arun struck at the right hand again. It was still folded. The stick cracked into the finger joints.

One hundred ... The car is driving itself. It is skittish, fickle. It demands free rein. He cannot feel his seat under him, cannot feel his body, is aware only of the roadway, the forest, a tingle in the skin of his fingertips. The slightest nudge will send the car hurtling off the road. Grasping the wheel will cause it to spin out of control. The slightest bump, the lightest gust of wind ... His heart begins to race and he thinks: Stop it now. Now!

Saman howled, jackknifing and hugging his hand against his belly. "No, *Prahib!* Please, *Prahib!*"

He presses in the clutch. Gingerly, so gingerly, flirts with the brake, presses his thumb and forefinger to the wheel. He can feel the car surrendering to him. Increases the pressure of his foot, wraps his fingers tight around the wheel. It vibrates and the car shudders, then slows perceptibly. The cleared ground sharpens in the corners of his eyes, the road and the forest harden. The needle backs down: ninety-eight, ninety-five, ninety, eighty-five, eighty ...

Suddenly a deafening racket filled Arun's head. The membrane was gone, as if shredded by Saman's keening. The distance closed. He could hear the pounding of the rain on the roof, the splattering of the drops on the ground. He could hear the wheezing of his own breath. A wave of nausea swept through him and an acrid taste seeped over his tongue. He threw the stick to the floor. "Saman," he said. "Saman."

The boy, cowering and hugging himself, would not respond.

Arun stood up. The chair fell back, clattered onto the wooden platform. "Saman, I'm sorry." He stepped off the platform, approached the boy with his arm outstretched.

Saman glanced wildly at him. "No!" He swirled and ran out of the schoolhouse. Arun rushed to the door. The air was milky with rain, the boy already far away and drenched, his stick-like legs churning through the mud towards the town.

He will never forget the seconds of exhilaration, the sense of time and existence teetering on the edge, that moment when his future depended absolutely on him and him alone. He will always wonder what would have happened had he not given in to fear. And part of him will always regret that he had.

Arun steadied himself against the doorsill, his breath shuddering. Then, through the rain, he saw another figure hurrying towards the schoolhouse, a piece of pink plastic held tight over his head and around his shoulders. He recognised Kumarsingh.

They wouldn't have found her had the rain not begun again. The drops slamming into her body had revived her, caused her to moan, the brief sound catching Mrs Jaisaram's ear just as the downpour turned harsh and obliterating. She had sat up in her bed, as suddenly alert, Mr Jaisaram said, as a stray dog sensing a mongoose. She'd looked around in great agitation, pointing at her ear then cupping her palm beside it, listening. Neither Mr Jaisaram nor Sona, who had brought her a cup of tea, had heard anything. They listened. They heard the rain. They agreed, through an exchange of sceptical glances, that she was beginning to crack under the strain. Sona caressed her head, Mr Jaisaram encouraged her to lie back down but she pushed them both away. Puzzled by her insistence, they let her clamber out of bed and followed her to the back door. When she opened it and peered out, Mr Jaisaram placed a restraining hand on her shoulder but his touch was too light to prevent her from launching herself into the rain. Bellowing her name, he dashed out after her, only to see her crouched beside a large bundle on the ground. He said that he had known immediately what it was. He scooped up the bundle and headed back into the house, his wife staggering along beside him, her hands clawing desperately at the soaked bedding. "She felt dead," Mr Jaisaram said, "but I knew she wasn't. A butcher always knows when there's breath left." He laid her on their bed and, for modesty's sake, left her to the care of his wife and Sona.

Arun ran the towel through his hair once more and handed it back to Mr Jaisaram. He had left his muddy shoes by the door. His clothes were still soaked but there was nothing to be done about that.

Behind him, Kumarsingh, stripped of his sheet of pink plastic, said, "That's when I arrived. He told me and I came to get you right away." He was crouched over a sheet of paper, scraping mud from his shoes with a stick.

Arun said, "How is she?"

"As I said, alive," Mr Jaisaram said. "For the rest, we'll see." He slung the wet towel over his shoulder.

"What can I do?"

"For Anji, nothing. But for me ..." He turned into the living room, sat heavily in his armchair.

Arun followed in his wet socks, perched on the edge of the sofa. His stomach still burned.

"I used to have a son, Anjani probably told you."

Arun nodded.

"She told you he ran away?"

"Yes."

"You know, there are those who say he didn't run away. They say he got blown up by a bomb, a bomb he was carrying."

"I've heard that too."

"Do you know, Arun, I'm not sure what the truth is. Maybe he's alive somewhere, maybe he got blown to pieces. But either way, I've lost a son." He dug into his pants pocket, emerging with a small photograph, which he passed to Arun. "My wife, she doesn't know I have it."

Arun held it up to the grey light coming in through the window: a young man a little older than himself with shadowed eyes, thick unruly hair and a short beard that framed tightened lips.

"His name was Nagarat. He had a talent for fixing things. He dreamed of becoming an electrical technician." He drew the back of his hand slowly across his eyes.

Arun said, "You say it's possible he was blown up by a bomb he was carrying. Then he was involved in ... you know."

"Everybody's involved in one way or another, Mr Arun. Some make bombs, some carry bombs, some give money."

From the door, Kumarsingh said, "There are some things it is better for Arun not to know, don't you think?" He stepped into the living room. "Please understand, Arun, it is not that I do not trust you, it is not even that we do anything wrong. But you see, giving money puts our lives in danger from one side and not giving money puts our lives in danger from the other side. The less you know about these things the better, yah?"

Arun said, "You have no reason to trust me or not trust me, Kumarsingh."

Mr Jaisaram sighed. "Perhaps you are right, Kumarsingh. These are our problems. Still, there is one thing I would like to ask Mr Arun."

Arun nodded.

"I have told you I am not a literate man, although I know many words. But there is one word I have never learnt and I want to know what it is."

"If I know it."

"Well, here it is. A man who loses his wife is a widow and a woman who loses her husband is a widower. Children who lose their parents are orphans." His voice wheezed and his eyes grew hooded. "What is a parent who loses a child?"

Arun was silent for a long time.

Kumarsingh, uneasy, tinkled loose change in his pants pocket.

Mr Jaisaram's breathing grew laboured, as if waiting for the answer were a burden.

"I don't believe there's a word for it," Arun said finally.

Mr Jaisaram nodded, his head rocking weightily back and forth as if this, too, like the army's refusal to help search for Anjani, was what he had expected all along.

Just then the bedroom door opened and Sona motioned to them. "You can come," she said.

The bedroom was small, glutted with furniture and dense with shadow, its air suffocating with dampness and body heat, stale breath, bay rum and coconut oil. When they had all squeezed in, it became claustrophobic. Arun found himself breathing through his mouth. Mrs Jaisaram, standing at the far side of the bed wringing a washcloth in an enamel basin, paid no attention to them.

At first, in the webby gloom, he thought Anjani was grinning at him. He smiled back, but the grin remained fixed. Then he saw that it wasn't a grin at all but a large cut that proceeded upwards from the left corner of her mouth. Her hair was haloed wet on the pillow and she stared dully at him through slits in the swollen flesh around her eyes. Light cuts and scrapes covered her forehead and cheeks. A bandage had been taped to her chin.

Sona said, "Her whole body, even her feet ..." Her voice cracked and she couldn't continue.

Arun said, "Can she speak?"

"A little. She asked for some water."

Another question came to him but he held it back. It was a question he could ask only Anjani herself. Instead, he said, "Did she recognise the men?"

"All she said is water."

"Have you sent for a doctor?"

Kumarsingh leaned in close to his ear. "We're not in the capital, Arun. You don't just send for a doctor. Sona's the closest thing we have."

Arun turned to the fleshy woman with a beak nose and close-set eyes. "You're a nurse?"

"I've had some training, a long time ago."

Kumarsingh said, "She can bandage cuts, fix broken bones, deliver babies. We're lucky to have her."

Sona shrugged. "Sometimes the army doctor helps, if it's very serious and if he has the time. They send a medical team through the area every four months or so, to do medical check-ups and inoculate the children against this or that and lecture us on birth-control. It would be the only good time to have a heart attack."

Kumarsingh said, "Timing is everything, yah?"

Ignoring him, Arun gestured towards Anjani. "How's she doing?"

"Her pulse is fast. Too fast. That's all I can say."

Arun turned to Kumarsingh. "Maybe the army'll help this time."

"I will get my car."

"No," Mr Jaisaram said. "We asked once. We will not ask twice."

Arun saw that his gaze was fixed on his wife, her body rigid, her face darkened by a frown.

Mr Jaisaram sat on the bed like a man settling in on the edge of a cliff. He looked puzzled, as if trying to find his daughter in the person lying under the white sheet. After a moment, he reached out his trembling fingers and brushed gently at an undamaged spot near her hairline. "Anji, you hear me?"

Her eyes blinked, found his face.

Arun, looking over his shoulder, couldn't read the look. Recognition or mere reaction to the sound of her father's voice? It seemed to him, with a leap of fright, that Anjani was absent from herself.

Mrs Jaisaram leaned forward and touched her husband's shoulder. She gestured with her hand that the visit was over.

Mr Jaisaram, with a long, searching look at Anjani, rose reluctantly. "We must let her sleep," he said.

As he turned to follow Mr Jaisaram and the others out, Arun let his eyes linger on Anjani's and he saw that that they hadn't budged from the now empty space where she had found her father's face.

Shame overtook him some hours later in the darkening living room. Across from him, Mr Jaisaram snuffled in restless sleep, his chin rolling into his chest.

Kumarsingh had left to attend to some business, promising to return towards the end of the afternoon. Sona had gone home to prepare dinner for her family. Mrs Jaisaram had emerged only once from the bedroom, to freshen the water in the basin.

Arun had been trying to distract himself with one of Mr Jaisaram's novels but it had failed to excite his interest. He shut the book, a wave of acid coruscating his stomach and inflaming his chest. How could he explain his actions to himself? How could he seek forgiveness from Saman, from his father? He'd never before been prey to such fury. Something deep within him had been rubbed raw. It was perhaps time for him to leave.

Mr Jaisaram stirred, his eyes blinking open, reddened and puzzled. For a moment, he stared at Arun as if at a stranger, then he sat up in the armchair and rubbed at his face with his palms. "Sorry," he mumbled. "I didn't mean to ... I mean, I'm very tired."

"Of course. There's no reason to apologise."

Mr Jaisaram glanced towards the bedroom.

Arun said, "She must be still asleep."

Mr Jaisaram nodded, pushed himself heavily up from the chair. Smacking his lips, he said, "Water?"

Arun rose to his feet, tossing the paperback onto the table. "Why don't I make us some tea?" He needed to move, needed action. It was the easiest way to flee thought.

Moving towards the kitchen, Mr Jaisaram said, "I'll show you where things are."

In the small kitchen, Arun filled a pot with water and put it on the stove while Mr Jaisaram searched the cupboards for the teapot. Through the open window above the sink, he saw his garden and his house as Mrs Jaisaram saw it every morning — the mud, the leafless stalks, the cement-block wall, the weathered wood — and he wondered whether it was the condition of the house itself or simply the dank, grey glow of late afternoon that suggested sadness and abandonment.

The pot began to hiss. Mr Jaisaram, crouching, finally found the cups and the can of tea. He said, "I will go check on them."

Arun had already filled the teapot when he returned and in a whisper said, "They're sleeping, both of them."

They took the teapot and cups back to the living room. Mr Jaisaram switched on a light and, perched on the edge of his armchair, poured the tea. "Sorry," he said, peering at the dark leaves floating on the surface. "I forgot about the strainer." He looked up at Arun with a faint smile. "You don't mind chewing your tea, do you?"

Arun smiled, less at the weak joke than at Mr Jaisaram's improving mood.

Sipping carefully at the tea, Mr Jaisaram said, "How are you holding up, Mr Arun?"

"I'm all right." But his stomach began to burn once more. He was tempted to tell Mr Jaisaram about Saman, about what he'd done to the boy, about the irresistible temptations of Nawaal. But what was he to say? Where was he to begin? A simple recitation of the facts would hardly suffice and all explanation still eluded him. Expiation was never a simple matter. He took a gulp of his tea, winced as it singed his tongue. He felt the leaves fluttering their way past his cheeks and down his throat. Some stuck to his teeth. He dislodged them with a finger, swallowing.

Mr Jaisaram leaned forward and picked up the paperback. He examined it for a moment, weighing it in his hand. "Mr Arun," he said, "when Anji wakes up, will you read to her sometimes?"

"Read to her? I'm not sure she would —"

"It will help her. It will take her mind off things."

Arun tried to imagine the scene — him sitting beside Anjani lying in bed, reading to her fantasies of other places, other lives — and he was surprised at how easily the image came to him. "If she wishes," he said.

"And will you read to me?"

"You can sit with us."

"No. I mean now." Mr Jaisaram held the book out to him.

Arun hesitated, then he reached out for it.

"Page fifty-two," Mr Jaisaram said.

Arun found the page, began reading. "Later that night, the winds turned violent. Roped to Captain Fabio's bed, Sapphire felt the ship lurch to the left and then to the right, its timbers creaking and —"

"Not there. Anji's already read that part. Lower down."

Arun skipped to the next paragraph. "Captain Fabio unbuckled his sabre and hung it beside the door —"

"Yes. There."

Mr Jaisaram settled back in his chair, his eyes half shut, already seduced away from the gloomy afternoon, the shadowy living room, and the pain of his beaten daughter asleep in the bedroom.

Arun read quietly on, page after page, pronouncing words that held no meaning for him, sentences and paragraphs that offered only hazy images of lovemaking and the clash of ships in high-seas battle and more lovemaking, concentrating on the sound of his voice, getting lost in the rhythms that banished for him, too, the cracking whip, the yelping boy, the chilling emptiness of Anjani's gaze.

He was on page seventy-five when an anguished wail smothered the sound of his voice. He looked up quickly into Mr Jaisaram's panicked eyes. The cry, primitive in its nakedness, had come from the bedroom.

SEVEN

O NCE THE PYRE had been lit, Arun commended Mr Jaisaram
to Kumarsingh's care and began easing his way through the crowd,
away from the chanting and the sobbing, past fists clenching
handkerchiefs, faces rigid with anger and fear, and into the vaulted
silence that he remembered so well from his parents' funeral —
that eerie, echoing emptiness that seemed to suggest a frontier
between unfriendly worlds. No one took notice of him as he made
his slow way across the dank ground, distancing himself with each
step from the thickening column of oily smoke roiling upward
like an eager tributary of the turbulent sky. All eyes were rapt on
the drama he could no longer bear: Mrs Jaisaram huddled in grief
among women as stricken as she; Mr Jaisaram, a tree trunk eaten
hollow, braced upright by a fraternity of hands and shoulders.

He followed the road back towards the town and soon found

himself on the beach, the horizon an indistinct smudge where cloud met the heaving, molten mass of the water. The surf spilled like dirty porridge onto the sand, leaving behind lengths of glistening seaweed and clumps of orange-hued foam. It was as if, deep beneath the surface, the seabed were being whipped and sundered by some unseen force. Here and there a crab slithered from beneath a rock, scampered sideways then lunged for the safety of another hole.

Watching a pincer disappear into the earth, he thought: *It's time.*

He imagined himself returning to his house, packing what he could get into his suitcase — he would abandon much that had accrued of this new life — and slipping away at night, as furtive as a fleeing salamander. He would be hated, of course, for running out. And he would confirm Mr Jaisaram's opinion of the rejects from the north. But was it his responsibility to redeem the faults of others? His goals had been much more modest, and perhaps, he saw now, naive. He had believed himself capable of living in a land of violence but remaining untouched by it, of the place but still on its margins, affecting its life but being unaffected by its imperatives. And yet there was Anjani, there was Saman, there was this sense of being soiled, infested. Somehow, in the end, he hadn't been able to resist Nawaal.

A light sprinkle of rain dusted across his face. He squinted up at the sky, at the dark, rumpled clouds and saw their pledge of pandemonium. He hoped it would not rain, not yet, not for many hours, for the ferocious deluge the clouds reserved would snuff out the flames of the pyre and the horror of Anjani scorched would compound the horror of Anjani dead.

He found himself at the outcropping of rock where he and Anjani had sat, where an unexpected intimacy had woven itself in the prying gaze of binoculars. Tugging with his hands, carefully placing his feet, he clambered up and sat facing the water. The rocks were damp and cold. The sea heaved like a wash of grey gruel. This spot, which he had thought he would long remember with fondness, struck him today as a place of great desolation, a place where no birds could fly or fish could swim or sunlight ever penetrate. It had become, like his parents' house after the explosion, an infinitely sadder place, possessed by shadow, haunted by absence. He reached into his pocket and wrapped the beach crystal in his fist. He pressed his fist to his lips and blew into it, his breath flowing warm over the crystal. Then, without hesitation, he raised his fist into the air and flung the crystal into the waves.

A breeze sprang up, full of salt and moisture, tugging at his hair, swiping at his skin. In the sky, the clouds heaved, began scudding along as if desperate to flee. Then, all at once, the breeze turned savage, a gale moaning in hard and noisy from the sea. His belly convulsed, convulsed again, and suddenly he was screaming into the wind, his throat aflame with the effort, his jaw stretched beyond endurance. The scream went on and on, like some beast forcing its own release, and when finally it stopped, leaving him breathless, he could feel the wind whipping away the tears as they fell from his eyes.

They were his first tears since Mrs Jaisaram's wail — the first sound she had uttered in years — had shattered the stillness of the late afternoon the day before. There had been no time. Every second had pulsed with a confusion of sound and movement. Mr Jaisaram kneeling beside his daughter's body, pummelling the mattress with his fists, his keening anguish cutting jagged through the encroaching darkness. A bustling of neighbours, the women crowded into the bedroom whispering and clucking around Mrs Jaisaram, the men gathered silent in the living room or smoking in the street out front. A shot of whisky thrust into his hand, another into Mr Jaisaram's, and the burning of the liquid through his constricted throat. At some point much later, sitting on the bench out back beside the stunned and haggard Mr Jaisaram, the night air fetid with soaked soil and vegetation, the house at their backs full of people and silence.

It was into that silence, broken occasionally by someone puttering in the kitchen, turning on the tap then turning it off, that

Mr Jaisaram had said, "Do you realise, Mr Arun, at this very moment somewhere a man and a woman are making love so that somewhere, someday, a child will be born? Do you realise that at this very moment some are taking their first breath? It is hidden from their parents that, in the blink of an eye, their baby will become a young child. And in another blink of an eye that young child will become a teenager. A third blink, an adult. In three blinks of an eye, those young parents will become old parents, grandparents if they are lucky." He paused, knuckles cracking like the snap of dry twigs. "A blink of an eye, Mr Arun. The measure of a man's life."

Arun had shifted uneasily on the hard bench. He felt disarmed by this unexpected vision of babies being conceived, babies being born, this vision of vitality and life, only to have it undercut by this other vision of the horrifying brevity of all that would follow.

Mr Jaisaram had snuffled, laid his head on Arun's shoulder, and immediately begun to snore.

Arun, dismayed, felt his body stiffen, felt it try to ease away.

Then he stopped himself.

A musty blend of sweat and coconut oil emanating from Mr Jaisaram's hair reached deep into his memory and flashed him back to a bedroom shuttered from light and fresh air, to an old man, his grandfather, lying in a bed beneath a blue blanket, enduring the effects of a stroke from which he would never recover, Arun bending forward at his father's urging to kiss the old man on the forehead and gagging at the smell of sweat and coconut oil, saying later to his father that grandpa smelled funny and his father saying that grandpa was *unwell*.

That was the word that came to him as he felt the weight and warmth of Mr Jaisaram's head on his shoulder. *Unwell.* Mr Jaisaram was unwell. When he'd lifted his lips from the damp forehead, his grandfather had managed a half smile.

So he'd remained there, dozing off from time to time, until the sky brightened into morning and they were gently awoken by a red-eyed Kumarsingh bringing mugs of hot tea and news that all arrangements had been made for Miss Anjani.

Exhausted, pummelled by the briny wind, he emptied himself of a rage he had not recognised. He wiped at his eyes, drew up his knees, let his head hang between them. His breath came in tiny gasps, as if his lungs couldn't accommodate more than a nibble of the sea air at a time. He thought: *Mr Jaisaram is unwell.* It was time to return, to the pyre, to the house, eventually to a life a long train ride away. He straightened his spine, inhaling deeply as he did so, looking for the strength to rise, to make his way back.

Suddenly his neck was wedged in the grip of something powerful, sinew and muscles crinkling in a laceration of sharp pain. His breath was pinched off. The embrace tightened. He heard himself gurgle. His fingers grappled at what had seized him. He felt a forearm, felt a fist. Felt himself go feeble. Felt night surging within him.

He remembered an explosion of light and a sense of hurtling along a bright, narrow tunnel.

The army doctor told him later that his eyes had flickered open while he was being wheeled to the examination room. "Being hustled along on a stretcher actually," she'd said. "Seeing the urgency of the matter."

The urgency of the matter: Her words had stayed with him, the way she had pronounced them hinting at foreign training or, at least, at the influence of another, more ordered world where chaos was defused, made manageable — a world, then, foreign in another way. He liked the phrase, the sound of it. For some unfathomable reason, it consoled him.

He wouldn't see her again, wouldn't even remember her name — she was being posted to the main defence-forces hospital near the capital — but he believed he would not forget the young woman in a khaki uniform and white coat, her long hair knotted into a bun and pinned at the nape of her neck, with eyes so frank he knew they could be fazed by nothing, they could be startled but would quickly register toughness: eyes that fought back.

She told him that he had also awoken on the second day, screaming. He had no memory of that, but he did remember a sweeter awakening, to sunlight and floating fibres that seemed to him as long and as fat and as graceful as earthworms. And voices, women's voices, conversing in low tones, an easy exchange, relaxed, sounds suggestive of women with hands engrossed in pleasant labour, acquainting each other with the details of their day, their hours, their families, the minutiae of their lives. Their voices waded over him for a long time as he watched the fibres drifting by like fish in the sea.

It was some time before he grew aware of a distant throbbing in his left thigh and an itch that was like the tickling of dozens of aroused ants, an anthill in a frenzy.

And then Seth was there. "At last. It's about time."

The voice seemed to come to him from a long way off, at the far end of a darkened roadway full of sharp obstacles. He forced his eyelids, willing them to rise. Only the right one obeyed. He saw, to the left, the slope of his own nose, the rest of his restricted vision offering a white ceiling, a white wall, and, dark against the whiteness, Seth gazing down at him with a weary smile.

"Arun, you hear me?"

He nodded. His mouth was parched, his lips when he passed his tongue across them felt thickened and cracked. Seth held a straw to his mouth so he could sip from a cup of water. As he turned his head to the side to take the straw, the muscles in his neck were so stiff they seemed to crackle. He sucked greedily at the water.

"Easy, Arun," Seth said. "A little at a time. Moisten your mouth first."

Gradually, he became aware that there were other people in the room. A man in a white coat flitted past the end of his bed. An increasing pressure tightened on his left arm, then was suddenly released.

Seth said, "How do you feel, Arun?"

"Exhausted. Sore." He could barely stir his tongue. "Where am I?"

"You're in the base hospital. You're going to be fine."

"What happened?"

A crisp female voice said, "Let's save that for another time. Pressure's normal, heartbeat's fine, but he needs to rest."

Seth said, "Time to sleep, Arun. You heard the doctor. I'll be back later."

Someone stirred beside him and he felt himself being pulled down into a delicious vortex.

When he awoke, he wondered what time it was. Both his eyes had opened. The only light in the room was the dull glow from a machine of some kind that stood sentinel beside his bed. He tried to sit up but it was as if he were welded to the mattress. The effort was beyond him and he soon gave up. He raised his left hand — a needle attached to a tube had been taped into his forearm — and felt his face. His fingers did not recognise the shapes they encountered. The area around his left eye was swollen and clammy and so badly bruised pain prevented him from removing a nub of grit stuck in the corner of his eye socket. He grew suddenly weary, his eyelids closing of their own volition, and for a few seconds he had once more that delicious sensation of slipping away into a velvety vortex.

It didn't last. At least, when he next opened his eyes, it seemed to him that only seconds had passed, but the room was bright now, daylight filtering in through a thin window blind.

The door opened, a young woman in a nurse's uniform came in. "Good afternoon," she said. She had a ready smile but dark eyes, wary with worry.

"Afternoon?"

"You slept a long time. Best thing for you."

"How long have I been here?"

"Three days."

"Three days!"

"Time flies by when you're having fun, doesn't it?"

Arun watched her as she eyed the blue machine beside his bed, adjusted something, checked the saline-solution bag to which he was attached by the tube in his forearm. "What happened to me?" he said.

"If you were a boxer I'd say you lost a prize fight. But since you're built more like a skipping rope, it's probably best you talk to Captain Jamadar about all that. We'll let him know you're awake. He came by dozens of times to check on you, you know, night and day. You must be a good friend, they don't even do that for the wounded."

Dozens of times: that puzzled Arun. Dozens of times went beyond a friendly concern. "Was my life in danger?"

"You really should talk to the doctor —"

"It's a simple question."

"A coma's always touch and go."

"Captain Jamadar was probably worried that I'd die."

"He certainly was worried. I'll have the orderly ring him. I'm sure he'll be right over."

Before leaving, she gave him a drink of water and asked what his favourite flavour of Jell-O was.

Seth arrived bearing a tray with an assortment of fruit and juices. He put an army duffel bag down on the floor beside the door. "I told the nurse to hold your order," he said, placing the tray on the night table. "I thought you might appreciate something more, ahh, robust. She'll be by soon to unhook you."

Arun, following him with his eyes, said, "I'm not that hungry."

"I'll crank you up. You're not allowed out of bed yet." He bent over and worked the lever.

Arun's head swam a little as the bed elevated him to a sitting position.

"All right like that?"

"That's fine."

Seth drew up a chair and sank heavily into it. "You had us concerned for a while there but you seem to be mending well. You'll be up and about in no time."

Arun glanced around the room. Bare white walls, a sink, a bottle of liquid soap, a paper towel dispenser attached to the wall. "What happened to me, Seth?"

"We were hoping you could tell us."

"I went for a walk on the beach after Anjani's cremation. That's the last thing I remember." He spoke with difficulty, as if somehow his mouth lacked sufficient space to accommodate his tongue.

"Ahh, yes, the girl. A terrible thing. Now that I'm a father, I can't imagine how Jaisaram can cope."

"You wife has given birth?"

"Yes, three days ago. A boy."

"Congratulations."

"Thanks."

"You haven't seen him yet."

"It's not a good time, too much going on, but I'll be able to take a few days in a couple of weeks."

"The evening Anjani died, Jaisaram said to me that a man's life is measured in the blinks of an eye. Your baby will be a man before you know it. Remember that. It's the only gift I can give you at the moment, I'm afraid."

Seth smiled, nodded. "Do you always turn into a philosopher when you're not well?"

"Second-hand philosophy, I'm afraid."

Seth laughed. "Well, second-hand or not, it's worth remembering. Thanks."

Arun glanced around the room again, at the walls so blank, so anonymous, that the words *tabula rasa* came to his mind. "How'd I get here?"

"You were spotted by a patrol boat, stretched out on some rocks on the beach, of all places. You were lucky, we have no idea how long you were there. You remember anything, anything at all?"

"I remember being grabbed around the neck. I remember not being able to breathe." The memory caused his neck to ache, the pain throbbing into his skull. "What happened to me?" he repeated.

"Somebody gave you a working over. Somebody who knew what he was doing. He hurt you but he didn't damage you, no broken bones or anything like that."

"The Boys?"

"You have any reason to think it might be them?"

Arun shook his head slowly.

"There's no evidence they had anything to do with it but it isn't out of the question. You're one of us, you're doing good work. You're winning hearts, maybe even minds, and they may not appreciate that. Still, it's unusual." Seth reached up to the tray, picked up a banana and began peeling it. "Have you crossed anybody? Maybe something to do with the girl? A student?"

"Anjani?" Arun shook his head again, but he thought: Saman. He could not bring himself to tell Seth of the incident. "No, not that I'm aware of. Maybe it was just a random attack, someone who doesn't like northerners." He thought of Saman's father, a meek man, but a man whose dreams had been whipped into nothingness.

Seth took a bite of the banana, chewed. "We don't think so." Rising slowly, he put the half-eaten banana on the tray and fetched the duffel bag. "Actually, Arun, when I said you'd be up and about soon, I was talking metaphorically, at least for now." He opened the bag — "This might be a little bit of a shock." — and turned it over above the empty space left in the mattress by Arun's absent leg.

A shoe tumbled out onto the white blanket.

Arun recognised it as his own.

Then he saw, with a jolt, that a few inches of plastic protruded from it. The rest of the prosthesis rolled out in three chunks.

Glancing quickly up at him, Seth said, "Sorry."

Arun's chest tightened in despair. "I don't understand," he said. "It couldn't have broken, it's too tough."

"It didn't." Seth picked up a chunk from the middle of the shin, held it out to him. "It was hacked up, see?"

Arun accepted the piece, his stomach beginning to bloat. He ran his fingertips around the cut edges: the hard plastic hadn't splintered, it had been sliced smooth and neat, like an animal's bone rent by a butcher's cleaver. His mouth went sour, he retched, and his eyes watered.

Three days later, strengthened by food and sleep and dressed in his own clothes, delivered by Kumarsingh, he was lifted into a wheelchair by an orderly and trundled along gravelled paths past the well-tended lawn to the officers' mess.

Weak sunlight filtered through the low clouds. Heavy rain before dawn had battered the world into a brew of dark browns and dull greens, into a landscape without subtlety. His head was clear, though much of his flesh remained sore and his eye discoloured. He'd spent the morning in dread of this ride and the prospect of being pushed along like so much cargo, not because he was ill, but because the army hadn't yet managed to drum up the pair of crutches Seth had promised. Still, after all that time confined to his room, after all the hours spent mourning his loss of mobility, being outdoors lifted his spirits.

Seth met him at the door. Nodding the orderly away, he took hold of the wheelchair and said, "Cool car."

"Depends on your perspective, I guess," Arun replied.

The dining room was half full, indifferent eyes darting at him as Seth wheeled him among the tables towards an open door in the far corner. Beyond it, in a wood-panelled room, the general sat at a table set for lunch. Pen in hand, he was hunched wearily over a stack of documents.

Leaning close to his ear, Seth said, "The general's private dining room, usually reserved for visiting dignitaries. It's to be a private lunch, just the three of us."

They entered the room. It was windowless, cooled by a small, humming air conditioner. Dozens of framed photographs covered the walls. The national and regimental flags occupied one corner, a bronze statuette of Aryadasha another. It smelled of aftershave.

The general looked up from his papers, swiped his glasses from his face. "Ah, my friend, welcome, welcome," he said. Turning his papers face down with one hand, he gestured at a chairless table setting with the other. He waited for Seth to wheel Arun into place before stretching out his open palm. Arun took it: less a shaking of hands than a joining of them in a gesture of reassurance, or, perhaps, a taking of his pulse.

Seth excused himself and went off to let the kitchen know that the lunch service could begin.

"So," the general said, sitting back in his chair and directing a fatherly gaze at Arun. "Captain Jamadar tells me you're mending well."

"Your medical people have been very kind."

"They've had a lot of experience, unfortunately."

"I'd like to thank you as well, for offering —"

The general waved off his words. "Least we could do. After all, you're one of us."

Arun immediately thought of the general's refusal to help search for Anjani — she had not been one of "us" — but he let his bitterness slide under his tongue. For now, the general was his benefactor. "Still," he said. "Thank you."

Fiddling with his fork, the general said, "You're not a religious man, I recall."

"Not much of one, that's right."

The general sighed, as if in regret. "You're young still but perhaps there will come a day." He replaced the fork, nudging it with his fingers until it was perfectly aligned with the edge of the plate. "You must not let this little incident get you down. Bruises will heal, a fake leg can be replaced. But black thoughts — now those are insidious. They are the first steps towards hell. It's all a question of how you view things. Tell me, have you ever visited the site of a firefight?"

Arun shook his head. In the main dining room, several voices competed to be heard before exploding in laughter.

"It's an impressive sight, even to us military men. You know, only two types of men relish the thought of combat: those who have never seen it and psychopaths. The destruction, the broken bodies, the smashed buildings. Very graphic testimony of what has happened, you see. It gets the imagination going. Difficult to deal with at first, but experience has taught me to appreciate the sight of a chewed-up wall."

Seth returned, closing the door behind him and sealing off the raucous voices in the adjoining room. As he took his place at the table, the general turned to him. "Captain, what's happening with the crutches for this young man?"

"They should be here within the week, sir."

"Why so long?"

Seth shrugged. "Demand is outstripping supply."

The general slipped his glasses back on, cleared his throat. "Now, where was I? Ah, yes, the wall. Some years before I was made a general, I joined a platoon under my command on a mission to free a rebel-held town. We surrounded them, cut off their supply lines and called on them to surrender. They didn't, of course. It isn't in their nature. Then they tried to break out. What followed was vicious and there were many casualties on both sides. In the end we won. When I found out the price we'd paid, though, I began having doubts."

He raised a fist to his mouth and coughed. When he coughed a second time, Seth reached for a sweating water pitcher and, starting with the general's, filled their glasses. The general took a long draught of the water and licked his lips.

"Or, not quite doubts," he continued. "I found myself brooding over all those families, more than a dozen, who didn't yet suspect that they were about to receive news that would change their lives forever. I found myself imagining them, all those mothers and sisters and wives and children going about their lives, doing the most ordinary things, cooking dinner or washing clothes or sweeping the house or scurrying around with their friends playing police-and-thief — all these people, so unsuspecting at that moment, brought tears to my eyes, there, in the middle of this town which stank of dust and gunpowder and blood. As the light began to fade, my eyes fell on a nearby house. Like every building in the town, it had been severely damaged, its walls heavily pockmarked by bullets. Like a gift from heaven, my vision changed. I realised that every one of those holes represented a bullet that had *not* hit someone. I felt better and swore never to forget that wall. It was a moment of great clarity, like suddenly seeing the hand of god."

Arun found himself discomfited by the story, by the passion that had entered the general's voice as he drew to its conclusion. He could feel Seth's eyes on him, looking for his response. After a brief silence, he said, "Is that what keeps you going? The hand of god?"

Seth looked away, unhappy.

"No, no, I'm not so full of myself as to think that I'm god's instrument. Considering the precedents, it's not a position I'd apply for. However, malevolent genies have been let out of their bottle and they're wreaking havoc in the land. Once genies are abroad, they can't be put back in. They have to be eliminated. And that is my duty, a question of loyalty, you see."

At a brief and discreet knock, the door opened. Two waiters entered, immediately shutting the door behind them. They made their way around the table, one holding a silver platter from which the other, moving with brisk efficiency, whisked china bowls of pakoras and tamarind chutney. They were served, Arun noticed, in order of protocol, beginning with the general, then him, and finally Seth. The waiters left, allowing in a brief gust of laughter from the main dining room.

Arun took a long sip of water, hoping to wash away the words that were dancing around his tongue. To no avail: "My father said something once, I don't remember in connection with what. He said the line between loyalty and complicity is often so fine as to be invisible."

The general glanced at Seth, then back at Arun. He pinched a pakora from his bowl, dipped it into the sauce. "It's time we had a frank talk, my friend, but that's for later. First we eat." He placed the morsel of food on his tongue and folded it back into his mouth, chewing with relish. Arun and Seth followed suit, Seth with his fork, Arun with his fingers. The chutney had an acidic bite to it, an excess of lemon juice, which caused the insides of Arun's mouth to pucker.

They ate in silence, the general sighing occasionally in appreciation of the food.

After a while, prompted by the general's mumbled inquiry, Seth began talking about his son. He told the story of the birth, which had begun when his wife's water broke one evening at the card table. His parents had called the doctor, helped her into their car, and driven her to the clinic. Labour proceeded normally, and eight hours later the boy emerged. Seth's mother, who had accompanied his wife through the entire process, squeezing her hand, feeding her crushed ice, had sent him photos she'd taken of the birth, but they were out of focus. In a note she'd included to apologise for her shaking hand, his mother had humorously accused her daughter-in-law of causing her water to break just at that very moment because she was about to lose yet another hand of bridge.

Arun thought: *The blink of an eye.*

The general laughed politely, as if to join Seth in the delight that showed on his face. Arun smiled, with a little effort. It was a birth story like any other, but Seth had told it with feeling. Yet, Arun couldn't escape the sense that the lunch — private, and so with a purpose unknown to him — had drifted into inconsequence.

The waiters arrived to clear away the plates and set others before them. They returned quickly with bowls of food: goat in a dark curry sauce, a thick dhal tarkari with chunks of cauliflower and potato a lighter yellow than the split peas, okra fried whole in onions, a coconut-and-milk pilao rice studded with hot peppers and raisins, a stack of naan bread.

Their arrivals and departures were accompanied by no further sound from the other room. He was, Arun felt with a touch of discomfort, alone in a deserted building with Seth and the general.

With a sweep of his hand, the general invited them to help themselves. As he spooned rice onto his plate, he said, "I am, I must tell you, a religious man and in every religion worthy of its name there lies an idea of apocalypse, a fear of annihilation. And it is that elemental fear, which we drape in intelligence and principle, theology of one kind or another, which inevitably triumphs." He drenched his rice in the lamb curry sauce. "Let there be no doubt, young man," he said, peering up at Arun above the rim of his glasses, "that fear, and not love, is the organising principle. *They* understand that, and so must we." A spoonful of dhal tarkari and a clutch of okra filled the rest of his plate.

Seth ripped a naan in two. "What the general means," he said, "is that nothing we do is unjustified. It may often be unsavoury —"

"You know the story of Noah's ark?" the general said, raising a forkful of tarkari to his mouth.

Arun chewed at a piece of the goat meat, and it reminded him of Mr Jaisaram, who had in all likelihood supplied it. "Of course."

"Most people see that as a story of survival, two of this, two of that, Noah and his family. But I've always been most impressed by the fact that god massacred millions of people, young and old, innocent and corrupt, the worst genocide the world has ever known, and people *still* said they loved him."

"That's the trick, you see," Seth added. "Getting people to smile and nod while you're slitting their throats."

"You mentioned your father earlier," the general said. "How did it go again, his little line about loyalty and complicity?"

"The dividing line is often so fine as to be invisible," Arun said.

The general appeared to turn the words over in his mind. Then he smiled. "I wonder where he saw himself in relation to that line, and whether it even mattered. He knew what his duty was, your father."

"My father?" A flutter in his throat betrayed Arun's surprise. "What do you know about my father?"

"I met him once some years ago. At your home. It was a business call. I didn't have the pleasure of meeting you, I'm afraid. I was with the PM."

"The PM?"

Nightfall.

"Sentimentality has no place in our business," Seth said. "Usefulness or potential usefulness, that's all that counts."

"Not to mention implication," said the general. "This complicity business of your father's."

"What complicity?" Arun's heart began to race. He balanced his knife and fork on the edge of the plate.

He is late returning home from an afternoon with friends. Already an evening freshness is beginning to lighten the humidity and in the west storm clouds are boiling above the setting sun. Trying to keep pace with the thickening darkness, he takes a shortcut from the road through the forest along a path so familiar he has no need of the light from his parents' house sparkling among the leaves to lead him home. As he approaches the point where trees will give way to lawn, he sees that several cars are idling in the driveway, their headlights lit, their engines grumbling. Silhouettes of helmeted men holding rifles stand beside them.

"You see, my friend, we deal with as many outside contractors as we can, suppliers of building materials, non-military vehicles, fuel, food, a whole range of stuff. The more people have a tangible stake, the more implicated they are in events, the less likely they are to kick up a fuss. They become more, shall we say, accepting. Most happily sign contracts and maintain enough distance to claim ignorance if they need to. We allow them the possibility of choosing not to know. Knowledge can be a dangerous thing."

Arun said, "But knowledge is my business."

"Have you ever wondered if you're teaching your students the right things? Might they not be better off with a certain amount of ignorance?"

"Ignorance can explode in your face, General."

"So can knowledge. Which one is more volatile, do you think?" He reached out for more okra.

Arun suddenly felt very tired. The general's question would have to wait. He said, "What does this have to do with my father?"

In the bluish glow of the porch light he sees his father sitting rigid in one of the wicker armchairs. Across from him, in the other chair, a man whose face is in shadow assumes a more relaxed posture, almost sprawled, his legs stretched out and crossed at the ankles, his hands clasped on his belly. Behind this man stands an army officer holding a briefcase. The man and his father are talking. On the carved teak table between them two large glasses of whisky sit untouched, an errant beam of light splattering gold along their rims. The man sitting across from his father turns his head as if to crack tension from his neck and Arun recognises the prime minister.

"Your father was one of our contractors."

Arun knew this. The printery had signed several lucrative contracts with the defence ministry. He waited for the general to go on.

Instead the general said, "You're not eating."

"I'm not hungry."

"The food isn't to your taste?"

"It's very good. I'm just not very hungry. I haven't eaten much in the last few days."

"Dessert, then? The cook makes a superb coconut ice cream."

When Arun did not respond, the general, with a light smile, turned his attention back to his own plate. "At the prime minister's request, your father made a verbal agreement with the government to import certain specialised equipment, certain implements our intelligence people needed, the kind of things we couldn't buy through official channels. Your father was most obliging. He ordered what we needed and had it shipped in as part of the printing equipment he regularly bought abroad. We paid for it all, of course, but it was important that none of it could be traced back to us, so those costs were included in the printing contracts we guaranteed him."

"This equipment, what was it exactly?"

"Can't get into that, I'm afraid. It's also knowledge you could do without."

Arun's body went rigid. "What kind of equipment was it?"

"Why don't we say they were tools for encouraging reluctant prisoners to give us information vital to national security. Does that satisfy you?"

"You're saying my father imported torture instruments for you."

"No, you're saying that. I wouldn't go around repeating it, if I were you. Some people might get the wrong idea."

Arun's head rocked on his shoulders.

The prime minister pushes himself up from his chair. The military man shuffles his feet. His father, after a moment of hesitation during which he seems to be gathering his strength, stands up. The prime minister, the shortest of the three, the plumpest, holds out his open hand to his father who, shoulders hunched, does not reciprocate. He lets his arms hang at his sides, lifeless. The prime minister's hand remains extended. His father's right arm slowly rises from the elbow alone and the prime minister seizes it, holds it tight. Then he drops it — even from a distance Arun cannot miss the contempt — turns on his heel, and, closely followed by the army officer, marches into the darkness towards his car. There is a flurry of movement as the bodyguards scramble at his approach. Engines rev, tires crunch on the gravel driveway and the vehicles, rear lights flaring red, speed away.

The general said, "Your brother-in-law has also been most cooperative. His contacts abroad have proven particularly useful."

Seth said, "Arun, you have to understand. We hit their encampments whenever we can, we send out patrols, but it's not enough. Sometimes we have to resort to unconventional methods. The funny thing is that at the beginning we didn't have all the technology we have now, we had to be creative. And now that we have all this technology, we find that the most effective methods are sometimes the most primitive." He cleared his throat and glanced at the general, who nodded at him. "Arun, you understand the implications of what we've just told you."

"Implications?" All he understood at this moment was that his father had been cornered.

"The bomb on the plane wasn't meant for some minister's wife. She wasn't the target."

A crevasse opened up before Arun, a cavern so deep he felt himself go dizzy.

"And now here you are, his son, involved with people you shouldn't be."

"What do you mean? What people?" He gripped the arms of the wheelchair in a vain attempt to steady himself. He could feel the crevasse tugging at him, attempting to suck him into its depths.

Arun remains among the trees at the edge of the lawn for a long time, for as long as his father remains in the porch, sitting once more, his head in his hands. Remains there even after his mother comes out, timidly, and leads his father back inside the house. Remains, there, shaken by the sight of his father undone. When he finally emerges, the house is silent. All the lights are blazing but his parents have locked themselves in their bedroom. Standing at their door, he hears them talking but their voices are too low for him to understand what they are saying. When he awakens the following morning, his father has already gone to the office and his mother has left word with the maid that she will be out for the day. That evening, when Arun asks about the prime minister's visit, his father replies, "We're diversifying the business a bit," before disappearing into his study. The visit is never mentioned again and eventually takes its place among the million and one things Arun supposes he will never fully understand.

"I tried to warn you, Arun," Seth said. "You see, we have every reason to believe that the girl, this Anjani, was the bomb maker."

His breath shallow, Arun pushed himself into the yielding leather back of the wheelchair. "You're out of your mind," he said quietly.

"We think she was introduced to a cell when she was at school in the capital. She got herself into some trouble —"

"What trouble?"

"That's classified. Political stuff. But then we got lucky — personal stuff too. Enough to get her tossed out of school. We've had our eye on her since then."

"Then you must know what happened to her."

"Stop right there, Arun. You don't want to go any further."

"Why are you telling me all of this?"

"You're your father's son," the general said. "I can see the resemblance. You must know where you stand, where your family stands. It's time you gave up all this foolishness. Besides, you can't stay here in your condition. You need to get a new prosthesis. Omeara isn't a place for crutches or a wheelchair."

"What about the children? Why did you build a school? Why let the education people send teachers here?"

"Oh, the children need an education but it has to be the right kind, with the right kind of teacher, one who knows his place. We thought you might be that person. We were wrong."

"You were wrong," Arun said.

"If it's any consolation, your father wasn't easy to convince either but he saw his duty in the end."

"Duty to what?"

"To his country."

Arun thought: *You didn't know my father.* But he kept the thought to himself.

"I've been on the phone to some colleagues at national defence headquarters. I've arranged for you to give literacy lessons to the garrison in the capital. You'll be well remunerated. You will leave as soon as things get back to normal."

"Why wait? Why not right away?"

"The train won't be making its regular run for a while. We've had to institute special security procedures for the foreseeable future."

"Why?"

"That's none of your business, Arun," Seth said. "Stick to your business. It's best for everyone."

There was a knock at the door and, at a word from Seth, the waiters came in.

The general rubbed his belly in contentment. Turning to one of the waiters, he said, "Bring our friend here a big bowl of coconut ice cream. He'll be leaving us soon and he won't have another chance to try it."

Arun looked long and hard at Seth. He could sense the crevasse beginning to fill in, could hear from deep within it the gurgle of a rising tide, a sound for him alone.

Seth, unflinching, returned the gaze.

"What's your son's name?" Arun said, layer after layer of sediment bubbling up and solidifying until the crevasse no longer existed and there opened up before him a stretch of rutted flats.

Seth, without replying, looked away.

Stick to your business.

One afternoon halfway through his final term, Arun stayed late to do some research at the school library. The sun was low in the sky, shadows lengthening but still soft in the buttery light, when he hefted the strap of his leather satchel onto his shoulder and began making his way along the silent corridors towards the evening gate.

He was halfway across the deserted parking lot when Mahadeo came trotting down the stairway from the teachers' lounge. Two books were trapped under his arm and he was frowning, preoccupied, like a man engaged in an intense conversation with himself. Lighting a cigarette, he acknowledged Arun with a nod and a gush of smoke, and, as was his habit, immediately launched into a discourse on some obscure historical event that he saw as invested — that he *sought* to invest, some said — with significance. Arun was pleased. Even, he acknowledged to himself, honoured. He fell into step with him.

They had just passed through the school gate into the street, stepping around the holes that had opened up in the crumbling sidewalk, when a gaggle of ragged children skittered up to them — boys and girls with oily hair and brightly coloured clothes; ninety-eight-percenters as Surein humorously referred to them. Jabbering sales pitches, they held out cans of pencils and pens, fistfuls of pink erasers and plastic ink cartridges. Cheap necklaces dangled from their fingers, bangles armoured their forearms from wrist to elbow.

Arun felt the rise of panic when he saw the reaching arms, the glittering eyes, cracked lips spilling words and spittle. Then he heard a growl from beside him and the children recoiled before Mahadeo's flailing arms. "Get away, get away! You fucking little animals!"

Eyes widened in fear, in puzzlement, in hurt. The children scattered. Mahadeo sucked at his cigarette, flung the butt away, lit another, and returned to his discourse as if he'd merely paused to flick lint from his shirt.

But Arun heard none of it. He couldn't get past the fear he'd seen on the children's faces, the puzzlement, the hurt. When Mahadeo, occasionally interrupting the flow of his words, said, "Don't you agree?" or "You see what I mean about this bullshit, don't you?" he found he could barely reply, squeezing out a "Yes" or coughing a grunt but no more. The fear, the puzzlement, the hurt: they seemed to him to be more incisive than Mahadeo's anger. But he was too ashamed to admit it. To be touched by the plight of those people was, after all, a weakness. For the rest of their walk together, until they parted ways at the statue of Aryadasha, Arun grunted and coughed and did his best to appear attentive.

Stick to your business. But what was his business?

EIGHT

"I HEAR YOU are leaving us. I knew you would. From the first time I set eyes on you, I knew you would not last."

Arun didn't know what to say. How could either of them have predicted the circumstances in which they now found themselves? The hurt showed in Mr Jaisaram's eyes. He had lost weight in the week since Arun had last seen him at the cremation ground. Dark hollows had sunk themselves around his eyes, his cheekbones had grown more prominent. His clothes hung on him. In the webby light of the butcher shop, a new stoop in his shoulders made him appear shorter, less imposing.

Into the silence deepened by the hum of the freezer, Arun said, "I have no choice."

"Every man has a choice," Mr Jaisaram growled. Outside, the world sat dank and colourless, sepia in a grey light.

"Look at me, Mr Jaisaram." Arun shifted the crutches closer to the counter, heaved himself forward. They were an old wooden pair a hospital orderly had come across in a storage room. "It took me half an hour to get here from my house. My leg feels as if all the muscles in it are ripping."

"I am sorry for your leg," Mr Jaisaram said without concern.

"Look at me, damn it! It rains everyday. I can't hold an umbrella."

"Madhu sells raincoats."

"It would take me an hour to get to the school, and an hour back."

"Kumarsingh will be happy to drive you, as he drives you to the army camp. I will pay."

Arun snorted in frustration. The crutches were sturdy but heavy, he found them difficult to manipulate, and the thinly padded armrests had chafed the skin of his armpits. He needed above all to be able to walk normally again.

"Mr Jaisaram, I need to get myself a new prosthesis."

"So have the army get you one."

"It's not that simple, not like buying a can of soup at Madhu's. It has to be ordered, fitted, tried out, adjusted to the wearer. It could take a long time. I have no choice. The work can be done only in the capital. I'm sorry."

"The children can wait a few weeks."

A gust of wind caused the light bulb to sway.

"I've been offered a job in the capital. It pays very well."

Mr Jaisaram was silent for a moment. Then he slapped the towel down onto the countertop and said, "A man must look after himself first. Thank you for what you have done here and good luck to you." He turned away.

"I haven't decided yet."

Mr Jaisaram paused at the door to the backyard, gazed over his shoulder at Arun. "So you might come back?"

"Please, Mr Jaisaram, I ..." He had gone too far. He didn't want to give the butcher hope where in truth there was none. But he didn't wish to be brutal either. On impulse, he said, "Mr Jaisaram, we must talk."

"What have we been doing now? I haven't heard you place an order."

"Please, Mr Jaisaram. In private. With your wife."

The butcher considered his plea for a moment. "Come by the house this evening. We will listen to what you have to say." He pushed at the back door and went out without closing it behind him.

Arun was perspiring heavily when he got to the school. The journey had been slow and painstaking. The crutches had slipped twice but he had managed, barely, to prevent himself from falling. In the car the previous afternoon, as they were returning from the camp, he had asked Kumarsingh to spread the word that classes would resume this morning.

They had driven for a while in silence. Slowing to negotiate a deep rut in the road, Kumarsingh said, "Your friend is not happy to see you leave the camp."

Seth had tried to dissuade him from returning to his house, had even pointed out that the general, as regional military commander in a war zone, had the authority to put him under house arrest for his own protection. But Arun had been insistent. If his attacker had wanted him dead, he pointed out, he would have killed him at the beach. In his time left in Omeara, he wanted to continue teaching. "It's the least I can do," he'd said to Seth, who had responded: "For whom?"

To Kumarsingh in the car, Arun had said, "He's worried for me."

Kumarsingh had nodded, swallowed. He glanced at Arun, his eyes brimming with tears. "After Miss Anjani, you. It is becoming too much. I am beginning to think of moving my base of operations, looking for greener pastures, as Jaisaram put it." He didn't know where he would go. "Someplace where the breathing is easier. Omeara is beginning to suffocate me. I cannot dream anymore, cannot plan anymore. Kumarsingh without his dreams and plans is not Kumarsingh. I need a place where I can find myself again."

Arun, wishing to comfort Kumarsingh, found words tumbling from his lips. "Or perhaps you need to make Omeara that place once more," he'd said, and wished immediately that he hadn't. The words confused him, troubled him, and he was relieved that Kumarsingh hadn't spat them back in his face.

He let himself into the schoolhouse, fetched the brass bell, and, balancing with some difficulty at the open door, rang it as loud and as long as he could. Then he sat at his table, placing the crutches beside him on the platform. The room was damp and full of shadow and it was perhaps because of the gloom that he didn't at first notice Nawaal. In the light, the stick almost blended in with the wooden tabletop. He stared at it for a long time, not daring to pick it up, and it seemed to him after a while that he could see it breathe, it seemed to him that if he held it he would feel the warmth and coursing of blood. He reached into his pocket for his knife, opened out the blade, and with it nudged the stick closer to him. Then, pinning the stick with his forearm, he began sawing at it an inch from the tip. It was slow going, like trying to slice through steel, but he bore down on the knife and eventually the blade worked its way through. The inch of stick rolled away, like a head severed from the body. He moved down another inch and began sawing once more. When that inch was detached, he moved down another.

And so he spent the day: dismembering both halves of Nawaal, rendering him harmless, useless, unrecognisable.

When he was done, it was already late afternoon. His fingers and arm and shoulder ached. He gathered the parts up into a pile in the middle of his table, put away his knife. Balancing himself on his crutches, he began making his slow way back to his house. No children had come. He didn't bother to lock the door of the schoolhouse.

Wearing his underpants, bracing himself on the wall with one hand then with the other, he showered as best he could. Through the space between the top of the walls and the roof of the shower stall, he saw day swiftly giving way to night. Stumbling back wet to the house, he let himself fall onto the bed. The clothes he'd removed before braving the shower lay piled on the floor, but he didn't have the strength to gather them up. He sat there for several minutes, the towel draped round his neck, catching his breath, letting the air dry his skin. He wasn't hungry but he felt weak. He had to eat. He rose on his one leg and hopped the short distance to the kitchen. Gnawing on a mango at the sink, he turned his thoughts to the words he would need later that evening.

He had known with conviction during Seth's unflinching stare — a moment during which something unidentifiable, a wall of some kind, seemed to have given way within him — that he would share with the Jaisarams the knowledge he'd been given. He would offer them Seth's suspicions and his own, unconfirmed. He didn't know what it might bring them — solace, anger, a pain unimaginable — but perhaps it would help them in the way that learning of his father's coerced role had helped him: with a strange relief, an unbuckling of the senselessness that had somehow cheapened his parents' deaths.

Still, standing there pressing his belly into the countertop for balance, the mango juice running through his fingers, doubt and confusion began assailing him, like birds of prey pecking at his certainty. What was the point of telling the Jaisarams what he knew? What would the knowledge change? Anjani was gone; might not suspicion about her killers lead merely to a deepening of bitterness and a strengthening of hatred? Would greater knowledge of brutality extirpate it or entrench it — knowledge not as light but as a deepening of the darkness? The questions cackled and squawked in his head like ravenous birds.

He sucked the last of the juice from the mango seed, pulling off the fibres with his teeth. The fruit had awoken his hunger, and from out of his hunger came impatience. Clarity — he needed clarity. It was, as Mahadeo had taught and as he himself had long believed, the hallmark of a vigorous mind. Those who did not strive for clarity, who hid their emptiness behind verbiage, were stupid men, and in this world stupid men had no place.

He tossed the seed into the sink, quickly washed his hands and mouth. Then he hopped over to the bed and pulled on a clean set of clothes.

Mr Jaisaram let him in. The house, dimly lit, was heavy with silence, with a sense of air unstirred. Something vital had been sucked out of it.

Mrs Jaisaram was in the living room, sitting rigid on the sofa like a knife stuck into a tabletop. Arun was momentarily taken aback: he had never seen her here before, it was as if she was out of place. As if, he thought with a shudder, she had chosen to fill the space usually occupied by Anjani.

With a nod of his head, Mr Jaisaram motioned him to his usual chair as he heavily lowered himself into the armchair across from him.

Arun eased into the chair then carefully placed the crutches on the floor. A cramp writhed briefly through his right thigh.

Mr Jaisaram said, "You want to talk to us about something." His voice was flat with aggression.

"There's something you should know," Arun said quickly. He knew that if he held back even for a second, the words would remain stuck like a fishbone in his throat. Without pausing to choose his words, he told them what he knew, what he suspected. When he said that the army believed Anjani to have been the bomb maker, Mrs Jaisaram's body jerked once and her palms folded into fists on her lap. Mr Jaisaram's eyelids fluttered down and clamped shut. They listened without comment, without further gesture.

When he was done, Arun's mouth was dry and his lips felt as if they were cracking.

A long silence followed.

A silence so long, it suggested to Arun he had made a mistake. He edged forward in the chair and reached down for the crutches. When his fingers touched the smooth wood, a low, hoarse voice said, "No. Do not go." Mrs Jaisaram leaned forward and put her hand on his shoulder. "There is something you should know too."

Mr Jaisaram turned to his wife. "No."

Without removing her glittering eyes from Arun, she said, "Yes. He must know."

"Why?"

"Because he is no longer just a schoolteacher from the north." She squeezed his shoulder. "Because he has seen our lives." She leaned in closer, her voice gravelly now. "Because he loved her."

Mr Jaisaram said as if in wonder, "Loved her?"

Mrs Jaisaram said, "Yes, loved her. Is that not so?"

Arun's eyes burned. His throat constricted. He nodded.

"So you must know," Mrs Jaisaram said, releasing his shoulder and sitting back on the sofa. "You must know first about my son."

Again Mr Jaisaram said, "Why?"

"Because we live in a place where we fear truth like fish fear the net. Because half a truth or a piece of truth is no truth at all. Because, my husband, we will be eaten alive by everything that is hiding inside of us and I have been silent for too long."

Mr Jaisaram nodded slowly. "Strange. I am the one who likes words but you are the one who does not fear them."

Arun said, "Anjani told me about her brother."

"Anjani knew nothing of her brother. She knew what we told her and what we told her was meant to protect her. We did not tell her that her brother was blown up when a bomb he was transporting exploded by accident, a bomb so powerful it left little of him. He knew the dangers."

Arun said, "Was he the bomb maker, then?"

"No, he was just the courier. He would deliver the bombs to the ones chosen either to place them or to wear them."

Mr Jaisaram said, "To be a bomb maker requires specialised knowledge. My son had no knowledge of such things."

Mrs Jaisaram said, "Special knowledge, yes. Knowledge you can get only in the liberated territories or in the capital."

Arun knew that travel to what they called the liberated territories farther south was next to impossible. He understood with hideous clarity what Mrs Jaisaram was saying. "So it was Anjani," he whispered. "The army was right."

"No," Mr Jaisaram said, "the army was wrong."

"So who —"

"Me," Mrs Jaisaram said.

The word, its implication, didn't register immediately. Confused, Arun said, "You ...?"

"I killed my son. I made a mistake with the timer."

"I don't understand. How could you know how to —"

"When Anjani was at school in the capital, my husband and I went there once. He visited the sights. I did not."

Arun pressed his fingertips to his temples. Was it Seth who had once said that nothing in Omeara was what it appeared to be?

"Afterwards," Mrs Jaisaram continued, "I remembered the last thing I said to him before he left. *Be careful.* He said nothing. *Be careful.* Again and again I heard my voice saying those words, when I was the one who had not been careful. From one moment to the next I grew to hate the sound of my voice and so I decided to shut it down."

"And the pictures," Arun said. "That explains the pictures."

"Yes."

"And the bomb on Kumarsingh's bus?"

"I do not always know the targets, or the reasons."

"Was it one of yours?"

"I do not know."

"That doesn't bother you?"

"I did not grow up a two-percenter. I was made one."

"But all those people. And now Anjani."

"Yes," Mrs Jaisaram said, her voice breaking. "All those people and now Anjani." She swallowed.

Across from Arun, Mr Jaisaram hid his face in his hands.

"You did not see her body," Mrs Jaisaram said in a harder voice. "There were strange marks on it, on her breasts and on her ... you know. We have seen those marks before. They say they're made by a machine, with electricity. To make people talk. So do not talk to me about all *those* people."

Arun's heart raced at the mention of a machine, electricity. He thought of his father sitting on the porch. He said, "Your children, then, Mrs Jaisaram."

"Your army, then, Mr Arun." Her tone hardened further, no longer that of the mother in pain but of someone harbouring a hatred that had impregnated her flesh. "I did not ask to be a two-percenter but they came to make sure that I and my husband and my children and my grandchildren would be one. If the soldiers hadn't come, I would not have had to become a bomb maker, my son would be alive, and my daughter would be giving me grandchildren."

Then, unexpectedly, she groaned, leaned forward and pulled at fistfuls of her hair. Mr Jaisaram eased out of his chair onto the sofa beside her. He put an arm around her shoulders.

"So why don't you stop?" Arun said.

She smoothed her hair back into place. "Did you hear what I said? Your people are telling me what I am. Do you know what it is like when others shape your life, when you cannot shape your own? We are not rich people here, we depend on the sun and the rain and the soil, and that is difficult enough. But when your heart and your mind and your soul are no longer yours, then you are truly lost, you are a slave to others." She shook her head. "It will stop when your people are ready for it to stop."

"There are people in the government who want peace."

"And there are even more who want war. We know. We hear them on the radio."

He knew she was right. "Was it your people who attacked me?"

"No. I cannot be sure, but I do not believe so. There was no reason. I think others want to frighten you, to make you go away."

"My prosthesis, it was sliced into several pieces, sliced clean, as if by — and I'm sorry, Mr Jaisaram, but it is the truth — as if by a butcher's cleaver."

Mr Jaisaram shrugged, leaned his chin into his palm. "Or perhaps by a machete," he said. "Every farmer has one. Many soldiers have one."

At his words, Arun saw a sheet of paper balanced on a machete blade so sharp it was sliced in two by the force of gravity. And suddenly it seemed to him that everyone was trying to drive him away.

Mr Jaisaram slid his arm from his wife's shoulder. "So," he said, "when are you leaving?"

"As soon as it can be arranged."

He reached down once more for his crutches and suddenly saw himself as a man sitting alone on a porch at night, his head sunk into his hands, his freedom to shape his own life removed from him. He wondered how it was that the free man who had taken a train from the capital had, without his being aware of it, become like a fish enmeshed in a net.

He straightened up, pulled himself erect with the aid of the crutches. Then he took a deep breath. He felt his lungs expand, his head rock a little. It was as if he hadn't really breathed in a long time, and he marvelled at the sense of well-being that came to him.

Each morning he returned to the schoolhouse, the physical effort getting no easier. Each morning he propped himself against the doorframe and rang the bell and still no children came. He was a hawker crying his wares in the land of the deaf. He would sit at his table, then, the crutches propped against the chalkboard behind him, and contemplate the pile of little sticks, each no longer than a match, which over the hours grew to resemble the makings of a cremation pyre.

Then, on the fourth morning, when the sky was glowing white with the promise of thinning cloud, a shadow darkened the open doorway. He looked up and saw that it was Saman's father. His first instinct was to hide the sticks — the shame of what they had once been. But he knew that would be foolish. He waited instead, unmoving, unsure of what was coming and trying to steel himself for it.

"Good morning, *Prahib*," the man called in an uncertain voice. His blue shirt was tucked carelessly into khaki pants. His left hand held a hat by the brim, his right a heavy paper bag. Behind him, the light grew phosphorescent.

Arun said, "How is your son?"

"Saman is … good," the man replied. He took two steps into the schoolhouse, his gait hesitant, as if he, too, were uncertain of what awaited him. He said, "I am sorry for your leg."

"You know about my leg?"

"Everybody knows about your leg, *Prahib*. Every morning we see you coming to the school."

"But the children don't come." The light behind the man was growing painful to his eyes. "Please come over here. I don't move very easily, as you've seen."

Four steps brought the man to his table. His clothes were clean but wrinkled. He was freshly washed, his silver-streaked hair plastered to his skull. He placed the bag in front of Arun. A large oil stain darkened the brown paper. "My wife sends some food. It is fresh. She cooked it this morning." Then he saw the pieces of stick on the tabletop and his eyes, narrowed, glittered in panic.

Arun picked up a fistful of the pieces, held them out. "Please give these to Saman."

The man held out his hand and watched uncomprehendingly as Arun let them fall into his cracked palm. "*Prahib?*"

"You know about Nawaal?"

"Yes, *Prahib*, everybody knows about Nawaal."

"I don't mean the woodcutter. I mean the stick."

The man's face darkened.

"You know what happened."

"Saman is a very bad student, *Prahib*. It is good to be strict with him."

"Strict, yes, but I was more than strict." Arun picked up a piece of stick from the table. "It won't happen again."

The man gazed in wonder at the pieces in his cupped palm. "This is Nawaal?"

Arun nodded.

"This is a bad thing you have done, *Prahib*."

"What do you mean?"

The man tilted his palm and let the pieces fall onto the table. "My son is a bad student. Now he will not learn."

"Of course he will. The next teacher —"

"No, *Prahib*. I know my son. He will not." His voice rose as he spoke, not in anger but growing desperation. He began wringing his hands. "Please, *Prahib*, you must make another Nawaal. I am here to beg your forgiveness for my son. He is a lazy boy, he gives trouble, he does not like to listen. But please take him back, I beg you. Do what you must to make him learn."

Do what you must. Arun saw himself slashing at the boy with the whip, heard its seething whisper, heard the boy's animal yelping. "Mister —" Arun didn't know the man's name. "Please, stop. No more."

But the man would not be calmed. Knotty fingers kneading hard at each other, he continued his pleading, his voice now rising and falling in a whine that Arun knew well from the beggars in the capital — a wail that gave voice to utter helplessness, utter despair, a death rattle of dignity. An ugly sight, an ugly sound: a man so undone, every seam that made him human had come unstitched.

A burning wound opened up within Arun. "Don't do this," he said, the wound suppurating now with shame and anger and fear. It made him want to lash out.

Spittle flew from the sides of the man's mouth, showering the words Arun could no longer grasp, falling through the gush of breath pungent with fried onions and salted fish.

Suddenly Arun understood Mahadeo — understood that snarl at the beggar children. And he understood, too, with revulsion, that he was now in a place he had never expected to be. He brought his palm sharply down onto the table, the blow causing the pieces of the whip to jump as if alive.

Startled, the man fell silent, his parted lips moist with spit. He looked at Arun, expecting to be struck.

"Look," Arun said, his voice hard, his eyes fastened on the man. "You must understand. I can do nothing for your son. I can do nothing for any of your children." He seized the bag of food, shoved it at him. "Now take your food and go. Leave me in peace."

The man grabbed the bag, backed away, then spun around and plunged into the glare irradiating the doorway.

With a growl of pain Arun swept the pieces of the whip from the tabletop, watched them plummet like dark confetti to the floor.

THE HOUSE WAS redolent with the burnt-sugar scent of stew. Sitting across the dining table from him, Mr Jaisaram said, "Kumarsingh has offered to sell me his taxi. He wants to leave Omeara." In the yellow light, his eyes appeared hooded, his cheeks hung slack on the bone. On the table beside his water glass one of his novels sat face down.

"He told me," Arun said. "I didn't really take him seriously."

When Mr Jaisaram had come knocking at his door earlier that evening, he'd been surprised, and had been even more so at the invitation to dinner. Mr Jaisaram, seeing him hesitate, said that he had a favour to ask of him. Shyly, he showed Arun the novel he'd been reading to him the evening of Anjani's death. Would Arun agree to finish reading it before he went away, this evening perhaps? He'd been unable to refuse.

Mr Jaisaram grunted dismissively. "He's just looking for possi-bilities. He knows I can't drive. What would I do with a car? Besides, it would be a mistake, I think, his going."

Arun bridled a little, as if Mr Jaisaram were speaking about him. "Why?"

From the kitchen, Mrs Jaisaram said, "Because wherever he goes, he will be a stranger." Her voice was still scratchy, a little uncertain, like machinery insufficiently oiled. She spooned food from a pot onto a plate. "These days, nobody trusts a stranger."

"But you've trusted me. I could have gone to the army with the identity of the bomb maker."

"But you didn't. I knew you wouldn't." She placed the plate in front of her husband, returned to the kitchen and began filling another.

"How could you know?" And he realised only then that the thought of running to Seth had not even occurred to him.

"We heard about Saman."

Mr Jaisaram, tucking into his food, grunted.

"I don't understand."

"We know what happened when Saman's father came to see you. That's when I knew I was right about you."

Arun shook his head in puzzlement.

Mr Jaisaram, chewing, looked up. "You understand about dignity. You are not a man who would sell yours."

Mrs Jaisaram stood in the kitchen doorway, a plate of steaming food in her hands. "Not even Kumarsingh knows about us. He is a good man, but a little simple. All he thinks about is money. Kumarsingh would have let himself believe that Saman was learn-ing, and he would have taken his father's food. I knew you would understand why I do what I must, and that you would take this secret away with you." She placed the plate in front of him. "Eat now," she said. "Our food costs you nothing."

Mr Jaisaram raised a finger in protest. "Except a little reading, of course. Nothing in this life is without cost."

Arun looked up from his plate. "Meat, Mrs Jaisaram?"

"Just for you, Mr Arun."

He saw that on their rice there were only vegetables. He picked up his fork and speared a piece of stewed goat. He would be sorry to leave these people. He promised himself that, once back in the capital, he would write to them. And it was from imagining them holding his letter, puzzling over his scribbling like archaeologists over some unknown hieroglyphic, that he said, "Mr Jaisaram, would you like to learn how to read?"

After dinner, Mr Jaisaram took the book and their cups of tea to the living room. Arun followed on his crutches. Mrs Jaisaram, sighing, cleared the table. Evenings were the hardest time for her, Mr Jaisaram whispered. Anjani's absence weighed most on her then as, alone, she cleaned up the kitchen. When she was done, she would go to bed and sleep lightly till dawn. When she got up, her pillowcase would be wet. He himself found the days alone at the shop difficult. He had hidden away Anjani's pencil and cross-word-puzzle book after the cremation and hadn't been able to bring himself to look at them since. "Evenings are long," he said, sitting on the sofa beside Arun. "Nights are longer."

Arun said, "That's what it was like after my parents died."

"But your evenings and nights grew shorter. For us, now, even life seems long." He weighed the book in his hand. "You know why I like stories, Mr Arun? Because every life is like a book. You can never tell what the next page will bring. Stories tell me that you can never know where the heart will lead the body."

Arun found it a simple and moving idea, beautiful and terrifying at the same time. He took the book from Mr Jaisaram, held it so that the thin light illuminated its pages, and, pointing to the first word of the new chapter, said, "This is the word *the*."

Mr Jaisaram peered at the word and nodded with the studied comprehension of a man utterly lost but unwilling to admit it.

"Do you know the alphabet, Mr Jaisaram?"

Mr Jaisaram stiffened his back and, summoning as much dignity as he could, intoned, "A is for apple, B is for bat, C is for cat ..."

From deep in the silent darkness, Arun heard Anjani laugh.

After an hour, Mr Jaisaram looked up bleary-eyed from the book. "Enough, Mr Arun. Perhaps I am too old to learn a new trick."

Despite his discouragement, Arun said, "No, no, Mr Jaisaram, you've made good progress. But you will have to practice every day." He had expected that, with his impressive vocabulary, Mr Jaisaram would have made an easy leap to the printed word. He had, under Arun's tutelage, worked his way through the pronunciation of every word on the page, his lips and tongue puzzling out their shapes, letting fall an occasional *ah!* when he connected a well-known word to the letters that represented it.

Mr Jaisaram pinched the bridge of his nose between thumb and forefinger. He said, "Writing has too many letters."

"You mean people write too many letters? I don't understand."

He cracked open the book, surveyed the page and pointed to a word. "Look at this. *Bree-ast.* Yet we must say *brest.*" His finger slid to another culprit. "And this one. *Slog-tear.* But we say *slaw-tur.* It is as if the language we speak is not the language we write."

Arun nodded in understanding. "When you know them both, you realise they're really the same even if they seem different. It's not so difficult."

Mr Jaisaram swung his head from side to side, noncommittal.

Arun said, "It's like ..." He stopped himself. He was about to say something foolish from an excess of fellow-feeling, something so simplistic that he once more heard Anjani's mocking laughter, directed this time at him. For he knew, despite what he had been about to say, that people treasured those singularities most obvious only to themselves and derided those particular to others. He remembered how an uncle, a man inordinately proud of his rotund belly, had once expressed distaste for the curly hair and darker skin of *rikshas*; how Mahadeo, who affected a style that suggested he had just rolled out of bed fully clothed, had mocked their speech in an attempt to suggest that people whose expression was more musical, less grave in tone and intonation than his, couldn't be taken seriously. He remembered the day that Surein, at a Sunday family lunch, had elicited approving laughter with a joke about two two-percenters coming to blows because each claimed to be the better liar and neither wished to relinquish the title, the joke being that each man, the recipient of government largesse, had successfully passed the bar exams — and this, as Arun now knew, from a man who trumpeted his business acumen while concealing his murky dealings with the grateful army.

Mr Jaisaram rubbed his eyes again. "Next time, you will read to me first, okay? We will do the lesson after."

Arun reached for the crutches.

"Wait, Mr Arun," Jaisaram said, getting to his feet with effort. "I have something for you." He lumbered to their bedroom and soon returned with a large, bulky package in his arms. Mrs Jaisaram accompanied him. He laid the package, awkwardly wrapped in butcher's paper and tied with string, on the coffee table. "This is for you."

"What is it?" Arun leaned forward, undid the string, peeled back the stiff paper. "What is it?" he repeated. Exposed on the table were two cylindrical pieces of wood linked in the middle by metal hinges. Attached to the top of the shorter piece was a metal bowl from which emerged what appeared to be a wide leather belt with buckles. The end of the longer, more slender piece had been carved into a club foot. A chill ran through Arun when he realised what it was.

"It belonged to my wife's grandmother," Mr Jaisaram said. "She lost her leg to Nawaal, the real Nawaal, or so they say. Anyway, it served her well through her eighty-seven years. She was tall for a woman, like Anji was, and vigorous. She lived a full life. And now it is yours if you want it. It won't be as comfortable as your old leg or the new one you will get when you return to the capital, but for now getting around Omeara will be easier than with the crutches."

Arun stared in wonder at the contraption, obviously handmade, probably heavy, but certainly serviceable. It appeared to be about the right length. "I don't know how to thank you," he said.

"Just use it well," Mrs Jaisaram said, her voice a growl.

Arun ran his hand along the wood. It was smooth and warm and he knew that if he closed his eyes he would feel life palpitating within it.

For a week, morning came bright and sunny. Bathed in sunlight and fragrant with a new richness, the fields had acquired an auspicious hue of dark cocoa. Families, dwarfed by the mist-veiled mountains, laboured at their lots, hoeing and raking and, crouched, churning manure into the soil. In the hours after midday, clouds would congregate, unleashing an angry afternoon downpour before retreating for the night.

The leg had been ingeniously made. At a ginger step forward, the knee would give just enough before tightening into place. Then he could move forward again or, with a little further pressure, cause it to give way, allowing him to kneel. It felt like an appendage in a way that his prosthesis had not and it gave him an awkward, rolling gait, but after a few days' practise he was confident enough to put aside the crutches.

Kumarsingh, watching him hobble in circles in front of his house, laughed. "Looks as if you've trained the beast. It does what you tell it to do. Now you can do anything you want, yah?"

Arun, perspiring, paused and put his hands on his hips. "Not that there's much for me to do," he said. He still returned to the schoolhouse every morning, rang the bell, but the only teaching he had left were his evening sessions with Mr Jaisaram. Classes still hadn't resumed at the camp and he'd had no word about his departure from Seth.

Kumarsingh said, "I hear the school bell every morning."

"Nobody comes."

"The children are busy. They have to help their parents. And the parents want to keep their children close to them, just in case."

The townspeople had noticed an increase in helicopter and spotter-plane flights. Army patrols, in trucks and jeeps, sometimes on foot, were now seen several times a day, barrelling through the town, tramping across the fields, dipping in and out of the forest. Night and day, two Navy patrol boats cruised the waters, coming closer to the shore than they had, binoculars bracketed on the houses and the shops and lingering on any townspeople they spotted. Rumours were circulating that something big was being planned — from a military operation against the Boys to an army withdrawal to the imminent arrival of foreign troops — and Arun sensed the rising tension. A new skittishness came to the town, the square less teeming on market day, the crowd less vociferous, as if people had begun talking exclusively in whispers.

"But it's not just that, is it, Kumarsingh?"

Kumarsingh shook his head inconclusively.

"It's Saman, isn't it?"

"Not everybody thinks like Jaisaram."

"And you?"

"I understand Jaisaram's way of thinking, but I understand the children's parents too. I think ..." He looked away, his gaze taking in the deserted road.

"You think what?"

"I think maybe it's a sign that it's time for you to go, too."

Arun nodded. There was nothing to be said. "And you? Are you leaving for sure?"

"Every businessman must know when it's time to pack up and leave. I have had a lot of losses here, Arun."

"Omeara has not been good to us, Kumarsingh."

"True. I always seem to be starting over. I am still thinking that it would be better to start over in some other place far from here."

Arun leant down and massaged his left thigh. It had grown accustomed to the leg — Mrs Jaisaram had sewn him a little cushion to pad the bowl and he was now less aware of the belt buckled tight against his stump — but the muscles still grew tired and sore after a few hours. "I hear what you're saying, Kumarsingh, but your voice tells me that those words are coming from your head and not your heart."

Kumarsingh shrugged, swiped the back of his hand across his glistening forehead. "Omeara has been good to me in other ways. I have friends here."

"Isn't that a good reason for staying?"

"It is a good reason, but is it good enough? You tell me, Arun."

"You'll have to decide that for yourself, I'm afraid. Now come inside, I've got to sit down. I've already put the things into a box for you, some cans of food and some clothes I won't be needing, and a briefcase you might find useful. You can pick up the fan and the radio when I leave. You will drive me to the train, won't you?"

"My head says yes, but my heart says I should make you walk. Which one should I listen to?"

"That too you'll have to decide on your own."

"All this thinking," Kumarsingh said. "It's beginning to make my head ache."

"Sometimes, my friend," Arun said, turning towards the house, "it's best just to make a decision and not think about it too much. Just pick a song, begin dancing to it and see what happens. Let the music guide you."

After Kumarsingh had left with his box, Arun unbuckled the leg and laid it on bed beside him. The stump was sore and the flesh bore the indentations of the straps. He squeezed a dollop of cream from the bottle Mrs Jaisaram had given him and spread it on the skin. It was cool, soothing. From across the room, the fan whirred hot air at him. He fell into a doze and dreamt that he was swimming underwater, breathing as fish do, his arms and legs, two whole legs, propelling him along the shadow-dappled ocean bed, the sand as soft as powder, the water as light as air. He awoke as a shadow descending swiftly from above was about to engulf him and he saw through the open window above the sink that night was falling.

Wearily, he buckled on the leg, switched on the light, and set about preparing himself a simple dinner: a can of tuna bought from Madhu's, a slice of bread, an overripe banana.

He found himself, without knowing why, trying to imagine Omeara as it might have been without the troubles. He saw sunshine on verdant fields, he saw colourful houses, he saw a glittering sea unfurling frilly waves on the pebbled beach. But he saw no people and he knew that, even in fantasy, the town would hardly be a happy place — too much labour, too little reward. He wondered then at the paint people had lavished on their houses, the blues, the reds, the startling greens, the yellows that were the colour of melting butter, colours that struck him now as an attempt to hold back the encroaching jungle. Could they sustain that combat? Did they have the spirit for it? Perhaps they did, he told himself, perhaps they did.

He spun for himself another fantasy of walking down the Omeara Main Road, the earth firm and battened down, the air sweet with the scents of bananas ripening in the sun, of mangoes and papayas and purple aubergines, of corn husked and ready for roasting and stacks of fresh coconuts ready for drinking, of the rich mustiness of paint freshly risen from the can, the liquid stirred and thickened for broad-stroked sloshing onto some sun-blanched wall. But there were no people on this Omeara Main Road just as, when the rains came, there were no people on the real Omeara Main Road.

Suddenly — puddles, mud, solitary tracks quickly washed away by thunderous showers, the brown, squelching muck rising to his ankles, filling his shoes, so that it seemed as if the earth itself were on the verge of claiming his entire being and if he didn't make a muscular effort he would be sucked down whole. He tugged hard, pulling his foot out to a sound that resembled the one Mr Jaisaram made when slurping at a cup of scorching tea.

The fantasy faded but a vibrant fragment of it remained and, there, he was held whole, deep within the earth, his arms stiff at his sides, his good leg and his false as if standing at attention. He knew that he was dead, preserved like the body he'd once seen on display in a travelling carnival — a balding old man with a wispy beard, his face as if asleep, his body all dark skin and fragile, complicated bones. The carnival master had pointed out, just below his ribcage, a mass of darker flesh as gouged and upturned as ploughed earth. A spear wound, the man in the sequinned tophat had said, the mortal blow inflicted in a battle between tribal armies in a land far away a hundred years before. He would have liked to touch the skin, the bruised flesh, the lips that hung slightly parted on a face that registered neither surprise nor pain nor fear nor relief, a face that revealed nothing of the long life that had been lived, the joys it had garnered and the hardships it had endured, that had ended abruptly in some forest clearing in a land unimaginable to him. But touching was not allowed and so, telling himself that the man was not a man at all but something confected by an artisan gifted in the creation of human bodies, he had turned away in disgust. It was in the image of this man, this doll, that he now saw himself encased below the surface of the earth, preserved, perhaps to be dug up one day, cleaned off, and displayed. What he couldn't imagine was the manner of his own death. He had once as a young child come close to drowning when his mother turned her attention from his metal bathtub to respond to a question from the maid. It was his earliest memory, impressionistic, so early his mother refused to believe he could actually recall it. He wondered whether the inhaling of mud would be like the inhaling of water: an obstreperous gushing into the nostrils, a sense that the body was being force-fed a substance that would claim for itself the heaving heart and the billowing lungs.

But that was not what he wanted — swallowing earth and a sucking down into a thick, liquid darkness. It was not the future-ended that he wished for himself. No, he wanted, with the fleeing of his spirit, the fleeing too of his body. He felt jealous that any of his flesh should remain behind, defenceless and abandoned. He wanted, when he departed this earth, that the departure be total and irrevocable.

He had just poured himself some water to wash down the unsatisfying meal when he heard the crunch of a vehicle pulling up outside his house. He listened, wary, but even so the discreet knock at the door startled him. He hesitated. He was wearing a light jersey and boxer shorts, would need time to pull on his pants. Another knock came and a low voice said his name.

"Who is it?" he called out.

"Seth."

He opened the door. Seth filled the doorway. In the greying light behind him, a jeep with a driver and two armed guards idled with its headlights extinguished. Seth pushed his way inside and firmly shut the door.

"Sorry I haven't been by," he said. "We've been kind of busy."

"We haven't missed all the activity." Arun followed him to the table. "What's going on?"

Seth batted the question away with his hand. "How are you coming along? Aches and pains all gone?" Then his eyes fell on the wooden leg. "What in hell is that thing?"

"A gift. Jaisaram happened to have a spare leg hanging around."

Seth leaned over for a closer look. "Looks like an antique. Does it work?"

"Well enough." He pointed to the crutches leaning against the wall beside the door. "You can have those back."

Seth straightened up. "Just wanted to let you know that there'll be a train in two days. Our compartment's been reserved."

"Our?"

"I'm finally going to be able to see my son."

"Good for you."

"One more thing. Tomorrow morning at ten, a detail will come to escort you to the camp. Be ready."

"Why the camp? It'd be easier to leave from here."

"There's going to be a ceremony honouring the regiment. Promotions, decorations, that kind of thing. Some important people are choppering down from the capital. The general expects you to be there. You'll be able to catch up on old times with a former teacher of yours."

"So that's what's been going on. You've been making preparations."

"Once this is over things'll be back to normal." He put his hand on the doorknob, opened the door a crack. A gust of hot wind blew in. "Two more things, Arun. One, keep it to yourself. Two, expect to be searched."

Arun stepped outside with him. In the last of the light, he could see heavy clouds raging in overhead, the stars that were already visible winking out. The wind was picking up, whistling through the trees. Seth climbed into his seat and the jeep drove off, tires crunching on the roadway, a moving shadow quickly swallowed by the night. When the sound of the engine had faded, Arun heard, from far off, the crash of rolling thunder and, beyond that, what sounded like the whisper of multitudes, an unyielding clamour that gave him the curious impression that his world was narrowing.

Without pausing to shut the door of his house, he walked slowly over to Mr Jaisaram's, the wind whipping fine sand against his exposed leg. He knocked at the door, hesitated through a moment of doubt, then knocked again, more forcefully. Waiting, he turned back to the night, stared into its blinding darkness and saw possibility.

NINE

S*CRATCH SCRATCH SCRATCH*

The sound was soft, suggestive of the passage of damp chalk on a chalkboard, and would have been soothing if not for the metallic edge that underlay it. For the last few minutes, each scratch had seemed to reverberate down through his pores, burning itself into his flesh like a drop of acid into soft tissue. Arun had been sitting for hours on the earthen floor of the hut, his back pressed against the wall of dried, powdery mud. At first the coolness of the wall had felt good, had eased the suffocating clutch of the surrounding jungle. But the warmth of the small fire Mr Jaisaram had set in a charcoal brazier had sucked that comfort away, and the smoke had exhausted the air, turning it acrid.

Despite his wife's protests, Mr Jaisaram had removed the jute covering from the doorway. "Listen," Mr Jaisaram had said, gesturing towards him. "He can hardly breathe. Besides, who's going to see the fire?"

Army patrols no longer ventured into the jungle after sundown unless given reason. The thick night air had billowed slowly in, thinning the smoke and sharpening the musky scents of earth and ripening vegetation. But breathing remained an effort. His nostrils felt singed.

Mr Jaisaram, sitting cross-legged at the edge of the fire, appeared unaffected by the burdened air. Sweat plastered the sleeveless cotton undershirt to his chest, but hardly more so than on those humid days when he spent hours carving up goat and lamb carcasses. He had laid the cylinder of polished wood across his thighs and had been working steadily at it — *scratch scratch scratch* — for all these hours. His fist and half of his forearm were deep inside the cylinder, the upper half of his forearm roiling at each authoritative twist of his wrist, his right bicep swelling tight. The implement was a half-moon of metal filed sharp, the flat edge fitted with a wooden handle. He assumed it to be a knife of some kind that Mr Jaisaram used in his work and to which he had ascribed a new purpose. The going was slow, but performed with unvarying deliberation.

Mrs Jaisaram was sitting slouched against the wall behind her husband. Her eyes were closed, and her head occasionally nodded as she dipped into sleep. But whenever this happened, she would jerk her chin back up with uncommon insistence. She had no intention of falling asleep. "Don't let her fool you," her husband had said at one point, his words rising above the rhythmic scratching. "Her ears are wide open. She hears everything. She hears a snake slithering in the grass, she hears spiders spinning webs."

"Some kind of supernatural power?"

"No, not supernatural. Only the Boys' leader has that gift. But she hears things you and I cannot." Then he fell silent again, his mind returning to his work, the sound methodical, unhurried, confident, the sound of an artisan at work, the final form clear in his head, imagination guiding the angle and force of the unseen blade.

The muscles in Arun's leg and back stiffened. He braced him-self on the heels of his palms, stretched his back, described circles with his head. His neck crackled. Mrs Jaisaram's eyes fluttered open and he saw that their suspicion was fastened on him: she had no doubt where the sound had come from.

The scratching stopped. Mr Jaisaram withdrew his arm from the cylinder, placed the tool on the floor beside him, turned the cylinder upside down and shook it out above the fire. Tiny chips and wood dust fell out. Flames flared briefly then died. He raised the cylinder to his lips and blew into the opening. The lonely lament of a conch shell resounded in the hut, but the sound was heavy, without reach. It simply hung there in the air where it had been made.

His wife stirred, looking up in expectation.

Mr Jaisaram glanced at his watch. "Just past midnight," he said. Then, as if speaking to himself, he added, "Patience. I will be some hours yet. It must be perfect. There is no other way." He placed the cylinder once more across his thighs, reached for the tool.

Behind him, his wife settled herself against the wall, her arms folded on her chest, her eyes reaching again past her husband's shoulder to settle on him.

"Sleep if you can," Mr Jaisaram said, speaking to them both and looking at neither.

Arun doubted he could sleep: the scorched air, the scrape of metal on wood, the stiffness in his muscles, and Mrs Jaisaram's gaze that would not release him.

After a while, the light in the hut appeared to diminish. It seemed to Arun that Mrs Jaisaram was consuming the brightness with her eyes.

A little later yet, the steadiness of her breathing, the regular rise and fall of her chest, told him that she was asleep. Deeply asleep. Her eyes wide open.

A tickle woke him, a runnel of sweat meandering past the roots of his hair, hesitating at his hairline like some timid creature surveying a clearing, then breaking out and striking a slow and determined path down his forehead. He had slid into a slouch. His lower back ached. He pressed himself up against the wall, straightening his spine, then took a deep breath of the exhausted air.

"Water?"

He opened his eyes.

Mr Jaisaram, face florid in the glow from the brazier, was crouched beside him, holding out a plastic tumbler. "It's not cool anymore, but it will revive you."

He took a sip of the tepid water then splashed the rest onto his face. "You could almost make tea with it," he said, fingers rubbing the gummy sleepiness from his eyes. He handed back the tumbler, waved away an offer of another. Then he saw that Mr Jaisaram had put away his tools and that his wife was no longer there.

Reading his gaze, Mr Jaisaram said, "She's outside, stretching."

"You're done? It's ready?"

"The rest is up to her."

"Will she be long?"

"She will be as long as she needs to be."

"It's hard to breathe in here."

"She likes it that way. It slows down her heart. She becomes calm. It is delicate work that she does."

Mr Jaisaram wearily straightened up, wandered over to the far side of the hut where his wife had sat. He glanced down at the jute sack tied at the mouth with a length of oily rope, which she had retrieved from its hiding place beneath a stack of firewood. At the bottom, where the bag was bulky, RICE was printed in red and, beneath it, in smaller letters, the words "Gift of the people of the United States of America." Arun wondered where the bag had come from. Their foreign aid came not in food but in arms and ammunition and tactical training. And then he knew it had come surreptitiously on one of those fishing trawlers the Navy patrol boats were continually seeking out. Mr Jaisaram yawned, scratched at his chest, and Arun wondered whether Mr Jaisaram himself knew what secrets the sack contained.

Suddenly, with the soundlessness of a ghost, Mrs Jaisaram glided back into the hut. She made straight for the bag, her husband stepping out of the way. Kneeling, she undid the rope, peeled back the mouth of the bag, and removed a small kerosene lantern, which she set on the ground beside her. Next she took out a miner's lamp, a small light attached to a head strap, the kind coalminers up north strapped to their helmets before going underground. Then, carefully, grasping each with both hands, a mayonnaise jar filled with a clear liquid and a few tins that had once held biscuits and tea leaves.

Mr Jaisaram turned to him. "We go outside now. The door will be covered, and we cannot come back in until she is done."

"I understand. Will you give me a hand?"

Mr Jaisaram stepped quickly over to him, took his arm in a powerful grip and helped him up. Arun slid an arm around his neck, found his balance. Awkwardly they made their way to the doorway. The moment they stepped through it, the jute covering fell into place and they were absorbed by a fetid darkness.

Mr Jaisaram helped him to a damp log, sat beside him. Only inches away, his presence was one of radiated warmth and dried sweat and a gentle stirring of the air. He took Arun's hand and put into it what felt like a dense table-tennis ball. "Eat it," he said. "It will give you energy."

He lifted it to his nose, sniffed a mingling of fruit — coconut? papaya? banana? — and flour, perhaps, *ghee*. "What is it?"

"My wife makes it. It is what hunters and woodcutters used to take into the forest with them. They lived on this day after day. The Boys use it too, to travel light."

He nibbled at the firm ball and its sweetness flooded his mouth. He chewed. Coconut, banana, papaya, yes, and fragments of cashew nuts and raisins and dried dates rolled into a floury paste. He said, "What is this place?"

"It's a woodcutter's hut. It's been here for a very long time. It belonged to Nawaal. The man I mean, not the stick." A grumble of laughter rose, lingered, then died away.

"He lived here?"

"I think it was where he felt at home."

"Is this where he ..."

"Yes. When my wife brought me here the first time, many years ago, I was afraid. I thought bad things always leave marks."

"Ghosts?"

"Yes. Or screams. A scream never really goes away, you know. It echoes forever."

"Is that the kind of thing your wife can hear?"

"Yes."

"But you're not afraid of this place anymore."

"No. The echoes are there, and the ghosts too. But I've made my peace with them. I think we need to, don't you? I mean, that's our big problem. We don't just remember the past, we live it. Our own past is killing us. Aryadasha, Nawaal. Sometimes I wish they would all just go away."

"Yet you're here now. You carved the wood."

Mr Jaisaram was silent for a while and Arun, nibbling still at the ball, thought that he had offended him.

"Yes, I'm here now," he said finally in a growl that failed to camouflage regret. "I carved the wood. And I am a butcher who does not eat meat. Life is like that sometimes, Mr Arun."

Arun read in his tone an observation of naïveté. Stung, he let the silence grow, let it inhabit the darkness.

After a while, Mr Jaisaram said, "Are you afraid, Mr Arun?"

Arun was not touched by the question. He was neither afraid nor joyous. He was, as best he could determine, indifferent. "When my parents died, I wondered whether they knew something I didn't, whether they'd solved the mystery we will all solve eventually, the mystery Anjani has solved. I got the feeling that they had — not a religious feeling, you understand, but a feeling that they were in a place where I'd join them one day, as if they'd made a journey ahead of me. My parents' death took away my own fear of dying. I'm a bit curious, if anything. But if there's nothing afterwards, I won't be around to be disappointed, will I?"

Mr Jaisaram gave a low, nervous laugh.

Arun wished he could have a sip of water, but the canteen was in the hut with Mrs Jaisaram. He ran his hand down his face. It came away wet.

Mr Jaisaram removed something from his back pocket. Before Arun could see what it was, he said, "I have the book, Mr Arun. When the light comes up, will you read to me?"

"We won't have time to get to the end."

"I will finish the book on my own. Kumarsingh will help me."

"If he stays."

"He will stay. The truth is Kumarsingh has no other place he wants to be."

The trees grew dark — at least that was how it appeared to him: that the jungle, unseen for so many hours, was suddenly looming. He was tired, and he was some minutes in realising that it was the lightening of the sky that had caused the trees to suddenly rise up in a cocoon around them. The discreet rustle of the night creatures diminished and in that silence he became aware that another quiet was descending. In trench-strewn and sandbagged jungle clearings, red eyes and tensed muscles were relaxing, hands growing less stringent on loaded weapons. In the army camp, as trench-strewn, as sandbagged, girded in barbed wire, weary shoulders could allow themselves to droop, cramped fingers to rub hallucinations from puzzled sight. In both places, tea was being brewed, rice being boiled, dough being kneaded. People began breathing more easily. They had survived the night. And now, as that darkness grew fragile, he sensed promise behind it.

Mr Jaisaram yawned and snuffled like a horse with its snout in water. He stretched his arms above his head, releasing a causticity of dried perspiration.

The jute covering was drawn back from the doorway of the hut and Mrs Jaisaram emerged. She looked grey in the thin light, her features drawn with fatigue. In her hands was the cylinder of wood restored to its purpose, the cushioned bowl with its network of leather straps reattached, the hinged knee screwed back into place.

Arun looked up. Through breaks in the branches, stars were still visible in the lightening sky and he understood that out of utter darkness could grow a beguiling beauty. When he took a breath — a hungry, lung-filling breath — he smelled sunshine and he was content, in the sticky morning air, to await the coming of the dawn.

NO ONE CAME to see him off. He had warned them that they couldn't. They weren't supposed to know. Still, as he drove off in the jeep with his escort, the wooden leg carefully placed so that it would remain as straight as possible, he couldn't help glancing backwards, towards the bedroom windows of the Jaisarams' house. Anjani's was shut, resolutely it seemed to him, but the other was levered up and he thought he saw through the soft morning sunshine a hint of movement in the darkened square. He thought of the first morning he had opened his window, startling Mrs Jaisaram at her sink and he resisted the urge to wave goodbye. What had begun with a wordless gaze would end in the same way.

All morning the skies and the water had been raucous with the whine of engines, the shudder of helicopter blades. Sensing a climax of some sort, the townspeople had remained indoors, few families working the fields, windows shuttered, doors closed.

He knew none of the soldiers accompanying him. Dressed in camouflage outfits, they stared out into the sun-dappled forest, weapons clutched on their laps, fingers caressing the triggers. Apart from the driver who had come to fetch him, they had not spoken a word.

As they proceeded through the forest, a feeling of lightness came to him. Images of his parents, his sister, his students left him unmoved, as if he had let go of them as he had let go of his fan and his clothes and his briefcase. When he thought of Anjani, it was with serenity, as if all that had passed between them, and all that had been inflicted on her, no longer inhabited him but were simply part of a larger fiction that had written itself out. Rarely had he felt so clear-headed, so unencumbered — not unlike the feeling that had come to him in the train months before when he began his journey to Omeara. He closed his eyes, his muscles jolted pleasantly by the shuddering jeep. He enjoyed the rattle and growl of its engine, the rush of the air against his skin, the fragrant warmth clinging to him like a freshly laundered blanket.

Sooner than he'd expected, they were at the camp. A glance revealed the heightened security. At the gate, the guards were dressed like his escort, as if for imminent combat, but with bayonets mounted, bandoliers of ammunition draped across their chests and faces painted green and black. Along the perimeter, armoured cars directed the snouts of heavy machine guns towards the tree line. Within the perimeter, three-man teams manned mortar tubes.

At the gate the soldier in charge asked him to step out of the jeep. He recognised Pande behind the camouflage paint. The machete was strapped to his waist.

Moving slowly, supporting the wooden leg with his hands and easing it out, he did as he was asked. He gave the appearance, he knew, of an invalid. From the near distance came the brassy sounds of the national anthem.

To the driver, Pande said, "You're late. They're starting." To Arun, Pande offered no greeting. His face remained inexpressive, dark eyes as wary and as cold as a fish's stare. "Raise your arms, please," he said.

Arun lifted his arms in the gesture of surrender.

Pande patted him down, along his arms, his ribs, around his waist, down his back, along his hips. There he paused, as if in surprise.

"Raise your pant leg, please."

Arun bent slightly at the waist and eased up the hem of his trousers.

Pande, squatting, squinted at the wooden leg. He batted his

343

palm at it. "Higher."

Arun tugged the hem past the knee joint. "It won't go any higher," he said.

A look of disgust crossed Pande's face before his mask quickly reasserted itself. He straightened up. "You can go," he said, turning away. He signalled to the men at the gate.

"Is it all right if I walk?" Arun said. "The jeep's cramped, it's not easy with my leg."

Pande, without looking at him, said, "Lalsingh, go with him."

One of his escorts leapt from the jeep and, just as the anthem reached its crescendo of trumpets, bugles, cymbals, and drums, they walked together through the open gates into the camp.

The parade ground was dense with ranks of soldiers standing at attention. They wore crisp green uniforms and peaked berets and each man held a shouldered weapon. Their clean-shaven cheeks glistened with sweat. Their boots gleamed.

His escort led him across the bare ground towards the front. When they arrived abreast of the first rank of soldiers he saw that a dais had been erected, perhaps the same one that had seen service at the burial ceremony not long after his arrival. On it, about a dozen men, military officers in dress uniform and civilians in shirtsleeves, sat on grey metal chairs in the sun, the officers staring straight ahead while the civilians fanned themselves with handkerchiefs or sheets of paper. A microphone stood at the edge of the dais. Arun recognised Seth among the officers. He was sitting in the last chair in the second row with a large crimson box on his lap. The chair beside him was empty: his own, Arun supposed. Facing the dais on the other side, the military band stood in wide-spaced formation.

The general, in a tight uniform sparkling with medals and a scarlet sash, the visor of his hat pulled low on his forehead, rose from his chair and planted himself before the microphone.

Arun's escort brought him up short with an outstretched arm

and signalled to him that they would wait there.

The public address system squealed once before amplifying the general's voice with the scratchy uncertainty of an old vinyl record: "Men of the Aryadasha Regiment! Valiant warriors! Today is a special day in the history of our heroic regiment. A special guest has come all the way from the capital to pay tribute to we who have fought so long and so hard and so courageously ..."

As he half listened to the general lauding the deeds of his men, a feeling of absurdity grew in Arun, a sense that all of this — the men standing rigid in the sun, the general as portly and picturesque as a prize-winning pig, the embroidered flags, the self-important solemnity — was somehow faintly ridiculous. His gaze left the general and settled on the men sitting behind him: the prime minister, in sunglasses, clutching his speech to his swollen belly, wearing his usual man-of-the-people uniform of a billowing royal-blue vest over a white collarless shirt and grey trousers; beside him, strangulated in a grey suit, the emaciated, vaguely frowning face of the minister of defence; and beside him, lounging on his chair in an attitude Arun would have recognised anywhere, Mahadeo, squinting through the smoke that rose from a cigarette drooping from his lips. He saw those eyes flicker towards him, saw them go by then wander back and settle. Mahadeo hadn't changed much. Still the spiky hair, if greyer now, still the unshaven cheeks, and still the fleshy lips twisting to the left in a grin so mirthless it might have been a grimace. Arun nodded ever so slightly in response. Once, a long time ago, he would have smiled.

The general ended his speech by announcing that "before the festivities begin," the band would play the regimental anthem in honour of fallen comrades. He returned to his seat. The band master raised his baton and launched the band into a tune that was rather sprightly, Arun thought, to serve the stated purpose.

Arun's guide tapped him once on the shoulder, gestured him forward.

He didn't have far to go. A dozen steps, fifteen perhaps.

He began the journey, feeling conspicuous with his awkward gait.

The general leaned in to the prime minister and whispered in his ear. The prime minister nodded, turned his sunglasses towards Arun.

The defence minister mopped his brow with his handkerchief and tossed a disinterested glance his way.

The brass instruments broke off, leaving the drums and cymbals to thrump through a stirring martial passage. Arun had visions of men marching to battle over an open field.

Mahadeo flicked his butt to the ground and extracted his cigarettes from his coat pocket. He tapped one from the box, placed it between his lips and reached into his coat pocket for his lighter. His eyes never left Arun, drew him closer. The bleary eyes of a man who slept too little, drank too much, eyes skittish with irony and wariness, constantly on the lookout for threat or weakness.

Arun stood in front of the dais, Seth smiling slightly at him over the general's shoulder. The general himself, with a grander smile, bidding him welcome.

The brass instruments opened up again, soaring above the drums and the cymbals. Visions now of the men charging across the open field, shells bursting around them.

Mahadeo's lighter flared, a curl of smoke rising from the tip of his cigarette.

Arun mounted onto the dais. He thought: *All you have to do is kneel.*

The prime minister leaned forward, reached out his hand. Pudgy fingers, nails neatly trimmed, skin accordioned at the knuckles.

His knee, the one of metal and wood, began to fold, descending towards the ground with the excruciating slowness of a flare descending through the night.

There would be a flash of light, he knew, and a roar such as he had never heard.

The prime minister looked puzzled for a moment and then his lips parted. In an oily, avuncular voice, he said, "No, no, my friend, there's no need for —"

Arun felt the knee jar against the wooden platform. He thought he heard a click.

ABOUT THE AUTHOR

Neil Bissoondath is the author of the novels *A Casual Brutality* (1988); *The Innocence of Age* (1992); *The Worlds Within Her* (1999); and *Doing the Heart Good* (2002) as well as the collections of short fiction *Digging Up the Mountains* (1985) and *On the Eve of Uncertain Tomorrows* (1990). His fiction has garnered many award nominations and wins, including, most recently, the Hugh MacLennan Prize for Fiction, awarded by the Quebec Writers' Federation. He has been published in the U.S. and the U.K., where his first novel was long-listed for the Booker Prize. He has published one work of non-fiction, *Selling Illusions: The Myth of Multiculturalism in Canada*, (1994), which won the Gordon Montador Award.

His work has been translated into French, German, and Dutch.

In addition to his book-length works of fiction and non-fiction, Neil has worked extensively in television. He has published reviews and essays in *The Globe and Mail*, *The Toronto Star*, *Saturday Night*,

The New York Times, La Presse, Le Monde, and *Le Nouvel Observateur,* among others. His short story, "Dancing," won a National Magazine Award (Gold) in 1985.

Born in Trinidad, Neil has lived in Toronto and Montreal. He was educated at St. Mary's College, Port of Spain, and York University, Toronto. He now makes his home in Quebec City, with his wife and daughter, and is a professor of creative writing in the Département des littératures at Université Laval.

Neil Bissoondath has published the following:

Digging Up the Mountains, short stories, 1985, short-listed for the City of Toronto Book Awards.

A Casual Brutality, a novel, 1988, long-listed for the Booker Prize, nominated for *The Guardian* Fiction Prize, the WH Smith/*Books in Canada* First Novel Award, and the Trillium Award.

On the Eve of Uncertain Tomorrows, short stories, 1990.

The Innocence of Age, a novel, 1992, winner of the Canadian Authors Association Prize for Fiction.

Selling Illusions: The Myth of Multiculturalism in Canada, opinion, (1994), winner of the Gordon Montador Award and the Prix Spirale de l'essai.

The Worlds Within Her, a novel, 1999, short-listed for the Governor General's Literary Award and the Hugh MacLennan Prize for Fiction.

Doing the Heart Good, a novel, 2002, winner of the Hugh MacLennan Prize for Fiction.